LEVERAGE

About the Author

Born in South Shields, Tyne & Weir, and raised in the Lake District, Katherine Black is the author of *Dark Around the Edges, A Question of Sanity* and *Pedigree Crush with a Twisted Gene*. After living in both Manchester and Farnworth, Katherine recently returned to the Lake District.

Alongside her psychological thrillers and suspense novels, she has published fast paced fantasy-adventure books for all the family under the name Kat Black, notably her series *Lizard's Leap*.

Find Katherine online at
www.katherineblack.co.uk

And on Facebook @authorkatherineblack

Also by Katherine Black

Pedigree Crush with a Twisted Gene
A Question of Sanity
Dark Around the Edges
People on the Edge

And writing as Kat Black

Lizard's Leap
Keepers of the Quantum

Leverage

Katherine Black

1 3 5 7 9 10 8 6 4 2

First published 2017

ISBN 978 154645034 4

In accordance with the Legal Deposit Libraries Act 2003, a copy of the publication has been lodged with the British Library, 96 Euston Road, London, England, NW1 2DB.

Acknowledgements

Special thanks to Peter, as usual. Need I say any more?

Chapter One

'Go on, Beth, it'll be a laugh.'

She laughed when she said it, too, sitting at my table with the newspaper open and a coffee stain on a Buy-One-Get-One-Free pizza advertisement. Her eyes were bright and sparkly and even when not vodka induced, that was never a good thing when it came to Maggie. Her ideas rarely panned out well.

Everything about it was wrong. Beth's instinct screamed at her to take heed for once in her stupid life. And so, with Margaret pumped and ready for anything, it started—the thing that destroyed them all began.

'You're joking, no way.'

Beth protested hard enough. She wasn't a pushover. The words came out of her mouth strong but, sparring with Margaret's enthusiasm, she stood no chance. Wasn't it Maggie who persuaded her to dye her hair green? That was a lifetime ago. They were young then, foolish.

'Look, Beth.' Look at the beginning of a sentence was a sure sign that Maggie was irritated with her. 'Every Wednesday night we go to the quiz at the Black Bull. Every Saturday we sing "I Will Bloody Survive" on the karaoke, and Christ knows how, but somehow, we always do survive. We watch Corrie on the telly and then dissect it over coffee and fags.'

This last sentiment sparked an inner reflex. Her right hand reached across the table and without pausing for breath or breaking eye contact, she helped herself to one of Beth's Superkings. She paused, long enough to spark up, absently flicking a second cigarette across the table.

'For Christ sake, Beth, let's do something different before we die.'

She blew a plume of hoary smoke into the air and Beth watched it unravelling as Margaret talked at her. The battle was won. They both knew it but went through the motions anyway, because that's how the game was played. Beth didn't hear what she said next.

Before we die. It seems prophetic now, those words, a portent to take with them on their mad adventure.

'...Isn't it?' She'd asked a question but didn't bother to wait for an answer. 'And anyway, it's at Club B in Barrow, a theme night to grab the punters early in the evening. But, I'll tell you now, I'm not paying three quid for a vodka.' She pulled a face. 'We'll take a half bottle out with us and sneak it into our cokes when we go to the loo. So, are we up for it then, or what?'

Beth loved Maggie even though she irritated the hell out of her. It's that love that you can only have with a life-long friend but nothing like the feelings Beth once had for Rob, or the way Margaret loves her kids.

Beth hasn't been to see the kids since it happened. It was something else to feel guilty about. But what would she say to Jess and Ben and little Barry? What could she say?

She knew where Colin was and one day, just that one thing, just knowing that, would probably drive her insane.

The following Tuesday, Beth was in a frazzle. Vodka is an evil beast, they had three large ones with diet coke as they dressed, and Beth was caught in the moment. It was exciting. She felt daring. She was alive, and for the first time in months, she didn't have to check her pulse to confirm it. She'd made Maggie promise that the evening was a one off. There was to be no follow-up of any kind; that was the deal. She wouldn't be bullied or pushed around.

That was the proviso; she only agreed to go if it was just a laugh for that night, something crazy that you do, just to see how it feels. 'After all,' she reasoned, 'the Yanks gave us bikini waxing and that wasn't a good move, was it?'

Maggie agreed, no follow-up, they were going for the experience and to see if they could still pull if they wanted to. It was a brief return to their youth. They felt the blood pump through their veins. It was seeing if they still had it.

Jess, Maggie's daughter, was horrified. 'Mu-um, speed dating? Ye-uk. How tacky. I can't believe you're doing this. How embarrassing. How could you, you've already got a boyfriend, and anyway—you're old.'

Maggie pushed her objections aside and said, 'Darling, I'd never do anything to hurt him—he'd have to be awake for that. It's just a laugh. And anyway, your Aunty Beth needs a man and I've made it my mission in life to find her one.'

Beth opted for tight black pants with flared bottoms. Can't go wrong with a good old pair of any time-any place black pants. Teamed with a tasselled belt and a black top with a playful motif, she hoped that a few years would melt away. Subdued lighting would help. If God was merciful, there would be a single low-wattage bulb. Oh, and no grids of any description—like drugs—grids and high heels don't work.

They got there early to have time for a drink before the evening descended into sleaze. Everybody had the same idea because there was already a school of women fishing at the bar. They were corralled away from the men. The women were eager. They were alive too. Some of them had done it before, speaking with an air of authority, imparting tales of caution and some unbelievable horror stories. Beth wanted to flee from the moment they arrived but Maggie was having none of it. She thought it was all good sport.

A woman approached the microphone. Beth commented that she 'looks like summat out of *Strictly Come Dancing*.' She wore a tight silver frock and her boobs only stayed in because gravity had taken its toll. She was a hoity-toity, with hair piled on top of her head. Beth nudged Maggie and said that she could have been Lily Savages' twin sister. That's when she learned that sound carried in the corridor.

'Good evening, ladies,' said Elaine, their hostess for the evening. She dropped Beth a withering look. 'We are about to start, but for those who don't already know, I'd just like to explain the rules.' She patted her hair with a manicured hand and smiled a simpering smile. 'In a moment, you will be given a number and escorted to your table. The men are lined up at the other side of the building and will join you shortly. You will have three minutes to find out as much as you can about each other. Keep the conversation flowing, ladies—flirt, and enjoy and remember it's all in fun. After three minutes the men will rotate and you will have a new partner to toy with.' She peered over her bifocals. 'As each man leaves you, ladies, you will be required to tick either the 'Yes' or the 'No' box on your form. He will do the same. Where two yeses match up, you will be given contact details for the men you've expressed an interest in with a view to meeting them for a proper date.' She went on to detail some rules of safety, like meeting in public places and always telling somebody where you are going. It was the stuff that parents tell their teenage daughters. 'I need you to make sure that you have all signed the disclaimer, given to you as you arrived. Have a good evening ladies and I'll see you in the bar.'

Have you seen what they've put in this disclaimer?' Beth whispered to Maggie. 'They don't want to be held responsible for anything. Did you see the clause about contracting an STD? What the hell have you got me into, Maggie? I'm not signing it, that's for sure—and the only clapping I'll be doing is when I give them a round of applause when this ordeal ends.' It was all very cloak and dagger and her feet were killing her.

'Right ladies, I'll show you to your tables.'

Maggie was number thirteen and Beth was fourteen. Maggie had to nudge her friend in the back to make her move. They passed the time leaning over and making whispered remarks about their female competition. Soon, there was a low hum of conversation as the men filtered in. Beth craned her neck to try and see what her man looked like but all she could see was the brassy perm of the blonde three tables down.

Maggie was already chatting to hers in full flow even though the dates hadn't started. Beth couldn't hear what they were saying but one look at him was enough to tell her that he wasn't dating material. If that was the standard of the meat for sale in this market then she needn't have worried about follow up dates.

She rose from her seat and shook the sweaty hand extended to her as number fourteen introduced himself. He was nothing to get excited about in the looks department and had *40-Year-Old Virgin* written all over him. Before he opened his mouth, Beth could see that he was a broken doll and wanted a replacement mummy. She told herself not to be so nasty. He was a nice enough bloke, sort of ordinary, tired looking, worn. 'Hello, number fourteen,' he mumbled, 'I'm Ron.'

Beth giggled and said in a Liverpudlian accent, 'Hello, number fourteen. What's your name and where d'you come from?'

'Oh, my mam loves Cilla Black, got all her records, she has. You'd love my mam. But she's got that senile disease now.'

As three minutes go, they were long ones. After talking about his mother and his border collie, conversation dried up. He replied to her questions with monosyllabic answers and his only other input to the conversation was a repeated, 'You?' At a loss, they took to gazing around the room. Beth caught Maggie's eye and Maggie pulled a face, it seemed the next one wasn't going to be much better than the first. The silence drew out uncomfortably. Beth reached into her vocabulary and pulled out the first constructed sentence she could find. 'I don't reckon much to number thirteen,' she said with a grin.

'That's my brother,' he answered. 'You'll like my brother'. The date wasn't a success. She felt that their relationship had run aground and it was time to kick him to the curb, along with his senile mother, his brother and his elderly border collie called Blackie.

It turned out number thirteen was an improvement on his brother. The man was passionate, fired up, enflamed—but his passion only extended as far as the wondrous joy of fishing. He droned on for the full three minutes about coarse fishing, sea fishing, fly fishing and angling. He didn't ask her name and she didn't get to speak—that was fine, she was fantasising about milky coffee and her comfy pyjamas. She noticed that his fingernails were filthy and could only imagine which poor fish had lost its guts under the long, dirty talons. It may have been her imagination, but she was sure that he had an unpleasant odour about him; imaginary or not, it was unmistakable, the coddled smell of dead fish. There would be no riverbank wedding.

Number twelve, who rode into town on his bicycle, was called Martin. He told her he could carry nearly as much on his handlebars as most people could fit in their cars and bragged that he'd once moved all his belongings from an old girlfriend's house to his new one using only his bike. Beth couldn't resist dropping her pen so that she could look under the table. One leg of his jeans was secured above the ankle with an elastic band—and he wore sandals. She saw no need for the purchase of a tandem.

Number three asked her if she was adventurous in the bedroom.

Four was in love with his ex-wife.

Five, six and seven were all okay but none of them were the type of men you could take home to meet your mother. Another glance at Maggie showed that she was enjoying herself to the hilt. She was animated and flirtatious, showing too much thigh and more than a hint of stocking top. Beth could only imagine what number three had asked her.

Number ten had soulful eyes.

Sixteen wanted a British passport.

Number twenty-one smiled, shook hands and hitched up his jeans at the knees before sitting down. He looked tired. He'd been introducing himself all night. 'I've been looking forward to getting to you,' he said, with a grin. 'You have a nice smile.'

Beth laughed. 'And how many times have you used that line this evening?' She wasn't sure whether to feel amused or insulted by the lame chat-up.

He chuckled. 'No, I mean it. I saw you on the way in. I might have been rude to the other girls. My only interest was getting to you. You don't belong here.'

He made the statement with an air of assurance and she bristled, who the hell was he to tell her where she did or didn't belong? She couldn't think of a single worthy retort and her cheeks burned. He exuded confidence and she felt a thrill mixed with a lot of caution at the thought that this man had been watching her from across the room. The small amount of confidence she had felt earlier fled, leaving her floundering and trying to come up with something intelligent to say but she couldn't think of a damned thing.

He smiled again, a slow, wide smile, making no secret of the fact that he was weighing her up, assessing her. 'Marc,' he said, offering his hand across the table, 'with a C.' They shook hands for the second time.

'Beth,' she replied, 'with a B.' His eyes darkened, it

seemed that number twenty-one didn't like to be teased.

His grip was firm and he neither kept his hand still nor shook with too much vigour. He left it to Beth to break contact. 'People will insist on spelling it with a K.' He grinned and relaxed into his seat. 'So, Elizabeth, tell me about you. Why does a lady who obviously finds this undignified set up distasteful agree to come along? Which of these painted beauties dragged you here tonight?' He glanced around the room and caught sight of Maggie bending backwards in her seat and giving Beth a thumbs-up, with shining eyes and wide grin. 'Ah,' he said, turning back and giving Beth his full attention. 'I see you are with the enthusiastic Margaret.'

'Don't let her hear you calling her that. She'll freak, it's Maggie, only ever Maggie. You've got me wrong too. It's Bethany, not Elizabeth. I much prefer Beth, though. I don't go in for all that formal stuff.'

Marc, with a C, said that people do insist on bastardising traditional names. He guided the conversation, asking her questions. He listened to her answers, interjecting with snippets of his life. He seemed interested in what she had to say and led her to reveal more about herself. They discovered that they both lived in Ulverston, quite close to each other, in fact, only a few streets apart. Beth wondered then, if she had been stupid for giving out the name of her street. She chastised herself and decided to exhibit more caution. Marc alternated between pompous and charming. He made her laugh despite her misgivings. The conversation flowed and Beth didn't notice that she was enjoying herself.

Along with jeans he wore a smart shirt, though he was the type of man who would be just as comfortable in a suit and tie. His shirt, fastened apart from the top two buttons, stretched over his pectorals, a small wisp of dark hair peeping from the neck opening leaving Beth to wonder how much more was concealed. The thought was enough to make her blush especially when he caught her taking in his masculinity. His hair was black—perhaps too black to be natural, and his grey eyes had a steel penetration that was severe until he smiled. His frame was broad, his waist slim and he carried self-assurance as an accessory. He stood out from the other men at the event with their cod and their collies. His confidence was impressive and daunting. She was like a self-conscious little girl sitting opposite him. She was attracted and intimidated by him. She was even a little bit turned on by him. He intrigued her and she was flattered that he'd singled her out from the other women. He was too perfect a man to be at the lost and found of lonely hearts. What was somebody like him doing speed-dating when he could have his choice of women from the classiest wine bars?

The gong, indicating the end of their time together, interrupted them. Beth jumped, not expecting the intrusive suddenness. She was sorry that the date had ended and felt a pang of something akin to jealousy.

He picked up her pen and handed it to her. 'I trust you'll want this, treasure. The yes box is the one on the right.'

He was patronising, arrogant and condescending but he was sexy as hell, and Beth was fascinated.

Marc turned his charm on the next lady and danger walked behind him, but all Beth saw was a tight-fitting pair of jeans.

Chapter Two

Beth hadn't ticked the yes box beside Marc's name; Maggie had done it for her in her usual brash manner. 'Well, it's not as if you actually have to date him, is it? I mean, nobody can force you, can they?' Beth thought that Maggie was born too late and missed her calling as one of Hitler's right hand men. She should have been firm. She should have said no, and meant it. She should have stood up to Maggie because Beth knew all too well, that to give her an inch was to find yourself sucked into Maggie-world and all it encompassed.

'You might as well give in,' mumbled Graham Clarke, Maggie's long-term boyfriend. 'You know what she's like.' Far from being annoyed at the thought of his woman going to a speed dating night, Graham viewed it with wry amusement. Maggie was a natural flirt, but she was harmless and was only ever up for a laugh. He wasn't much for socialising, and liked the home life with the football and a can of beer.

'We can double date,' Maggie had continued, trying to wind Graham up. 'That Steve was cute, you know, Graham. Maybe I'll go out with him.'

'You go for it love, just remember to bring me a kebab on your way home. God help the poor sod.' Graham knew that Maggie was only going along with this so that Beth would go on a real date. Maggie had told all the men that she'd talked to at the speed dating, that she was in a happy relationship and was only there looking for friendship, and to help her friend. Beth had been single for over five years and Maggie felt that it had gone on long enough.

Maggie pushed and goaded and even went as far as ringing Marc's number. She held out the phone to Beth. There was no escape.

Beth's voice trembled, stammering like an awkward teenager. Marc had laughed at her nervousness. 'Bethany, you have no idea how appealing you are, have you?' The words were patronising, but, like a fool, she was thrilled by the compliment and irritated that she couldn't think of a sophisticated and witty retort.

With Maggie nudging and prodding beside her, Beth had brought up the idea of a double date. They could go out with Maggie and whichever of her thirteen 'ticks' she had decided to test drive.

'Beth, dear, I couldn't imagine anything worse than wanting time to get to know you and finding myself, instead, embroiled in the life and times of the overbearing Maggie.' Beth shuffled and held the phone closer to her ear. 'I would much prefer to meet you alone,' he said. 'There will be plenty of time for us to socialise as a couple, later.'

Beth's first thought was that he jumped to a lot of assumptions, this Marc fella. Their joint life experience together amounted to three minutes and here he was talking about them as a couple. Yes, she was irritated, and no, when faced with his confidence she couldn't think of anything to say in reply. But over and above the irritation, she was flattered and felt an uncomfortable warmth crawling onto her cheeks and seeking harbour there.

She moved the phone onto her other ear, and stepped

a few feet away from Maggie who was trying to get closer to hear what Marc was saying. They would meet the following afternoon for coffee at The Lancastrian. It was close for both and on a Saturday afternoon there would be plenty of diners giving the requisite safety in numbers.

Maggie sniffed in disdain as Beth tried to smooth her ruffled feathers. 'Well, he looks like a right ponce, anyway.' She was still coming to terms with the fact that Marc hadn't ticked her as possible dating material and two rebuffs from him in one day were too much for the effusive Maggie to deal with.

Beth's bedroom resembled delivery day at Debenhams by the time she had dressed for her date. Her wardrobe, doors flung wide, displayed a rack of empty coat hangers, and the bed was piled high with discarded clothing. She settled on a calf-length black skirt with a print of tiny pink roses and a pale pink top that accentuated her figure. She wore black knee-length boots and Maggie said that she looked 'mumsie' and offered a black Lycra mini skirt, which Beth declined.

He was waiting for her outside the bar. He held out a bouquet of a dozen pink roses that matched the print of her skirt. He told her that she looked beautiful and kissed her on the cheek before guiding her by her elbow into the lounge. He escorted her to a table by a bay window and ordered their coffee. He had suggested lunch at first but then, as if sensing that Beth was a person who moved cautiously, he had said, 'Or we can just meet for coffee and see how it goes.' Beth appreciated the act of thoughtfulness. He had good, old fashioned manners, rare in a man of his age. He seemed assured and strong.

She felt out of her depth, yet protected by him.

Coffee did stretch into lunch and one hour became three. Lunch lapsed into red wine and after her third glass she felt the effects of the alcohol warming her and loosening her tongue. The conversation, never stilted, came more easily with every sip. He was adept at filling any awkward gap with a witty quip or a relevant question. They talked and laughed and made eyes at each other as the afternoon shadows moved around the room with the passing of the day. He showed an interest in her life, but Beth never felt under fire.

She didn't want to be the one to end the date and he seemed comfortable. After six hours, Beth wanted to see him again.

She didn't want any more to drink though, she'd had enough. As he poured the last drips of the wine into her half full glass, he asked if he should get another bottle, 'Or...,' he tailed off lamely, 'do you have things to do?' She didn't want more wine, but it gave them a reason to sit and talk even though Marc was driving. He only had one glass and she was the one doing the drinking.

The second bottle came and he poured it, suggesting that they make a night of it, that they move on from there to see a film at the cinema. She nodded. He handed her the glass that hadn't needed replenishing and as she reached to take it, his knee knocked against the table causing her to fumble. The glass tipped and she watched in horror as the contents emptied down the front of his shirt.

He jumped up and grabbed a serviette to dab it.

Beth stood too, 'Oh, I'm sorry. I don't know how that happened.' She tried to blot the stain and made it worse.

His smile when he looked at her was forced and stiff. He glanced around the room, openly embarrassed by the disturbance and of the spreading stain to his shirt. Beth thought he was being flamboyant and making an unnecessary fuss. It was only a shirt but she felt clumsy and stupid.

He managed a tight-lipped smile. 'Oh, don't worry about it. I'm sure they'll be able to do something with it at the dry cleaners. It was an accident, it could have happened to anybody. I'll have to go home to change, though.'

Beth was irritated; he was blaming her, as though it was her fault that he'd knocked the table.

'Look,' he continued, there was that word again, 'I'm not sure that the cinema is a good idea tonight, maybe we should leave it for another evening.'

She tried not to let the disappointment show. 'Oh, okay, yes, of course. I'm sorry about your shirt.' She was humiliated. Should she offer to replace it? How much did something like that cost? She'd blown it. He obviously regretted being seen in public with a woman as clumsy as her. It seemed to Beth that he couldn't wait to get away. The date had started out so well, too.

He was still talking. 'Unless, of course, you wouldn't mind waiting? It'll only take me a couple of minutes to change.'

She smiled, 'Of course not. Do you want me to wait here?'

'No, I think we should get out of here, don't you? People are staring at us.'

There was reproach in his words and she felt the sting of having been told off like a naughty child.

'I suppose it would be best if you came home with me. You know I live just around the corner from you and I've got the car outside. We can go straight to the cinema from there. I can get you some water at my house; it might help to steady your hand.'

His words were barbed. Christ, she thought, it was an accident, get over it, man. Jesus, she'd only had two thirds of a bottle of wine and a brandy after lunch. She liked him but, fuck, he was overbearing. She wasn't sure if she wanted to go to the cinema after that, the condescending arse, but he was already guiding her out of the pub.

He saw the uncertainty cross her face and settle in the folds of her brow. 'I'm sorry, Beth, that was stupid of me. Of course, you shouldn't get in a stranger's car. You don't know me. We'll do this properly and I'll call you soon.'

'Yes, that's probably best,' Beth said, reaching for her purse. 'But I insist on paying the cost of your dry-cleaning.'

'Now I've offended you. I've enjoyed this afternoon. Let's not let one silly little incident spoil a perfect date.' He winked. 'We'll go to the cinema as planned and to salve your conscience, you can buy the popcorn. How's that?'

She gave herself a mental ticking off. Marc was okay. He wasn't one of the dating agency weirdo's that she'd heard about. He was just particular about appearances and needed to lighten the hell up.

'Okay, deal.'

His good mood returned in the car. He'd been stiff and uncomfortable when he'd paid the bill. He refused

Beth's offer to split the cost between them and said that when he was treating a woman to lunch, he didn't expect her to pay for it. Beth always liked to pay her way, but she would tackle her independence issues another, more appropriate time.

She was looking forward to seeing inside his house. As a child growing up on Croftland's Estate she had passed it on her way to school. The house was old, gothic, and lacking a gardener. It crouched at the top of Springfield Road and was a remnant of times past. A wall of Lakeland stone surrounded the two-acre property, but the ominous turrets of the west-wing tower were visible over the top. She remembered visiting the house one Halloween. They had been very daring then, egging each other on. Maggie was brash, claiming to the world that she wasn't scared, but she was back at the road before Beth had time to turn from ringing the bell. Beth had always been in awe of the great house covered in emerald green ivy. It was anti-climactic when nobody answered the door that Halloween, they'd retreated, half disappointed and half terrified, convincing each other that curtains twitched in the upstairs rooms and sinister old ladies embroiled in dark deeds, lurked behind them.

For years, the old place was a nursing home. Marc bought it with a view, he said, to development and returning it to a grand family home.

'What are you smiling at?' He pulled up in front of the house.

'Oh, nothing really, you know, just ghosts from the past.' She felt stupid under his gaze.

He indulged her with a smile. 'I want to hear about all of your memories, Beth. All your dreams, too. I want to know everything there is to know about Bethany Armstrong. Well, don't just stand there, come in and I'll get changed.'

The house was a work in progress but it was already spectacular. Marc and his team of designers were working to keep the character of the old house, while giving it a fresh, modern twist. The furniture that lined the hallway would have cost more than the contents of Beth's house, and her car to boot. The light was fading but Beth could imagine sunshine streaming through the front door in full daylight. Antique and modern sculpture complemented each other. The attention to detail in the refurbishment was sublime and no cost had been spared to make the ambiance just right.

He ushered her into the main lounge. The room was vast with bay windows looking onto the garden. Marc explained that everything was on a centrally controlled timing device. At dusk the curtains closed and the lights came on. Water features were popular in people's lounges. Praying hands, elephant herds and earthenware gourds were on sale in any market hall with their tiny waterfalls and up-lit prisms. Marc had taken the concept a step further. The right-hand corner of the room was dominated by the sculpture of a dancing lady in treated bronze. She was in a classic ballerina pose, hands high, almost meeting in an arch above her head, left leg, slim and pointed, sticking out high in front of her, the positioning and delicate point of the foot a testament to the fact that this home was not child friendly. The golden curves of the dancer's body were subtly lit with unseen coloured bulbs in the trough below. Water cascaded over her breasts and a filter controlled how much pressure was forced through the fountain heads for whichever mood was desired. The water trickled, sighing and gurgling as it made its way into the font at the base of the statue. The statue was life-sized, the fountain containing her monumental, a lesser room could never get away with something of this size and flamboyance.

Experts say that a room should have one dramatic focal point. This room had two. An enormous open fire was laid with wood and coal, ready to have a match put to it if the evening should turn chilly. The hearth was set with old fashioned irons. The fire-surround dominated its fore, hewn from Lakeland stone and set with small alcoves and deep recesses where ferns had been placed far enough into the cool rock to be protected from the heat of the fire when lit.

The polished real-wood floor shone. Five plush leather sofas were placed with care at angles to encourage conversation. There was no visible entertainment system in this room, no television, until Marc went to a discrete control panel hidden in trunking by the side of the fireplace. Beth could see that he loved showing off his home to new people. He reminded her of the ringmaster at a circus she had attended as a child. He pressed a couple of buttons on the panel and the huge oil painting on the wall—by the Lakeland artist, Len Mein—slid up to the ceiling on silent motorised tracks and settled into its new niche on the wall. A television of cinematic proportions, and the best in home entertainment centres, lay snugly where the oil painting had been.

Marc handed Beth an ordinary remote control and told her to help herself. He pushed buttons on the panel and four racks of CDs trundled from the wall cavity to show thousands of albums. More buttons released a similar array of DVDs. He showed her to a room off the lounge—a fully equipped bar. He said that he was going for the quickest shower in living history and would be back very shortly. He told her to help herself to anything she wanted and asked her to pour him two fingers of bourbon over ice for when he came down and said that they would take a taxi into town.

When Marc left the room, Beth looked at the remote control in her hand. Way too many buttons, she decided, and put it on the arm of one of the sofas. She wandered into the bar. Looking through the array of bottles on the shelving, some on optic some standing free, she shook her head, she couldn't see one that said 'bourbon' on the label. She knew it was some sort of whiskey, but had no idea in what form it presented itself. Oh, bugger, she thought, where's Maggie when I need her? She grinned. Maggie would have loved all this. She could just see her friend gazing around in awe and calling Marc a posh twat.

Beth had a vague idea that Bourbon was American whiskey. She settled on a bottle of Wild Turkey that looked sort of American and would just have to do. He probably couldn't tell the difference between one whiskey and another, anyway. She poured him what she figured was probably about two of his big chunky fingers and couldn't find any ice. She poured herself a smaller glass of the nasty looking brown liquid, smelled it, pulled a face and poured her drink into his. She put her glass on the bar and went back into the lounge.

He had left the door open. She walked to the threshold and listened to see if she could locate the sound of running water. His bathroom was too far away to hear anything and the house hunkered over her with a dense silence. She felt uncomfortable and couldn't pinpoint why. Shivering, she went back into the warm atmosphere of the lounge.

She was running her finger along the spines of his CD collection when she heard whistling followed by footsteps coming down the stairs.

'There, that's better,' he said, coming in through the door and leaving it open behind him. 'I feel clean again.' He stopped in the middle of the room and stared around him. 'Oh, Bethany, I expected you to put things away after you'd finished with them. Look at all these racks left out to collect dust. You're not a very tidy person, are you? We'll have to do something about that, you know.'

Beth didn't hear a word he said. When she heard him coming, she'd turned towards the door smiling. She had moved on from his CDs to his DVDs and held his copy of *Dirty Dancing*. She was going to tell him that it was one of her favourite films; she was going to ask him if he knew Swayze's mother owned a dance school; she was going to ask him if he was ready to go. She didn't say any of these things.

He shut the door with a soft click.

She only caught a glimpse of the lower half of his body. While she was dragging her eyes up to search for answers in his face, she had only looked down for a second, but she knew exactly what she'd seen.

Instead of coming into the lounge dressed in a clean shirt, ready to go, he was half naked. He wore a short, satin, dressing gown. The front had come apart showing his torso, covered in curly black hair. She fought her eyes, demanding they stay locked on his face.

She'd seen it though—his erection. It was big and ugly. She had seen the definition of it beneath the thin material of the robe. It stuck straight out from his body, a small ring of the cloth darkening, wet around the head, turning the silk from a rich deep red, to a brown colour. The bulge of his penis was distressing the hang of the dressing gown. Although his erection was covered, it had pulled the gown open and the top of his thigh was exposed. He had hairy upper thighs, and as her mind replayed what it had seen in that split-second glance, she remembered the tiny mole below his navel. She shuddered.

He was smiling at her, amused.

'Come on, Bethany, don't be coy. You're not going to go all precious on me, are you? We both know that this is what it's all about. This is what you're here for isn't it? It's all about sex. Don't play Miss Innocent with me, after all, you went to the speed dating knowing full well that the brash, Lady Margaret had a man waiting for her at home, didn't you? Yes, I've been checking you out. You aren't married, but do you have a man waiting for you at home as well? Does he know that you go out alone, like an alley cat? Not that it makes any difference to me.'

She was shaking her head, feeling out of her depth, but he carried on talking.

'If you wish, we'll play the game. You can act horrified, I'll break through your defences, and then, when we're bored with the game, we'll have some great sex.'

'I don't understand. Look, there's been a misunderstanding. I'm just going to leave, okay?' She was backing up as he advanced towards her, one step for every three words.

'You aren't going anywhere, my dear. You don't even want to. Isn't this delicious? The tension, Bethany, can you feel it? Can you feel the vibes in the room?' He drew in a deep breath and shuddered. 'I'm very excited, Bethany. You've done this to me. You are so very sexy with your big scared eyes and your "Don't touch" attitude. You have no idea of your power, have you? We're going to be so good together. We're going to be—electric.'

He was between her and the door. She'd have to push past him to get out. She was terrified. She didn't think he was going to let her leave. Gathering all her determination and courage, she hugged herself, her body language closing in, shutting down, blocking him out. 'I'm leaving,' she said.

His only reply was to smile that infuriating smile. The edge of her vision caught his hard-on as she was striding towards the door.

Marc stepped aside to let her pass, his own arms folded, but crossed loosely, his expression arrogant and assured as she fled. She was surprised. She expected him to grab her and stop her from leaving. Perhaps it was just a misunderstanding after all. She would kill Maggie for this, tomorrow. She had learned her lesson. All these things were scrolling through her mind as she reached for the door handle. And then her mind voided, all thoughts blasted violently away as a hurricane of fear blew into town.

The door was locked.

She remembered the click, thought nothing of it at the time, was too preoccupied with Marc's state of undress. She knew that she wasn't going to be able to walk away from this with no more repercussion than a feeling of shame and embarrassment.

She faced the locked door. She didn't want to turn around and knew that when she did, she needed all her wits about her. She breathed, drawing the scent of furniture polish into her lungs and exhaling it slowly. He hadn't moved. She was attuned, listening. She sensed him leaning against the maple and stone fire surround, smiling—smug and waiting, much as a snake will wait for its prey to move, biding its time, knowing that the result will fall in its favour. This was foreplay.

She took another breath and turned. Her eyes hardened, her face set in a mask of resolve.

'Let me out.' She said it with a steady voice, hoping that her no-nonsense attitude would bring Marc to his senses.

He didn't say a word. His smile fixed, teeth strong and white. Teeth that had seemed so attractive to Beth earlier, flashed menacingly, forcing the image of the predator. He was a shark.

He dropped his left arm to his side and brought his right hand up his body. He pushed away the raw silk material and snaked his hand across his naked chest. He was taunting her with a display of self-caressing, his fingertips curling through the thick chest hair, finding his nipple and fingering it until it budded. His mouth dropped open, his eyes half closing for a second. He released a long breath, the hand at his thigh moving, in a slow, circular motion.

His eyes snapped open, making her jump. They locked onto hers, hard and threatening. Beth was aware of the door behind her. She leaned into it, wanting it to support her, but she pulled away to stand unsupported, realising that this was more about power than it was about sex.

'I want to go home. Let me out, please, or I'll call the police.'

'And how are you going to do that, my dear?' He was still smiling, his hands still moving, his eyes still cruel.

'I'll scream.'

'Feel free. Nobody will hear you.'

She felt tears well in her eyes. She willed herself not to cry. 'Why are you doing this to me? I just want to go home.' The word 'home' was broken by a sob and she was annoyed with herself.

She wheeled around, turning to face the door, searching for a mechanism to unlock it and let herself out. It was self-locking with a Yale type catch but there was no release chamber on the inside of the door. She could feel hysteria rising inside her and hammered with both fists. She was screaming and the tears fell as she yelled to be let out.

Marc didn't move. He had stopped stroking himself; his audience was inattentive so there was no point. He watched the woman beating on the heavy door until her fists were red and swollen and her voice was strained.

'I want to go home,' she finished quietly, when the last of her energy was spent.

'There are three ways to open the door,' he said, conversationally. He had opened a panel in the wall at the other side of the fireplace where the column of controls was inlaid into the trunking. 'You can open this and press this button. Or, you can use this, like this.' He had picked up a black remote control and held it out towards her. He was showing off, enjoying her terror and confusion.

She wasn't thinking. Her mind was blank, all her efforts focused on the remote control. She ran towards him ready to snatch it from his hand. He was offering it, holding it out to her, smiling.

She reached for it, moving forwards. Her fingertips were closing around the plastic as he flung his hand into the air, taking the control out of her reach, tossing it backwards into the room. It clattered to the floor, overended once, and lay still.

'Or, Bethany,' he continued, 'the best way to get out of here is to just be nice to me. I want you to be nice to me, Bethany. You want that, too, don't you? We can be so good together.' He grabbed her, his arms encircling her body, chest to chest, breath to breath, grunting into her face as his hard chest pressed against the softness of her body. 'Can you do that, Bethany? Can you do that for me? Can you be nice to me?' She was struggling, fighting against the closure around her, trying to loosen the grip of his arms. She tried to get loose to gouge his eyes but he had her pinned. Her hands fluttered birdlike and useless against his chest. She lifted a leg to kick him but he anticipated the movement. As her leg moved, he wrapped his calf around her weight-bearing leg and pulled it from under her. They fell to the floor in a tangle. With nothing to break her fall, she fell on her back. Contact with the ground drove the breath from her and she was winded. Her head hit the floor and bounced off, catching the side of his cheek with her chin as he came down on top of her. She felt sick. Her eyes stung. The void in her chest, left by her breath's wake, burned. It swelled inside her and as she tried to inhale, it caught under her rib cage and held. She couldn't exhale; fringes of blackness were billowing at her peripheral vision. Her mouth was opening and closing but no air passed in either direction.

He was on top of her. The fall distracted her from what he was doing. Her concentration was focused on drawing breath and she didn't struggle as he took first one arm and then the other and fastened them under his knees. Her eyes were bulging and her lips tinged with blue as she dragged the first jagged breath down her throat. It brought her no relief. It had a serrated edge and caught all the way to her lungs. Once inside her, the dirty air rolled with the burning heat and expanded. She tried to get rid of it, tried to push it out, but it stuck, big and heavy inside her. He was talking but she couldn't understand the words, all she was aware of was being winded, the incredible weight inside her body and her inability to breathe. Her muscles contracted, trapping the air inside her. In panic, she tensed, further cramping her tortured body. Her eyes were bulging, bloodshot with bursting vessels. Her focus was hazing. The world was swimming around her, moving, and she felt herself surrendering to unconsciousness. She slumped, relaxing the tension and the stale air left her body in a rush as the muscles released their cargo. The next inhalation was easier but still raw and it dragged. The one after that was smoother. The fire waned and the darkness lifted, deserting her—just when she needed it most. She couldn't fight him and if she was going to be raped, she wanted to be unconscious.

Her eyes refocused. He was on top of her, sitting

across her chest. The dressing gown was gone. As she brought order to her mind, she could feel the cool softness of satin against her lower right calf. He must have thrown it behind him. She could feel his buttocks on her abdomen. She felt him there, her body supporting him and cushioning the definition of his balls below her breasts. She could smell the musk scent of his sex underneath the aroma of magnolia shower gel. The base of his penis was touching her. His foreskin was stretched back as he pushed the head forward into her chest. He leaked pre-cum onto her blouse. The glans smooth and shining with his moisture, purple in colour as the blood was forced to the head of his dick.

She felt sick. As the panic of not being able to breathe and the intense burning pain left her body, she was aware of the pain in her head. She had banged it hard. His weight on top of her exasperated the momentum and the fall was heavy. Her body shifted, the wave of motion causing him to resettle his buttocks, she felt the bones of his backside digging into her sternum. She could feel her heartbeat in the rush of blood to her ears. The pain in her head knocked against the back of her eyes. She was sleepy. All she wanted to do was to go to sleep. She shook her head, causing a wave of nausea to surge through her body, banishing the sleepy feeling and bringing her back to the hard floor beneath her—and the monster on top of her.

He was sitting over her, watching, waiting for her to gather her wits. When Beth came through the stages of inertia to alertness, he grinned. It was clear that he wanted a lively participant. She was aware; she saw his erection pulse back to full attention.

He bent his head and covered her mouth with his, grinding his teeth into the flesh of her lower lip, drawing blood and forcing his tongue against hers, tasting saliva as it filled her mouth. She thrashed her head from side to side. He stayed with her, his mouth on hers, riding her attempts to stave him off. Her legs kicked and hips bucked. She almost threw him and he had to rebalance. He was grunting into her mouth, tasting her breath, his tongue probing and retracting between his mouth and hers. He brought his hands up to the sides of her face, holding her jaws with his palms, stopping her from biting and maiming him. A dribble of saliva-thinned blood trickled onto her chin. She whimpered, the small bleat of desperation resonating inside his mouth, sending a shudder of lust into his loins. He fed on her weakness.

He tore his mouth from the unreciprocated kiss. His finger grazed across the cup of her bra. 'I want to see them; how hard would you like me to bite your nipples?' Humiliation tracked across her face. He sat straight and ran his hands over the front of her blouse. She pushed her shoulders into the floor and twisted her spine to get him off her.

Marc grimaced. 'Little boobies. Deceptively small. Bethany Baby-tits. I've seen chubby boys with bigger knockers than you. No matter, if they are responsive, we can make do until we can get you some surgery. They remind me of the breasts of a pre-pubescent child,' His face had a far-away expression, as though he was reliving a memory from the past, '...like somebody's little sister.' and then he was back in the moment, 'I'll spank you later.' With a single motion, he brought his hands up in front of her and ripped her blouse open. A button flew away to the left. Beth followed it with her eyes. She wanted to see where it went, where it stopped. It might be useful as evidence, later. He'd had this planned, the spilled wine an excuse to get her back here.

Her push-up bra gave her a false cleavage. He grabbed at the lacy black cups with both hands and wrenched them down her body. His fingernail caught on her upper chest and gouged an inch-long trench in her flesh. For a second, the exposed capillaries blinked at the world, pink and empty, but with the next heartbeat they filled with blood. It oozed down her chest and pooled around his penis. It was only a small cut but like many small skin breaks, it bled greater than it's worth.

Her breasts were exposed, but she was encumbered by the bra which, when covering her, had looked feminine and elegant, but left to flap below her ribs showed its deception. Forced down, the straps tore into her arms above the elbow.

'Stupid bitch, you should have worn a front fastening bra, you knew you were meeting me.' He pulled at the straps in temper, stretching them and causing her to cry out in pain as they dug into her flesh. He couldn't risk letting her arm go, she was stronger and had regained some strength as the instinct of survival kicked in. He wouldn't be able to secure her so easily a second time if he let his guard down. Beth was waiting for any opportunity to get away. The stitching gave on one strap and he could get the clothing far enough down to push under his thighs and out of sight.

She was naked to the waist, displayed before him. Her face was red with humiliation and her eyes burned with hatred and terror. His hands shook as he reached out to stroke her breasts. They were small but had large responsive nipples. They hardened as he ran his fingers over them. She hated her body for this betrayal.

'See, under the prissy attitude, you are a little slut, aren't you?' He kneaded her flesh with brutal fingers, hurting her.

He left red finger marks in her breast. They would bruise later, but the skin was flushed and angry. He saw the welts and they heightened his excitement. He pummelled her body with his hands, grunting and thrusting his hips forward so that the head of his penis pushed through the valley of her cleavage.

The friction caused him to leak more semen and he gathered the meat of her breasts together as he thrust harder and faster into the slippery crevice. She was weeping, tears rolling down either side of her face and dropping onto her shoulders. Each time she begged him to stop he thrust harder. For twenty seconds, he rode the cleft between her beasts as she bucked and fought to dislodge him. He groaned and shuddered. His torso stiffened and he stopped moving, forcing his penis through the resistance of her breasts and his hands. The end of his dick appeared and the first jet of his ejaculate hit her in the face.

'Oh, yes,' he moaned, 'Oh Bethany, I'm coming on you.'

Each new rope of spunk lessened and spilled over her chest. She felt his buttocks tense and shudder under her and the damp stickiness of his balls felt slick as they lifted and then dropped on to her body. She hadn't stopped fighting him. Her legs thrashed and her body swivelled, but he was six-foot-tall, his body was firm and dense, his weight more than fourteen stone, to her nine stone seven. She couldn't budge him.

He sat up, his eyes closed, and he licked his lips. His brow was shining with perspiration and his breath was rasping after his orgasm. He opened his eyes and if she dared hope that the ordeal was over, and that he would let her go, his eyes told her that he was far from finished with her. His face settled into a new expression—one of black, furious anger.

'I didn't want to do that. Why did you make me do that? You little whore. I wanted our first time to be so -' he stopped and rolled his eyes to the ceiling searching for the correct word '- intense. I wanted it to be intense and memorable. And what do you give to me? Your pathetic baby tits, that's what. Flaunting them at me, like a brazen bitch in heat, begging me with your soulful eyes to touch them, to ride them. Thrusting them out at me, and all the time playing your little "Oh, please don't touch" game. I didn't want to come like that. I didn't want to make a mess of you. It was supposed to be special. You ruined it, you spoiled our first time. You're filthy—disgusting. You repulse me.'

He was ranting, forcing his knees into her shoulders, shifting his weight to release the tension in his muscles where cramp threatened. She was telling him no, asking him to let her up.

'Please, let me go home. I promise I won't tell anyone. I won't go to the police. Please, just let me go.'

'And have you telling that low-grade wench, Margaret that I'm an unsatisfactory lover? That I come too quickly? Have you mocking me to her? Would you be that disloyal to me, Bethany? Have I judged you wrong?' His shoulders slumped and for the first time she sensed a change in his demeanour. His rapid ejaculation had taken some of his power and arrogance.

She shook her head vehemently. 'No, no, I won't tell anyone, I promise.' She was scrambling around in her vocabulary. This might be her one chance of escape. She had to find the right words to pacify the lunatic. 'Don't worry about it. Next time will be better, you'll see.'

His head had dropped to his chest in a posture of abject self pity. It shot up, fire blazing in his eyes. 'You mock me already. Not only do you strip me of my masculinity, but you take me for a fool. You think I'm going to let you go? And as for next time—next time? My dear Bethany, only I will decide if there is to be a next time. What pull do you think you have, lying there broken and used with filthy stuff dripping from your ugly body?'

He shuffled back and pulled her up by the shoulders until her face was in line with his. She thought he was going to kiss her. He dropped his forehead and she moved her face a fraction of an inch to avoid his mouth, saving herself from the worst as he head-butted her in the face. Her movement saved her nose and deflected the worst of the impact, but her already bruised bottom lip split like an orange segment ripe with juice. 'Next time, restrain yourself, woman, until I tell you I'm ready. If I can ever stand to look at you again, next time we will take our orgasm together. We will forget about this initial unpleasantness. We will go back to our taunt and tease game and it will be our first time, just as I had it planned. It will be so good, Bethany... so intense.'

He was more compliant. Not thinking about how she would get out of the room and, after that, the house, she saw only her chance for her first move towards freedom. She wanted to explore her ruined face, probe with her fingertip to find out how badly hurt she was. But instead, when she felt him shift his weight on her body, she gave an almighty heave of chest and hip. He toppled and struck out a hand. Too late to balance himself, he fell to the right. Beth was out from underneath him. She was scrambling across the floor towards the remote control that would activate the door, whimpering like a beaten dog but resolute in her need to escape. Her knees grazed the hard floor. She reached out and almost toppled over. She had the remote in her hand, pulling it into her body and balancing on both legs and one arm.

But he was on her, tackling her from behind, bringing her down. His arms were tight around her waist. She kicked out, wasting energy, pummelling her leg muscles into free air. His legs were pulled close to his waist, giving him purchase and the power to attack her again. Shifting his position, he grabbed her hair with one hand while the other strengthened its grip around her waist. He pulled her by the hair until her back arched, and he continued to yank until her body contorted into the shape of an archer's bow. Both legs were straight out behind her, kicking furiously. Her right foot connected with the base of the life-sized bronze sculpture. She brought her other foot to meet it. She had something to provide an anchor to push against. Bracing both feet against the statue she put every calorie of energy into twisting her body. He had her by the hair. The movement wrenched at her scalp. Her force, not his, rived follicles from their bed, tearing the hair from her head. The agony added impetus to her action. She bunched her fist for added force and drove her elbow backwards into the tender flesh of his groin. She missed her target on the first attempt but heard a satisfying whoosh of breath as she connected instead with his belly. She got him in the balls the second time. He curled, cradling the hurt with his forearms crossed around his middle.

She was up, facing him, on her knees, on her feet, swinging her foot behind her, grateful for her choice of knee-length boots over open-toed sandals. He was occupied with the fire in his belly and didn't see the kick coming. He didn't move to deflect the blow. She planted her foot full in the bastard's face. She hopped on her pivotal foot as the velocity of the kick carried her forwards. The crunch of bone was satisfying.

He didn't bleed as much as she expected. It didn't spurt as her lip had done. It was more of a gush down his chest. Deep red, capillary bleeding released in a flood from the burst vessels in his nose. She dropped into a relaxed stance, her legs three feet apart, bent at the knee with her hands on her thighs. Taking a breath to inflate her lungs, she took the weight on her left leg and swung with the right, kicking him in the head.

She watched him slump and turned towards the door, but before she could point the remote control he was on his feet, black fire in his eyes. His face, cruel before, bore a look that any fool could read as murderous.

He was going to kill her.

She knew it.

He knew it.

Bethany Armstrong was going to die, tonight, in this house, and nobody would know where the hell she was.

He didn't say anything. He wasn't playing. The game was over. He'd spat the dummy out and, like all babies who don't get their own way, he didn't want to play any more. The silence was broken by their combined rasping breath. He moved towards her. She turned, one step at a time, circling, keeping space between them, ancient wrestlers of the Acropolis, swathed in blood, fighting to the death. She had turned ninety degrees and was facing the statue when he ran her. She was still holding the remote, pointing it towards him, ready to fire. It was the only weapon she had. Gone was her moment of surprise, where his lapse in concentration had counterbalanced the ratio of their strength and gave her a split-second advantage. No ifs, no buts—she was going to die.

Her mind was clear when his body hit hers. She stepped back on her left foot for balance and went with the momentum of his body in a graceful dance-like movement, rather than stiffening and trying to absorb the shock of his bulk. She remained on her feet. He shook his head to clear his fuzzed vision and speckles of bone, blood and snot splattered her face. He was pushing her, using his weight to cannon her backwards. He tripped as his foot tangled with the CD rack. He didn't fall but tottered, grabbing onto her for balance rather than wheeling her away like a supermarket trolley. She grabbed at this second chance, turning the tables on him, taking his own tactic and switching it against him. She was slight and lithe, and had nothing much to work with, but she found strength in desperation. Beth had never fought in her life. Her only experience came from a few lessons in self-defence at the local Community Centre but now she was fighting for her life and a primal instinct drove her.

Moving on intuition, she took a deep breath into her diaphragm. At that moment, when she had to take her advantage and make it work for her, she felt an energy that she didn't know she possessed, and used it. She pushed him backwards, just as he had done to her. His upper body was rigid but his legs pummelled across the floor, trying to get purchase, finding none, three steps, four steps, five, building speed, cannoning backwards.

It wasn't planned. She didn't mean to do it. She didn't even see what was going to happen. She was fighting to stay alive, living one second to the next, not expecting to ever see further than that room, working only to keep his feet moving backwards from this second to the next, and forever so that he couldn't lay his filthy hands on her again.

The bronze lady was smiling at her, willing her to beat him, willing her to live. Beth pushed with everything she had, moving him—moving him—moving him, until, suddenly, he stopped.

It was quiet.

His eyes opened wide. His mouth gaped, he screamed, but Beth didn't stop, she was still pushing him backwards, fighting against the barrier that was holding him. It wouldn't give.

But he did.

She heard the sharp, pointed foot of the ballerina pierce his back. His feet were paddling in the font at the base of the fountain. Fresh blood bubbled from his mouth, different from last time, brighter, freshly oxygenated, arterial. He blew red airy bubbles at her, wheezing a reedy cry like the whistle of a boiling kettle.

Burst lung.

He looked like an extension of the sculpture. He was impaled on her extended leg, the workmanship fine, elegant, slim, tapered and as thin as a stiletto knife adorned with a ballerina's slipper.

She watched him die, exultant, victorious, horrified. She witnessed the split second that his essence left the wreckage of his body. He was stuck to the front of the sculpture, dancing with the ballerina, one leg lifted, brow furrowed, eyes wide in agony and with the horror of realisation. His body danced with the lady but his eyes belonged to Beth. He pleaded with her silently to help him—and then he was gone.

She didn't suspect that he was dead, didn't have an inkling that he was dead. She simply knew that Marc, with a C, no longer inhabited the bloodied body. The font filled up with the dying man's blood and by the time his heart stopped pumping, the water in the trough was cloudy and red. The bulbs, at the base pointed upwards, changing colour every five seconds. The blood was purple, then orange, then blue.

Beth had her forever back. Her future was destined to last longer than the next few seconds, yet she could have spent forever watching water play in rainbows over a dead man's body.

She heard a noise. It sounded like a child – somewhere a child was laughing. It couldn't be. Her mind was playing with her, creating illusions like that of the violet blood splashing in front of her eyes.

She turned towards the source of the imagined noise

and the previously locked door hung open.

She ran from the room, ran from the house, ran from the nightmare. She ran until vomit rose in her throat and until her feet buckled and caused her to fall. She ran all the way home and then stopped only because there was nowhere else to run.

Chapter Three

'If you're there, pick up. C'mon Beth, get out of your pit and pick up the Goddamn phone, I want all the gory details. Oh, my God, you're not in bed with him, are you? Okay, so you're not there. I'm burning with curiosity here. Meet me at the market caff at ten, yeah? Colin hasn't put my money in the bank, the bastard, so I'm going to call in at the garage. A bit of public humiliation will remind him of his parental responsibilities. Catch you at ten, babe. Bye.'

The phone was beside the chair where Beth sat, numbly ignoring it. It was only eight thirty. She'd been in the same position all night without moving. She hadn't noticed the passage of time; she could have been there for one night or three weeks. On the rare occasion that her mind filled with thought, the only thing taking space was a detached haze. She was amazed that her mind wasn't racing. She killed a man. She watched life seep away from another human being and yet, she didn't feel anything. She wasn't frightened. On getting home she prepared for what was coming and then she sat down to wait.

She ran home in panic, but the moment she shut her front door on the world—on him—the fear left, clinical shock jumped into its place and she was filled with an empty calm. She went to her bedroom and stripped out of her bloody clothing, folding the items into a neat pile and putting them in a suitcase. As well as all the blood on her outer garments, there was a small blood stain on the front of her underwear, a drop that had smeared through her skirt from either one of her cuts or one of his. She was humiliated and wanted to throw them away, but they'd have to examine her underwear too. She put her boots on top of the clothing, zipped the case and dressed in jog pants and a jumper. She wanted to shower. She could smell him on her, that sickly magnolia shower gel. It made her gag and she thought she was going to vomit. She wanted to shower but she'd seen enough cop programmes to know it wasn't the right thing to do. She didn't want to incriminate herself further, or make things any worse for when she stood in the dock a murderess.

She'd put on a coat because it was cold, took her suitcase, put it beside her chair and sat down—waiting. She didn't contemplate ringing the police; thought took effort and she had no effort to give. She didn't feel numb in the way that media stories describe, this was different. She was blank. She wasn't thinking because she'd lost the ability to think, she had no thoughts in her head. She had no vocabulary. A lifetime of learning was gone and she was an empty vessel.

Coming out of her fugue was like waking in an unfamiliar world. It took effort, she pulled out of The Empty—and her mind resisted. She should meet Maggie, live for an hour as a normal woman on a normal Monday morning. Maggie said she wanted the gory details of her date. If gore was what she wanted she wouldn't be disappointed.

She expected them to come, flashing blue, almost immediately. But Marc might not be found for ages, it could be days and then they had to connect him to her. It would save a lot of time if she went to them. But it would be good to have a coffee with Maggie first. For once, she had something to tell that Maggie couldn't beat.

After hours of empty nothingness, the thought of seeing Maggie opened a small part of her functioning. She wasn't cold, she was freezing. She noticed that she hurt all over her body. Letting the hurt in created a channel for simple thought. She'd meet Maggie and then she would hand herself to the police. That was the right thing to do in these unfortunate circumstances.

She left a note for the arresting officers saying that she was going to give herself in but had to nip out first. It was the polite thing to do—even murderers should use their manners. She had no idea how fast the police would break down doors in cases of cold-blooded murder. It might look as though she'd run away.

She felt as if she had a cold, the type of cold that people exaggerate to flu. She was tired but not sleepy, heavy and encumbered. Her head ached from the beating and her few intermittent thoughts couldn't get through the swelling in her synapses to make themselves understood.

She looked at the clock to see what time the next bus was due. The time went from her eyes to her brain and was lost. She read the clock again, this time keeping the information on its lead, but she struggled to do the calculation of current time to bus time. It was irrelevant, more white noise in a head crammed full of the stuff. The buses ran every fifteen minutes so she wouldn't have long to wait.

As she left the house, she saw somebody sitting on

the strip of council owned grass opposite her house. She panicked, figuring a police stakeout, but it was only a teenager. Her bottom must have been wet, sitting on the grass like that. It was a dismal day. As she cut across Maple Avenue and onto Acacia Terrace, she tried to face the enormity of what she'd done. She had to make herself think about it, but she wondered instead if it was worth buying a meat and potato pie from the market—would she have time to eat it?

'I killed a man last night,' she whispered. But it didn't feel big. She needed to buy tampons and that seemed like a much bigger deal if she was going to be arrested. The girl from the grass was walking behind her. Beth glanced around, worried that the kid might have heard her admitting to murder, but she was far enough behind that, at worst, she might have seen a crazy woman talking to herself. She couldn't hear what Beth said.

She turned towards Croftland's shops and the bus stop. It was quiet for a Monday morning. An old lady waited in the shelter with her head bent against the autumn chill. The young girl walked past and disappeared into Buywrights. Beth envied her youth. She probably didn't have a worry worth frowning over.

There was plenty of room on the bus. She took the first forward facing seat, crossed her legs and turned her face to the window. The driver released the air breaks and the bus rolled away from the kerb. She watched without interest as the girl from the grass ran from the shop and hopped onto the bus as it was pulling away. After paying, she plonked herself on the seat facing Beth.

'Phew, just made it.'

Beth tried for a polite smile. It turned into a grimace

as the clotted blood at the side of her mouth split. The girl was looking at her. She felt herself colouring. It dawned on her that she hadn't washed. Apart from pulling on some clean clothes, she was as she had been when she fled Marc's house. Her hair wasn't brushed, her mouth was stale and her battered face unclean, the blood was left to dry as it had fallen. She had dried semen between her breasts. What would her mother have said about that?

The girl took a canvas bag from her shoulder and rummaged inside. 'Here.' She held out a white cotton handkerchief, 'You might want to…,' she tailed off, motioning to the dribble of fresh blood escaping from the cracked scab on Beth's face. 'It's clean.'

'Thank you.' Beth took it and dabbed at her face, she winced. Talking hurt, touching it hurt—thinking about it was agony. She brought her hand down, went to pass the handkerchief back and saw that it was stained with blood. She shrugged an apology and dropped her hand, not knowing what to do.

'Keep it, I've got plenty more.'

The small kindness was too much for Beth. She hadn't cried, but on the bus, surrounded by people, she felt tears welling. Not now, she pleaded, silently. Dear God, please not now. Her prayers were unanswered and the tears exploded from her eyes. She was going to be hysterical if she didn't get a grip. She felt a noise rising inside her and, until it mixed with air, she had no way of knowing if it was going to be a sob or a scream. She swallowed it and brushed at her face with the hanky. She took some breaths, aware that the girl was looking at her, hoping that nobody else had noticed the exchange between them. She had to get herself under control.

'Are you okay?' The girl's eyes were sympathetic—and they were curious.

'Yes, I'm fine thanks.' What she wanted to say was, 'Please, leave me alone. Don't look at me. In fact, please sit somewhere else,' but she couldn't say any of that so she scrambled around for something else, any distraction from the state she was in.

'Not many people use them these days.'

The girl looked blank.

'Lace handkerchiefs. I mean, not many people have them.'

'Oh, right.'

'We live in a disposable world and will probably be swallowed by things that won't biodegrade.' It was a big sentence, and the part of her brain that hadn't been beaten to chopped liver congratulated her.

The girl didn't look like a hanky user. Beth turned her face to discourage more conversation. She saw the girl—staring at her in the reflection of the window. Beth's reflection made a point of giving the girl's reflection the cold shoulder. She looked about thirteen. She was tiny and elfin. Her complexion was pale and she had a mop of unnatural jet black spiked hair, cut short. Her eyes were lined with black eye liner and she had black nail varnish. The black theme didn't stop at her makeup. She wore flared black trousers with a tartan mini skirt over the top and a black t-shirt with the slogan *'You've been a naughty boy—go to my room!'* printed on it. Her eyes were huge, dominant in a round pixie face. She looked confident and carefree. Beth envied her.

'It looks sore.' She was peering at Beth and every explanation that came to mind was implausible. Beth felt that she should give some account of her injuries to the stranger, but she couldn't come up with a lie that would fit, so she said nothing.

'My name's Jennifer.' She held out her hand for Beth to shake. 'It means White Phantom in Hebrew. I like it. When I was a little girl my nanny used to call me it. She said I was like a ghost creeping around. I'd like to be a ghost, wouldn't you? It'd be great being able to appear anywhere you like and listen into conversations and stuff? I see things that I'm not meant to see. You can call me Phantom if you want to.'

'Beth,' she replied, ignoring the girl's hand. She hadn't intended calling her anything at all, and Phantom was ridiculous.

'Are you going to the doctor? I could walk with you, if you like. I mean, you might be unsteady on your feet, it would be no trouble to see you get there okay.'

'No,' Beth spoke too loud. Her voice bounced off the windows of the bus. She saw people looking, alert to the possibility of some in-travel entertainment in the form of a row between passengers. She forced a smile, 'I'm sorry, no, I'm not going to the doctors. It's only a little cut, it looks worse than it is. Stupid really, I fell over the cat after a few too many drinks last night. The cat came off worse. I'm just meeting my friend in the market café. I'm all right, really. Thank you.'

'Well, at least let me walk with you to the market, it's on my way, I'm going in there anyway.'

She was persistent and Beth was irritated. Why couldn't the nosy little Goth freak just leave her alone and mind her own business? Why wasn't this kid the stereotypical doped-up teenager for whom the term 'self-absorption' was invented? Beth shrugged; the bus was pulling in and it would be churlish to refuse the girl's company when they were going in the same direction. She smiled her thanks and they left the bus together. Beth was surprised that she didn't feel shaky. She was cold, though, and shivered into her coat. Jennifer chatted all the way to the market hall and Beth was grateful that she didn't pry. She was content to ramble about a book she was looking for but didn't want to pay full price on. Patricia Cornwell's latest page-turner was a book that Beth had read and, despite herself, she found the conversation interesting.

'Everyone's talking about it. Apparently, it's really cool,' Jennifer commented.

'Yes, it's not bad. I think I've got a copy lying around somewhere. I'll hunt it out for you, if you like.'

'Really? Oh, that'd be fantastic. Thank you. I've been looking for it for weeks. You live on Maple, don't you? I could call around for it some time.'

Beth switched off from the girl's rambling chatter. They were walking through the outdoor market, picking their way between stalls. She could make Maggie out through the throng of people. She was waiting for Beth at one of the coffee stall tables. Beth hurried towards her.

'`Bout time you got here. Well, that showed the bastard he can't mess with me,' Maggie was already talking as she waved Beth over. 'I said to him… Oh my God, Beth, what the hell's happened?' she stood up and Beth waved her into her seat.

'Sit down, don't fuss, it's nothing.'

'Nothing, my arse. Je-sus, Beth, did he do this to

you?'

Jennifer was hovering beside her and she turned to thank the girl again, willing Maggie not to say anymore until Jennifer left.

'Hi, I'm White Phantom. I've been looking after Beth. You should have seen the state of her on the bus—proper white, she was. I thought she was going to faint right there and I'd have to do the kiss of life and everything.' She pulled out a chair and sat down. 'I was just saying to Beth that she ought to go and see the doctor. It looks nasty, doesn't it?' Beth and Maggie exchanged glances and Beth spread her hands behind Jennifer's back to indicate that she hadn't really brought her.

'Oh, look, they have lime milkshake,' Jennifer was oblivious to her lack of welcome. 'Don't you just love lime milkshake? Most people just stock strawberry and chocolate these days, even banana is scarce. If you're going up, I'd love one. Here, let me give you some money for it.' She scrambled around for her purse at the bottom of her bag.

'Oh, don't bother,' said Beth. 'It's all right, I'll stand you a shake. Um, we're not staying long though. I have to walk Maggie to work, don't I, Maggie? You have to be at work in quarter of an hour, don't forget.'

'Yes,' Maggie picked up Beth's attempt to get rid of the girl. 'Yes, right old git my boss is. Can't risk being late.'

'What do you do?' asked Jennifer, straightening up from her bag and lighting a cigarette. She shielded the cigarette with her hand against the wind in the open air café.

'Barmaid,' said Beth, while in unison Maggie said,

'accountant.'

'Um, I'll get the coffees in,' muttered Beth. She mouthed the word 'accountant' over Jennifer's head and shook her own. Maggie looked like many things but she would never be the first thing that sprang to mind on the mention of accountancy. She couldn't add up for toffee.

'Well, what I mean is,' Maggie didn't take so much as a heartbeat's break between lies, 'I work behind the bar at The Grapes, but I do the pub accounts on a Saturday.'

'It's Monday.'

'Oh. Yeah—well sometimes I do them on a Monday too. There's a lot of accounts.' The mother in Maggie came to the fore, 'Are you old enough to be smoking that?'

Beth was soon back with two coffees and a lime milkshake and could see that Maggie was jumping out of her seat with frustration. She had a head full of questions and was impatient to get rid of the Goth who sat with a froth moustache, oblivious to the fact that she wasn't welcome. Jennifer controlled the conversation for the next ten minutes.

'Right, come on then,' said Maggie, draining the last of her piping hot coffee and burning the roof of her mouth. 'Let's go.'

Beth tried to say goodbye to Phantom—but the girl was as sticky as Sticky Vicky.

'Oh, I'll wander round that way with you. I've got nothing better to do and you'll need someone to help with Beth if she gets wobbly.'

'No,' said the women together.

'Really, I'm fine. Steady as a rock. There's no need and I've got Maggie if I need anything.'

Maggie used her take-no-prisoners voice. 'Actually, we have some things that we'd like to discuss in private. It's been very nice meeting you though, Spirit.'

Beth cringed; she couldn't be that blunt. Maggie was straight-talking to the point of rudeness. But, she'd been polite for fifteen minutes when she was dying to know what happened to Beth. Under the circumstances, she was remarkably restrained.

'It's Phantom,' said Jennifer, but Maggie was unrepentant.

'Oh well, see you then, kid. Hey, try it with a dollop of ice-cream next time. It's to die for.' And they were away, waving behind them. Beth heard Phantom say that she'd call round to pick up the book, but Maggie was pushing her hard from behind.

'What a bloody fruitcake, where the hell did you get her from?' Maggie didn't wait for an answer. 'Right Missy, what the hell's happened to you? My car's in the car park, we'll go to yours and you can tell me all about it.'

Beth flopped into Maggie's car seat after moving Ben's football boots and a soggy cheese Wotsit, sucked and discarded by Barry. She didn't know what to say—how to begin. She felt tears forming and couldn't stop them from falling. 'Wait until we get home Maggie, I just want to sit quietly for a second.' Maggie scowled before patting her knee and turning her attention back to the road.

Beth was confused. She had wanted to see Maggie before she turned herself in. She was going to tell her everything. She knew Maggie would support her and would insist on going with her when she went to the police station. Since leaving the market and walking down the street, all the feelings that Beth should have been feeling were coming to her. It was a normal Monday morning in Ulverston. People were doing their thing: traders were selling, shoppers were shopping and impatient drivers were flicking the bone at the idiots in front of them. These people weren't thinking about being sent to prison for murder. They were wondering if they should do sausage casserole for dinner. The women might be working out if they could spirit some money from the housekeeping to buy a pair of jeans in the sale. The men might be thinking about sneaking off for an hour with the bit on the side they had stashed away, but they almost certainly weren't thinking about a man they had killed the night before.

Beth didn't want to go to prison. A furtive emotion that was new to her was tunnelling through her mind. It was self-preservation. She'd never needed to use it before; she'd never thought of it as an emotion and didn't know that she had it. But it was there. It was every bit as strong as the fear that was causing her to tremble in a steady, but increasing, panic. Maggie saw her shaking and turned on the heater. 'Hang in there Beth, nearly home, darling.'

In that instant Beth knew that she wasn't going to go to the police and she wasn't going to tell Maggie what happened. When the police came—if the police came—she'd tell them that Marc had dropped her at home straight after the pub. She'd never been arrested so they had no record of her DNA. They might never connect her with anything. What if, by some miracle she could get away with it?

What the hell was she going to say to Maggie? She'd never been able to lie to her and she couldn't use the tripping-over-the-cat story—she didn't have one. Her best friend for twenty-eight years, and the mother of three children, had a nose for ferreting out lies. She could see the colour of them before they were fully spoken. Beth was going to have to come up with something plausible.

Once in the house, and when the coffee was poured, and when the fags were lit, the stalling was over. Maggie came into the room with two mugs of coffee. She sat opposite Beth and threw her a cigarette. Beth winced, lighting it through cracked lips.

'Did that Marc bastard do this to you? I knew from the second I saw his squinty little eyes that he was no good.'

Beth tried for a laugh and failed. 'No, don't be daft. He was lovely, the perfect gentleman. I'm seeing him again, next week. No, I was walking home.'

'He let you walk home alone?'

Shit. Not good enough. Change of plan.

'No. He brought me home at about eight thirty because he had to go and, um, see his mother. It was her birthday—prearranged—unavoidable—couldn't get out of it.' Beth had too many unnecessary details flooding her mouth. 'I made myself something to eat.'

'He didn't feed you?'

'Oh, shut up and listen, will you? You sound like a Yiddish mother. I'm trying to tell you. I had a snack, made a brew and realised that I had no cigarettes. I had to go out to get some, so I nipped to the shop.'

Maggie looked at the almost empty packet of cigarettes on the table beside them and raised an eyebrow. 'That's some heavy smoking you've done since, lass.'

Beth ignored her and carried on with her story, focusing on what she wanted to say and not allowing herself to be side-tracked. 'And on the way back I cut through the garages and some boy grabbed me.'

'Oh, my God, Beth.'

'He only wanted my bag, but stupidly I had it over my shoulder and hung onto it. So, he hit me. He was only young, just a kid really. Drug addict, I think.'

'What did the police say? Have they caught him?'

Bugger. It was going to get tricky. Beth felt panic rising. Her palms were soaking and she wiped them on her legs. She brushed some non-existent hair out of her eyes and shifted in her seat, then shifted back again.

'I didn't go to the police.'

'What? Are you mad? Why not?'

'What's the point? I haven't a clue who he is. It was dark. I didn't get a good look at him.'

'Beth, he hit you. You've got to go to the police. What if he does this to somebody else? What did he get away with? What about your credit cards and all that? Shit, Beth he didn't touch you, did he?'

'No.' Beth tackled the last of the barrage of questions first. 'Look, Maggie. I just want to forget it. He didn't get my bag in the end because a man came around the corner and he ran away.'

'A man came? You have a witness? The police can find him and get a statement. We can nail this little bastard before he hurts someone else.'

'He didn't see anything. The lad ran off as soon as he saw him and the man didn't even look our way. It's over. I just want to forget about it.'

Maggie was relentless.

'But Beth, you can't let him do this to you and get away with it. Don't you want to see him in court? Hell, don't you want to kick the little shit in his tiny, teenage bollocks?'

Beth was losing control of the situation, her body was jerking in spasms, tears welled in her eyes. She just wanted Maggie to leave so that she could crumble and think. 'For Christ's sake, Maggie, drop it, will you? I've made my decision. It's nothing. It looks worse than it is. Look, if we ever see him again we'll drag him down a back alley and beat the crap out of him, okay?'

'I thought you wouldn't recognise him?'

'I won't. Now shut up and give me another fag.'

'You can smoke it on the way to the hospital. Come on you, this is bloody ridiculous. What would you say to one of your patients if you saw them in this state?'

'I'd tell them to quit smoking.'

Beth's tone hardened, she made a valiant effort to bring the trembling down to a shivering. 'Drop it, Maggie. In fact, if you're just going to poke your fucking nose in and badger me into doing what you want me to do, you can get out. Go on, fuck off. I can't cope with this. It happened, it's over. I just want to forget it, and that's my choice—not yours. Okay?'

'But you're not going to forget it, are you? Look at the state of you, pet. I won't leave you like this, you know I won't.'

'I'm sorry, Maggie. I just can't, okay?' She was losing it. While she was angry with Maggie she'd felt more in control but under her friend's pitying look and gentle words, Beth could feel herself turning into a basket case. She gulped at the air. The room was too hot. Everything was closing around her and she felt as though she might be sick.

'Please, Beth. Please let me take you.'

'Seriously Maggie, I'm okay. Just a bit shaken, that's all. I'll be fine in the morning.'

'I don't like it, Beth, but if you can't be swayed at least get a good night's sleep.' She picked up her handbag and rummaged through it pulling a bottle of tablets from its depths. 'I've got some pills. Just something to help you get through tonight and we'll see how you are tomorrow, yes?' She thrust the bottle into Beth's hands. 'You only need one.'

'Flurazepam, Jesus Christ, Maggie, I can't take benzodiazepines, there's nothing wrong with me. These would knock an elephant out. They're prescription drugs, where did you get them?'

'Postnatal depression, darling, remember? Plays havoc with your sleep patterns. They've been at the bottom of my bag since Bazzie was born—probably out of date by now, but they'll be okay, get one down you and ring me as soon as you wake up tomorrow.'

They moved on to other subjects and Beth deflected Maggie every time she tried to stray back. She was on edge. She had things to do. She'd pack a bag and run away to Morocco. She had no ties here. There was enough money in her savings to build a modest life. She'd call Maggie when the dust settled. Get her to come and visit. She'd get a new identity, or amnesty, or do whatever it is that other murderers do to avoid being caught – if only she knew what that was.

She felt dirty. She wanted a shower and some clean clothes. She just wanted to be left alone to think.

It seemed like forever before Maggie left. She gathered Beth into a bear hug and Beth stiffened so as not to cry out in pain or wince when she felt bruising to her ribs and back. She didn't realise that she was hurt there.

'Are you sure you're all right?'

'Yes, yes, now go and see to those kids before you have Social Services banging your door down. I'll ring you in the morning.'

'Okay, but you're sure, now?'

'Yes, go on, bugger off.' She forced a laugh and waved Maggie out of the gate.

Beth shut the door and sighed. It looked as though she'd got away with it – for now. Not Marc's death, she knew that wasn't going to be so easy to cover up, but at least Maggie didn't appear to smell a rat.

She was by the door still holding the bottle of pills in her hand. She'd clutched them, holding onto them tightly since Maggie had passed them to her, much as a child will grip a rattle for comfort, Beth had squeezed on the bottle while Maggie talked, subconsciously channelling her feelings into the plastic—anything to keep her focused on that moment, that second. She looked at them as though they'd just appeared in her hand. Her brow furrowed. Sleeping pills? Bloody ridiculous, she told herself. She didn't need them, but she did need sleep. She couldn't think further than a shower, soft pillows and a warm duvet. One pill wouldn't hurt. If it blotted out the awful images that flooded her mind, she wouldn't have to watch her very own snuff film looping behind her eyes, seeing Marc die a hundred times.

She poured a glass of water, the noise of the tap running echoing the water in the fountain. She heard the trickling, saw it thickened with blood, passing over the breast of the statue and Marc's dead eyes. Her gorge rose and she clutched the stainless steel of the sink, gulping air. Battling with the childproof cap, she swore into the silence of the room. The lid gave and she cupped her hand, letting the few tablets in the bottom of the bottle empty onto her palm. One pill be buggered. She wanted complete blackout for at least twelve hours. If the police came, they would have to hole her up in a cell until the fugue lifted. She was beyond caring and wanted it to go away. Before she could talk herself out of it, she tilted her hand to her mouth and tipped four of the eight capsules in, swallowing them down with a gulp of water. Her only thought was of falling into a long, deep sleep and waking the next day with this far behind her.

She heard the pounding as she was putting the rest of the pills back into the bottle. They spilled onto the kitchen floor, the bottle crashing among them as she was startled by the insistent banging.

She crept into the living room and hoped that whoever it was would go away if she ignored them. The first knock was forceful, the second was demanding, louder than the first. It wasn't the knock of a neighbour wanting to borrow a cup of sugar.

It was the police. It had to be. She'd plead self-defence. It was an accident. It really was an accident. She hadn't wanted to kill anybody. She felt sick. Her heart was thudding. Her knees threatened to give way. It was Monday afternoon. She should be watching *Corrie* on catch-up and making a mess of a crossword puzzle. This time yesterday, her life was boring and normal. Now she had police hammering on her door.

'Just coming.' Her voice trembled, she didn't recognise it. She was shaking. Could the pills be working already? Nonsense.

She opened the door.

'I followed you. You lied to me. Why did you lie to me?'

The weird kid from the bus was on the doorstep.

Beth was relieved – and annoyed. But she was so bloody grateful that it was only the girl with the ridiculous name and not the police.

'Oh, hello. Can I help you?'

'Why did you lie to me?'

'Oh, yes. I'm sorry about that. You see, Maggie and I, we had some things that we wanted to discuss and... Oh look, I'm sorry, but you understand, don't you?'

'But you're my best friend.'

Chapter Four

Her friend!

What the hell was she on about? Her friend. She'd only met the girl that morning. She was just a kid. Beth couldn't get her head around why a teenager would want to befriend a woman twice her age. Beth had killed a man and here was this silly little girl having histrionics on her doorstep. She didn't have time for this.

'Look, I'm sorry, Jennifer, but it isn't a good time. I was about to get in the bath and I've got some stuff to do.'

'I think you should let me in. We need to talk.'

Beth laughed. Her head was swimming. They couldn't be working yet, it was too soon. 'What about, Jennifer? Is it about the book? I'll have to hunt it out for you. I'll tell you what, call back tomorrow and I'll have it ready.' Beth was fighting the temptation to shut the door in her face. She'd killed a man; after that, bad manners and rudeness were nothing. She was going to follow through with her thoughts when the girl's stance hardened.

'Don't patronise me. This isn't about a stupid book. This is about friendship and loyalty and it's about not lying to somebody who is supposed to be your friend.'

There she goes with that friendship word again.

'You'd better let me in. It wouldn't be in your best interests to annoy me. That would be a very stupid mistake. Who knows what I could say.' Her face was granite hard. 'I might have friends that you wouldn't like.'

Beth was dizzy. She gripped the door-casing for support. This kid, who she'd met on the bus that morning, was threatening her. What the fuck. Did she know something? What could she possibly know? She couldn't have an inkling about last night. It was just coincidence. Some kid was having a hissy fit and Beth was jumping at shadows. She couldn't think straight. Thoughts were jumbled and reality was blurring at the edges, everything was jazzy colours and sounds were distorted, her mind was made up of pretty strands of pink candy floss—Beth was high.

'There are things we need to discuss,' said Jennifer. She'd seen the change in Beth and her attitude altered. She had a calm cunning in her eyes. Her anger was replaced with a matter of fact voice. 'Let me in, Beth.'

Beth was going to fall over; her feet were bouncy castles. She opened the door because she'd lost the ability to argue. 'You'd better come in then, I suppose, but I don't know what all this is about. I really am very busy.' The words came out, but her mouth wasn't working properly.

Leading the way through the house, she stumbled into the table beside her chair. The note that she left for the police that morning was on it. She picked it up and pushed it into her pocket as she motioned Jennifer to a seat.

Jennifer raised her eyebrow. 'Secrets, Beth? Secrets and lies?' she chanted in a sing song voice. 'Secrets and lies and alibis.'

Beth was aware of a tremor above the thickness when she replied. She tried to keep calm but the girl was freaking her out. 'What are you talking about? It's nothing, none of your business.' Her voice sounded different in her head. She was slurring and her mouth was rubbery. She straightened up and tried to collect herself. Jennifer looked amused, she was smiling. 'What are you saying? What's all this about?' Beth repeated.

'Oh, nothing, nothing at all. You just looked guilty about something. Calm down, you'll give yourself ulcers.'

Beth let out her breath in a whoosh. She laughed. Jennifer didn't know anything. She was jumping at nothing and if she didn't get herself under control, despite the pills, she might as well go and shout to the world that she had committed murder. If a young lass could pick up something suspicious by her attitude then what the hell would the police make of her?

'Would you like a drink?' It seemed appropriate to offer something, ever the effusive host. 'Coffee, maybe? Or tea?' What the hell was she doing?

'Have you got any Lexicon Fruit Fizz?'

'No.'

'You'll have to get some in. It's what I drink.'

Beth's life was blurred. She saw Jennifer in triplicate. She tried to follow the three girls separating each one from the paper dolly of the next and then she blinked and the world snapped into focus.

'Where will I be sleeping?'

'What? Did you just ask…?'

'I don't do sofas. They make me restless and then I sleepwalk and shout out in my sleep really loud. There was this one time when I leapt off the sofa at my aunt's house and I ran into the kitchen. I started going through all the draw–'

'Stop! Will you just stop talking for one second? Jennifer, I don't know what the hell you're thinking but you can't stay here.' She swayed, drunkenly.

Jennifer rolled her eyes and pouted. 'Now, here was me thinking we'd got this name thing all sorted out. It's very rude you know, calling somebody by a name that they don't want to be called. It's Phantom, okay? Phantom. I'll tell you what, let's play a little game. You'll like this. Every time you call me Jennifer, I'll call you Beth Bathory. How's that?' She didn't wait for an answer but ran to the windowsill where Beth kept a collection of Wade animals. She'd thought of getting rid of them but the collection had grown from childhood. Jennifer picked up one of the larger pieces. 'And,' she continued, elongating the word, 'every time you call me Jennifer, I'm going to smash one of these stupid things. I can see you aren't very bright, Beth Bathory, so I'm going to have to educate you.'

Jennifer was nuts. On top of everything else that she had to cope with, Beth had the misfortune of taking the number six bus. If only she had gone for six pills, too. 'Okay, Miss, that's it… Out! I want you out of my house right now. Go on, get out.'

'I can't. Nowhere to go.'

'I don't care, Jennifer. Get out.' Beth moved towards the girl to grab her and physically move her to the door but her feet refused to obey. She felt awful. The pills were taking full effect. Her head swam. She had to get rid of her before she fell over.

'Oh dear, Jennifer again. Just remember, this is going to hurt the polar bear far more than it'll hurt you.' She swung her arm back and flung the ornament hard against the wall. It broke in two and lay on the carpet by Beth's feet. Jennifer put a finger to her mouth and giggled. 'Oops, sorry.'

'What the fuck are you doing? How dare you…' She wanted to say more but the thought got lost before reaching her mouth. She had to focus on the words to get the bitch out of her house while she could. She was unsteady and the air was filled with a blanket of vagueness.

The girl turned on Beth and stood with her left hand on her hip in a stance of defiance, challenging. It was Beth's move but she didn't know what to do. This was ridiculous; she was intimidated and frightened of a child. Her instinct was to slap the girl but the kid was deranged. The best course of action was to reason with her.

'Look, Phantom, you can't stay here. I don't even know how you came up with the idea. I've got to be up early in the morning for work. I'm not prepared for visitors and, like I said earlier…' She was struggling. Reasoning with her was hard. Her brain was fogged and she felt woozy. 'I've got a lot of stuff on and have plans for this evening.' She took a step forward. She didn't want to sit down. She needed to be upright to get her out but she had to sit. She couldn't stand any longer. As she moved towards her chair, she collapsed.

When Beth fell unconscious to the floor Jennifer jumped. She recovered herself quickly and went to the prone figure. She remained standing, observing. Beth breathed and watched for a few seconds. She picked up Beth's handbag, rifling through it. She pulled out her driving license and put it on the arm of the chair. She went to the dresser and flung open the first of two drawers. Glancing at Beth, she went through papers and documents and after looking at – and discarding – several letters she picked up a recent British Gas bill, grabbed a pen from the front of the drawer and scrawled Beth's driving licence number before putting it back where she found it. She pocketed the bill with the scrawled number, shut the drawer and looked through the second drawer. She saw Beth's address book and hesitated for a second then shoved it down the front of her skirt, pulling the loose T-shirt over to mask it.

Kneeling beside Beth, she watched her chest rise and fall for two breaths and then grabbed her arm, raising it a foot from the salmon carpet. She let it go and smirked as it slammed to the ground. She shook Beth and shouted her name. When she didn't stir, Jennifer slapped her across the face. She sat on her heels and waited. No reaction. She frowned, stood and walked into the kitchen, taking in the spilled pill bottle.

'All too much for you, Bethany? Oh, no you don't.'

After picking up the empty bottle and stuffing it into her pocket, she went back to the living room. She grabbed the front of Beth's jumper with both hands and lifted her head and shoulders off the floor. She shook her violently, Beth's head wagged on a limp neck.

Beth responded, her breath caught and her eyelids opened.

Jennifer hooked her arm under Beth's head and pulled the pill bottle from her pocket. She shook it in front of Beth's unfocused gaze. 'How many of these have you taken?'

'Huh?'

'Come on, get up. Flurazepam, it says on the bottle. Flurazepam. What are they?' She shook Beth again but not as roughly. 'They're prescribed to Margaret Johnson. What are they, Beth? How many have you taken?'

'Pills.'

'Duh, I know they're pills, stupid. What do they do? What are they for?'

'Sedative.'

'Sleeping pills, right? How many have you taken? I'm ringing an ambulance.'

Beth lurched forward, grabbing her by the wrist. 'No ambulance.' She licked her lips and tried to produce some saliva to swallow but couldn't. Her eyes opened wide and stayed in focus. 'I'm a nurse, no ambulance. I work at the hospital. Reputation...'

'Oh well that's all right then, job done. I'll just leave you here to die, shall I?'

'Four.' She tried to swallow, her voice cracking like her lips. 'Not die, only took four. Sleep. Need Sleep.'

'Some bloody nurse. You've taken too many. What do I do?'

'Emetic.'

'What? What're you on about?'

'Need to throw up.'

'Oh, fucking delightful.'

Jennifer moved behind her and grabbed her under the breasts trying to lift her onto her feet. 'Come on help me. I need you up and moving.

With no effort from Beth, Jennifer got her to her feet.

Beth's legs were dead and useless.

'One foot after the other, that's the way,' Jennifer

said.

They staggered to the kitchen and Jennifer led her to the sink. Holding Beth with a supporting arm, she took the two empty mugs from the basin and sat them on the draining board.

'In there, go on.'

'Can't.'

'Yes, you can. It's easy. Think of that size-eight dress and just do it.'

Beth shook her head, her vision spinning. 'Water.'

'Later. Come on, bring it all up.'

Beth leaned over the sink, her hands steadying her balance on the countertop, and dry heaved. Other than a coffee or two, her stomach was empty. It had nothing to give. 'No good,' she said.

'For heaven's sake, Beth, what're you like?' Jennifer took Beth's chin, turned her head to face her, and prised her jaw open. Beth tried to back away, wobbled, lurched, and Jennifer stuck two slender fingers in her mouth.

Beth retched. The fingers were deep. Her head buzzed, her stomach contracted and she felt the bile volcano from her gut. Jennifer pulled her fingers out and forced Beth's head towards the sink in time for the splatter of thin vomit. The wave of nausea that flushed up through Beth's chest to her head made her dizzy and a second heave produced more contents of a largely-empty stomach.

When the retching stopped and her body had expelled two cups of coffee and four sleeping pills, Jennifer rubbed a tea towel over Beth's mouth and chin. 'There, that wasn't so difficult, was it? Is there anything else I need to do? Are you in the clear now?'

Beth shrugged and shook her head. When her vision settled again, she said, 'Sleep.'

'Haven't you just had some?'

'Need rest.'

'We need to talk. If you've got to sleep, you'd best sleep it off fast.'

She helped Beth to the bedroom and threw her onto the bed. 'I'll wake you at seven, and don't think I'm leaving, I'm not going anywhere.'

Beth didn't care.

When she woke, it was to the sound of a strange voice yelling up her stairs. She was disorientated and felt fuzzy. It took her a few seconds to make sense of the fact that a stranger was in her house. Once she had put a face to the voice, she groaned. And then she remembered Marc and the groan wasn't enough.

'Beth, I'm not waiting any longer, you're making me angry. Come on, get down here. With your playing up we didn't get to finish our chat.'

Beth got out of bed carefully, to find that although she was stiff and sore, her legs were working. With new resolve to get rid of the unwelcome guest, she put on her dressing gown and sat on the bed as the sickness hit her. Still under the effects of the sleeping pills, she was muzzy and brain-addled. She wanted to go downstairs fighting, but couldn't find the words for combat amongst the noise in her head. She walked into the living room to find Jennifer sitting on the sofa, eating a packet of crisps from the kitchen cupboard.

'Well, halle-bloody-lujah, it rises. Feeling alive again, are we? Right, sit down. We need to pick up our little talk where we left off.'

Beth sat in her chair and looked around the room in a daze.

'You said I can come and stay with you.'

'Over my dead body.'

'Maybe it would have been if I hadn't saved your life, and anyway somebody's going to have to look after me, I'm too young to be on my own and I get frightened.'

'What are you talking about? I can't look after you, I don't even know you. Where are your family? Where do you live? How old are you?'

'My parents are away skiing in San Moritz. They won't be back until next week. So, you see, I'll have to stay here until then. You're my friend and I have nobody else.'

'But, it's not convenient, I'm sorry, Jen…Phantom. You must have some family that you can stay with. Why on earth did your parents go off without making proper arrangements for you? It's ridiculous.'

'Oh, I lied to them. I said I was staying with a friend from school, but that didn't work out.'

'Oh, there you go then. You'll just have to go and see this friend and sort things out with her family. Would you like to use my phone to ring her? If you've fallen out, I'm sure she'll be just as happy as you to make up.'

'I can't,' Jennifer's voice trembled and her bottom lip crumpled. 'She died yesterday and in all the fuss her parents have forgotten about me. I don't blame them, it's understandable. I don't suppose they've even noticed that I've gone.'

'What? Oh, come on you can't expect me to believe that.' She looked at Jennifer's teary eyes. 'Really? Phantom, that's awful. What happened?' Beth tried to focus.

She couldn't make sense of the words coming out of Jennifer's mouth and made a valiant effort to keep hold of the conversation.

'Well, I just left and walked around all night and then this morning I met you and you seemed nice and –'

'No, I mean what happened to your friend?'

'Oh, she stepped out in front of a Mazda 323. It was red and had a really cool *Don't bump me, dude!* sticker on the bumper. I think it's a mistake though, it didn't look right. I think they should get a re-spray and have it black.'

'And your friend was killed?'

'Yes, poor Carrie. It cut her head right off and they had to put it in a separate bag.'

Beth couldn't believe what she was hearing, if even the gist of the story was true then no wonder Jennifer was acting oddly. 'That's terrible. Were you there? Did you see it?' Beth didn't know if the girl was telling the truth or not, but she seemed distressed.

'Yeah, there was a lot of blood, like, and all these people ran around the road screaming and getting all hysterical and stuff, like. So, can I stay?'

Beth was spaced out; the pills had made her bilious. She wanted to go back to bed. What could she do? She felt that she couldn't turn a distressed child out onto the street without being able to hand her over to a responsible adult. As much as she hated the idea of taking in this odd stranger, she had little choice. Her head felt as though it was about to explode. Jennifer was looking at her, waiting for an answer. All her instincts were screaming that it wasn't her problem—but the problem was sitting on her couch. She felt so ill and didn't have the strength to go through whatever channels had to be gone through to act responsibly and get in touch with the girl's parents.

'All right, if you've got nowhere to go. But only for tonight. I'm going to have to ring your parents, and these other people. They must be worried about you, and on top of everything that's happened they must be frantic.'

'Oh, no, it's cool. I told them that mum had broken her leg skiing and had come back early.'

'But you said that they wouldn't notice you've gone? You said that you didn't tell anybody.'

'No, you said that. I said that it wouldn't make any difference if I was there or not. They won't notice that I'm not there because they've got funerals and stuff to sort out.'

'Oh, right.' All kinds of alarm bells were ringing. Had she been thinking straight Beth would have perused the matter further, possibly even called on Social Services for their help, but under the circumstances, she couldn't think about her own problems never mind having to deal with somebody else's.

'You can't get in touch with my parents. They are in a ski lodge up a mountain, there's no phone signal, I've tried.'

Beth was trapped. The girl was traumatised, they were both traumatised. The accident didn't seem to have hit Jennifer properly. She'd have to tell somebody that the girl was here tomorrow, but who to tell? Social Services, or her school? She'd ring the school and let them know. But she couldn't do that until Monday and she didn't want to be stuck with her until then. Beth felt guilty—the poor kid was going through hell and all she wanted to do was to get rid of her. Maybe she could find a way to contact Jennifer's parents and explain to them what had happened.

'Have you spoken to your parents at all since they went on holiday?'

'Nah, they've left their mobiles at home on account of the fact there's no signal. Don't you listen?'

'Well couldn't we ring the resort?'

'Don't know where they're staying.'

'Are you telling me they've gone away without leaving any contact details in case of an emergency? That seems unlikely; surely they must have left something?'

'Well, see, my brother was supposed to be at home this week, but something came up and he's gone away too.'

'Well can we ring him?'

'Don't know his number. What's for tea? I'm starving.' The discussion was going around in circles and Beth gave up. She went into the kitchen on unsteady legs to make something to eat, it gave her thinking time. Jennifer was fussy, she didn't like this and didn't like that, they settled on pizza and chips. Her visitor had only been with her for a few hours and already Beth was in trouble with work after ringing in sick. It was the bi-annual audit. Her boss was annoyed when Beth rang to call in sick for the following morning. She had never lied to her employer before but said that she had come down with a stomach bug that had knocked her off her feet. No, she didn't think she'd be feeling better by the morning. Yes, of course, if she was, she'd come right in. It was something else for her to feel guilty about, but at least it was sorted and she could cross it off the worry list.

As she cut the pizza, she tried to pull her thoughts into order. Her life was usually so staid and disciplined. She lived by routine, nothing much ever changed and the only unpredictable aspect was Maggie. In twenty-four hours everything had changed and she was out of control.

What was she going to do about Jennifer? The police could arrive at any minute. She was going to run away. Should she pack a bag and go while Jennifer was asleep, stick to the plan? The girl wasn't her responsibility. It was messed up and she was so tired. Another thought struck her about the friend that had been killed. There would be a police investigation. Jennifer was a witness. They'd want to speak to her, wouldn't they? Had she been taken to the hospital, checked over? Beth had no idea how to deal with a traumatised teenager. It was obvious that the accident had upset Jennifer, even though she wasn't showing it much. Her behaviour since the moment they met had been very odd, but then, Beth of all people could understand that.

Where the hell did she go from here?

She wanted to do what she always did when she couldn't think straight, she wanted to ring Maggie and ask her advice. But, she didn't need to, she knew exactly what Maggie would say and the tone of voice she'd use to say it. She'd say, 'For Christ sake, Beth, why do you always let people walk all over you? You're too soft. Tell her to piss off and find some other sucker to take pity on her. She's not your problem.' She couldn't ring Maggie, it would only complicate matters.

After they had eaten their meal and Beth had picked

up the plate that Jennifer put on the floor, she broached the subject of her stay again.

'So, Phantom, I'll sort the spare bed out for you for tonight, but tomorrow we are going to have to make some alternative arrangements. I work, you see, and I'm not used to young people. I mean, what about school, for instance?'

'Oh, that's no problem, its half term.'

'Really? Which school do you go to?'

'Ulverston, Victoria high school, why?'

'Well, Maggie's kids go there and I know for a fact that they were off for half term two weeks ago. So that isn't true, is it?'

'No, I lied. Got any ice-cream?'

'Oh, for God's sake Jennifer, how can I help you when you won't even tell me the truth?'

Jennifer glared at her. She ran to the window sill and picked up a Wade figure. It was the otter, one of Beth's favourites. Her father had bought it for her when they visited Lowther Wildlife Park, the year before he died.

'Don't,' yelled Beth, but it was too late, the otter lay in pieces on the carpet.

Jennifer turned around with a smug smile and sang a nursery rhyme.

'Elizabeth Bathory hired me.

'Put me in a vat of tea.

'Left me there `till half past three.

'Wicked Elizabeth Bathory.'

Beth was crying. 'I can't cope with you. I'm sorry, I've changed my mind. You'll have to go.'

'Oh,' said Jennifer, slyly, 'but I can't, Beth, because, you see, I know what happened last night.'

Chapter Five

She felt faint and sick and lost all at the same time.

'What are you talking about?' Her voice was sharp with terror. 'I didn't do anything last night. I watched telly, did my ironing.' She thought back to the lie she'd told about falling over the cat after a few too many drinks. At least she'd only come across as a sad, lonely old lush.

'Right, of course you did. Oh, by the way, sweetie—Marc says hi.'

Beth's legs buckled, she had two choices: to lower herself into the chair she was clutching, or wilt to the floor because her legs had lost the ability to hold her. She sat down.

The last of the colour drained from her face. She stared at Jennifer.

'Marc's...'

'Marc's what, Beth? Marc's dead? Is that what you were going to say?'

Beth didn't respond.

'Of course, he is. Silly me. You left him doing Swan Lake in the water, didn't you? Oops, I must have lied, then. Maybe he didn't say hi, maybe he just had a glassy look in his big dead eyes.'

Beth thought she might be sick. She wasn't living her life; she was trapped in the corner of a warped mind. She owned a pair of blue, fluffy slippers, shopped at Asda, and she always donated to Barnardos. All these horrible things couldn't happen to a fluffy-slipper type of person.

'It was an accident,' she muttered.

'Let the prosecution note that the defendant has submitted a plea of guilty, your honour. Some bloody accident. Christ, you really know how to make effective use of the understatement, don't you?'

'How do you know?'

'Never mind that. The question you should be asking, the question you need to ask, is—what are we going to do about it?'

'I'm waiting for the police, they should be here soon. I'm giving myself in.'

'Have you called them?'

'No.'

'Well then, they aren't coming, are they?'

Beth looked up, not knowing if this was a positive statement or just something else to drag her deeper into the quagmire that she'd crawled into.

'Somebody must have found him by now. They'll be doing tests and things... Those forensic people, my fingerprints. They'll be coming soon.'

'No, they won't. People don't tend to visit us very often. We aren't the sort of neighbours who have the vicar to tea on a Saturday afternoon, and you aren't the sort of murderer to have ever had your fingerprints taken. Trust me; he's still dancing with Miss Bronzy Tits. What do you think of that statue, by the way? I've never really liked it myself.'

This Grimm fairy tale was moving and changing. It was morphing into something different and Beth was trying to get a grip on what Jennifer was saying. The girl used possessive words like 'us' and 'we'. This was Beth's nightmare; Jennifer had fallen into it by chance, but here she was staking her claim as a legitimate character. She had seen Marc's body. She was at the house either after he was dead or during the accident. It made sense of the feeling when she went to the stairs to listen for Marc coming down. She didn't identify the sensation at the time, but it was the sinister presence felt when you think somebody's watching you. She remembered the door unlocking to let her out. How did Jennifer tie in to this?

'Who are you Jennifer?'

Jennifer smiled. Calmly she threw three more of Beth's Wade figures crashing to the floor. Beth didn't care. They had always meant something to her, but now they were just pieces of pot.

'You really don't learn, do you? For the last time, my chosen name is Phantom and I won't answer to anything else. Now, will you remember the rules?'

The scale of Beth's fear didn't diminish. It stamped its mark at the uppermost point of her emotion-meter and then moved one place to the left, making way for anger to take its seat at the same heightened level. She couldn't take anymore and wouldn't play stupid games with her.

'Fuck your rules,' she screamed. 'And tell me what the hell's going on. Now.' Her voice cracked on the last word because she'd yelled it with such force. Her throat would be sore for days as her vocal chords stretched to unaccustomed levels. She reached behind her and grabbed the cushion at her back hurling it with all her force at Jennifer.

Jennifer laughed and ducked long before the soft cushion came anywhere near her. 'Beth, is that all you've got? The temper's good, mate. Bravo. It's just the choice of missile that needs work. Here, let me show you how to do it properly.'

Jennifer picked up a heavy candle in a glass holder from the shelf behind her. She threw it against the wall to the left of Beth's head. Beth screamed and ducked as glass shattered around her.

'See?' said Jennifer. 'That's how you get a reaction. You need to make your temper work for you otherwise it's just wasted energy. Did you know that you can run a car on cow shit?'

'Who are you? What are you doing here?' Beth repeated, the temper finished and replaced with nothing. She had nothing left to feel. 'This has gone on long enough. I'm putting an end to it. I'm going to call the police.' She went to the phone and picked up the handset. She didn't know whether to ring 999, or to ask directory enquiries for the number of the local station. While she was pondering what to do, Jennifer pulled the cable from the wall and held it up in her hand.

'Don't be so bloody stupid. You're not calling anyone. What do you think is going to happen? Do you think they'll pat you on the head and say, "There, there, dear, it's all right"? You'll go to prison. A mental institution, maybe. How long do you think you'd last? You're pathetic.'

'It was self-defence. It was an accident. I'll make them see.' An idea formed in her mind. She jumped up and grabbed Jennifer by the wrists, mania and terrorised euphoria lighting her eyes. 'You were there, weren't you?' She was excited, she screeched out the accusation in a high-pitched voice. Hope returned and she thrust at it greedily. 'You can tell them. You can tell them that it was just an accident.'

Jennifer shook herself loose. 'Hey, I'm not telling the cops anything, because you're not going to ring them. Oh, and you might as well know the truth, I'm not a kid. I'm older than I look. I'm seventeen. And my parents have both been dead for years—that's the truth of it. It was just me and my brother, so guess what, Bethie? I'm all yours. You took full responsibility when you sexy-danced with my brother. Shut your mouth, there's no point in arguing and, anyway, that's not the issue, is it? We've got to do something about Marc. We're going to get rid of the body. We'll go tonight, in a couple of hours when there aren't so many people about.'

'What? I can't. I can't go back into that house. I can't touch…'

'Oh, stop snivelling. You want help, don't you? You want somebody to make it all right and make everything go away? Well, here I am, your fairy fucking Godmother come to grant you three wishes. I mean, we could leave it until tomorrow if you like, and go in daylight, but I wouldn't fancy your chances. Too many nosy neighbours around here. People carting dead bodies up and down the streets would tend to get noticed. And anyway, you really don't want to leave it much longer. Do you know what happens to a piece of meat two days after it's been slaughtered? It's not going to be pretty, Beth. I'd go as soon as possible if I were you.' Her voice was sickeningly conversational. Beth was disgusted more by her tone and attitude than by what she was saying. They could have been discussing the removal of a mouse from a mousetrap.

Before Jennifer burst into her life, she was clear about

what she was going to do. Now, too many words were clouding her judgement and she was groggy after the sleeping pills. 'You were there, you know what happened. Why haven't you called the police?' Her voice held no tone of curiosity or interest; it was just words to fill the empty space.

'Oh, believe me, I have reasons of my own, but mainly, I suppose, it's because I know what he was. I mean, okay, yes, he might have been my father… but that doesn't make him good, does it?'

'Your father,' Beth was stunned. 'But you said he was your brother, he can't be your father. He would have told me, surely. He's too young...'

'Okay then, not my father, my brother, but he was like a father to me since my parents were killed in the Omagh bombing when they were on their second honeymoon.'

'Stop it, stop lying to me. Please stop torturing me like this. Just tell me the truth. Your parents aren't dead, they're on a skiing holiday. You said so.'

'Aw, come on Beth. Don't be boring, I'm only playing with you. I tell lies. It's what I do for fun. You must work out which story is real and which is a lie. For instance, I watched a little girl burn to death, once. Do you believe me? She had long blonde hair and it caught fire along with her dress. In seconds, she was bald and I watched her melt. Do you believe me, Beth? Have you ever seen a person melt? She looked like goats cheese on toast. Your turn; go on, tell me a story and I'll guess if it's true or not. Go on.'

'You're mad. A man is dead and you're playing stupid games. What the hell is wrong with you? Give me the phone. I want to ring Maggie, she'll come and get rid of you and then we'll go to the police.'

'Now, that would be really stupid. You think that Saint Maggie can help you now? With varicose veins like hers, you'd think she'd do something to help herself. Wrong. The only person that can get you out of this mess is me. You need me, and that's why I'm here. If you wanted me out you'd have screamed for help or something stupid. See, you're playing the "Saying the right thing" game, but that's all you're doing, you're just playing at it. If you had any intention of ringing the police, or telling Maggie about your nasty little secret, you'd have done it straight away. You need me to go back to the house with you and help you to get rid of the body. When you've done that, it all goes away, doesn't it? You can go back to normal and pretend like it never happened. You'd like that, wouldn't you? I'm the only one who can help you now. I'm all you've got, Beth.'

'Give me the phone.'

Jennifer bent down to the wall and connected the telephone. She held out the receiver. Beth's hand trembled as she reached out to take it. Jennifer smiled, her face was strong and her arm steady. Beth let her hand fall in defeat. 'Dear God, help me.' She sat down and sobbed.

'Right, first rule. You need to toughen up. Let me tell you something, Beth, I'm a compulsive liar. Do you know what that means? It means that I'm also the most truthful person that you'll ever meet. You see, when I tell the truth, I tell it straight. I don't wrap it up with excuses and transparencies. What is it people say in these circumstances? "But it wasn't my fault", "But I was provoked", "But they made me do it." There is no 'but' in the truth. I don't wrap the truth up in convenient little escape routes. So, let me tell you some truths now. Feel free to put me right if I'm wrong but the way I see it is this: One, you have no intention of going to the police. Two, you don't want to do what's right. You want to get your arse out of trouble. Three, you'll do whatever it takes to get through this. Am I right?'

Beth looked up, her face was tearstained but her eyes were hard. 'Yes.'

'That's more like it, but not yet. It's too early. We need to wait until people have settled for the night. And anyway, there's something that I need from you first. My services don't come free. What's in this for me? I mean, sure, if you want to go to the police now, bring it on, we can do that. I can feel myself tearing up. Oh, the trauma, the way you've made me suffer. You've ruined my life, Bethie. I had my loving brother, my guardian. Now I have nothing. I'm all for going to the police. But if we do, I won't be protecting you. Why would I? You killed my only family.'

'You can't do that. You know what happened. You know the truth.'

'I know what I saw Beth. I know that I saw you lose the plot and kill my dear, sweet brother in cold blood. I'll tell them how you ranted when Marc said he didn't want to see you again. You know what they say about a woman scorned. When I've finished with you, sweetheart, there won't be a dry eye in the courtroom and you'll be spending the next twenty years professing your innocence to your lesbian cellmate.'

'No, wait. You must believe me, it wasn't like that. Please help me. I can't go to prison.'

'Which brings us full circle. I ask you again, what's in it for me?'

'Blackmail? Is that what this is about? I don't have any money.'

Jennifer laughed. 'I don't want money. I want assurances. You haven't been very friendly to me so far. I want to help you, but once we step out of that door, we're in this together. I need to know that you are going to stick by me. This is going to be a big secret to keep. I'll do everything I can to help you, but I've got a loose mouth, Beth. We've got to trust each other. I need an incentive to keep my trap shut. I need to know that when all this is over you aren't going to shaft me. Are you my friend, Beth?'

Beth looked at the girl's earnest face and gave a little laugh. 'Of course, we're friends. If you can help me through this, we'll be friends forever.' Beth didn't think about the words. She just spouted what the crazy bitch wanted to hear. Jennifer had offered her a way out, if there was a way to get through this and save her skin she was going to take it.

'Promise?' She spat into the palm of her hand and offered the spit-shake to Beth. 'Will you be my friend forever, Beth?'

Chapter Six

'I can't do this.'

'Yes, you can. You've got to.' Jennifer pushed her through the front door and let it close behind them.

Beth felt faint. An overpowering heat met her inside the door. It was hot; she had to gulp a lungful of air. She felt the force of the heat burning as it hit the back of her throat. It was like being in the butterfly house of a stately home, or getting into a small car that had been parked in the sun too long on a scorching day.

They could smell him. In the ventilated hall, it wasn't unbearable but the air was tight and musty. It wasn't instantly recognisable as the aroma of meat left to putrefy for thirty hours, it was foisty, similar to the air around damp clothes left too long in the wash basket, or autumn leaves desiccated to the point of crumbling, yet still retaining the tinge of the wet pulp they'd been. Above the musty smell Beth detected the whiff of blood. She could taste iron at the back of her throat. And on top of all these other scents was the smell of eggs, as though somebody had boiled some and mashed them while warm and pungent.

'You go and reacquaint yourself with my dear brother and I'll find us something to wear. Don't touch anything,' said Jennifer.

'Don't leave me. I'm not going in there alone.'

Jennifer laughed. 'No, I don't suppose you will. Stay here then and I'll be back in a sec.' She went in the direction of what appeared to be the kitchen and Beth heard a key rattling in a lock. She sat on the bottom stair and hugged her knees to her chest. She was terrified and her body trembled as she rocked on her tailbone.

True to her word, Jennifer came back quickly. She threw a pair of dark blue overalls towards her. 'Here, put this on. It might be too big so there's a belt there, too.'

Beth caught the overalls. They smelled of engine oil and grease. Normally it would have been a comforting, manly scent, but any aroma from this house was going to repulse her. 'I can't wear these. They belong to him. I can't.'

'Beth, in a minute you are going to be lifting his body down from that statue. It might be messy and we don't want to risk being covered in incriminating evidence should the shit hit the fan at some point. Wearing a pair of his overalls is the least of your problems.'

'I can't touch him. I can't. I can't go in there.'

'Okay,' Jennifer walked towards the front door. 'I can't lift him by myself, so if you won't help, well, you're on your own, girl. Good luck.'

'Wait, don't leave me. I'll try.'

On taking charge of the situation, Jennifer seemed older than the devious child she had shown at Beth's house. With her self-assurance came coldness. She turned around, smiling. What they were about to do didn't seem to bother her. Beth noticed that the set of overalls she was scrambling into fit her tiny frame. Jennifer saw Beth looking as she did up the last of the poppers.

'He was interested in restoring classic cars. We both were.' For the first time, Beth saw a fleeting glint of emotion pass across Jennifer's face. 'We do them up together—did, it was our thing. Come on.' She donned a cheerful tone. 'Let's get to work.' She tapped Beth on the arm to chivvy her along and laughed. 'I've got a surprise for you.'

She stepped forward and flung open the doors to the lounge. A force of additional heat blasted from the room blowing into the hall and bringing with it a foul odour, the same as before but increased in strength tenfold. The smell of eggs was stronger but they didn't smell freshly shelled, the stench was rotten and putrid. Beth gagged and covered her mouth with her hand, afraid that she was going to vomit.

'Oh God, that's a bit intoxicating,' said Jennifer, behind a muffling hand. 'I thought I'd lay on a surprise for you—maybe surprise is the wrong word, it's more of a punishment. I have the right to play judge and jury after all. So, before I followed you the other night, I turned the heating up. Besides, I wanted to see how fast he'd decompose. Don't puke. They'll get your DNA from it.' Jennifer crossed the threshold but Beth stayed in the hall, unable to move.

'C`mon. I want you to see this.' Jennifer grabbed her arm and pulled her into the room. Beth made no attempt to dig her heels into the floor or hold back and she allowed herself to be led. It's said that a human being can only sustain terror for two minutes before either going into shock or getting over it. Beth's mind had removed the terror and replaced it with a cushion of shock. She was meek and compliant. Had this state evaded her, she would have run from the house screaming and crying. Nothing could have prepared her for the image of grotesquery.

'Ta-dah,' said Jennifer, throwing her arms wide in revelation. 'See, he's not so scary now, is he?' Beth's mind wasn't playing so she made no comment either way and stood, looking, her hands clasped together at the front of her belt.

'Wow, this is interesting. Normally it would take four to six days for a body to reach this level of decomposition. I read up on it on the Net. It said that in the tropics decomposition is accelerated, so I thought it would be fun to bring a little Tropicana into our hum-drum existence. What do you think, Beth? All that's missing is some rum and Calypso music.'

'Sick,' mumbled Beth, but it wasn't clear whether she meant that she was going to be sick or was expressing her opinion of Jennifer's character.

'See, now you were pretty damned creative positioning him like that. The fountain lights are so pretty, the overall effect is visual and clever but he was lacking something, don't you think?' She stepped back a couple of paces and pointed her forefinger to her chin in a pose of evaluation. 'I hope you don't mind my collaboration, but I felt that I could improve on the canvas.' The tiara on his head sparkled under the canopy of ceiling lights. 'The intense heat was a master stroke. We wouldn't have seen it like this if we'd left nature to take its course. You did good, but together we are amazing. Look at this, it's perfect. It's a shame we can't share it with the world. Lucien Freud painted corpses. This blasts his concept out of the water.'

Beth couldn't help but look. Jennifer's words were wasted on her; she didn't hear any of them. One horror was as much as her brain could accommodate and her visual sense was overtaking the audible hands down.

His head was slumped forward. The tiara that Jennifer had put on him had slipped so that it fell over his left eye. She frowned and leaned over the fountain, arm outstretched. She repositioned it, stood back, squinted, and positioned it again before giving a nod, satisfied.

For the most part his upper body was pale. The higher blood vessels had emptied, causing the dried-putty appearance of his skin. Fluid from his lungs had emptied from his nose and mouth to crust and discolour on his lips and chin. The area around his eye sockets had blackened and where his chin rested, a pool of blood had collected below the epidermis. The area had bloated to form what looked like a lurid purple and black blister. The same had happened to his abdomen. The day before his stomach had been firm and toned; now he had the appearance of a five-month gestation pregnancy. At the lowest point of his stomach, the blood had pooled and blackened. His penis was shrivelled and yet at the same time stiff, pointing out from his body, the head exposed and purple. His legs dangled but not loosely, rigor mortis had claimed them.

Although impaled, the stiletto-sharp point of the dancer's foot had not pierced through to the front of his body. There was no exit wound, her toe was buried somewhere inside Marc, tangled with decomposing offal, up hard against rack of rib and sternum.

'Come on then, Daydreaming Dottie, let's get on with it.' Jennifer went to the back of the statue and looked at the body from behind. 'Ugh, messy. You mashed him up good.' Jennifer sized up the corpse of her brother. 'You know, Beth, you have never once asked me what we're going to do with him. You're in this as well, you know. Have you given this any thought at all? No, I don't suppose you have. You just think that you can stand there looking pretty and that Phantom will make all your problems go away. What would you do without me, eh?'

If she was expecting an answer, there was none forthcoming. Beth was immobile with her eyes fixed on Marc and the statue. Somewhere in her mind she was elsewhere. She had the merest hint of a smile playing around the corners of her mouth, nothing definite or defined, but wherever she was, the sun was shining and birds twittered in the trees.

'We're taking him back to your house, you see. He can sit on the sofa tonight and watch *Who Wants to be a Millionaire* with us.

The birds weren't singing anymore. Ugly words seeped through the fog. Marc was coming home with them to watch the television. That couldn't happen, she hadn't vacuumed and there were still bits of broken pottery all over her living room. What would he think of her? But he was dead. He wasn't going to think anything. He was just going to prop stiffly on her sofa, stinking and rotting. Beth came out of the fugue and wailed.

'No, you can't. He can't. He mustn't.'

'Don't worry, only joking. Gave you a scare though, didn't it? That woke you up a bit. Ha, ha, you should see your face. So, now that I've got your attention, try and stay with me, eh? I need you to help me. I can't do it on my own and the sooner you get your act together, the sooner we can get this done and get out of here. There's a room upstairs, a vault, it's a sort of panic room thing. Marc's paranoid as hell. Well, he was. Always reckoned that somebody might come and kill him in his home. If only he knew. He built the vault for his protection and safety, but he didn't reckon on you popping up, did he? We can take him there. It's hidden. Nobody would ever find it, even if they came looking for him.'

Beth was still, horribly pale, but her eyes were focused and she dried her tears. 'Okay. What do I have to do?'

'I've dragged a tarpaulin in from the garage. It's just by the interconnecting door. Go and get that for starters. We can roll him in it and use it as a stretcher to get him up the stairs.'

Beth nodded to show that she understood the instruction. She even grinned at Jennifer, glad of the opportunity to get out of the room. Fetching and carrying she could do. Anything rather than touching the body. Getting a tarpaulin was easy work. Having to come back in afterwards was not going to be so easy.

Despite her conviction, getting the tarp was not easy work. It weighed more than Beth did and getting it into the lounge was a huge effort. She admitted that Jennifer was one tough little cookie, though she doubted that they would be able to move it with the added weight of Marc's body inside. When she returned, Jennifer was standing in the fountain. The water had a film of crud on the top and where her feet had disturbed it, an oily slick, thick with blood, pooled around her ankles. Where the water level had risen, a ring of scum mottled the basin.

'Bring the tarp over and spread it out along the base of the fountain. We need to make sure that nothing gets spilled on the floor. He's going to be heavy so it'll take both of us to get him down. Are you up for it?' She smiled at Beth.

She sounded almost kind. It was the first time that she'd shown any concern at all for Beth's state of mind.

'Yes, I think so.' Beth made sure there was good coverage of the tarpaulin on the floor. She stood at the rim of the fountain and tried to lean over; making sure that her hands would connect with statue, and not with Marc's body. She screwed her face up in distaste, hating what she was about to do and hating what she had already done.

'That's no good, Beth. I'm going to need you closer so that you can help me take the weight when we get him down. You're going to have to get your feet wet. Just imagine you are at Bardsea Beach—only difference is there's no Roy's Ices.'

Beth didn't want to step into the blood-thickened water. She didn't want to feel the weight of Marc's body against her again. She felt her gorge rising. 'I think I'm going to be sick,' she said.

'No, you're not. Come on, take some deep breaths and go for it.'

It was sound advice but easier said than done with the dead-Marc stink. She drew in and expelled foetid air, trying not to taste dead-body sweat in her mouth. She didn't look down as she stepped into the water, keeping her eyes level with a metal fold in the dancer's tutu. The smooth surface of the fountain base had never been intended for footwear and the marble bottom was coated in a film of blood. With one foot in the fountain, Beth's trainer squelched and shifted in the silt. She lifted her left leg before her position was stable and her right foot slipped from under her. Her body slewed forwards and she slid like a figure skater along the base of the fountain.

She was falling.

Her head was going to sink into the body-fluid water. She opened her mouth to scream and put out her hands to save herself. Her left hand grabbed onto the smooth bronze finish of the dancer's dress. There was nothing to hold and she felt herself falling. Her right hand reached out, clutching at the flesh of Marc's chest, piercing his clammy skin with her nails. Her fingers curled into his chest hair, clutching and snatching to stay upright. She felt Jennifer's arm under her elbow, steadying her. Her relief at not falling into the mire of Marc's mess staved her revulsion. When the moment of contact with the body had come, it hadn't been so bad, it was better than drinking him. He felt unnaturally cold. He was hard and unyielding, like a mannequin, but her fingers had not pierced the blackened flesh of his necrotic blisters, only his bloodless chest-flesh. She was thankful for that—it could have been a lot worse.

When she was steady she turned to Jennifer and mumbled, 'Thanks.'

'S'okay. I considered letting you swim, but at least now you've got over the thing about touching him. Let's get him out of here.'

Jennifer moved to the front of the body. If she had expected to fling his arms over her shoulders she hadn't reckoned on the stiffness of his limbs. Rigor mortis had given the body the density and immovability of somebody frozen. She inched towards his chest and tried to pull him from the spiked foot of the sculpture but she hadn't the strength to move him.

They worked together to release him. When he came away from the statue, it was sudden. His body popped free of the ballerina's foot and the unexpected sound made Beth scream.

As he fell on top of her, stiff with rigor, Jennifer staggered backwards. Marc had weighed thirteen stone; dead, he felt heavier. Jennifer was slight. Her knees caught at the back of the fountain base and she stumbled with Marc heavy on top of her. Beth was taken along with the rush of movement. She was still hanging onto Marc's disgusting body but having his bloated penis against her abdomen was better than her face penetrating the contaminated water. Nothing on earth could have been worse than that.

Gases had built in Marc's body after his death. It was this escaping methane that caused the unbearable rotten egg smell. As he fell on top of Jennifer, the remainder of the methane was forced up his airways and came out of his mouth with a loud *ughhhhh* sound. The expulsion of gas smothered Jennifer's face and, winded by his weight on top of her, she inhaled and gulped it in. To this point she had shown no concern or emotion at the demise of her brother. Her only reaction had been a morbid fascination in his death and decomposition. Beth felt no sympathy as she watched the girl's mounting panic. Jennifer struggled violently beneath the dead weight on top of her, fighting to get out.

Beth had fallen to her knees in the fountain. She stood gingerly, conscious of the slippery basin, and climbed out of the water onto an uncontaminated corner of the tarpaulin. She watched Jennifer's struggles to free herself, making no move to help the girl. Jennifer was grunting. It had taken seconds from Marc flying free of the statue, to Jennifer crawling out from underneath him and getting back onto the safety of the floor, but it seemed like longer. Beth felt a malicious satisfaction as the tables turned.

Still on her knees, Jennifer crawled to the side of the fountain. She was grunting and heaving and she flung the top half of her body over the rim and vomited into the water. It splashed back into her face and she retched again, emptying herself into the pool.

'Ah, ah, ah. DNA, remember.'

Jennifer threw up a third time and wiped her mouth on the sleeve of her overall. 'Fuck off,' she replied, before resting her back against the wall of the fountain, drawing her knees into her chest and lowering her head onto them.

Marc was lying on his side, one arm sticking stiffly up at an unnatural angle. Beth lowered herself to the floor with her back towards the body and took a moment of rest too.

'So much for throwing your weight around; all you've thrown is your supper.'

Jennifer was petulant and shot back in a sulky tone, 'I'll throw you back in the fountain in a minute. You're going to be sorry for that.' She leaned round and spat in the water. Beth watched her body relax. As Jennifer turned to her, she had a sly smile on her face. 'Oh yes. You're going to be sorry for that.'

'Oh, get over yourself,' she muttered. 'Anyway, surely the worst is over now.'

'Don't you believe it. We've got to carry him up two flights of stairs yet.'

Beth shuddered as she looked at Marc's extended arm, would they have to break it to make it lie flat in the tarp? A new horror caused her bile to rise as she noticed that his index finger on that hand was missing. There were no jagged edges; the finger appeared to have been chopped through cleanly. The stump, close to the main knuckles of the hand, was bloodless but blackened.

'Oh, my God, his finger,'

'His finger? What about it?'

'It's missing,'

'It must have dropped off.'

'Don't be so bloody ridiculous, it can't just drop off. Where is it, Jennifer? Jesus, where is it? It must be in the fountain somewhere, we've got to find it.' Beth felt her hysteria rising again. Every time she felt a glimmer of hope for her future, something came along to hinder it.

'Chill,' said Jennifer. Her nose was wrinkled and she wiped at her front with a pulled down sleeve to remove a blot of vomit. 'It's not in there. I've got it somewhere nice and safe.'

'You chopped his finger off?' Beth couldn't keep the revulsion from her voice. 'How could you do that? Why?'

Jennifer snapped her head towards Beth, 'Do you know what it feels like to have somebody's finger hurting you…there?' She motioned downwards. 'I was twelve years old. He raped me. Do you know what it's like to be a scared little girl waiting for your bedroom door to open in the night? No, of course you don't, `cause you had the charmed life, didn't you? I remember him inside me, hurting me. I had no use for his dick, but his finger is very valuable. And anyway, I made sure that finger is never going to do any girl-caving again, not in this life, or the next. But I had other reasons, too,' she frowned, 'big ones—over half a million of them.'

'What do you mean?'

'Nothing,' her face had set hard and standing, she busied herself trying to cover Marc's body with the tarp,' We're going to have to break this arm,' she said, confirming the nightmare premonition that Beth had already had.

They discussed their next steps. Beth was shaky but Jennifer was regaining her composure. 'Don't know what the hell that was all about,' she said, harking back to the vomit-fest of minutes before to regain the upper hand. 'The food at yours must have been dodgy.'

Getting Marc into the vault was going to be difficult. The tarpaulin was enormous, made of heavy canvas, and that, added to the weight of the body, meant that they would have to lug almost twenty-stone up to the top of the house. Jennifer had broken Marc's arm with a hammer to make it lie flat while Beth had hidden her face. She would never forget that sound, she was sure it would haunt her dreams for the rest of her life. Jennifer suggested using the tarpaulin like a blanket, keeping it open and dragging Marc up by each of them holding two corners. Beth said that it would be impossible to do it like that. They decided to wrap him up in the canvas, Persian carpet style.

Jennifer left Beth alone with the body while she went in search of rope or a thick twine to bind the ends. Beth didn't fly into hysterics. She had dehumanised Marc and thought of him only as a body. She was terrified, but her concerns were all for self-preservation. She had to see this through so that she wouldn't be held accountable for his death. As much as she detested Jennifer, she had to admit that without her none of this would have been possible. Jennifer terrified her. She was so cold and emotionless. She had proven herself to be cruel and manipulative, with her veiled threats and insinuations. Yet she had still gone to great lengths to help Beth. Why? What were her motives? Beth had killed her brother. Instead of wanting vengeance and the hand of justice to crush her, she was putting herself out on a limb to keep her from being answerable. None of it made sense and Beth wanted time to sit and think things through. She had questions that Jennifer must answer, but this wasn't the time. She cleared her mind. She had to function rather than think. There would be plenty of time to worry and work out where she went from here when they had concealed Marc's body.

When Jennifer returned, she brought with her two steaming mugs of strong tea and had a nylon washing line draped around her neck. 'A is for apple, tea is for trauma. That's what Marc always said.' She offered one of the mugs to Beth.

Beth shook her head and turned in disgust. She couldn't face the thought of drinking anything.

'Suit yourself,' Jennifer, pulled a chocolate digestive out of her pocket and picked the fluff from it. 'But it's going to be thirsty work.' Somewhere a pipe gurgled as it cooled and Beth was glad that while she was out of the room, Jennifer had turned off the heating.

Wrapping Marc in the tarpaulin and binding the ends

took half an hour. They were sweating and he looked like a Christmas cracker by the time they finished.

'Won't we be leaving a trail of evidence in our wake if we carry him up the stairs?' asked Beth.

'Well, what do you suggest, Einstein? Flying him up there?'

'The tarp's dirty, what if it leaves oil stains on the stairs? What if he bleeds through it?'

'What if he comes back to life and takes a shit on the third step from the top? Stop letting your imagination get the better of you. There shouldn't be any blood now,' said Jennifer, 'Once the heart stops circulating, the blood, it can't flow, can it? As for the rest, we'll just have to clean up after us. We're going to have to empty and re-fill the fountain. Moving him is just the first stage of the operation.'

'But what about forensics? Just cleaning the floor isn't going to be enough, is it? They'll find fibres and oil stains and they'll have ultra violet detectors to identify blood and stuff, won't they?' Beth's voice had risen as a feeling of overwhelming panic rose in her.

'Calm down, for Christ sake, you're making me jittery. This is Ulverston, arse-end of nowhere. The police are going to be in-bred Neanderthals. They won't have all that high-tech equipment and stuff here. Relax, it'll be okay.'

'What if they bring people in? Won't they call in Scotland Yard, or a big murder squad, or something? We're going to get caught, I know we are.'

'Listen, I'm telling you. It'll be all right. My brother and I led a secluded life. We have no friends. His work was freelance. Nobody will even miss him. Listen to me.

Nobody is even going to come looking for him. That's the way he designed his life.'

Beth would like to have taken a moment to fathom out the deep and meaningful of the last statement. She wanted to try and weed the fact from the lies; Jennifer was a skilfully adept liar. She was small and pixie-like but her vocabulary and manner of taking charge exceeded that of most teenagers. Had Marc raped her? Thoughts and conflicting questions were flying around Beth's head but time was against them. They had to get things done before night turned into day, and after the removal was done, the cleaning and returning things to order had to start.

It took them a long time to get Marc's body up the first flight of stairs, turn the corner at the stained-glass window and then haul him up a second, even longer flight and along an endless corridor to the full length mirror that hid the secret vault. Several times, one or other of them let go and precious space was lost as the tarpaulin-covered body bounced back down a few stairs with a sickening thud. Beth ached all over. She felt that the smell of the house had permeated not only her clothing but also her skin. She had never craved a bath so much in her life. And never had she felt the urge to empty full bottles of thick bleach into the water before getting in.

It was with pomp that Jennifer fiddled with the hidden mechanism that sent the mirror trundling along rails set into the floor, revealing an inner door with an electronic keypad lock and a small retinal scanner. Jennifer enjoyed showing off with childish exuberance as she tapped the security code into the keypad. As she did this she explained that the inner room was twelve feet smaller than the space it occupied because of the three-foot thickness of the reinforced steel and concrete walls. The keypad bleeped and a red light flashed on the scanner. It had been put in place for Marc, as Jennifer had to stretch on her tiptoes to align her left eye with the sensor.

'It's a dual-purpose room, acting as both a vault for our valuables and secrets, and a panic room for the family. When you're outside, unless you're coded into the scanner, it's impossible to get in, and when you're inside, unless I activate the release button, it's impossible to get out.'

When the retinal scanner had analysed her eye, there was another beep and the sound of a lock releasing.

'Air circulates in the vault through one-way filters. It's fitted with its own generator in case the electricity is cut, an independent phone line, emergency rations enough for two people for six months, and an extensive first aid kit to cover all eventualities.'

Jennifer pushed the steel door open with a single finger and said, 'Welcome to my vision.'

'Can we just get on with it?' Beth asked.

They hefted the body for the last time, pulling it into the centre of the room, and then straightening up to ease out the kinks in their backs. Beth looked around, noting the rows of blank wall-to-wall monitors, the boxes and crates marked 'Provisions', and a bed along one wall—one bed for two people? Had Marc raped his sister from the age of twelve? The room scared her. It was only a room and she couldn't understand why she was so nervous of it.

'In short,' Jennifer finished, 'it would make the perfect prison.'

Beth realised why she was on edge. She looked up at Jennifer and saw the familiar cruel glint in her eye.

'Three times this evening, at your house, you called me Jennifer. And then we had your display of cockiness when I got sick. I've asked you so politely not to call me that. I've told you my preferred name, yet still you choose to ignore my wishes. You know there's always going to be consequences, Beth, don't you? But you flout the rules.' Beth had backed into the room with the body ahead of Jennifer. To get out she had to get past her.

Jennifer was already over the threshold before Beth realised what was happening. She had pushed a button to close the door and it was moving quickly on its tracks.

'Remember, Beth. There's no way out.'

Beth made a lunge for the gap in the closing door, not caring that she trampled over Marc's body to get there. 'Jennifer.' she screamed, but it was too late. The door finished its movement and came to a perfect and silent close.

Chapter Seven

Beth screamed and cried and banged but it was useless. No sound could escape that room, nothing could. She hoped that this was just another of Jennifer's childish jokes, but as the minutes ticked by, she felt her faith dwindling. Was this what it had all been about? Was her punishment to die a long and slow death locked in a nine-foot square room with the rotting corpse of the man she'd murdered?

Jennifer told her that air was filtered through vents into the vault but she was convinced that the air supply had packed up, or that Jennifer had helped it to pack up. Her throat tightened. Her body trembled and she felt faint. The room was shrinking, the walls closing in like a fist tightening around her lungs. With her back against the wall, she let her legs buckle and she slid to the floor, her bones were liquid. Her eyelids flickered and a darkness seeped across her vision as the world slipped away from her. Her last conscious thought was wondering if her death—when it came months from now, would feel like fainting.

She didn't feel as though she'd been out long but she came to, slowly. Her joints were stiff and ached from the unaccustomed exertion of moving a dead weight around and her injuries from the attack were raw and agonising. The cold of the concrete floor penetrated her body and chilled her. For a few seconds, she had no idea where she was, or who she was, but reality bit hard.

Jennifer told her there was enough food and water to

last two adults for six months. That meant that, realistically, she could live in the vault for a year and then for however long she lasted once the rations ran out. This thought terrified her more than the concept of dying ever could. Would she go mad?

Maybe Jennifer's conscience would prick her and she'd relent and let Beth out.

She could cling to this hope. It could be enough to keep her sane in the face of Jennifer's insanity. Her mind drifted to the medical provisions. There'd be drugs, maybe lots of drugs. It wouldn't be long before suicide was the only solution.

She wanted to hammer on the door, to try and reason with Jennifer, but she knew that it would do no good. Fainting had cured her of the initial panic attack and she was able to breathe. The first waft of Marc's pungency was leaking from the tarpaulin. It wasn't free enough to be an overpowering stench yet, but it was there, it felt tangible and made her feel sick.

To take her mind off the need to vomit, she studied her surroundings. The bank of monitors occupied one wall, thirteen of them in all. She flicked a switch at the side of the bank. The monitors spluttered to life and thirteen views of the house showed on the screens. She could see Jennifer in a massive kitchen making herself a sandwich. At the bottom of each monitor was a button with a speaker icon. She pushed the button on the monitor for the kitchen. Jennifer had the radio on and Beth could see her dancing and hear her singing along to Korn's *Word Up*.

Beth imagined Jennifer sitting in the vault watching everything that had happened between Marc and her, hearing every word. Marc went upstairs for his shower. Did he know that Jennifer was watching? Did he get off on that? Had he done it before as Jennifer had suggested? She wondered what would have happened if things had played out differently. What if Beth had agreed to have sex with Marc? Would Jennifer have been sitting in this vault munching on chocolate biscuits and drinking fizzy pop as though she was at the cinema? Beth gave herself a mental shake-up. She'd only been locked in the vault a matter of minutes and paranoia was running rampant and playing with her mind.

At least there was a comfortable bed. She had the monitors to watch and could see everything that happened in the house. There was a selection of books and magazines. Half of the room was taken up with the compact chests of rations. It might not be so bad, she mused. And she couldn't really be left to die here, could she? Not really. Beth decided that for the time being, she would play Jennifer at her own game. Unlike Marc, people would report her missing. She'd been seen on the bus with the distinctive Jennifer. Maggie knew about her, and sooner or later Beth would be linked with her and somehow or other she'd be traced back to here—which brought problems of its own. When she was found alive and well in this vault, Marc would be found with her.

To the back of the vault was a spare section of wall, it lay in the shadows of the packing chests and was partially covered from view. Beth decided that she would move Marc into that space. He wouldn't be out of sight, or out of mind or smell, but at least she didn't have to keep stepping over him to get from one side of the room to the other. Another thing that she'd need to sort out was the whole uncomfortable issue of toileting. As soon as this problem arose in her mind, she felt the first twinge of needing to pee. She couldn't see a flushable loo, or indeed a bucket. Something would have to be done. How long would it be before rescue came, a day, two, three? Surely it couldn't be more than that. In her nursing, she'd seen death many times, which helped to calm her. Sharing this vault with a putrefying carcass was only horrific because she'd killed him. Already she was becoming accustomed to the smell which, due to the thickness of the tarpaulin, wasn't that bad. All she had to do was stay calm, not give her captor the entertainment she was hoping for and sit it out until rescue arrived. She might be Jennifer's prisoner but she did have the upper hand in one respect, she could see and hear everything that was going on outside the vault. The situation might be terrifying, but all she had to do was keep calm and wait.

Calm? She felt the scream building but the noise took her by surprise when it left her mouth.

The green door-release mocked her from its position on the wall. In desperation, she would press it many times over the coming hours, days and weeks. Beth couldn't be optimistic. Her positive outlook crumbled as she remembered that she was dealing with somebody who was deranged. Two days earlier, her life had been sedentary and boring. She'd longed for something exciting to happen. She was a murderer on the run, with nowhere to run and a body to step over when she took a few steps across her cell.

She cried. Then she shouted, screaming to be let out.

She punched hard on the release button in temper and the door slid open on its tracks.

Jennifer was sitting against the wall in the corridor laughing until tears rolled down her cheek. 'Bloody hell, it took you long enough, you silly cow. I thought you were going to stay in there forever.' She bit into her sandwich.

'It wasn't locked,' said Beth.

'Don't be stupid. Of course, it wasn't locked. It'd be bloody dangerous if you got locked in a sealed room that you couldn't get out of.'

Beth's voice rose in anger. 'You said it was locked. You said that you had to know the combination to get out. I thought you'd left me there to die.' Her fists balled at the side of her legs. 'You fucking retard.'

'I'm a retard? And yet you were the one who couldn't get out of an open door.' Jennifer laughed so hard that she couldn't speak for a while. 'No, you idiot, you can't get *into* it from the outside without the code.'

Beth wanted to hit her. She didn't know how to punch somebody, she'd never hit anybody in her life before scuffling with Marc the previous evening. But she wanted to take her fist and ram it into the pretty girl's face. She wanted to do acute damage. She wanted to feel the skin split on her knuckles as her fist encountered teeth. But she didn't do anything. She let Jennifer lead her downstairs. She begged that she be allowed to go home. She reasoned that she'd return the next day to help Jennifer clean up. She wanted her Happy Mug with the smiley face and her dressing gown and her duvet. They went into the lounge and Beth marvelled at how perceptions change and adapt. The night before, that room was the worst place that she'd been in her life—but now she was so happy to be there—anything other than the panic room until death from starvation claimed her.

'What are we going to do about Marc?' she asked. 'We can't leave him there forever, can we?'

'Don't see why not. We don't have to think about it, yet. It's the best place for him for now.'

'But what about the house? Are you going to continue living here? What if you move?'

'I have no plans for the future. Let's just get over today and leave it at that.'

Beth had no energy to argue.

Jennifer insisted that they do everything that needed to be done that night. 'You need to cover your tracks. Leave nothing to chance. Successful murderers only walk away if they are fastidious and careful. When you slip up, you get caught. I've read a lot of books on the subject.'

Beth worked alongside Jennifer in stony silence. She was sulking and recovering from the shock of the last couple of days. Jennifer, in contrast, chatted as she worked, as though they were an external domestic company doing an ordinary night's work.

'I can't wait to get home. We can get a fish supper on the way,' she chirruped, as they cleared the last of the cleaning products and burned their soiled clothes and overalls in the cellar's incinerator.

'What are you on about? You are home.' Beth knew that she wasn't going to like Jennifer's reply. She saw it coming and it wasn't going to be good.

'No, home with you, stupid, I'm coming to live with

you. And you know what? You can't stop me because you've just ruined any chance you had of screaming self-defence and getting off lightly with a sympathetic jury. Any court in the land would have taken pity on you — but guess what? You blew it. You have just lost your last chance of legal freedom and you walked right into my trap. You thought you were going to get away with killing my brother. Not a chance, sweetheart. If you want to stay out of prison now, your only chance is to keep me sweet. But, don't worry, I'm not going to tell because you're my friend and everything's going to be good. I think I'd like to decorate my own bedroom, if you don't mind. All that mauve's a bit much for me. God, I'm tired. C'mon, Beth, let's go home.'

Chapter Eight

The banging was persistent. Whoever it was, they weren't for going away until they got an answer. Beth didn't want to move. She was cosy. She liked her days off when she didn't have to wake up while it was still murky. Sunlight was coming through the chink in the curtains and she felt safe. But it wasn't her day off. It was Tuesday morning and she should have been up and out for a seven thirty shift.

She heard voices in the hall downstairs. A malignant Goth had taken over her house and this was no nightmare. It was with resignation that she reached for her dressing gown and made her way downstairs, fastening the belt as she went.

Maggie and Jennifer had progressed from the hall to the living room. The broken ornaments still littered the carpet from the night before. Maggie had a face like thunder and Jennifer was waffling about her plans for decorating Beth's spare room.

'What the hell's going on, Beth? I called until after midnight last night and was worried sick when I didn't get an answer.'

Beth flopped into her chair. She was still groggy from sleep and could do without the third degree from Maggie. She was trying to think of something to say when the phone rang. She reached over to answer it and met more trouble head on.

'I'm so sorry. No, no, you're right, I didn't ring in this morning to say that I haven't improved through the night and wouldn't be in. I know I said I would. It's unforgivable with us being so short staffed. It's just that I was up all night, ah, throwing up and this morning when I finally got to sleep I forgot to set my alarm. I overslept. I'm sorry.' She nodded in response to the angry hospital administrator. 'Yes, yes, I should be okay for tomorrow. It depends on this awful diarrhoea. I'll ring in if I'm no better.'

'Are you sick?' Maggie asked before Beth had replaced the handset on the phone. It was no friendly concern, this was pointed accusation.

'Yes. No. Well, sort of,' replied Beth, but her voice was drowned out by Jennifer's.

'God, yes, she was sick. I've spent half the night cleaning the bathroom. Up the walls and everywhere, it was. And the smell –' she pinched her nose '– you really don't want to go in there.'

Maggie glared. 'Look, toots, I have every intention of being rude here, will you just fuck off so that I can talk to Beth?'

Jennifer turned to face Maggie. She straightened her posture, gaining a couple of inches. Her face was cold and set and for a second Beth thought that she was going to square up to Maggie and challenge her. Then her cheeks dimpled as she smiled and the words that dripped from her tongue were honey sweet. 'Oh sure, you two have a lot to talk about. I don't want you to think that I'm trying to take over your best friend, Maggie. I'll go up to my room and start stripping the wallpaper. I'm having three walls painted purple and the ceiling and window wall done in black. I can't wait to get it done. Don't forget you promised that we could go to Homebase and get the paint today, Beth. I'll leave you to it, then. Tell her what we've been up to since you saw her yesterday.'

Beth hadn't promised to take Jennifer anywhere. She watched her leave the room and felt a panic rise, twisting the signet ring on her finger and avoiding eye contact.

'What's she on about?' Maggie asked. 'What've you been doing?'

Jennifer would know what to say to Maggie, she could think on her feet and falsehoods came as second nature to her. Beth didn't have a clue what to say. She'd never lied to her before all this mess and knew that Maggie was going to ask probing questions and wouldn't be fobbed off lightly.

'Oh, nothing. You know what she's like.'

'No, I don't have a clue what she's like. What the bloody hell's going on? What's she doing here? Who is she, Beth? And for God's sake why are you letting her wreck your house? You spent a fortune last year getting that spare room the way you wanted it.' Beth opened her mouth to speak, though she had no idea what to say. But Maggie's eyes had gone back to the broken ornaments on the floor. 'And what's happening in here? It looks as though there's been a fight. Are you in some sort of trouble, Beth? Talk to me.'

'Well, I will, if you'll let me get a bloody word in edgeways.' She knelt to the safari park of broken animals and picked up the larger pieces. She was glad to avert her eyes and having something to focus on would make the lying easier.

'She's had a bit of a hard time of it at home. I work

with her, you know? We took her on last month. She's a live wire, she was always going to be a bit of a gamble, but she's a good kid and giving her a go is paying off. She's fantastic with the old people.' Now that she had started, the lies came easier. 'She left home. Parents didn't approve of her boyfriend, that sort of thing. Anyway, she moved in with him and things haven't worked out very well.' She lowered her voice to a whisper. 'Drugs, I think; him, not her, of course. It all ended badly and the poor kid had nowhere to go. So, I said that she could hole up here for a while until she sorts herself out.'

Her ramble had come out in a rush and Beth found herself holding broken words and broken pottery. She was terrified of taking a breath. She knew that as soon as she stopped talking Maggie was going to fill the silence and what she had to say might be tricky. Beth risked a look at her.

'Hang on a minute. In the café, you made out that you didn't know her. In fact, you distinctly said that you hadn't a clue who she is.'

'Yes, well, Jennifer was a bit embarrassed about it all. She didn't want anyone to know what had happened with her boyfriend. And she was supportive about the whole, you know, mugging thing.' Beth fingered her damaged face and mentally kicked herself for bringing the subject up. She was rambling and needed to get a grip.

'Huh, she doesn't come across as the modest type to me,' muttered Maggie. 'More edge than a broken piss pot, that one.' She lit a cigarette and tossed one to Beth. 'How long's she staying?' she disappeared in a haze of smoke.

'Oh, not long. Just until she sorts herself out. You know what kids are like. She'll probably be back home in a few days.'

'I don't like her, Beth. And I'm not convinced that you're telling me the whole truth. We've never kept secrets but if you have something that you don't want to tell me, well, that's your business. I think that one's trouble. I'd kick her out on the streets, if I were you. She's not your responsibility. But you won't, because you're soft. Any old dosser wanting free bed and board can come to you and they can put their feet up in comfort. If you're too pussy to tell her to pack her bags, I bloody well will.'

'No, no, it's all right, it's in hand. Maggie, there's nothing else to know. The kid's in trouble and I'm just seeing her over the worst of it. She'll be gone soon and then we can get back to normal.'

'She's using you, Beth.' Maggie went into repeat cycle which was good because at least she was sticking to the one line of fire and not asking anything awkward. 'I don't like her. She's a head-the-ball.' And then, in typical Maggie fashion, she tired of the subject and changed it in a heartbeat. 'Let's go out this weekend. Just the two of us. Tequila!' She jumped on the chair with an air saxophone and saxxed the old Champs song.

'Get down before you break my chair, you nutter.'

'Come on, we need some rhythm and booze.'

Beth couldn't think of anything worse, except for going back into the sealed vault.

'Have you heard from that Marc guy? How's it going? Still keen? When are you seeing him again?' Maggie fired the question-bombs and Beth defused them before they exploded in her face.

After draining the dregs of her coffee, Maggie said that she had better make a move. Beth stood to see her out, something that she hadn't done for years. Maggie treated Beth's house like a second home.

'There's something not right with you, Beth. What happened to, "Oh, just stay another five minutes"?' They often joked that the inscription on Beth's epitaph was going to read, *She only wanted another five minutes*. 'Babe,' Maggie said, 'I'm here for you. You know that, right? If something's wrong you can talk to me. Any time, day or night. Well, except tomorrow night because I'm having my bikini line waxed.'

When Beth closed the door, she sat on the stairs opposite the front door and put her head into her hands. It was aching and the dull, persistent throb was resistant to both Paracetamol and cursing.

'Huh, so she doesn't like me, eh?'

Jennifer was on the landing amongst the shadows.

'How long have you been listening? Don't you know that it's rude to listen at doors and that a sneak is not likely to hear anything complimentary about themselves?'

'I've been there long enough to hear what that stuck up cow said about me. Who does she think she is coming across all la-de-da? She's nothing. I'll bloody show her, the bitch.'

Normally Beth would have found this exchange amusing. Maggie was the least stuck up person that Beth had ever met, but Jennifer's last sentence worried her.

'What do you mean, you'll show her? I'm telling you Je... Phantom, Maggie's my oldest friend and I don't want her upset or dragged into this mess. And don't you be fooled by her. She may not look it, but she's sharp and she's already suspicious of you. We need to keep a low profile and the less involvement you have with her the better it's going to be for both of us. Don't forget for one second that you're in this up to your neck as well.'

Jennifer laughed. 'Sweetheart, don't try the blackmail card with me, because I've got the full suit.' Her face crumpled and she sobbed. Her eyes misted over and although tears didn't fall, her shoulders convulsed and her body trembled. 'Oh, Mister Policeman, sir. Please don't send me to prison. She made me. She made me do it.' Her arms flailed and she let out a wail. 'That woman killed my brother. I loved my brother so much and she killed him. She held me hostage in my own house, forced me to tell her where the vault was, and then, and then, she made me hide his body.' Quick as a flash she was laughing. She took a bow, 'Well, how was I?' She'd managed to squeeze a tear from her left eye and it hung from her lashes.

Beth was appalled.

'Oh, come on, Beth, lighten up. I won't do it, will I? I'm just saying, that's all. Now then, where does that bitch Maggie live?'

'You're not going to go to her house. There's no way you're going around there to cause a scene. She's got children. Maggie's nice; if you knew her you'd like her. All I'm saying is keep away from her. Try not to see too much of her because she has a way of ferreting things out.'

Jennifer's attitude changed again. She looked as though she was giving Beth's advice some thought.

'Maybe, you're right. She was a bit nasty about me but maybe she was just looking out for you. I did sort of drop in from nowhere, didn't I? You see, somebody murdered my brother and I have nowhere else to go. It's horrible for me, too. You don't care that I'm suffering just as much as you are. More; he was my brother. I can't stay at the house, can I? Not with… not with…' She tailed off.

'I'm sorry, Phantom. You're right. It's terrible for you. I'm so sorry for what happened to Marc.'

'It's horrible when she's nasty about me. I only want to stay for a little while. Just until I get on my feet and I don't want things to be awkward. Maggie's going to be coming round, isn't she? You see a lot of each other. I think that we need to clear the air. Let's go around there later. We could take a bottle of wine. I'll say that I'm sorry and we can all get to know each other. What do you say?'

'Oh, hang on. I don't think that's a clever idea. Graham will be getting ready for work. He works nights and she'll be busy sorting the kids out. I'm not sure that she'd appreciate us just dropping in on her like that.' Beth knew that she'd always be welcome but could imagine Maggie's face if she walked in with Jennifer in tow. 'I'll tell you what. She wants to go out on Friday night. How about if I make a nice supper and suggest a girlie night in with a soppy DVD?'

'Oh wonderful. Can we dress up? I'll be Barbie.' The sarcasm in Jennifer's tone made Beth wince but Jennifer changed her attitude again. 'Does she have far to come? We could send a taxi for her and then she can have a drink.'

'No, it's okay. She only lives on Sands Road.'

Jennifer's smile grew and she seemed to be genuinely trying to make amends. 'Really? Wow. Top end or bottom? My aunty lives on Sands Road, maybe they know each other.' She giggled, 'They might be neighbours.'

'Top end, just off Birchwood. What's your Aunty called?' Beth stopped talking. Jennifer's face was like granite and Beth realised that she'd been tricked. She felt stupid to have fallen for such an obvious con, but she wasn't used to dealing with anybody as duplicitous and sly as Jennifer. She was getting wise to her houseguest and wouldn't be caught again.

Jennifer was fighting her way into her denim jacket, 'Right, I'm going to go and get the bitch.'

Chapter Nine

Beth ran down the street to keep up with Jennifer. 'Phantom, stop, look, just wait a minute, will you. What are you going to do?'

She didn't slow her pace; she was striding down Oakwood Drive with furious determination. 'Oh, I'm not going to do anything, mate—you are.'

Beth pleaded with Jennifer all the way to Maggie's house. She had no idea what was going on in the girl's head but she knew that it wasn't going to be nice. She played with the idea of turning around and going back home. Maybe Jennifer would run out of steam if she didn't have an audience to play to. She was trying to decide what to do for the best when Jennifer stopped. They had been running along Birchwood Drive and had rounded the corner of Sands Road.

'What number?'

'What're you going to do?'

'Number.'

Beth tried not to glance at Maggie's house but had already given herself away.

'Ha ha, gotcha.' Jennifer smiled in triumph and set off.

Number sixty-four was the house on the corner. Jennifer stopped short of the manicured lawn as Beth caught her up.

'Wait,' Beth said.

'Wait for what? Christmas?'

The curtains in the master bedroom upstairs were

closed. Graham was in bed after his night shift. Somebody was trimming the front hedge of the house two doors down. A young boy was walking along the other side of the street with a dog. There was nobody milling around number sixty-four.

They were on the side road. Jennifer was looking up at the back of the house. 'Hmm, they never had the back done when they double glazed the front then, that's typical of her type, all show, rotten windows at the back and a pretty façade to show to the neighbours. I bet they save all year for a three-star trip to the Costas. Her type has a houseful of cheap ornaments and a piggy bank to save for a bidet.'

Beth wasn't sure how old Jennifer was, she'd been given three different versions and rather than pandering to her lies, she'd given up asking. Jennifer was older than she'd at first thought, though. Sixteen, she figured, maybe eighteen at a push, but she was astute. Maggie and Graham did struggle all year to have a cheap package in Spain.

Jennifer bent over and picked up a large stone from the rockery edging the side lawn. 'Follow me,' she ordered Beth. She stepped over the two-foot wall and across the lawn to the back of the house. Peering into the kitchen window she made sure that nobody was in the room and straightened up. The house was secluded from their adjoining neighbour by a high fence that trailed clematis. It suited her purpose. Beth knew what was coming and felt powerless to stop it. 'Come here,' Jennifer hissed. 'You've got three seconds before I scream the place down and bring out the whole street.'

Beth followed her into Maggie's garden. 'Here,' said

Jennifer and thrust the rock into Beth's hand. 'Smash the window with it, and don't even think of missing because I'll come up with something a lot worse if you do. I wonder—Does Maggie's youngest go to that playgroup down the road?'

'Please don't do anything to those kids. Surely you wouldn't hurt a baby?'

'Throw the stone.'

'I can't,' Beth dropped it, 'I won't.' She was going to go on to tell Jennifer how childish and stupid this was when Jennifer bent, picked up the stone and lobbed it through the kitchen window.

She didn't stop to survey the damage; she was running before the broken glass had time to settle. Beth panicked. She was standing in Maggie's garden looking at the jagged hole in the window. She heard the lounge door opening. In a few seconds, somebody would burst into the kitchen to see what had happened.

She ran.

She hit the street, not bothering to avoid Maggie's newly planted azaleas and she turned the corner just as the back door was thrown open. Across the street, Jennifer was disappearing into an alley. Beth followed and then they ran neck and neck until they emerged at the far end of Oakwood Drive. Beth hadn't run like this for years. She felt sick and didn't know if it was because of the vandalism they'd just done to her friend's property or because of the pain in her chest and the stitch in her side. She wanted to stop but Jennifer grabbed her by the arm and dragged her on.

Jennifer was laughing. 'Oh, you should have seen your face.' She giggled, still pulling Beth. They took another back alley to the entrance of the park and then slowed to a walk.

'That was evil,' said Beth between gasps. 'I want you gone.'

'I'm not going anywhere. You're stuck with me and you know it. I refuse to leave. Call the police if you have a problem with it.'

Beth was near to tears. She wondered what Maggie would have done in her situation. How would Maggie have played it differently? All Beth wanted to do was go to her and talk everything through. Maggie would have the answers; she'd know what to do. Beth felt spineless and weak.

Jennifer was still talking. 'In fact,' she said, 'seeing as I had to do all the work back there, there's going to be a penalty. I feel like going shopping. Come on, have you got your purse?'

'After what you've just done, forget it. I'm not going anywhere with you and I'm certainly not buying you anything.'

Jennifer was excited. She was like a five-year-old jiggling about on the seat of the bus into Barrow. Beth expected her to insist on going to Homebase to get the stuff for her bedroom makeover. Jennifer refused to tell her where they were going and Beth was beyond caring until Jennifer dragged her into the pet shop Feather and Fur.

'What are we doing in here,' Beth said dumbly, 'You know I haven't got any pets.'

'Not yet, we haven't. Not even a cat to fall over.' She was animated and her eyes danced with excitement. She was walking down the aisle picking things up and putting them down after scant examination. 'A coat for a poodle? I ask you, who would put a poodle in a fucking parka? I could just see you with a poodle, Beth. You'd call it Foo-foo and it'd be a spoiled substitute for a child.' She put the dog coat down and walked to the next shelving unit displaying treats and toys for cage-birds. 'When you were a little girl, did you ever steal a fiver from your mum's purse?'

'No, of course not. Can we get out of here now, please?'

Without looking around Jennifer picked up a seed bar marketed for budgies and slipped it into her jacket pocket.

'What the hell are you doing? Put it back. Are you mad?' hissed Beth.

'Nope.' Jennifer looked smug. 'See? It's easy.'

'Put it back, Phantom. She'll see you.'

Jennifer looked at Beth. 'Your turn.'

'Absolutely not. I'm not a thief.' She was still whispering but her voice had risen in indignation. She turned and walked towards the door of the shop without looking behind her to see if Jennifer was following. She heard a sigh and jumped when she felt Jennifer linking arms with her. Relief that she was accompanying her out of the shop was mixed with the fear of them being caught with the stolen goods in Jennifer's pocket.

The till was to the left of the door and the shop assistant was labelling some books, the pricing gun clicking rhythmically as she worked.

'Excuse me,' said Jennifer in an unnecessarily loud voice. The girl looked up and smiled. Beth blushed and turned her attention to the display of chew toys. 'I was supposed to be meeting my brother in here,' Jennifer continued. 'Don't suppose you've seen him, have you? He's tall.' She raised her hand to indicate a height far taller than her own. 'Dark hair.'

'No, sorry love. There's been nobody in for about half an hour.'

'Not to worry. Sometimes you'd think he'd died he's that slow. Oh, Beth, before we leave didn't you want to look at something over there?' Beth nodded. She had no choice but to follow Jennifer back to the budgie section.

Beth picked up a tiny mirror and looked around the shop.

'No, no, no,' Jennifer said, grinning. She reached up to the top shelf and picked up a large brass bell that would hang from a parrot cage. Beth focused on the gaping space left between two smaller parrot bells. Jennifer rang the bell and the sound echoed around the small shop. The assistant raised her head and smiled. Jennifer smiled back. She put the bell back in its place. 'I want that bell,' she said in a conversational tone.

'We don't have a parrot.'

'Parrots are lovely, aren't they? All that talking—saying things they shouldn't. Now, get me the bell.'

'Okay, but I'm paying for it.'

'That's not an option.'

'I can't, it's massive.'

'Course you can. You could fit the bell, a cage and the bloody parrot in that bag of yours. I wonder if Marc's coming yet?'

'It's too big and it makes a noise. What if it goes off in my bag?'

'It's not a bomb. You should be more worried that parrots can talk, Beth.'

Beth lifted the bell down from the shelf. She felt the sweat in her armpits. Her face was burning. The clapper hit the side of the bell and rang once as she brought it down to waist level. She glanced towards the assistant.

'Stop looking round, you look like a shoplifter,' whispered Jennifer. 'Just get it in your bag, quick.'

Beth opened the zip on her handbag, aware of the sound it made. She shoved the bell inside, pushed it down as far as she could and zipped it up. She was breathing heavily and felt sick. 'Let's get out of here,' she muttered, gripping the bag against her side.

'Not yet. I want to look at the animals, we might even buy one.' She wandered away. Beth wanted to walk out of the shop. She could wait for Jennifer outside, or just carry on walking until she was as far away from the shop as she could get, but while she had the incriminating bell in her handbag she didn't have the courage to walk past the assistant on her own and she couldn't trust Jennifer's unpredictability. The bell clanged repeatedly in her head.

Jennifer bypassed the rabbits and guinea pigs with barely a glance. The chipmunks didn't interest her, either. That only left the birds and rodents. Beth felt that if she was going to argue about a pet then it was better to be refusing a budgie than a Great Dane. Along with the tolling bell inside her head, a voice was shouting loud and clear that pet buying wasn't something that a guest staying a couple of days should be doing.

Beth had never ventured into the animal section at the back of the shop. She'd only ever been in once when she'd been with Maggie to pick up food for Blue, her Irish Setter. She wasn't aware that the back room existed and if she had known what it contained nothing could have persuaded her to venture in. Jennifer held the door open for her.

Beth was terrified as Jennifer went from vivarium to vivarium. She was terrified of snakes, hated them. She'd never given any thought to whether she was frightened of lizards, but seeing all those beady eyes staring at her she knew that she was. They looked menacing and some of them were massive. At least the snakes didn't bother to turn their heads and stare at her as she walked by. They looked slimy; the big ones were terrifying but the little ones were, if anything, worse. They were thin and had a look about them that Beth could only think of as spiteful. It was hot, the air was thick. She couldn't breathe. She remembered being locked in the vault and the feeling was similar. But the vault hadn't smelled like this. It wasn't strong or even horribly unpleasant, but it was a cloying aroma that made her feel claustrophobic. She wanted to get out.

Jennifer was wittering. 'That's a Burmese python. They grow huge but are very docile and quite easy to keep if you've got the room for them. Oh, look, that's an olive indigo snake. They are the most beautiful things. This one's a beauty. They're fast though, always bloody escaping. I wonder how much he is.' Before Beth could ponder the horrific implication behind the innocent question, Jennifer had moved on to the next vivarium. 'Corn snakes. They make a good starter pet, but they're boring. We want something' – she paused – 'special.'

Beth didn't want anything at all, unless it came as a

double in a long glass with ice. Her first attempt to speak came out as a croak. Even to her the half-formed word sounded weak and lacking in authority. She tried again, 'Phantom, this is ridiculous. I'm going to wait outside. I don't like it in here. I don't mind you looking around. Take your time, I'm going to have a fag. This place bloody stinks. I'll see you outside when you've had your fill of creepy crawlies and stuff.'

She hadn't said anything about not buying any of the awful creatures because she realised that Jennifer was playing one of her mind games. Well, she wasn't about to fall for it. She almost laughed at her gullibility. As if you could keep a reptile in a little house like hers. It was ridiculous.

Jennifer turned away from the viv that contained two boa constrictors. 'I really don't want us to fall out over this, Beth,' she said sweetly. 'You know I don't make idle threats. I need a small pet to help me get over the death of my brother. Call it therapy, if you like. And let's not forget what you've got in your bag as we speak.' She started to sing. 'Ding dong bell, I'm gonna tell.' Her tone hardened, 'I'm not leaving this shop without Rosy.'

She pointed at the snake nearest to the viewing panel of the largest vivarium. The laminated card on the front of the viv read, *Rosy Boa, Lichanura trivirgata.*

Beth thought she might be sick. She'd always been frightened of snakes, though she'd never been close enough to one for it to be more than a revulsion. She wondered where discomfort turned into a titled phobia. Just looking at the horrible creature had made her palms clammy, her breath was coming in short heavy gasps, pulling the smell of the place into her throat until she could taste it. The heat was making her dizzy and she still didn't know if Jennifer was playing with her or if the demon who had invaded her life did intend on bringing this horrendous animal into her home.

'I'm not having a snake, Phantom, and that's final. Please, let's just get out of here.'

'Okay, come on then.' Jennifer was laughing. She wasn't laughing at Beth, nor was she yelling, throwing a tantrum, or brandishing threats to get her own way. Her eyes were shining with excitement. She was in good humour. Beth had just refused her something and she seemed happy to just let it go and concede to Beth's authority, but Beth wouldn't trust her any more than she'd trust the snake.

Jennifer grabbed Beth's hand and skipped her out of the reptile room and into the main shop where the air-con was buzzing and the breeze was fresh and cool. Jennifer was pulling her along the shop. 'Well, if I can't have a snake. Can I have one of these?' She was pointing again, this time at a glass tank filled with half a dozen rats. They were horrible and vicious, but at least Beth comforted herself with the fact that they had fur, well, apart from their ugly tails that looked as though they'd been skinned.

Jennifer was bouncing up and down beside her. 'Oh look, look, it's a Kaluki Blue. I've got to have that one. Oh, please Beth, please. I'll do anything to have that one there. It's rare. I'll keep it in my room. You won't even ever know that she's there. Please, it's only a fiver. I'll pay you back. It's a Kaluki. It'll probably be ages before she has another one of those in.'

Beth couldn't have cared less if she never had another

one in and the shop went bust for lack of them. She had to admit that Jennifer seemed to know what she was talking about. There was no card saying that the rat was a Kaleeky Blue or whatever the hell it was called. She couldn't believe that she was standing in a pet shop considering having a dirty-filthy rat in her house. But, she reasoned, it would be in a cage. It wouldn't need walking. It wouldn't pee all over her carpets and a rat wouldn't cost much to feed. If it kept Jennifer off her back it was small price to pay. Best of all – the very, very best thing of all – thought Beth, it isn't a damn snake. But rats are vermin. She didn't like rats.

Maybe there was room for compromise here.

'How about a hamster? I had a hamster when I was a kid. He was called –'

'Are you serious? A hamster?' said Jennifer, her voice dripping disdain. 'A hamster? What the hell would I do with a hamster? Do you know how stupid they are?'

Beth refused to think of the implications of what Jennifer might do with a rat. She couldn't imagine that she'd want to do anything with it. 'Well, admittedly,' she mused, 'I've never heard of a hamster with a university degree, but...'

Jennifer cut her off. 'Rats are superior rodents. They are the most intelligent of them all. Hell, they make better pets than any other cage animal. Do you know that once a rat is tame it will rarely bite unless it's cornered? Bloody hamsters bite for the hell of it.'

Beth had to admit that Jennifer was right. She'd only ever handled her hamster once. It bit her hard and she'd bled for hours and cried for ages. Was Jennifer right? Would this horrible rat never bite? And would that come in writing with a guarantee? She had no intention of getting anywhere near the dirty creature to give it the opportunity to bite her. She felt herself caving in. How far would Jennifer go if she put her foot down and refused? She gripped her handbag tighter, terrified that the bell inside it might tilt and jangle. She felt as though she was holding onto a ticking time bomb. What if the shop girl went over to that shelf and saw the bell-sized hole?

'Okay, go on then, you can have it.' Was she mad? She couldn't believe that she'd just agreed to buy a rat— A rat, for God's sake.

Jennifer screeched with excitement. She grabbed Beth and cuddled her. 'Oh, thank you, thank you, thank you. You won't regret it.'

Beth already did.

And within seconds she came to regret it even more. Jennifer shot across the shop. She grabbed the girl from behind the till and reeled off lists of things that she would need, while Beth stood back horrified. She didn't want to go near the shop lady because of the bell but she tried to interject some reason into the proceedings when Jennifer ordered the biggest rodent house in the shop. It was four-foot square at the base and three storeys high, with ladders and slides and bloody hammocks connecting the levels. The shop assistant explained that you could buy tunnels and add-ons to make the tank even bigger. Jennifer wanted them all and ordered a second house with two tunnels that would connect them both. The equipment in the deluxe houses could be moved around to introduce different stimuli into the rat's life. Beth didn't like the idea of an intelligent rodent with access to a ladder. She liked even less that Jennifer was buying half the shop while they both had stolen items on them. Jennifer was high on the thrill of her shopping trip and nothing was going to stop her. She bought sawdust and hay, a sack of rat food, two heavy ceramic dishes and two water bottles.

'All this for one little rat?' Beth couldn't believe it.

'It's not much, Mum.'

Beth's face withered at the thought.

'Just think, if we'd bought a snake it would have cost you two hundred pounds before all the equipment it needs, so you've saved money, haven't you?' They loaded all the gear into the car. The back seats had to be put down to accommodate one of the massive enclosures and Beth assured the shop assistant that they'd be back for the other. At the till, Beth had to go into her bag to get her purse out. She couldn't have been more terrified if the stolen clanger at the bottom of her bag was the Liberty bell. She removed her purse very carefully, if she dislodged the bell and it made a noise the game would be up. After handing over her credit card, the assistant brought a little box with holes to the tank with all the female rats in. Jennifer pointed to the one she wanted and it was put in the box for her. 'Oh and...'

Jennifer moved along to the next tank. She glanced once, slyly, at Beth. 'That one, please,' she said. The girl dipped into the second tank and pulled out another rat. It was predominantly white with chocolate brown patches.

'What are you doing? We agreed one rat.'

'Don't be daft; you can't keep one rat by itself. It would be cruel. They are sociable creatures.'

'Oh aye,' interjected the girl, 'they like a bit of comp'ny.'

'But, that one's a boy, isn't it?' asked Beth, eyeing the enormous balls protruding from the back end of the rat. 'Won't they have babies?'

'Oh, no, not for years yet, and I'll have left home by then.'

The assistant opened her mouth to speak and Jennifer shot her a warning look. She closed it again. Jennifer winked at her.

Even as they left the shop, Beth expected to hear the girl running out after them shouting, 'Thief, thief.' Only when they got in the car and drove out of the car park did she breathe freely since putting the bell in her bag. 'I have never stolen anything in my life until today. Shame on you for making me do that,' she said.

'Making you do it? Seemed to me you took to it like a pro, sticking things in bags and pockets like a proper Artful Dodger.'

She turned in her seat to look at Jennifer, 'What do you mean? You're the thief. I only…'

Jennifer grinned at her. 'Pockets feeling a little heavy, are they?'

Beth put her hand into her pocket and pulled out the seed bar that Jennifer had stolen and the poodle coat. From her other pocket she took out a diamante dog collar.

'I never stole a bloody thing from that shop,' Jennifer said. 'There's only one thief in this car, love.' She turned her attention back to the rats on her knee. Beth was terrified that they'd chew through the thin cardboard and get loose in the car while she was driving.

At home, when the eight-foot rat houses had been set up, loaded with sawdust and hay and sat resplendent with two inhabitants in the living room, Jennifer said, 'I'm going to call the boy Riff-Raff and the girl Magenta.' When Beth complained about their placement, Jennifer said, 'Well, it won't fit in my room, will it?'

Beth's Welsh dresser had to be moved into the small dining room and one armchair was too close to the sofa. Her spacious living room, dressed just as she wanted it, was cramped and uncomfortable and the bloody rats had more damned space to move around than she did. The large brass bell dangling from the top of the cage added insult to injury. However, she had to grudgingly admit that she was fascinated watching them running around exploring their new home and getting acquainted with each other.

'Oh, oh they're fighting,' Beth said as Riff-Raff grabbed Magenta at the back of the neck and made her squeal.

'No, they're not, they're having sex, but don't worry, they're too young to have babies.'

'Oh, that's all right then,' muttered Beth, dubiously.

She'd watched as Jennifer set up home for her new pets. It was as though she was sharing her life with a different girl. Jennifer was happy and spoke to her differently. For the first time, Beth didn't see the manipulative monster but a young girl, excited and buoyant. Beth was a reluctant foster mother. How the hell was she going to cope with her career as a busy nurse along with the demands of a troubled teenager? How long was she going to have to do this? And given the way that it had come about, what the hell did the future hold for her?

'Do you want to hold one?' asked Jennifer.

'No.'

Chapter Ten

The next few days passed without incident. Despite a lack of trust, Beth went back to work, leaving Jennifer to her own devices. The girl was calm and made few demands on her, nothing that you wouldn't get from any teenager and without the previous veiled threats. Beth tried to live normally and the only thing that gave her away was waking from her nightmares bathed in sweat. Jennifer was decorating her bedroom and in the evenings Beth helped her. They were playing at being normal. It was the next phase in the game, a role that Jennifer could never keep up for long.

Maggie and Beth spoke most days on the phone although Beth tried to make the calls from work whenever possible. Maggie would always ask if the little freeloading freak had gone yet and Beth would tell her to give the girl a break. The phone line crackled with tension whenever Jennifer was mentioned and eventually, to Beth's relief, they soon avoided the subject. Beth had killed a man, she'd hidden his body, she'd been blackmailed into taking his strange sister into her home and yet, as the days passed, her life became an overcoat with a label that read *Normal*. Despite misgivings, she found the antics of Riff-Raff and Magenta charming. Madge chewed a hole in one of Beth's good scatter cushions and made a nest. Riffy left droppings the size of bullets on her cream sofa but, far from being disgusted, the rats were so loveable that within days Beth would have forgiven them anything. Jennifer had told her on the first night that once a rat is tame it won't bite unless cornered and this seemed to be the case. Soon Beth was brave enough to let them out of their penthouse suite to run around and get into mischief. She loved it when they'd crawl onto her shoulder and chatter into her ear.

Maggie called around one evening with two bottles of Lambrini and a Chinese takeaway. She had teenagers herself and knew what they could be like but that didn't stop her having a lot to say about the rats running around the living room. She was cool with Jennifer, who moaned about the curry being too mild and having peas in it, despite putting away a third of the contents. Maggie had only bought for the two of them and was annoyed when Beth, trying to avoid confrontation, spread the food between three.

'I mean, it's not right, is it? Whoever heard of Indians putting peas in their curry?'

'Do they have peas in India?' Beth asked. She thought that garden peas were part of a purely British heritage. 'After all, they don't have cottage pie, do they? And where would a good cottage pie be without peas?' They crunched on prawn crackers and pondered the thought for a moment.

'Oh, I forgot to tell you,' said Maggie around a mouthful of fried rice, 'I had my window put through, last week.'

Beth concentrated on spearing a piece of beef with her fork and felt her cheeks warming.

'Shut up,' shrieked Jennifer. 'That's awful, Maggie. Have you any idea who did it? I'd zap their balls in a blender till they screamed like little girls.'

'You're kidding, aren't you?' said Maggie with a

laugh. 'I'd shake their hands and drop them a fiver if I knew who it was. I've been nagging the bastard for ages for double glazing at the back and if they hadn't smashed it, he'd have made me wait another two years. We got a bargain in the end with one of those deals off the telly. I'm just hoping the vandals come back and trash my bathroom suite.'

'I bet they didn't think they were doing you a favour at the time,' Beth laughed, looking boldly at Jennifer.

In response, Jennifer leaned across the table and poured herself a third glass of wine.

'Are you old enough to drink? Shouldn't you still be at school, or something? How old are you, anyway?' asked Maggie.

'I'm twenty-one, twenty-two in May. See, I'm not as young as I look.'

Maggie and Beth raised their eyebrows. 'Yeah right,' said Maggie, 'and I'm Jesus of Nazareth. Listen, I've got kids of my own, sweetheart, so don't come that with me.'

Jennifer was sulking. 'Okay, I'm almost eighteen, but I'm not some snot nosed brat, you know. I've seen things that you could only imagine.'

Maggie sneered. 'Such as?'

Beth shot Jennifer a warning look. It didn't go unnoticed by Maggie.

'Such as wouldn't you like to know,' countered Jennifer.

'Oh, isn't it past your bedtime, little girl? Go on, run along now and let the grown-ups talk.'

Beth saw the animosity flash between them and tried to be peacemaker. 'Pack it in you two. Can't you just play nicely without bickering?'

It was Maggie's nature to blurt out whatever came into her head. Fuelled by cheap wine and bothered by the looks that passed between Beth and Jennifer, she couldn't hold her tongue. 'This is bent all out of shape, Beth. I'm not buying this set up. You're touting happy families but I'm seeing Jeremy Kyle. Have you been in touch with your folks, kid? Do they know that you're here? Where are they, anyway?'

'Overseas,' said Beth.

'Dead,' said Jennifer at the same time.

Maggie's eyes opened wide, her face set with a look of triumph. She had them now and she wanted answers. Something was going on and Beth knew she wouldn't let up until she found out what it was.

Jennifer forestalled her. 'They're overseas really. I tell lies to get attention. My brother's dead though, and that's the truth. He died after a tragic accident with a ballerina.'

'Did she die too?'

'Oh no, she's still dancing. My mum went loopy and drinks gin, so my dad takes her abroad to see Betty Ford.'

'He must be quite a celebrity, this dad of yours, seeing as The Betty Ford clinic only panders to the very famous and very rich. Been in the charts, has he?'

'No, but my mum was a top model before she was horribly disfigured. One of the other models was jealous of her and threw acid in her face. That's what happens to bitches.'

Maggie had had enough, 'Yeah, whatever.' Beth saw Jennifer relax; the girl was shrewd and had clearly done what she had set out to do. The probing questions, once deflected, had stopped. Turning her back to Jennifer, Maggie said to Beth, 'So, how's work going, mate? Any fatalities or mad medical dramas since you've been back?'

'Yeah, we lost Elsie. You know, the little lady I told you about who fell and broke her hip. And I went out to a bloke the other day and found him in a diabetic coma. I told you about it, didn't I, Phantom?' Beth tried to bring Jennifer back into the conversation.

'Yep, dirty old git had shit himself. I don't know how you do it. I couldn't. And all those dead people that you have to touch. How do you do that? Ugh, I could never touch a dead person.'

Beth laughed, it was high pitched and unnatural, 'Hah, I'm a care in the community nurse, Jennifer, not a bloody mortician. It's not often that I have dealings with anyone that has died.'

'But what do they feel like? Dead bodies, I mean. I've never seen one. Are they all cold and stiff?'

'Shut up, Je... Phantom.' She had an edge to her voice. She spoke too sharply and covered herself with another laugh. The curry rose in her throat and she pushed her plate away swallowing hard. Maggie was staring at her, waiting for her to speak. 'Hah, ever the Goth, eh? Always dwelling on death and destruction. What about life? Where does that fit into the Gothic creed? Let's all lighten up a bit. This is supposed to be fun.' She bent under the table to feed Riffy a prawn cracker.

'You seem uptight, Beth. What's the matter?' Jennifer wasn't about to let up. 'I haven't touched a sore spot have I. Oh my God, you haven't lost somebody close to you, have you? A boyfriend or something?'

'No, I haven't. Now for Christ's sake shut up, will you? It's getting boring. I'm going to sit in the living room. You two coming?'

Maggie hadn't spoken but she was watching. Beth knew she saw her hand shaking as she stood up, scraping her chair back from the table and splashing wine onto the floor.

The following Thursday Beth came home to hear the unmelodious strains of Marilyn Manson belting from the house. She heard what she could only describe as devil music before she'd turned off the car's engine. The neighbours would be demented.

Once in the hallway she shouted twice for Jennifer to turn her music down but the girl would never hear her over the racket. Beth mounted the stairs two at a time. She knocked on Jennifer's door, but there was no answer. After another attempt at respecting the girl's privacy by knocking first, she threw the door open and marched inside.

'Will you turn that bloody mus—'

The words dried in her throat and Beth stared in horror at the girl lying on the single bed. She took in the room at a glance but no relevant words rose to express herself.

Jennifer turned to look at her and a wide smile broke across her face. 'Beth, I'm glad you're home. I've been shopping. She stood up awkwardly, dragging the monstrosity with her. 'Beth, I'd like to introduce you to Darklord. Isn't he beautiful? Would you like to pet him?'

Jennifer took two steps towards her and Beth backed

out of the doorway slamming the door hard to form a safety barrier between her and the massive snake. 'What's that fucking thing doing in my house? It can't stay. You do realise that, don't you? I mean, Phantom, I know you live in your own world with your own warped set of rules and ideals but even you must see that this is completely unacceptable. Get rid of it.'

The door between them opened and phantom stepped through, closing it quietly behind her. Beth was glad that the thing was no longer draped around her neck. Jennifer had a smile on her face and spoke to Beth as though she was addressing a small child. 'Oh, now calm down and stop overreacting. Let's go downstairs and talk this through quietly. There's no need for all this drama.'

'Where is it? Where's the snake?' blurted Beth, fighting back tears.

'It's okay, don't panic. He's back in his vivarium and I've been responsible, Beth. I've bought glass locks and everything so that he can't get out. He's a Burmese python.'

The enormous wooden contraption taking up most of the space in Phantom's room must be the vivarium and was presumably what housed the beast.

Jennifer took Beth by the hand and led her down the stairs. Beth ranted and gave ultimatums as she was guided into a chair. Jennifer was all quiet domesticity. She prattled on to herself while she made a big production of putting on the kettle. Beth began her rant several times but Jennifer shushed her and said that they'd thrash it all through once they had a nice cup of tea. Beth didn't need tea; she needed to get that fucking snake out of her house. Now.

'Now then,' said Jennifer, putting a cup between Beth's hands as you might a frail and elderly lady, 'Let's not shout or get excited because there's no need and I've got something far more important that I want to talk to you about.'

'It's a snake,' said Beth in a small voice, as though defining the intrusion into her home explained everything that needed to be said on the matter. She wanted it out. She refused to be blackmailed by Jennifer.

'Yes, he is and he's magnificent. You didn't want the rats, remember.' She shot this across the room as an accusation. 'And now look. I can't get a second with them. They love you and you love them and it all worked out for the best, just like this will.'

It was true; she had come to love Riff-Raff and Magenta. Since the first few days after the novelty of the pets had worn off for Jennifer, Beth had cleaned them, played with them every night after work and saved scraps for them from the evening meal. Left to Jennifer, they would have died from neglect. She tried to pull herself together and gain some control of the situation. Her next words were strong and direct, stating her intensions and brooking no argument. The discovery of a huge snake loose in her house had had a profound effect on her and she was still trying to get over seeing it.

'I don't like snakes. Get rid of it. I won't have it in my house. What if it escapes and gets into my room? I won't be able to sleep with that here. I want my life back. Jennifer, just get it out. And while we're on the subject, it's time you were thinking of moving on too. This was only ever a short-term arrangement.'

'Everything's yours isn't it, Beth? Your house, your room, your life. I need security. I need to feel as though I belong. From now on, I really would like it to be our house, our rooms, our lives. You can be very selfish sometimes. I expect you're going to go mad again when the credit card bill comes and you see that I've charged seven hundred pounds to it. Haven't you seen the adverts? You should never write your pin number down like that.'

'You've done what?'

'Shush, I'm talking. I need to feel wanted and you can afford it. I hope you don't make a big deal out of this because it really is very insignificant. We need to find a way to be happy together and Darklord makes me very happy, Beth. You want me to be happy, don't you?' Without waiting for a response, she carried on. 'I'm glad we've got all that sorted out, I feel better for our little chat. Right, before you say anything at all, I want you to hear me out. You might balk at the idea of this but it's necessary for us to move on.'

Beth was processing the confession that Jennifer had used credit card fraud to buy the snake. Seven hundred pounds was over half of her monthly salary. How was she going to pay the bills at the end of the month? They'd try to take direct debits and, when they bounced, there'd be bank charges on top of that. Her mind was reeling. And now Jennifer was attacking her with something else that she wasn't going to like. How bad could it be? A Bengali tiger to lie in front of the fire, a great white shark for the bath? Maybe Jennifer wanted to commit bank robbery, grand larceny—murder!

'I can't take anymore. Please take your snake and go

back to your own house.'

'Stop giving me a hard time and listen. I want you to get me something. It's no big deal and you can do it easily, you being a nurse and everything.'

Jennifer waited. Beth noticed that she was pausing for her to interject, wanting to gauge the reaction thus far and work out how best to formulate her next sentence. Beth looked in her direction but she didn't say anything.

'I want you to get me a little bit of morphine.'

Chapter Eleven

She hadn't slept. Driving to work in a trance, she didn't see the road; she didn't see other vehicles on the road. All she saw was the map of her life with no exit route. She contemplated driving into a wall—and hated herself for being too much of a coward to do it.

Her job was structured to work three days in people's homes with her community care patients and two days in the local hospital. She was on her way to begin a full day shift.

She went to the staff room and exchanged the usual greetings without any awareness of anything that she said. Smoothing down her uniform out of habit, she made her way to the nurse's station for the shift handover. Charts and papers were thrust into her hand as Debbie, the previous shift staff nurse, took her through the night's events and traumas.

'Mrs Gleaston had a bad night, very restless and complaining of abdo pain. She's been written up for an extra two milligrams of Diazepam, and Voltarol four times a day. Mrs Beck, fine. Josie Taylor, fine. Mrs Davies, her wound looked a bit sloughy last night, swabs sent off and wounds re-dressed. We need to keep an eye on it. Beth? Are you okay? You seem miles away? Beth?'

'What? Oh, yes, fine thanks; just had a late one last night. What were you saying about Josie?'

She pulled herself together for surgical rounds. Mr Bell, the consultant, demanded full attention and required all the ward sisters to hear what he said first time, every time. Her mind was on the job and she was grateful for the distraction.

She wasn't going to do it. She had no intention of jeopardising a fifteen-year, unblemished career. She had trained and worked hard to gain the position of ward sister. She was caring and compassionate, firm and strict with the junior nurses and respected and liked by every member of staff from the consultants to the ward domestics. In fifteen years on the job, she had never stolen so much as a biro. She had never stepped out of line or had a discipline attached to her record. She knew the job and did it well with a sense of pride in doing what she had to do to the best of her ability. No freaky little Goth was going to change that. Beth could no more steal from the hospital, or cause suffering to her patients, than kick a dog in the street.

But—If Jennifer demanded that she kick a defenceless dog, would she?

All morning her mind played out how she could do it. The safest time would be during the night-time drug round, but her shift would be long finished by then, she was working until three o'clock. Morning drugs were hectic, but the lunch time round was usually quieter. Some of the patients would doze off after their three-course lunch and before their relatives came for afternoon visiting.

She did the drugs round with Fiona working alongside her. She was a qualified nurse who would double sign for all the drugs dispensed. Her hand shook as she gave Molly Jones her two paracetamol, one diuretic and a measure of lactulose for her bowels. She couldn't understand why she was shaking, she wasn't going to do anything wrong.

'We're in a rush today, Fi. If you do the beds on that side of the bay I'll take this side, it'll be quicker and we can be finished up by two.'

She could have kicked herself for saying it. They weren't busy, but Fiona was used to taking orders and didn't question the request. Protocol decreed that they stayed together and both oversaw each drug administration to each patient, but when they were rushed it was customary practice to split and take one side of the ward each. As they came back to the drug trolley at the top of the bay, Beth would sign and Fiona would countersign for the next two patient's drugs.

Annie Ryden in bed 1 was unconscious. She'd been in for three days after a fall. They didn't expect her to wake up, let alone recover. She was sleeping peacefully thanks to the morphine infusion fed through her drip and replenished every four hours.

Beth looked around the bay. Ethel in the next bed was talking to the woman who'd come in for bariatric surgery the following day. The obese lady looked bored as Ethel explained, at length, how she'd come about her broken hip. Fiona hadn't reached bed 6 yet. The lady from bed 5 was telling her some tale about a flooded cottage at Newbiggin. Fiona had her back to Beth and looked as though she'd be awhile disentangling herself from the description of soggy carpets.

Beth put the vial and the syringe on Annie's table. She put on a pair of latex gloves and did Annie's observations, marking the results on her chart. She hesitated for a moment and then wrote the patient up for her lunchtime dose of morphine. She checked Annie's cannula, ensuring that the vein hadn't tissued and that the flow of saline and morphine were getting through the thready old vein. She checked on the regulator controlling the speed that the fluid dripped into her arm. So far, she had followed procedure to the letter. She hadn't done a thing wrong apart from writing up the morphine and saline before it was administered, a small oversight—but one that she had never done before. The protocol was clear—check, administer, write up.

She pulled the wheel on the regulator to the bottom of the slide; this stopped the fluid from entering the delivery tube, holding it steady in the bag. She took the syringe pack and opened it releasing the sterile needle. Holding the vial of morphine upside down she inserted the tip of the needle into the circle of mesh on the top of the vial. She drew up half of the 50ml dose. Annie was heavily sedated and Beth prayed that half the dose would be enough to keep the old lady unconscious and free from pain.

Ward 4 housed six bays of six beds and four single private rooms. By the time they had finished their drug round, she had used the other half of the first vial on another patient and had added two more vials of morphine to her uniform pocket by short-changing most of her patients. She could feel them against her thigh as she walked. She considered going to her locker and transferring the stolen drugs to her handbag in the ladies' toilet during her break, but she didn't dare. If suspicion was aroused and anybody challenged her about the missing drugs she would stand a better chance of coming up with a plausible cover story if they were on her person. In her handbag, they were stolen; on her person, they were just 'not administered' despite being signed off. She heard the little glass jars clink together. To her ears the noise sounded like a church bell calling the faithful to worship, or a stolen parrot bell proclaiming her a thief. She was convinced that everybody on the ward could hear the almost imperceptible sound that they made. By the time her shift finished, she felt sick.

Fiona asked her to wait while she got something from her locker, saying that she would walk to their cars with Beth. Beth didn't want to walk out of the hospital with Fiona. She didn't wait and rushed down the endless corridors to her car. With every step, she expected security to stop her.

She drove out of the hospital grounds with the vials of morphine in her pocket. She took two left turns and then a right to envelop herself in a nearby housing estate to shake off the security men that she was convinced were following her. She was attuned, listening for the scream of police sirens. She drove, turning here and there into the warren of identical streets. When she was far away from the hospital, she parked alongside a children's play area and, surrounded by the happy cries of children playing on the swings, she transferred the stolen drugs from her uniform pocket to a zip pouch in her handbag.

Lowering her head into her hands, she wondered what the fuck she was doing. She probably had enough Morphine to kill somebody if they were frail and vulnerable. A single drop was enough to kill her career. Beth had always been content, her life was never exciting or heady, but it had behaved itself. She ran along neat, well-tended tramlines and, if asked, would have said that she was happy with her lot. And then—with one stupid advert in the local paper for a ridiculous date night, it had all changed. First, she was a murderer, now she was a contemptible drug lord. Beth didn't want to go home, it was no sanctuary for her, but she had nowhere else to go.

For the second time in her life—and both that day—she considered suicide as her only way out.

Chapter Twelve

Jennifer was waiting for her when she put her key in the lock.

'Well?' she demanded, before Beth had got through the door. 'Did you get any?'

Beth answered in a dull monotone. 'Yes, I've got you some.'

Jennifer jiggled like a little girl whose mummy had brought home the latest edition of *Moon Girl* comic. 'Let's see it, then. Come on Beth, give it to me.' She was impatient. Beth took the vials of morphine from her handbag and laid them on the coffee table. 'You have no idea what it has cost me stealing those.'

'Oh, do you have to pay for stolen goods these days? Seriously, though, you didn't get caught, did you? Nobody saw you? That could ruin everything.'

'No, nobody saw me,' she replied in the same dull monotone and was about to explain that she had sold out everything that she claimed to hold dear, but realised it would be wasted breath, Jennifer had stolen her integrity, but what was the point in saying so? In her self-absorption, she didn't care.

Jennifer scooped up the vials and held one to her face. She beamed with pleasure. Peering into the tiny amount of clear liquid, she gave a cross-eyed smile. 'Good day's work, Bethie. Will you be able to get this much every day?'

'I'm not getting any more.' There was no intonation, no inflection and no emotion in her voice.

Jennifer laughed. The sound was too loud in the stillness of the room. 'Oh, don't start all that again, it's a waste of time and we both know it. Of course, you're going to get more, lots more lovely drugs so that we can move on to the next stage.'

'If you're planning to take it yourself, it'll kill you.' Beth wanted her to take it. All of it. She would have stolen more – as much as she could get to take this monster out of her life – but right now, she was beyond feeling anything and only gave the warning because she was a nurse and nursing is a vocation. It couldn't be left behind at the hospital doors and she'd be failing in her duty if she didn't advocate precaution when handing out stolen class-A drugs.

Jennifer looked bemused that Beth could even consider the idea. 'Don't be so ridiculous, I'm not going to take them myself. Is that what you were hoping, Beth? Do you want me to kill myself, let you off the hook, relieve you of all responsibility? No, I don't want to know. I want to believe that you love me. You're all I have.'

Beth didn't respond.

'It's an interesting concept though, isn't it? I mean, what if you had to play God and choose to save one person's life over another? For instance, if you had to choose between your mother and your father, who would be allowed to live and which of them would you let die?'

Beth was used to these morbid flights of fancy. She was lost in her own troubled thoughts.

'Come on, answer me, which one?'

'Oh, don't be ridiculous, it's a stupid question. My

parents are both dead. You know that. And if they weren't, I'd never be able to choose one over the other. Just give me some space, please, Phantom. I'm not in the mood for your games tonight.'

'All right, then, let's make it simpler. Maggie and her ex-husband Colin Johnson. Only one can live, but to save that person the other must be sacrificed. Which one?'

'Haven't you got some death's-head poetry to write? Just leave me alone, will you?'

'Not until you answer me. If you had to pass sentence on Colin or Maggie, which would it be?'

Beth sighed. 'Colin of course. Maggie and I have been friends since we were three. If I had to choose whose life I would save, it would be Maggie.'

'But I wasn't asking who you would save. I was asking which of them you would kill.'

'Oh, I've had enough of this.' Beth walked out of the room.

'So be it. The cloth is cut.' Beth couldn't be bothered humouring her. She ignored the remark and, foregoing anything to eat or drink, made for the solitude of her bedroom.

Days turned into weeks and Beth stole enough morphine and other drugs to stock a pharmacy. For the most part there was no noticeable difference in the status or wellbeing of her patients. She commented on this one evening to Jennifer.

'That is so negligent,' Jennifer said. 'It just goes to show how hospitals overprescribe drugs.'

On the rare occasion that a patient did wake, writhing in agony, they would be labelled LPT, or HDT—'low pain threshold' or 'high drug tolerance'—and their medication would be upped to accommodate the change. No questions were asked and Beth learned to breathe again.

'People should be allowed to experience pain,' mused Jennifer. 'It's their right. They shouldn't be denied it. I'd want to feel it.'

Some days Beth couldn't steal anything and she would incur the wrath of Phantom. Other days she brought home the bacon and a few chops on the side and it was smiles all round. She stopped asking what the drugs were for. She didn't care. She only ever asked when it would end. She admitted that as the weeks passed without getting caught it had become easier. The crime was the same and yet, her conscience pricked less and her need for survival carried her through the days. In bed, when she was alone with her demons, she mused that Phantom was the perfect nickname for Jennifer because since the day that girl had taken over her life she had been haunted. She wasn't sleeping and when she dropped off, she was plagued with nightmares about Jennifer coming into her room at night to kill her.

Magenta was fat. Beth commented on it. 'Yes, I've noticed that, too. I know what's happening. The female is always the dominant rat. You see, the greedy cow's taking all the food and leaving Riff Raff with nothing.' Beth was horrified and ran her hands over Riffy's body to check for starvation or malnutrition. He didn't seem any different but Beth noticed that Magenta was nasty with him. They had always slept together curled around each other's body like lovers in the night, but now, if Riffy tried to get into the bedding box she screeched at him and turned him out to sleep in a corner of the cage by himself. 'She's just a fat bully,' said Jennifer with the air of one who knows. 'Perhaps we should separate them for a week or two. That restores the balance; she'll miss him.'

The following day, Beth bought a smaller cage and Riffy was shown into his new home. He seemed happy enough – but then, he hadn't seemed unhappy with his previous hen-pecked existence. The rats were only agitated when Jennifer brought Darklord into the living room and insisted on taunting them by letting him slither over their cages. The rats would take fright and hide in their bedding boxes while Darklord tried to squeeze through the bars to reach them. His tongue would flicker, tasting the smell of lunch but not being able to locate it. Afterwards Jennifer would have to headlock him to stop him from biting her in frustration. Beth told her it was cruel, but Jennifer laughed at Beth and taunted her for her continued fear of the snake.

Jennifer pounced on Beth as she walked through the door. It was a ritual. 'Well, what did you get today?'

'I told you this morning that I wouldn't be able to get anything because I was shadowed by an examiner for my upgrade.'

Jennifer pulled a face. 'You should have given her the slip and tried harder.'

'Yes, and if I got caught and ended up without a job – and had my arse hauled in jail to boot – then where would we be?'

Jennifer stomped into the living room in a foul mood and Beth heard her banging up the stairs. Jennifer was in a rage, so Beth was surprised when she shouted from the top of the stairs, 'Beth, could you come up a minute please, hun? I've got something to show you.'

After knocking on the bedroom door and being told to go in, Jennifer motioned for Beth to sit down. Forgetting about the potatoes she was peeling, Beth sat on the edge of the bed. Jennifer's moods usually lasted much longer than a few minutes and Beth was grateful that something had distracted the temperamental teenager.

'Well, what's up?'

Jennifer was holding Riff-Raff and stroking him. 'He's such a character, isn't he? So gentle and curious about everything. It's such a shame.'

'What is?'

Jennifer crossed the room and stood beside Darklord's vivarium. The snake, sensing motion and smelling rat on his flickering tongue, was uncoiling.

'That he has to die.' With a deft movement, she put the key into the glass lock, turned it and slid open the door by six inches. She did it smoothly and with one hand while cradling Riff-Raff in the other.

She grabbed the rat by the tail and swung him from her supporting hand. Shocked, it screamed and writhed, trying to curl his body back up to safety. If Jennifer hadn't moved so fast, the weight of his body hanging suspended from his tail would have de-gloved the skin leaving just the bone. Given a week, that would have desiccated and dropped off if the rat hadn't died from shock or infection before then—but Riff-Raff didn't have a week to live.

In the second that it took for Beth to cry out and rise from the bed, Jennifer, with a deftness borne of practice, had forced the frightened rat through the gap in the vivarium door and dropped him onto a log at the mercy of Darklord. Riff-Raff sensed death the second his feet touched the branch.

'Oh, my God, what the hell are you doing? Get him out. Get him out of there.'

The snake was excited; he'd unwound the top third of his body and his eyes were fixed on the rat. Riff-Raff was petrified. He was staring at the snake, whiskers erect, body trembling. The snake was moving towards him, slowly, psyching his meal out, only his flickering tongue giving away any impression of urgency. It was moving fast, sensing out the rat, smelling and tasting the air. He was within a foot of his prey.

Darklord lifted his head so that he rose from eye level with the rat to look down on him from half a foot above. The snake's head swayed, almost imperceptibly in a slow, hypnotic rhythm.

Beth was screaming but couldn't move. She wanted to rush to the vivarium, pull open the door and thrust her hand in to retrieve the terrified rat, but she couldn't. Her fear of Darklord was too great. Any sudden movement and the snake was going to lunge with frightening speed. She'd be badly bitten not only by the snake but also by the rat if she even got as far as grabbing him. Only Jennifer would have the guts to put her hand into the snake's domain. 'It's going to kill him. The bastard's going to kill Riff-Raff.' She was sobbing, tears streaming down her face. 'Please, Jennifer, do something.' Jennifer didn't respond. The hypnotic sway of the snake and its prey had entranced her. She was erect, a smile turning up the edges of her mouth. 'Jennifer, I'll do anything—anything you want, please just get Riffy out.'

Darklord was within striking range. He pulled his head back. Beth shrieked in despair. Riff-Raff shrieked in terror. Jennifer shrieked in delight.

Before the snake touched the rat, he let out a single high pitched scream made more grotesque by the fact that he hadn't made any attempt to move. He knew that any effort to save himself was futile.

The snake struck, moving only the first foot and a half of his length. Beth gasped and held her breath. Her hands flew to her mouth, not making it all the way up to cover her eyes. There was silence in the room, broken only by the sound of Jennifer breathing.

The snake was unbelievably fast, but Riff-raff, despite being in shock and stilled by fear and the swaying movement of Darklord, was attuned and ready for the movement. The instinct of survival had overtaken conscious reasoning. Darklord's mouth was open as he struck, his upper body blurred with the speed of his lunge. As his head made contact with the quivering form of the trembling rat, Riff-Raff squealed and jumped vertically into the air. He landed on the snake's back. Darklord spun, infuriated. He hissed and recoiled in anger. Lashing out at the rat, he missed him as Riff-Raff bounced all over the vivarium in blind panic.

His next attack missed and, as the rat took flight, Darklord grazed his own body with the sharp impaling fangs. Raff-Raff jumped and scurried up one of the thick branches. Darklord was frenzied. He didn't stalk the rat but made a third fast strike. He wanted to tire the animal. On the branch, the prey was trembling, but now his reaction to the snake was different. Whereas before he was unable to move and his fear held him fast to the spot, now he knew that there was nowhere to escape. His eyes were darting while never leaving the breadth of the snake, always aware of his positioning within the vivarium but seeking any means of flight. His mouth was open, showing his sharp teeth. His body heaved from the diaphragm with the effort of panting and his rapid heartbeat was visible as it beat through his fur.

Darklord was moving. He needed to get the rat down from the branch to enable him to constrict around its body once he had him impaled. Riff-Raff didn't let him get close and leaped from the branch, scurrying into the farthest corner of the vivarium. This final flight sealed his fate. He was open and exposed. Darklord had him cornered and moved to stake his claim.

He struck with precision a fourth and final time, taking the rat by the side of his neck. As suddenly as it began, the war dance was over. Riff-Raff kicked out with his back legs but only fought against air. The snake was too experienced and wily to expose part of his body where it could be kicked and clawed. He held Riff-Raff to the floor of the vivarium with the muscles in his jaw and the mass of his body moved over and around the rat, encircling him. Riff-Raff screamed as the fangs pierced his neck and he'd tried to twist from the grip of the snake, but it was a wasted effort. As the snake wrapped his thick body around the rat, Riff-Raff's small, black eyes bulged from their sockets and his tongue was forced from his mouth. The snake's mouth was open showing pure white convex fangs. Holding the rat by the neck, Darklord loosened his coils a hair's breadth allowing Riff-Raff the luxury of inhalation. The rat gasped greedily for air, taking in a huge lungful. Then, before he could exhale, Darklord went in for the death cuddle. He tensed his muscles and increased the pressure on the creature, tightening his coils and pulling them into a taut blanket around the dying rat's body. Riff-Raff knew it was hopeless. He gave up struggling and waited for death to relieve him of his suffering. His eyes bulged deeply out of their sockets as the pressure was increased.

All he could do was fix his eyes through the glass of the vivarium and plead with them for help from his owners. Beth let out her captive breath. She hadn't breathed once since Darklord had made his first strike. Now she was yelling incoherently through her sobs. 'You bitch, you fucking evil bitch. How could you do this to him?' She knew that it was already too late. The rat was crushed with bone-breaking force beneath the snake's coils, his internal organs squeezed and bursting. He wouldn't survive even if they could get him out. 'Do something, please. Please, Jennifer, do something.'

Riff-Raff's insides were crushed long before he went limp. Immense coils increased the pressure on his heart. It took ages for him to die and although Beth wanted to turn and run, she felt compelled to watch. She owed him her suffering for not having the guts to save him. Hatred for both Jennifer and her bastard snake burned inside her. The python increased his hold for another minute. A kill was to be savoured.

From the second he had made the first coil, his gastric acids had been releasing for breaking down the flesh, fur and bones of the rat.

A minute after Riff-Raff was dead, Darklord pulled his long, curled fangs from the rat's neck. They made a loud plopping sound as they came away from the prey's flesh. The snake uncurled and looked at his prize.

He seemed lazy now that the kill was over. He was taking his time, enjoying his moment. He glided over the still body of the rat. Much as a mortician measures his corpse, so Darklord measured his kill. He nudged it with his blunt nose down both sides and along its rump, straightening the rat out, making it streamlined. Once the carcass was in line, the snake gauged the size of his lunch. When he was satisfied with the position and sizing of his meal, he moved very slowly towards the rat's nose.

Lining himself up, he raised his head off the floor and opened his mouth.

With extended maw, he moved his lower mandible to either side, loosening his jaw so that it fell back as though on a hinge. He seemed to be yawning as his mouth opened wider. The Jacob's organ, a tube that allows a snake to breathe when his windpipe is covered by the carcass of his kill, glistened white along the bottom of his mouth. He was ready to begin the slow business of swallowing his prize. He took the rat's nose into his mouth. Gradually, by moving his mouth side to side, the rat's head sunk further in until its nose had passed into Darklord's neck. At that point, Darklord stopped and contracted every muscle in his body, as he squeezed down on the carcass of the kill. It moved further down the snake's gullet. He opened his mouth, stretched it a little further and moved the rat an inch further in. This cycle of inching his catch down his digestional tract was repeated, clenching muscles and taking the prey down with brute force. Alternating between mouthing up the rat's body and using his muscles to manoeuvre it down his gullet, the rat disappeared inside Darklord. By the time the snake had reached the large rat's shoulders, Darklord's skin around the bulge of the kill stretched until it was translucent.

Beth was convinced that the snake was going to split. She willed it, wanting to watch the snake die in front of her eyes as Riff-Raff had. Darklord's markings became elongated, much as the pattern on a Lycra dress stretches on an obese lady.

It took the snake twenty minutes to swallow the rat and he lay with the obscene bulge moving down the inside him. Beth could trace Riff-Raff's head, feet and body through the skin of the snake.

Darklord was sated, and would not feed again for ten days. Beth didn't feel as though she'd ever eat again.

The black spurs either side of Darklord's cloaca dug into the soft substrate. He stretched his dislocated jaw a couple more times. With an audible click he snapped it back into position. He slithered into his fibreglass cave. For the next couple of days, he would be watchful, dangerous, at his most vulnerable. He lay in the darkness of the cavern and slept.

Beth had never seen such cold cruelty, she hated the snake but he was only following his instincts. The focus of her anger was turned towards Jennifer. She tried to swallow the fury inside her; she wanted to find out what drove the girl. 'I don't understand what's inside you. What part of you is it that's so evil? Has it always been there? Is it some kickback reaction to the blows that life has dealt you? Do you want to be like this or is there some part of you that wants to change and be a good person?'

'Oh, Beth, don't be so infantile. You see everything in black and white terms. The rat's no big deal. We've still got Magenta and I have a surprise for you when we go downstairs. Hell, I'll buy you another rat if it meant that much to you. Come on, come and see what I've got for you.'

'When is this going to end, Jennifer? I want you to leave my house. I just want you to go and get out of my life.'

'Stop sulking, Beth, or I'm going to get angry and I'm in a good mood tonight. You know I can't leave here; we're inextricably tied together. There's too much between us for us to ever be apart. How could either one of us trust the other not to talk? We need to keep a close eye on each other, don't we, Beth? It's just the way it is. And anyway, all best friends fall out sometimes; it's natural and makes the friendship stronger. Now come on.'

Jennifer left the room but Beth made no move to follow her. She went into the bathroom and knelt in front of the toilet waiting for the moment when her stomach would empty. Afterwards she stood and washed her face with icy water. She cleaned her teeth, brushed her hair and felt no better. She understood what it meant to feel desolate.

She walked into the living room with a sense of dread. She didn't want to see Jennifer, didn't want to have to speak to her. She felt as trapped as Riff-Raff had been in the snake's vivarium. She had imagined murdering Jennifer many times; she'd done it once, why not again? She had enough morphine to kill a hundred people, but tonight she wanted to stab her. Her hatred was so strong that she wanted to take a knife and thrust it into Jennifer's body until she collapsed with fatigue.

She heard the unfamiliar noises as she entered the room. Jennifer was sitting on the armchair nearest the rat cage with a self-satisfied grin on her face. 'Well, about time. Come on. Come see what we've got. Thirteen of them. Look.'

Beth couldn't see much, magenta was inside her bedding box and the multiple high pitched squeals came from there. 'See, I told you it didn't matter about Riff-Raff. Magenta's had a litter of babies. Don't you see? We'll save a fortune in snake food. This is the start of our breeding empire. We can set up more cages and breeding boxes in the garage. We'll keep one male and all the females from each litter. We can introduce new bloodlines later. We'll grow the males out until they're fully grown and then use them to feed Darklord. He so enjoys live food.'

Beth's brain was taking a minute to catch up with the excited ramble. 'Stop. For God's sake, stop. I don't want to be overrun with rats. And after seeing the suffering that you inflicted on Riff-Raff today, how can you even contemplate putting other animals through that?'

'Ah, I expected the pious, holier-than-thou act. Who went to the pet shop and bought three frozen rats for Darklord last week? Let me think. Yes, that would be you. Of course, those rats didn't suffer, did they, Bethie? Taken from their mothers too young, farmed in battery boxes, fifty to a foot square box. Do you know they eat each other when they go mad with frustration? And then they are put into a tank and gassed. No, of course those animals don't suffer. They're just born frozen in cellophane.'

Beth was trapped like the rats. She looked ahead and saw no way that she could ever be free from this monster, or the terrible course of events her life had taken.

Since that first suicidal moment weeks earlier, Beth had been thinking ever more often about how it would be best to end her life. It would take five seconds to fill her vein with enough morphine to kill ten men. The end would be quick and painless. Jennifer made her life unbearable, but worse was the guilt that she lived with.

If only she wasn't a coward.

Chapter Thirteen

'Come on, admit it, he's fit, isn't he? I bet you fancy him.'

'Oh, you're not on about Colin again, are you? I warn you, you stay well clear of that garage.'

Jennifer was relentless. 'I can't see what he ever saw in that trollop Maggie. And that's another thing, how could she prefer that piss weak drip of a thing that she's with now after being married to Col?'

'Well, Colin and Maggie had a lot of problems. He's not the saint you think he is.'

'I don't blame him, who'd want to shag that? He winked at me last week. I bet I could get him if I wanted to.'

'Jennifer, he's thirty years old, what would he have in common with a young girl? And no offence, love, but you're not exactly the type he'd go for anyway.'

Life had settled over a few weeks. Beth was coping with what her life had become in the best way she knew how. She still had nightmares and during her waking hours she took the outlook that she was under siege and being held hostage by a deranged captor. For the most part she had fallen into the habit of trying to keep Jennifer's moods sweet and stable. The one-night-only stay had stretched and it was over six months since the night her life changed forever. She had been living this non-existence for half a year. Inside she was dead, just a body getting through one day and dreading the dawn of the next, but to anybody looking in, she was normal—just Beth Armstrong, nurse, friend—unofficial foster mother.

Maggie, despairing of the situation and not understanding why Beth had lumped herself with Jennifer, had become an infrequent visitor. Beth never went to see her. Their friendship was strained and distant. However, Maggie's ex-husband, Colin, was a regular topic of conversation and Beth realised that Jennifer was fixated on him. She hoped that it was just a girl crush and that it would soon pass. It was the only normal teenager thing that had happened since Jennifer came into her life. But her obsession with Colin was worrying – everything that concerned Jennifer was worrying – but at least fantasising about the opposite sex was exactly what a young girl should be doing and it seemed to have calmed her in recent weeks.

Beth had been stealing drugs from the hospital daily for over two months. She stole them, brought them home and then did her best to forget about them. She was adept at sleight-of-hand dexterity when it came to using only half doses.

She was paranoid that Jennifer was going to use them to kill her. She didn't fear death. She actively wanted to die and would have used them herself long before now if she'd had the guts. But if she was too scared to commit suicide, she was even more terrified that Jennifer would come into her room at night and stick needles of morphine into her. She took to sleeping with the light on. She would only eat food that she had prepared herself and never allowed Jennifer to make her a cup of coffee. The paranoia amused Jennifer and she'd play to it, it was one more game to taunt Beth with. Beth had stolen other things from the hospital, too – catheter kits, dressings, suturing packs, scalpels, nasal gastric tubes and a bottle of chloroform.

Each new request brought a new argument. It didn't matter how much Beth lamented that she couldn't walk into stores and take these things, that there were procedures and things had to be signed for. Jennifer would be adamant that they had to be produced. She pulled the best friend routine. 'Beth, just say if you don't want to be my best friend any more and I'll be on my way.' It was her way of saying, 'If you don't do what I say, I'll report you to the police for the murder of my brother.' Friendship with Jennifer was her sentence and it was life without any chance of parole.

Beth had no future. She had each day as it came and couldn't see anyway that her life was going to improve. Jennifer seemed happy enough but she often had days where she was sullen and attitudinal.

These were the days when Beth's thoughts most often turned to murder. She'd done it once. What was to stop her doing it again? She'd be in no more trouble having two deaths on her curriculum vitae. She would lie in bed at night thinking about the best way to rid herself of Jennifer forever. Marc hadn't been discovered. She could put Jennifer's body in the same place as her brother and forget about them both.

One night Jennifer overheard Beth talking to her boss on the phone. After she hung up, she made a second call to social services.

'What was all that about?' asked Jennifer, feigning disinterest.

'I have a patient due for release tomorrow but we're worried about her going home and how she'll manage. She's an elderly lady living alone.'

'So, what's the problem?'

'You know I can't discuss my patients with you.'

'Oh, like I'm going to go blabbing about some piss-stinky old bag. Come on tell me, I want to know.'

'Jesus, Phantom, it's nothing. Just work stuff. You wouldn't be interested.'

'If you don't tell me, Darklord might escape from his viv tonight and make his way into your bedroom when you're asleep.'

'Fuck off, Phantom. I'm not in the mood.'

'Don't swear. You know I don't like it. It's not lady-like. Tell me, I'm waiting.'

'For Christ sake, it's an old lady. Her son is in hospital after having a nervous breakdown and she came to us with pneumonia and malnutrition. She lives on a farm along the Coast Road, she's isolated and we're worried about her aftercare. She's having home carers four times a day and I was sorting out what equipment she would need. Orthopaedic bed, hoist and such like.'

'See, that wasn't so hard, was it? I only wanted a little bit of civilised conversation. So, this old lass'll be all on her own while her son's in the whack house?'

'Yes. She'd be better off in a home, but she's too stubborn to give in. she's lived on that farm all her married life, and since her husband died it's just been her and her son. The son's wife ran off and left him, and then the foot-and-mouth outbreak just about did them in financially. It hasn't been easy for them.'

'Tell me about the bed.'

'What?'

'The special bed she's getting, tell me about it.'

This was typical of Jennifer, she'd hone in on the

smallest detail and interrogate about it until she was satisfied. Beth wanted to shut Jennifer up so that she could get back to writing up case notes that she had to have fresh in her mind the following day. 'It's a bed, for God's sake. Just a bed. It goes up and down and has a pressure-sore prevention mattress. It tilts and has cot sides so that the patient can't fall out of it.'

'Or, if needed, to be restrained in?'

'Well, yes in extreme cases that can happen, but I don't think it'll be relevant for Mary.'

'I want that bed.'

'What?'

'The bed, I want it.'

Beth was cold. An icy tremor ran the length of her spine, but what Jennifer said was so ridiculous that she laughed.

'Yeah, right. Of course, you do Jennifer.'

'That's right. And you're going to get it for me.'

Chapter Fourteen

Jennifer's cheeks were red and her demeanour could only be described as joyful. Beth hated her. She was repulsed both by the girl and by what they were about to do.

'I've waited to put my plan into operation for so long.' Jennifer laughed, 'you know me, I'm not good at being patient, but we're close now. Once I've got this bed, I think I've got everything we need.'

Beth had to make one last attempt to get through to her. 'Please, Phantom, don't make me do this. She's a frail old lady; the shock might be enough to kill her.' Beth tried pleading with Jennifer but even to her ears, the fake Scottish accent that she'd been forced to adopt sounded ridiculous.

'I'm not making you do anything, Bethie.' Jennifer was staring at her with wide-eyed innocence. 'If you don't want to help me that's okay, sweetie. I just thought you were my friend, that's all.'

Beth chanted the required mantra. 'I am your friend, White Phantom. I am your best friend.'

She'd learned it was easier to go along with it. Chanting her mantra like an idiot was one thing – what the hell, she could do that, it was no biggie – but evicting an old lady from her death bed was another matter. Beth had offered to buy an orthopaedic bed for Jennifer, but she was having none of it. She wanted that bed and no other and Beth was in too damned deep to be able to refuse. They'd had the usual screaming match. It was like a play, conducted in three scenes. The first was Beth refusing to do it. The second was Jennifer pointing out that Beth was the most stupid murderer on the planet, and if she'd gone to the police immediately after Marc's death, she would have walked away without a sentence, but because she'd gone along with Jennifer's idea to hide the body, she had sealed her fate and would be looking at life. It ended with Jennifer asking if Beth didn't want to be her friend anymore, and Beth assuring her that she did.

Beth took an analytical look at what she was doing and couldn't comprehend how she'd sunk so low.

She hated going to the house at the top of Springfield Road. Jennifer made her go back many times, sometimes to clean and give the impression of occupancy and sometimes to indulge in one of her sick games. One day, she forced Beth to look at photographs of Marc. She didn't have many to show, but the ones she had depicted a young, handsome man. He smiled, with his white teeth on show. Jennifer had the pictures spaced out in a part-filled album. She turned the pages and each image brought back so many horrors for Beth. The last photograph in the album almost stopped Beth's heart. She hadn't expected it. It showed Marc, half unwrapped from the dirty tarpaulin. He was propped in a sitting position with a cardboard smiley-face on a stick in his hand. The lettering on the big, yellow smiley read "Get your tits out for the lads, Beth."

That game was a punishment for refusing to go into the vault where Marc's body lay. Beth didn't refuse again.

Going didn't get easier. It was more of an ordeal every time. She was terrified of the memories and petrified of what Jennifer might do to her on her home turf, but there was also the fear of being seen. Going to that house stopped the façade of normal that she lived in-between visits. The man she'd killed, and later tried to dispose of, lay in a vault upstairs. It was the connection linking her to the crime.

Jennifer pointed the remote key, and the garage doors slid open. 'See? I told you we had a van.'

Inside the garage was a soft-top Porsche, a sleek Jaguar and a large white Mercedes panel van.

'And you can drive this thing?' asked Beth. The van was enormous and Jennifer was having trouble sliding open the side door to put the things they'd need inside.

Just getting out of the garage nearly caused Beth to have a coronary. They hit the back wall of the garage when Jennifer popped it in reverse instead of first, causing a shelf full of tools and tins of nails to come crashing down all over the van. Jennifer tried to go forwards in a straight line but the van went into a lurch and hit the Porsche. She didn't stop and rammed the car out of the way to force the van out of the garage, The scream of metal grinding on metal reverberated around the interior of the garage. Beth expected people to charge down the drive to investigate. 'Oops. Marc's gonna be pissed. Sorry bro,' she muttered, rolling her eyes towards the roof of the van.

Three gouges ran the length of the Porsche's red bodywork. She had no idea whether it amounted to hundreds or thousands of pound's worth of damage. 'There's going to be red paint on the van, it'll show signs of being in an accident and raise suspicion. It's going to draw attention and get us pulled by the police.' She was panicking.

'Oh, stop being such an old woman. It's nothing to worry about; it just gives the van a bit of character. Right, let's see how we actually work this thing.' She swung the wheel hard to the left and screamed out of the driveway without looking for oncoming traffic. They took half a laburnum bush with them. She beamed at Beth, giving every impression of having a fun day out.

By the time they'd lurched and bunny hopped to the end of Rake Lane and turned right onto Priory Road, Jennifer gained something that might just be considered control of the vehicle. Beth was terrified.

'Turn the radio on,' demanded Jennifer. Beth leaned forward and pushed the button. *Mr Brightside* by The Killers burst into life.

'Louder.'

Three times Jennifer ordered that the music be turned up. She wound down her window and draped her elbow over the edge as she drove with one hand, her foot pressing down harder on the accelerator. The road ahead was clear but Beth knew it was twisty in parts.

'Slow down, Phantom.'

'What?'

'Stop. Let me drive.'

Jennifer grinned, flooring the accelerator. The speedometer went from forty to seventy. They passed the cemetery and the first sharp corner was looming towards them. Beth braced and pushed back into her seat, both feet pressing into the floor and ramming home imaginary brake pedals.

At the last moment, Jennifer braked hard. The back

end of the van flew out towards the centre line. Half way into the bend, she took her foot off the break and gave the van a hit of gas. The van righted and came out of the curve with power.

'See, told you I can drive. Just needed to get used to it again. Marc taught me.' Her face clouded—'But then you killed him.'

Beth wasn't immune to the accusation and every time Jennifer used it against her it stung, but she'd pulled the 'You killed my only brother' card out of the hat so many times that she had learned to ignore it. 'You're driving too fast. It's going to draw attention to us.'

'Rubbish. Everybody drives like this.' She gave the accelerator a workout as they came out of another tight curve.

Beth was relieved when they made it to the farm. The narrow track leading to the farmyard was difficult to negotiate due to neglect and overhanging trees. Jennifer told her not to moan because it served their purpose by adding greater seclusion. There were no immediate neighbours and the farm was covered on three sides by fields and bushes. Unless somebody paid a visit to the old lady while they were there, they weren't going to be seen.

They had timed the bed raid carefully. The teatime staff would have left and the carers due to settle her for the night would not arrive until nine o'clock. Beth checked her watch. It was seven forty-five. There were no other vehicles outside and none of the staff could come to this call on foot, but as a precaution she rang the bell. She could legitimately say that she'd called to see the old lady if anybody answered. They didn't. She motioned to Jennifer that it was okay to continue.

Beth put on her gloves and took the key from the hanging basket by the front door. She knew it was there because she'd made the arrangements for one to be left so that carers and nursing staff could let themselves in until an electronic keypad was installed. Jennifer had thought of everything else. Because the old lady might recognise her voice, for nearly twenty-four hours Beth had been speaking in a soft Scottish accent. It wasn't good, but Jennifer decreed that it was 'passable'. She'd changed both her usual deodorant and perfume. They both wore gloves and unremarkable clothing, jeans and plain black jumpers. Beth opened the front door and they stepped into the shadowy hall. The final precaution was to put on Ski masks before going into the makeshift bedroom that Beth had set up downstairs. She said that Mary would be terrified and might die and Jennifer's only answer was that Beth had better apply her best bedside manner and keep the old cow calm.

Beth tapped on the door with a light showing from underneath. Jennifer laughed. She found it funny that they were going to rob the old Lady but still knocked politely on the door. She pushed Beth from behind and told her to get on with it. 'We're not here for a cup o' tea and cucumber sandwiches, you know.'

They walked up to the bed, tiptoeing past china dogs and chintzy armchairs. The room was cluttered but the bed was on castors and would wheel out to the van. The only time they'd have to lift it was to get it in.

Mary was asleep, propped high on pillows to aid her breathing. Her chin had lowered to her chest. Her mouth was open. Her teeth grinned from a jar on the table beside her. Jennifer screwed up her nose in disgust. The frill at the top of Mary's flowered nightie raised and fell with the breath from each snore. Beth's eyes filled with tears. She didn't want to do this but had no choice. This was the evil that she'd become.

'With a bit of luck, we can lift her onto that sofa and the senile old bat won't even wake up,' said Jennifer.

'I wish we could, it would be better for her,' mused Beth. 'But it'd be too dangerous if she woke while we are lifting her. It'll be quicker and less stressful for her if we don't use the hoist. But if she wakes in the middle of the lift and struggled she might be hurt.'

'Whatever,' said Jennifer, bored. 'Let's just get it done and get out of here.'

Beth tapped Mary on the shoulder and had to remind herself not to use the lady's name. She spoke softly using her adopted accent. 'Lady, come on. Wake up, lady.'

As she stirred, Beth covered Mary's eyes with a gloved hand. 'Wake up, but don't open your eyes yet... sweetheart.' She'd paused, she had been going to say doll. She called all her patients doll to calm them. 'Come on, love, wake up. Nice and easy now.' Mary was awake. 'Right, I'm going to move my hand, but don't be frightened. We're not going to hurt you. It looks scary do—darling, but don't you worry, we'll be out of here in two minutes and we're going to make you nice and comfortable before we leave. Everything's all right.' Jennifer nudged her in the back to get on with it.

'Right, we're just going to lift you out of bed and move you onto the sofa over there.'

Mary was awake, her eyes wide and terrified. 'What's going on? Who are you? What are you doing in my house? Oh, don't hurt me. Please don't hurt me.' Beth rolled the blankets down to the bottom of the bed. A smell of stale urine rose from the soiled bed sheets and Beth noted with disgust that the previous carers had changed the old lady's incontinence pad but left her in a damp under sheet. She couldn't help herself from picking up the record book beside the bed to find out the names of the two carers. She'd remember them for future reference and see what could be done about them. Beth hated sloppy care and wouldn't tolerate it in the controlled setting of the hospital. She knew it was harder to monitor in home-care circumstances where the staff were sent out on trust.

Jennifer was making up a makeshift bed on the sofa. Beth instructed her to put extra pillows down and showed her how to position the draw sheet until it was placed just right to lie under Mary's bottom. 'Right, I'll take her shoulders. You get that scarf over there.' She motioned to a long tartan scarf hanging over the back of the armchair.

Jennifer had said that she wasn't going to speak while they were with Mary. She'd said that the less sensory perception Mary could recall the better, but she couldn't help herself. 'Why, are we going to strangle her?'

Mary tried to raise herself in alarm. 'My son John's coming. He'll be here any second. He's just gone to lock down the animals.' Beth knew that the animals were long gone and that John was resting in a drug-induced slumber. 'It's okay, sweetheart. She was only joking. Take no notice of her. I promise you, we are not going to hurt you. You have my word.'

Beth could have hit Jennifer. 'Shut up and get the

scarf. Put it under Mary's legs. Elderly people bruise easily and by using the scarf to lift her you'll have a better grip and minimise the risk of hurting her.'

For once Jennifer did as she was told, allowing Beth to take a leading role in the proceedings. She eyed Mary's twisted, sparrow legs with distaste and was obviously glad to have the scarf to lift her with rather than having to touch her skin. Beth told her how to put the scarf under Mary's legs above the knee and lift from both ends of it. The lift went well and Beth repositioned pillows and tucked Mary in, making sure she was comfortable while Jennifer ripped off the soiled bedding and fiddled with the brakes on the bed to unlock them.

'We'd better take some stuff to make it look like an ordinary burglary,' she said. 'The old bird's got some decent bits here. We'd better take her watch and rings and stuff.'

Mary was sobbing. The tears hadn't been far away but at the thought of her wedding ring being taken she was distraught. 'Oh please, don't take my wedding ring. You can have anything else, but please leave me that.'

Beth almost came out of Scottish character when she yelled at Jennifer. 'We take nothing but what we came for. You wanted this bloody bed and we're getting it. But you do not take anything else. I swear to God, Ph—' She stopped herself from calling Jennifer by her chosen name, 'I swear to God, I'll—'

'What will you do? Go on. What will you do?' Jennifer's voice was menacing. 'What can you do?'

'I can walk out of here right now and leave you to your sick games.' She wasn't about to argue with Jennifer, 'Come on, get the other end of the bed. We take nothing else.'

She assured Mary that her night care would be coming soon. Jennifer glared at her. They weren't supposed to know details like that and she'd already called Mary by name. Beth put two chairs against the sofa to stop Mary from falling out and said goodbye on the way out. They left, taking the bed with them.

It was an easy job getting it up to and loaded into the van. Beth was sickened by what they'd done and wanted to get home. She felt the need of a long cleansing bath and a stiff glass of wine to take away the filthy taste of corruption from her mouth.

'She's got one of those yucky commode things, hasn't she? That chair thing by the bed was one, wasn't it?'

'Yes, why?'

'While I'm breaking the window in the door to make it look like a break-in, you go back and get it. I need it.'

Argument was useless and fell on deaf ears. They were wasting valuable time and it was easier to just get the toilet chair for Beth than stand locked in a battle of wills.

Beth didn't want to go back into Mary's bedroom. She didn't want to see her accusing eyes. Mary flinched at the sound of the breaking glass. Beth was half way across the room with the chair.

'It's all right, hen, it was just a little window at the side of the front door. You try and have a wee sleep now, and when you wake up your carers will be here.'

As Beth passed the sofa, Mary put out her hand and grabbed her shirt. 'Wait.'

'Yes, love, what is it? Are you comfortable? Can I get you anything before I go?' This was surreal, it was ridiculous. She had broken into the old lady's home and was standing over her in ski mask and gloves asking her if she wanted a cup of fucking tea.

'Thank you for not taking my wedding ring. Thank you, Beth.'

Beth's eyes flew open. She was terrified. Mary patted her hand, 'You can hide your voice, but you can't hide who you are, Beth. You're a good girl, I know that and as soon as I knew that it was you, I wasn't frightened. You must be in a lot of trouble. I hope you come out of it soon.' With that, Mary closed her eyes and Beth grabbed back her hand and fled the room with the commode, sickness and self-disgust welling inside her.

Beth wasn't a good girl; she was a murderer and a thief, and now an abuser of elderly ladies. And there was nobody in the world that she could turn to for help.

Chapter Fifteen

They left the van at Marc's house with the bed and commode still inside. The next morning, Jennifer said that they would have to move it. She wanted it 'set up and ready' but she still refused to say what she wanted it for. Beth's mind took her back to a conversation with Jennifer about the bed. She asked if the bed was suitable for restraining somebody. Beth assumed that the 'somebody' in question was going to be her. Something was coming to a head. A plan was ready to be put into action—but what was it? Beth determined to have her wits about her and to remain vigilant. But what about when she slept?

'Everything's coming together beautifully, Beth. We're ready. I'm excited and you're terrified, which is to be expected because you're so dull.'

'What are you going to do to me? What's all this about?'

'Do to you? Beth, I've told you not to ask questions. It's a surprise. Just wait and see what happens. Now, then, there's one last thing that I need.'

'You said the bed was the last thing.'

'I lied. I don't suppose for one second that you've got Colin's mobile number, have you?'

'No, of course not, why would I?'

'As expected, Beth, as expected. Never mind. You'll just have to pay a visit to Maggie and get it for me. But, and this is most important if you want to stay out of prison, you can't ask her for it. You've got to steal it.'

'Why can't you just ring the garage to speak to him, why does everything have to be such a fucking drama?'

'Because, my dim friend, we can't have anything linking back to us afterwards. Contact has to be made through his mobile.'

'What's all this mess got to do with Colin? Oh, my God, you're not going to dope him and force him to go out with you, are you? It'll never work. You're just going to make an almighty fool of yourself, Phantom.'

Jennifer didn't like criticism. Her temper snapped and Beth knew when to back off.

The girl ranted. 'Don't be so stupid. Credit me with a little bit more maturity than that. I've told you to stop asking questions. You're going to spoil the surprise and I've spent a long time setting this up for us. Just shut up and make the tea, will you?'

The phrase 'fuck off and make your own tea, you psychotic munchkin' sprang to mind but Beth sighed and opted for the quiet life.

Beth knew that Maggie was hurt and confused by the cooling of their friendship. Maggie hadn't let go easily and for weeks after Jennifer came on the scene she would ring up to suggest going to see a band or sometimes just going out for coffee. Beth always made an excuse not to. Long after she'd stopped calling at the house, Maggie continued phone contact and always ended the brief conversation by asking Beth to go to see her. Beth would be evasive on the phone, always in the middle of doing something. She never took up the invitations to visit.

She paused on the doorstep. She'd always just tapped and walked in. After six months of absence she couldn't do that now. She rang the bell and waited. Maggie came to the door, drying her hands on a tea towel. Her face played a conflagration of emotions one after the other. Her immediate reaction was to break into a huge grin. The smile left as suddenly as it had come. 'Oh, you're here then,' were her first words. 'Do you want to come in or are you selling Avon or something?'

Beth tried for a smile but failed as Maggie stepped back and motioned her through to the living room as though she'd never been in before. Maggie prepared coffee and they made small talk through the door. 'How are the kids? Did Graham get his promotion? The garden looks good, is that lobelia in the corner?'

When the coffee was on the table, Maggie sat down and reached for her packet of cigarettes. She took one and threw one across to Beth. It was so like old times that it wasn't like them at all.

'Has the goth freak gone?'

'No, Phan—Jennifer's still with me. It shouldn't be for much longer. She's getting her life sorted out and will be moving into her own place soon.' It was a pack of lies and they both knew it.

'What's the hold that she's got on you, Beth? Look at you, you're skin and bone, your clothes are falling off you. Where's your smile and the sunshine that you always brought out? What's she done to you? I just want to understand why you've taken this freeloader on, but I don't get it.'

'Oh, Maggie, please don't let's talk about it again. I don't want to fight.'

'Okay, okay. End of conversation. But I just want you to know that any time you want to talk—any time you need me, I'm here, okay? We go back too far for me not to be, even though you've dropped me like yesterday's shit and really pissed me off.'

Beth looked out of the window at the garden. Her eyes were too full of tears and her throat too thick to speak. She just nodded miserably.

Knowing that she wasn't going to get anywhere, Maggie brought the conversation back onto safe ground, 'So, have you been watching Corrie lately? That new bloke's bloody fit, isn't he?'

They chatted and drank coffee with a wall of barriers between them.

'What's happened to us, Beth? What can I do to put it right?'

Beth was saved from answering by the grizzly crying coming from upstairs. 'Oh, that's Barry awake. He's not well. Running a temperature. He was sent home from nursery this morning. I'll go and get him. Won't be a sec.'

Beth waited for the door to click shut behind her and the sound of feet pounding up the stairs. She leapt from her seat and grabbed Maggie's handbag. She'd never rifled through another woman's bag before. It felt like messing in her mother's knicker drawer. Groping through tampons, a purse, receipts and a baby's dummy, she saw Maggie's phone at the bottom of the bag.

She pulled it out and opened her own phone, working her way through the system to add a new contact. She was all fingers and thumbs and dropped it. Twice she clicked the wrong button and had to begin again. It took three attempts to get the numbers in the right order. By the time she clicked the phones shut, she could hear

Maggie coming downstairs, talking to her toddler.

She opened the handbag and thrust her hand to the bottom to put the phone back exactly where she'd found it. The door opened.

Maggie was in the doorway with Barry resting on her right hip. The little boy's face was flushed and his enormous brown eyes were heavy with fat tears. Normally he'd have wriggled to get down and run to Beth shouting, 'Beffie, Beffie,' but he clung to his mother and stared with the open curiosity of a child weighing up a stranger. Maggie took in the situation.

'Oh Maggie, I was looking to see if you had a nail file. I hope you don't mind, got a ragger here.' she held up her hand as though to validate her excuse. When the door opened, she'd jumped back from the handbag but not before Maggie had seen her with her hand inside.

'What's going on, Beth?'

'Nothing. Nothing at all, mate. Look you've got your hands full with little fella. Ha, literally. I'll let you get on and see you again soon, eh? Ring me, yeah? We'll sort something out.'

She couldn't get out of the house fast enough and Maggie did nothing to stop her going. Beth was sobbing before she'd turned the corner of the street, knowing that Maggie watched from her front door with the baby on her hip.

Chapter Sixteen

After everything that Jennifer had put Beth through, when Beth flipped, it was over nothing.

She returned from Maggie's in a state. Her lifelong best friend had caught Beth with her hand in her bag. Their friendship, which had withstood childbirth, divorce and every one of Maggie's melodramas over the years, lay in tatters. Beth missed her more than she could put into words. If only she'd gone to the police that first morning. Maggie would have supported her through everything. She'd have stood by Beth through whatever legal issues arose and she'd have screamed self-defence from every roof top in town on Beth's behalf.

At what point would she have washed her hands of me? Beth wondered. She'd probably have accepted her taking Jennifer in, the smashed kitchen window and even the removal of Marc's body. Beth knew exactly where Maggie's friendship would have ended: the day she took her first vial of morphine from the hospital. Beth realised that that was her point of no return. Everything up to that moment could have been justifiable. With a good solicitor, she may even have escaped a long jail sentence. Everything Beth had done up to that point, Maggie would have forgiven and explained as misguided survival instinct. But theft of controlled drugs from a county hospital was beyond even Beth's level of forgiveness, never mind Maggie's. Beth could only imagine what her oldest friend would make of breaking into a defenceless old lady's home and robbing her of her bed and toilet. Beth was deeply ashamed. She was worried how the previous evening might have affected Mary's health and on top of all that worry she was heartsick and heartbroken.

Walking to Maggie's house and back, she'd been hit by a paranoia so intense that she felt as though she might have to find somewhere to vomit.

Mary must have spoken to the police. Why hadn't they come for her? To be taken from her home would have been a sweet release. The worst women's prison in England couldn't have been any worse than the sentence she was living, but to be taken from the street would be terrifying. Every second of the walk home she expected to hear the sirens of police cars screeching up beside her. She imagined eight strong men running from cars and rugby tackling her to the ground. By the time she put her key in the door, she was a mess.

'God, you've been ages. Did you get Colin's number?' It was as though Jennifer was asking her if she'd remembered to pick up a pint of milk.

'Yes, I got it. That's right, Phantom, selfish to the end.'

'What's that?'

'I said I got it.'

'Knew you would.'

'Did I ever have a choice?'

'Oh, don't start. If you're making a cuppa, I'll have one, please, but hurry up because the news is coming on soon and I want to see if there's anything on about the bed.'

Beth didn't scream. She didn't yell. Her voice was solid and neutral as she said, 'If you want a brew, why don't you get up off your lazy fucking arse and make one?' She took off her coat and was in the living room, glaring at Jennifer as she sat with that damn snake wrapped around her. 'Move. You're in my chair.'

'Ooh, get you. I take it you and Maggie had a lover's tiff, then?' Jennifer didn't come back at Beth with threats and mantras as she normally would. She uncoiled from the armchair and slouched towards the kitchen with Darklord draped across her shoulders. Beth didn't flinch at the sight of the snake as she flopped into the soft chair.

'Crikey, Beth, you're shaking like a leaf. What's happened?'

'What's happened?' Beth parroted. 'Oh nothing, I've just killed and stolen. And if that's not bad enough, I can add to my repertoire beating up old ladies and getting caught with my hand in my best friend's bag. That's all.'

Jennifer snorted. 'Well, aren't we full of the joys of spring tonight? And anyway, you didn't beat her up. You were very nice to her. You got the number, though, and Maggie doesn't know what you were taking?'

'Fuck off, Phantom.' Beth had never been one for swearing much except for the odd 'shit' if she dropped something. When, she wondered, had this foul language come about? She couldn't say it was a rub off from Jennifer because she didn't swear much either, which surprised Beth. She'd always assumed that all teenagers swore as a matter of habit. 'I'm sorry, I didn't mean to swear at you. Look, just give me a few minutes and I'll be okay.' And then she thought of Mary's eyes filling up when Jennifer had said to take her wedding ring. She saw the look on Maggie's face when she'd walked into the room, and the way her godson looked at her, as though she was a stranger. Beth felt the anger surging up from her gallbladder where it had mixed thoroughly with bile and stomach acid. 'No, no, Phantom. That's not true. Actually, I do mean it. I mean every fucking word of it. I wish you'd just fuck off and die.'

Jennifer looked at her warily and left the room without saying a word. Beth heard the screech of the vivarium door as it opened. Jennifer bounded back down the stairs taking them two at a time and went into the kitchen for a few minutes, reappearing as the news was beginning with two cups of coffee and a plate of toast on a tray with two side plates. 'You feeling any better? Thought this might help.' Beth didn't want the toast, and she couldn't have cared less if the coffee was poisoned. In fact, after yelling at the girl, there would no doubt be some punishment and it was likely that it was poisoned coffee with a teaspoon of rat droppings instead of sugar. Beth was beyond caring – she needed the caffeine.

They sat through the forty-five-minute programme without saying much. Jennifer commented on a couple of the items reported but Beth did little more than grunt in reply.

'And finally,' the anchorman said. 'We're crossing over to our local correspondent in Barrow-in-Furness.'

'Well, James, as you can see, it's glorious weather for the ducks here in Barrow.' The good-looking man with too many teeth and his coat collar turned up gave a chuckle and then composed his face into an expression of grave concern. 'I am just about to enter the farmhouse of Mrs Mary Baker. As you can see from the state of the front door beside me, she was broken into and burgled last night. Mrs Baker is eighty-nine years old and has recently come out of hospital to spend the last of her days at her beloved farm. Last night, she was the victim of a cruel and vicious crime. I'll pass you over to Mary to tell you in her own words what happened in this, one of the strangest news reports of the year.'

Beth was sitting on the edge of her seat, her coffee cup cradled with both hands. Her knuckles had whitened around the mug. Her face was pale, her eyes huge in her face. She couldn't stop shaking despite turning the gas fire up full.

'We're famous, eh, kid?' said Phantom, enjoying every second of the interview. 'Hey, there she is, there's old Mary. I bet she's never had so much attention in all her long life. She'll be loving the sympathy.'

'Shut up,' snarled Beth. 'Don't say another word.'

Jennifer opened her mouth to reply, but stopped when the camera cut to a facial shot of Mary, bundled up in blankets and a shawl. 'Well, son, it was all proper peculiar, it was,' Mary said. 'I opened me eyes and there they was, three of 'em all stood over me, shoutin' and tellin' me off. They had black masks covering their faces and they all wore gloves.'

Beth couldn't understand what was going on. Mary didn't normally speak like this. She sounded confused, where did she get three from? She wasn't given to exaggeration and was particular about her grammar and diction. She was normally as sharp as a button. Beth was worried that the burglary had upset her more than she'd feared.

'And did you get a good look at the burglars, Mary?'

'Well, son, there wasn't much to see, see. Been as my eyes are bad, I couldn't see much. They all had masks. All's I can tell you is there was three men. Big brutes they was, too. One of them picked me right up and carried me clean across the room in his arms. Oh, wait, there is something. I did happen to notice that he had one of them horrible tattoo things on his arm. It was a heart with the name Mary written across it. I remember it because it was the same as my name, see.'

'And what happened next, Mary?'

'Well, they huffed me onto the sofa and stole me bed right from under me, the brutes. Said something about selling it on Tebay. There's not much at Tebay, though. Me and my Jimmy – that's my late husband, you know – we stopped at Tebay for a cup a tea once. But it was wishy-washy stuff. You could tell they didn't make it in a proper teapot. I don't think there's even a market at Tebay.' Beth knew Mary well enough to know that this waffling was an act. She was directing the conversation away from awkward questions.

The interview closed. 'Back to you, James,' said the reporter. 'And maybe we should be charging "Tebay.com" for the mention.'

Beth felt humbled. Why would Mary protect her? She didn't deserve it. She felt the tears spill over her cheeks and felt as though she could cry in shame, forever.

Phantom was hugging herself and laughing. 'Classic, absolute classic. Well, would you credit it? The crazy old bitch has just saved our bacon without even knowing it.'

Beth didn't tell Jennifer that Mary recognised her the night before. Jennifer's words forced through Beth's shame and she felt her rage building.

Jennifer was still talking. 'The stupid, crazy old cow. What she can't remember she's just made up. How could she mistake us for men? I could kiss the senile old trout if she didn't smell of pee.'

Beth wasn't aware of moving, one second she was sitting on the rim of the chair, the next she flew towards Jennifer. The girl moved her head in shock, presenting her face towards Beth as she looked up at the sudden flurry of movement.

The slap was hard. The sound cracked loudly enough to drown out the voices on the television and cause the cage full of rats to stop their business and stare.

Beth moved so fast that Jennifer had no time to protect herself from the blow. She gasped and flung both hands up to her left cheek. Her eyes filled with tears and the imprint of Beth's hand was already visible in a deepening stain across her cheek. 'You bitch,' she whispered. 'That's the first and last time you'll ever hit me. I'll make you pay for this.'

Striking Jennifer felt good. Beth's hand stung so badly that she had to pin it under the opposite armpit to cushion the throbbing—but it felt good. 'I don't doubt for one second that you will, Jennifer? Yes, I called you Jennifer. What are you going to do about that? Plenty of ornaments about. Help yourself. Are you going to go to the police? Well, you know what? I'm finished. You fill your boots, darling, because I'm done fighting and I couldn't care less. Tell you what, I'll save you a place beside me and if it isn't in jail—then it'll be in hell.'

Jennifer flew out of the room in a rage, Beth heard her thumping up the stairs, she heard a door opening and then Jennifer came flying back into the living room. She was breathing hard. 'See this?' She waved a piece of paper in front of Beth's face and then stuffed it in her pocket before Beth could see what was written on it. 'You'll be sorry. You don't want to fight any more? Okay. Well, let's see how true that is because you know what, Beth? I don't believe you.'

Jennifer strode over to the phone and dialled a number. Beth didn't attempt to stop her. She sank into the chair. The fight ebbed out of her. She told the truth – she really didn't care what happened to her.

Jennifer had pale skin but four ugly welts stood out proud and red on her cheek. Beth noticed that she'd caught the side of her mouth when she'd struck her. A small cut was bleeding at the corner of her lip.

Beth was lightheaded. So, this is it then, she thought as she listened to Jennifer say, 'Hello... Hello. Yes. I'd like to report an offence please.'

Chapter Seventeen

'That's right. Yes, I'll hold.' While on hold, Jennifer smirked at Beth. 'Didn't think I'd do it, did you?'

'I couldn't give a damn what you do.'

'Oh, yes, sorry. I was talking to my friend. Yes, that's right. I've been attacked and I'd like to report it.' Jennifer launched into a lengthy description. 'It happened about an hour ago. See, I was crossing at the zebra and a woman nearly ran me over.'

Beth looked up from her chair, what the hell was she talking about? Jennifer continued talking and Beth came out of her slump to listen as lies poured from the girl's mouth.

'Yes, I did look for traffic and when I crossed the road there were no cars. And then suddenly this red car came around the corner. She didn't stop and the zebra is just around that bend and she didn't look at all. Just drove straight into me. Yes, my lip's cut and I have a big hand print on my face. No, no, the car didn't hit me much—she did. The woman slammed her breaks on and got out of the car and started shouting at me for being in the road. I said that I was on the crossing and that it was my right of way,' at this point Jennifer sniffed a couple of times and pretended to cry, 'and then officer… and then... she hit me,' she sobbed. 'I've seen the woman before. She takes her kids to the same school as my little brother. I think they live on Sands Road. No, I don't know their name. But think I can remember the car's registration number if that's any help.'

Jenner took the piece of paper out of her pocket and read out Maggie's registration number to the police. What the hell was she doing? This was just the kind of attention that they didn't need.

'My name? Oh, yes, it's Lorraine Vidal. Yes, Vidal. Like the shampoo. Address? Well I'm staying with a friend. I'm at Twenty-six Maple Avenue. That's Right. No, I'm sorry I don't think I will be in. There's no need to come. We've got to go out, you see. No really, you don't need to come here. I just wanted to report it in case she does this to anybody else.' Jennifer's voice had changed. During the conversation. She went from being full of confidence to backtracking at a million miles an hour. 'Well, um, can't you just go and talk to her? Give her a warning or something? Serious offence? Well, it was just a little slap really; it shocked me more than anything. Oh really, there's no need. Okay, yes, yes if you have to. In the next five minutes, then. Thank you.' She hung up the phone and turned around slowly. She was chewing her lower lip and looked pensive.

'You stupid, stupid little bitch. You've shot yourself in the foot now, haven't you?'

'Well you shouldn't have hit me.'

'You do realise, don't you, that by bringing the police to my door you've opened up the very can of worms that I've suffered hell for over these last six months to keep closed. That's it now, Jennifer. Your power's gone, the hold you've had over me all this time is broken. In fact, you've already told the police that you've been hit and marked so what's one more slap, eh?' She raised her hand. She had no intention of hitting Jennifer, only of showing her what it was like to feel bullied and scared.

Jennifer flinched out of the way and raised her arm to protect her head. 'Not so big and hard now, are you, little girl?' Beth finished her tirade. She'd risen from her chair and was busying herself with putting her purse and cigarettes into her handbag.

'I'm sorry. I didn't mean to ring them. You just got me mad, that's all.'

'You didn't mean to ring them? Don't be so bloody stupid. You don't mean to stub your toe. You don't mean to drop a cup. But picking up a telephone and ringing the police is a conscious decision. You've done it now, you damn fool. And what do you suppose Maggie's going to say when they turn up on her doorstep accusing her of all sorts. "Oh yes, officer. I was driving my car over that zebra crossing this afternoon and I did almost run somebody over and then got out of my car and belted her. Please arrest me now." No, she isn't. The first thing she's going to ask is who has made the ridiculous allegation? And then she's going to drop us both right in it. Before you know it, the police will smell a rat and start poking into other stuff and then we're finished. Maggie probably thinks my 'affair' with your brother fizzled out over a matter of weeks, but what if the police ask questions and his name is mentioned in relation to yours? How soon before Maggie puts two and two together and makes a connection between me, you and him. You've done it now. Bravo, little girl. Bravo.'

'It'll be okay. It's all right, we can sort this out. I gave them a false name. I'll tell them that I was drunk, that I read the number plate wrong. We can tell them that it wasn't Maggie. I won't press charges. That way, they can't do anything. We can tell them it was just a big mistake.'

'We? Hang on a second, did you say "we"? No, no, no. You're on your own. I'm not even going to be here, because while you're spinning your web of lies to the police, I'm going round to Maggie's to warn her that she's about to be visited by the bloody cops and to try and sort out some kind of damage limitation.'

'I'll tell them everything.' Phantom changed tack and was shouting; her voice hardened and her usual bullying tone returned. 'Don't you dare leave me, Beth. If you don't stay and help me, I'll tell them about Marc. And everything else. Don't you want to be my friend any–?'

'Go for it,' shouted Beth over her shoulder as she stormed out of the house and slammed the door behind her.

On the way to Maggie's house, Beth wracked her brains to try and come up with some story that sounded anywhere near plausible. She had no idea what she was going to say when she saw Maggie but she had to come up with something to get them all – Maggie included – off the hook with the minimum amount of fuss.

Beth hammered on the door. There was no immediate answer so she knocked again.

The living room door opened and she watched Maggie through the frosted glass. 'Okay, okay, I'm coming,' Beth heard her grumble. 'Beth? This is getting to be a regular thing. I'm hoping you've come with some kind of explanation, but you'll excuse me if I don't leave my bag unattended.' Although her voice was thick with sarcasm, Beth knew that she was hurt and confused and was striking out. Beth pushed the door open and rushed into the living room, grabbing Maggie by the sleeve and dragging her in with her.

'The police are on their way.' Beth was out of breath and couldn't get her words out. 'We haven't got long. They might be here any second and I've got to talk to you.'

'Oh, Jesus, Beth what have you done? This has got something to do with that kid, hasn't it? What's going on?'

'Huh, it's not what I've done that's the problem. It's what you've done.' Beth stopped and ran a hand through her hair.

'Me? I don't under–'

'Ugh, I'm not telling this well. No, you haven't done anything. But the thing is, well, the police think that you have.'

'What? What are you on about?'

'I'm trying to tell you, aren't I? Just shut the fuck up and listen.' Beth's voice had risen in frustration.

Maggie sat down. 'I swear Beth, you've changed. You've changed so much and it's not a change for the better. I can count the times you've said 'fuck' on one hand and most of them were when we were kids.'

'Are you going to let me speak, or are we going to have a half hour episode of The Maggie Show because I really don't have time for this. Listen, Phantom has grassed you up to the police for something you didn't do. She's told them some cock and bull story about you nearly running her over this afternoon and then getting out of your car and hitting her.'

'What?' Maggie was dumbfounded and it took her a second to stock up on verbal missiles to fire at Beth. 'Well the fucked-up little Goth freak bastard. I can fucking-well prove that I didn't lay a hand on her. My car's been in Col's garage all day for its M.O.T. I swear down I never touched her. I can prove it.'

Beth couldn't believe her good fortune. Maggie could prove that she hadn't been out in her car at the time of the supposed assault. That should make it easier to get the police off their backs. Now all she had to do was get Maggie to make light of the false accusation to the police and to help her get rid of them. That might not be so easy.

Maggie was still ranting. 'What a pack of lies. I tell you, Beth, when I get hold of her, I will fucking kill her. I'll make her wish she'd never been born. I haven't even seen the little bitch. How could I have hit her?'

'I know you didn't hit her. I did it.'

'You hit her? Beth, what the fuck's going on? You've never hit anybody in your life. Not even me—and Christ knows, if anyone can push your buttons, it's me. I think you'd better start talking to me, Beth, and fast because I've got a thing or two to say to the police if they arrive.'

'That's just it, Maggie. I need you to help me. I need you to prove that you didn't do anything and then leave it at that. I need you to get rid of them before they start asking too many questions.'

'Questions about what? C'mon, Beth, if I'm going to lie to the police and defend you, then I want to know what I'm defending you against. Let me get this straight. Are you asking me to protect that stupid little cow after she's told the police a pack of lies about me? Because that's what it's sounding like. Why did she say that I hit her? And anyway, Beth, why the hell should I help you after the way you've treated me? We used to be best friends and now I don't even know you.'

'I know, I know, everything you've said is true. I can't explain it all now, Maggie, but please, please, I'm begging you, just help me out this once. All you need to know is that Phantom and I had an argument. I lost my temper and hit her. She wanted to get back at me and she felt that the best way to hurt me was by hurting you. She rang the police in temper without thinking. Please, Maggie, just tell the police that it wasn't you and then don't make waves. Just back me up, okay?'

'Why, though? Why ring the police and say that I'd hit her when I very obviously haven't? She's not right in the head.' They heard a car pulling up outside and looked out of the window.

'Oh shit, it's them, it's the police. Please, Maggie, just help me get rid of them.'

Beth sat on the edge of the settee while Maggie answered the door. She heard her talking in the hall and then the door opened and Maggie showed two police officers into the living room. Beth stood up.

'Hello,' she began as Maggie rooted through her bag for the M.O.T certificate that would prove that her car had spent the afternoon in the garage. Beth continued talking, 'Look, this is all a huge misunderstanding. You should never have been called out. It was just a silly teenager having a tantrum because she couldn't get her own way. What happened was –'

'And you are?' asked the officer, with a pen poised over her notebook. Beth didn't want to give her name. She especially didn't want the police to write it down anywhere where they might pull it up later.

'The thing is it was my niece who rang you. She's at

that age, you know. Everything's a drama.'

'Can I have your name, please, madam?' asked the policewoman a second time. 'You can tell your version of the story, but first I must have your name for my records.'

'Beth,' said Beth reluctantly.

'Beth?'

'Beth Armstrong.'

'Address please?' Beth gave her address. She felt that each word spoken was taking her closer to life imprisonment.

'And your niece is the complainant, you say?'

'Yes, that's right. Well, no not exactly, she's not my real nice. She's my, um, cousin's daughter and she's staying with me for a few days while her parents are away on a skiing holiday.' The heat in the room was suffocating. She was immobile, determined not to give her nervousness away by fidgeting. She wanted to get away from the subject of Jennifer's parents, what if she was asked their names? She employed a trick of distraction that she'd learned from Jennifer herself. 'Jennifer rang you. What happened was Jennifer and I were having an argument.' She hoped that offering up Jennifer's real name would pay off. The police officer pounced on the new name thrown into the mix.

'Jennifer? We have the complainant listed here as a, Miss Lorraine Vidal.'

'Yes, I know, you see she was playing games there, too. She gave you a false name. Her real name is Jennifer Brown.' Beth stuck with Jennifer's real Christian name but plucked the first ordinary surname out of the air that she could think of and hoped that she could distract the police from names. She was gratified to note that the policewoman didn't write this new information down. 'Jennifer is the typical angsty teenager. Always wanting to be the centre of attention, always wanting her own way. Maggie and I are going out tonight.' Beth looked towards her friend. 'Aren't we, Maggie?'

'Yeah, that's right. Long overdue night out.'

Beth picked up the story again, 'Well, Jennifer decided that she wanted to come, too. I told her she couldn't because she's too young and she threw a tantrum. She doesn't like Maggie.'

'That's the understatement of the year.'

'Anyway, she said that if we didn't let her come with us tonight, she'd ring the police and say that I'd hit her. I laughed and told her to go for it because she'd never be believed and I suppose that's when she made up the stupid story about the car and Maggie.'

The policewoman turned towards Maggie. 'And you corroborate this?'

'Well, I certainly didn't hit the little freak. I corroborate that much. I haven't seen her, but I tell you, she wants her arse kicking for a stunt like this.' Beth was willing Maggie to stop talking. 'I've never laid a finger on the idiot, but if you get called back in an hour saying that I've hit her again—it'll probably be true.'

'And this girl, she's what age?'

'Seventeen,' Beth said. 'You know what they're like at that age.'

'I do, love. I've got one of my own.' The officer closed her notebook and pocketed it. 'Look, fair enough. We'll need to speak to her. Officers should be with her now, but we've had a few serious issues to deal with today.

But…' She looked at her watch. 'Just make sure she keeps her nose clean, yeah?' She turned to Maggie. 'And you're happy to let the matter drop if we give Miss Brown a good talking to?'

Maggie opened her mouth to speak, caught the look that Beth was flashing her, and closed it again. She nodded her head. Beth assured the police that they needn't waste any more time on Jennifer and that she'd see that she was punished and didn't pull a stunt like that again. Maggie saw them out and watched them drive away. Beth didn't like the look on her face one little bit when she came back.

'You owe me. You either tell me what the hell's going on, and I mean everything—or you walk out of that door and we're finished. I've had enough, Beth. Christ, I've got a family to think about. What are you doing, bringing the police to my door like that? Come on, sit down and talk to me.'

'I can't, Maggie.' Beth realised that this was the last chance she had to save her friendship with Maggie and she was going to let it go. 'Believe me. You're better off not knowing.'

Maggie's voice was almost a whisper and she wouldn't look at Beth. 'That's it then. Get out, Beth, and don't come to my house again.' She didn't move from the sofa as Beth stood up to let herself out.

'Bye, Maggie.'

As Beth closed the door, Maggie's hand was already reaching for the phone book. She thumbed to the listings for Brown.

Beth was glad that Maggie had severed ties between them. It was the one thing she could do for her friend.

Six months earlier she wouldn't have believed anything could come between their friendship. Since the night she had killed Marc, Beth worried that Maggie would come too close to the truth and be dragged into the mess that her life had become. She felt that it was one less loose end to trip her up. Maggie was dangerous and instead of feeling heartbroken about losing the one person who might have been able to help her, Beth only felt relief.

Chapter Eighteen

Four days passed since the police were called. The atmosphere in the house was strained at best. Beth was furious with Jennifer. She gave her a month's notice to sort her life out and find somewhere else to live. Jennifer came back at her with all the usual lines about going to the police. Beth called her bluff and told her to go ahead.

The night she came back from Maggie's, and in the aftermath of her rage, Beth was prepared to confess and go to prison for her crimes—if Jennifer was taken off the streets, too. As she lay in bed knowing she'd thrown the police off the scent, self-preservation kicked in. It was six months since Marc died and there were no repercussions. She'd done bad things in tandem with Jennifer, but they walked away without being apprehended. The colder the scent, the more chance she had of returning to normal life. She'd stood up to Jennifer and refused to be bullied. Despite all Jennifer's threats and promises, she didn't go to the police– because that would bring about her own downfall and there was no way Jennifer was going to do that. For the first time since Marc's death, Beth thought about a future that didn't contain either Jennifer or a police cell.

Jennifer once told Beth that they had to stay together to keep an eye on each other because neither one of them could ever trust the other was keeping her counsel. This was her meal ticket, her bargaining token and she had embroiled Beth in more and more trouble so that their lives were tangled and intertwined. She kept Beth malleable with threats and innuendo. It took her until now to understand that she'd been a fool. Jennifer never had any intention of going to the police. For months, Beth believed that the girl was crazy enough to not care about her own incrimination and trot off to the police for the attention and acclaim it would bring. Beth could see without clouds for the first time. Jennifer was too self-serving to risk her own safety, and unless she did, she couldn't accuse Beth of anything—it was stalemate. There was nothing to stop Beth from throwing Jennifer under the bus. She told Jennifer that she had thirty days to find herself a job and a flat. Jennifer used every blackmail trick going and said that she couldn't go home because of the body in the vault. If she didn't want to go back to the big house, that was her problem. One way or another, she was moving out.

Relations were unpleasant. Jennifer wheedled and cajoled, sulked and cried, and screamed and shouted. Beth's retort was to throw the local paper on the table, open at the property section.

Beth let herself into the house after finishing an evening shift. She wasn't greeted by the blare of Jennifer's music. She walked through the living room, dropping her bag by the chair. Jennifer was sitting by the light of the lamp. She didn't have the television on, she wasn't reading and she didn't have the snake draped all over her. She was just sitting. Walking through to the kitchen and putting on the kettle, Beth barely gave her a glance. 'I hope you've spent the day looking for a job,' she shouted, as she spooned coffee into a cup. 'Do you want a brew?'

'You need to come in here, Beth. I've got something

to tell you.'

'Not interested, Jennifer. Couldn't give a shit what you've got to say unless it's something to do with employment and flats.' She tapped the spoon on the edge of her cup and, picking the coffee up wandered back into the living room. She plonked herself in her chair by the fire and grabbed the remote. She was pointing it at the telly when Jennifer threw something across the room at her.

She caught it and frowned. 'What's this?' She turned the child's coat in her hands. It was a tiny blue anorak. On the inside, stitched just below the hanging loop was a nametag that said, Barry Park.

'It's Barry's coat. Has Maggie been here? What did she want? Oh, God, what have you said to her? What's going on, Phantom?'

Jennifer ignored her questions and said, conversationally, 'I'll tell you what, Beth, you want to have a word with Maggie about that nursery she sends sweet little Barry to. I'm very concerned and think she should take him out of it. You see, the security is lax and the poor children are in terrible danger.' She smirked at Beth and threw her mobile phone to her. 'Anybody can walk in off the street and snatch one of those kiddies. I thought after all that Dunblane malarkey that they had to keep the gates and what-not locked. Wasn't there a law passed? Well, that place doesn't lock the gates, that's for sure. I could have been anybody. Heck I could have been a –'

Beth was looking at the photograph on Jennifer's phone and felt dread crawling along her spine as the implications of her words sank in. She cut in on the girl's ramble, 'What have you done? Is Barry here? Is he upstairs? Have you taken him? Oh, Jesus, Maggie will be frantic if anything's happened to him.'

The picture showed Jennifer kneeling down beside Maggie's youngest son. She had her arm around him and she was smiling. Barry looked anxious. In the background of the tiny snap, Beth could see the day care centre that Barry attended two afternoons a week in preparation for going to school. In the photograph, Jennifer had a copy of the local newspaper in her hand.

'You can't see the date on that picture it's too small but if you enlarge it, you'll see that it's today's.'

Beth flung the phone on the floor and pounded up the stairs. She checked her room, Jennifer's, the bathroom, but the child wasn't in the house. She didn't know whether to be relieved or terrified. Jennifer was at the school, she was in the cloakroom, she'd been alone with Barry long enough to take the photo. How had she done it? Had she told staff she was a family friend come to pick the child up? Surely the proprietor wouldn't let one of the children leave with a stranger. Beth was confused

'You're bluffing,' she said without conviction. 'You haven't got him at all.'

'Did I say that I had him?'

'No, but –'

'Well then. Of course, I haven't got him.'

'Oh, thank God for that.'

'Mind, you might want to give Maggie a bell. I think you'll find that she could use a friend about now. Those roads are dangerous.'

'Oh, God. What have you done?'

'Then again, maybe the police will want her to keep

the phone lines free. You know... just in case.'

Beth clenched her hands together to prevent them from shaking. 'What have you done? What have you done? What have you done?' She spoke in a dull monotone. 'Where's Barry?'

'I'm sorry, Beth, he had a little accident. But it's all your fault. You pushed me to it with all this talk of jobs and moving out. You made me do it.'

'No,' Beth moaned. 'Please, tell me he's all right.'

'Er, 'friad not. It's tragic, really. Cars and roads and that. Kids being allowed to wander off willy-nilly, anything can happen.' She threw another object across the room.

Beth caught it and wiped at her streaming eyes so that she could focus. It was something in a plastic bag. She took out the T-shirt. It smelled of her perfume. She recoiled in horror as she held it up and saw the blood stain across the front. Her mind told her it was a trick, that it might be tomato ketchup. But she knew it was blood.

Jennifer handed over a second bag. Beth could see what was in it before she took it. It was a kitchen knife – her kitchen knife, the one with the broad steel blade. It was blood-stained. She saw something attached to the clear edge of the blade. It looked like a piece of sinew or muscle.

Beth clamped her hands over her mouth but was vomiting through her fingers before she made it out of the door.

She came down in clean clothes ten minutes later. She was pale and tearful. 'You know that you can't beat me, don't you, Beth?' said Jennifer coldly.

'I really am going to the police this time. This had nothing to do with me. I can prove it.'

'Can you? If you look at the knife it's not a moulded sheath, the handle is fastened on with screws. I carefully unscrewed it. Afterwards, well I just re-screwed the handle to the blade. Whose fingerprints are all over that knife, Beth? Whose is the blood-stained shirt? Who has fallen out with her best friend? People have killed for less, you know.'

'The nursery has security cameras. They'll have caught you on tape.' Beth was clutching at straws.

Jennifer laughed, 'I doubt it. But even so, we do everything together, don't we, Beth? If it comes out, I'll just tell them how you forced me to take him for you. It'll be your word against mine, Bethie.'

'It's his birthday next month.' It was an irrelevant detail, but it meant the world to Beth.

'We are going to the big house tonight. We'll stay in the vault. We can monitor anybody coming in. If the police know anything, they'll come straight here for us and then—if they're clever they'll go there. But at least there we can be prepared for them. They'll never find us in the vault, but we can keep an eye on their comings and goings until we decide what we're going to do. It was a direct order and Beth knew it.

She shut down. She'd been here before. She knew how the numb mode went. It was allowing herself to be led astray in this condition that got her into this mess in the first place. She needed to do what was right this time.

'I'm not going, Jennifer. You'll have to take that knife and use it on me to stop me. I'm going to the police and

I'm going to tell them everything.'

Jennifer laughed. 'I don't need a knife to stop you using that phone, mate. I'm leaving here in two minutes and you're coming with me. I don't have to force you. It'll be your choice. Can you imagine what women in prison do to a child killer? How do you think they'll treat you when they find out you took a toddler and stabbed him over thirty times before dumping his little body on waste ground? Don't you remember the Jamie Bulger case? And all to get revenge on his mother after a squabble?' Jennifer handed Beth her coat and she put it on.

'He's not in the vault, is he?' Beth sobbed as they walked up the stairs of the big house. 'Please, promise me that Barry's not dead in the vault? I couldn't bear that.'

Jennifer activated the mechanism to open the vault door. 'Oh, stop snivelling,' she said and pushed Beth inside.

She looked around. 'He's not here. What have you done with him?' Jennifer smirked in reply. There were two beds in there now. Beth lay on one bunk, and turned her face away from Marc's decayed body and cried into the pillow. She wasn't crying for herself, she was crying for Maggie and little Barry.

'Oi.' Jennifer was talking to her but she didn't respond. 'Oi, look at me.' Jennifer repeated.

'I can't stand to look at you. You disgust me.'

'Your choice. Anyway, thing is, thought I'd let you know you'd better get your head down. We've got a big day tomorrow. We're going to kidnap Colin. So be ready.'

Beth couldn't believe what she was hearing, but after murdering a small child, why wouldn't Jennifer want to try her luck again. 'You crazy, deranged animal.'

'Be ready in the morning to do exactly what I tell you.'

'Why, Phantom? Why more hurt and more pain? What are you going to do with him?'

'Just shut up with the questions, all right?'

'You're on your own. I'm not doing anything with you.'

'Oh, yes, you are, my friend. Because, you see, I'm going to throw you a big, fat lifeline. What if I could make it all right again, eh? What if I could help you out of trouble, just like I did last time?'

'You didn't get me out of trouble. All you did was lead me slap bang into it.'

'Ah, but what if I could turn back time?'

'What are you talking about?'

'Now, don't be miserable, Beth. Let me show you how I'm going to help you. What if I could turn back the clock to three thirty this afternoon?'

Beth raised her head.

'What if,' continued Jennifer in a sing-song voice, 'What if I sneaked into that house thing that pretends to be a school and nicked the kid's coat and then waited outside for them to have playtime. There's only about three kids. The teacher-come-housewife woman nipped in with one of them, didn't she? What if I just took little Barry's photo and legged it. What then, eh? Beth. What if Barry's safely at home with his dad and that fat bitch, Maggie? Wouldn't that make you happy?'

Beth wasn't falling for it, but her heart was pounding.

She'd gladly have given her life at that moment to know that Barry was safe and sound at home where he should be. 'But the T-shirt, the knife, all that blood. I know you've killed him. Barry's dead and you're playing your sick games.'

'See, now that's where you're right.'

Beth wailed. Wasn't it enough that Jennifer had done something so evil without bragging about it?

'You're right about the mind games, anyway. See, I must play this one out to keep you in line. I need you to do what I tell you. You've had a power trip lately, Beth, and I have to show you that it's not on. Maybe I killed the kid—maybe I didn't. You're stuck in this vault, away from the real world. You don't know what's happening out there, and I'm not going to give you access to the television to show you.'

'Stop it, Phantom. Just stop it. You're torturing me. Please tell me, is Barry alive or dead. What about the knife?'

'Stage props darling. It's amazing what you can do with a big piece of bloody steak from Tyson's, the butcher. Did you like the little touch with the piece of sinew stuck to the blade?'

Hope welled up inside of Beth. She would do whatever Jennifer wanted if Barry wasn't dead. 'Is he alive?' she whispered.

'That's what I can't tell you. If you do exactly what I ask of you tomorrow, I promise you, I give you my word faithfully, that tomorrow night I'll tell you the truth.

But—you've got to do what I say. You have tonight to mull it over. He might be dead, he might not. If you disobey me, I will kill him—if I haven't already. I've shown you how easy it is. As far as you're concerned, the kid's dead. He might be very much alive, but if that's the case, I've got him locked away somewhere, doped and dreaming morphine dreams. Possibly somewhere in this house. He won't wake up. You don't know, do you, Beth? But to have any chance of saving him, you must play the game. My game. Do exactly as I tell you and who knows, maybe by this time tomorrow we'll have turned back time and he'll be alive and well and eating spaghetti hoops at his mum's table. Your call, Beth.'

Beth put her head down on the hard pillow and closed her eyes. Tears streamed from beneath them. She shut out Jennifer and the world.

Chapter Nineteen

After a restless night on the hard bunk of the vault, Beth woke feeling wasted. Several times through the night she thought that she'd heard a child crying somewhere in the cavernous house, but she may have been dreaming. Between brief spells of troubled sleep, she strained her ears, listening to the nothingness in the dark.

As Jennifer hustled her out of the house that morning, Beth pulled away from her. She ran along the corridor, flinging open doors and calling out Barry's name. Jennifer scorned her, filling her head with doubts, asking if she'd really be so stupid as to have the kid lying in the open where Beth could find him. 'You'd better follow me right now. We're going to do this and if you don't, then the blood of that little boy will be on your hands forever. I mean it Beth, I'm not messing around.'

'He'll be scared and hungry. Please, Jennifer, let me see him. Give me two minutes with him and I'll do anything you ask.'

'I might not have him at all. He may be at home sitting on his mummy's fat knee inhaling cigarette smoke into his precious little lungs—but you can't take my word on that so, I'd come now, if I were you.'

Beth abandoned her search and left the house seething. She was furious and for the first time in her life, she was scared of the temper that was boiling in her blood. She was somebody different.

The drive to secluded Priory Beach was no less hair-raising than last time Beth was in the van with Jennifer.

The Goth had gone to extra pains with her appearance wearing twice as much black makeup as normal and she had on a long black trench coat with clumpy boots. She had a new piercing through her cheek which wasn't there the night before. She'd done it herself with a needle and the skin around it was red and inflamed. She struck Beth as a Tribeswoman painting herself up to go into battle. They were about to kidnap a man in daylight, but if Beth expected Jennifer to look inconspicuous then this certainly wasn't it. Jennifer drove fast with the windows down and *Theory of a Deadman* blasting out and drawing attention. Beth was trying to think. They were on their way to attempt violence on an innocent man. The psychotic girl next to her might already have the toddler locked away somewhere. She felt the madness spiralling out of control. Why were they taking Colin? Jennifer had briefed her on what she had to do to play her part, but no matter how many times Beth asked her, she couldn't get any straight answers about what she was going to do with him, or why she was taking him. Colin wasn't a big man by any means, but he was strong. What if it all went wrong? What then? Jennifer had forced her to cut down on smoking but she needed a cigarette and lit up, resting her arm out of the window.

'No smoking in the van, I've told you to quit. You stink.'

'Oh, fuck off. I need it.'

'Okay,' said Jennifer, pleasantly, pushing her foot harder on the accelerator. 'Your lungs.' She flung the van into a hard turn and made Beth scream in fear as it slewed across the road. 'Every action has a consequence, Beth, you know that.'

She had to reduce her speed when they turned off the main road onto a narrow service track to the beach. It was little more than a rut. Jennifer drove too fast, almost putting them into the deep ditch at the side of the hedgerow. Beth said nothing, but she was blazing. She flicked her used fag butt out of the window.

'Littering as well. My, how our little goody two shoes is changing.' Beth didn't grace Jennifer with a reply, she satisfied herself with wondering if it would sizzle if she put her next fag out on Jennifer's eyeball.

The beach was fed by a single entrance and exit. At the end of the road, leading onto the shore front, was a solitary house. Only the rear of the two-storey and a few outbuildings overlooked the beach. One car sat on the expansive drive. A moderate rain fell and the skies were grey. Only the most ardent dog walkers would be out today.

Fastening their coats, Jennifer and Beth got out of the van on the rutted track, interspersed with bushes running alongside the sand line. Jennifer parked between two clumps of gorse so they would be as secluded as possible. On a sand dune, some distance away and in profile to them, a fisherman sat beneath a green umbrella. They could see him through the gorse but the van and the bushes would be enough to obscure them from his view.

'Do it,' Jennifer ordered.

Beth took the new mobile phone that she'd bought at a supermarket on a trip out to Lancaster, fifty miles away. She'd paid cash for both the phone and its credit, making it untraceable.

Her hands shook as she rang Colin's number and the

tinge of fear in her voice when he answered was entirely genuine. 'Colin?'

'Yes?'

'Oh, hi, it's Beth.'

'Beth?'

'Yes, Beth Armstrong. You know, Maggie's mate? Sorry, I know it's been awhile. The thing is –'

'Oh, Beth. Yes, um, how are you? How's things?' Beth could tell from Colin's voice that he was trying to work out why Beth would be ringing him after all this time.

'The thing is,' she went on, ignoring his salutations, 'my van's broken down and I wondered if you'd be able to come and help me. I'm at Priory Beach.'

'Oh, I'm sorry, hun, there's no chance today. I'm snowed under here and I'm at work on my own. Listen, ring Mason's garage. Hang on, I'll get you the number. Tell them I sent you and they'll look after you.'

Beth was prepared for this. 'Oh, that's good of you. Thank you, Colin. Who do I ask for?' Beth gave a half scream and moaned. 'Oh my God, he's back.' She raised her voice and screamed, though not loud enough to draw the attention of the fisherman. 'Don't come any closer. I'm warning you. I'll ring the police.' She was crying and pleading. 'Oh, please. Leave me alone. What do you want?'

'Beth. Beth.' Colin was shouting down the phone. 'Beth, get in your van. Lock all the doors and ring the police. Then sound your horn until they come. I'm on my way.' The phone went dead.

'He's coming,' Beth said.

They watched a man with a black Labrador turn the corner into Priory Wood and disappear. 'I hope he's not planning a return journey in the next half hour,' Jennifer said from the coverage of the gorse bush in front of the van. She was in position and ready.

Beth, in a state of agitation, paced up and down until she heard a van coming fast along the track. 'This is it,' she murmured. 'Stay out of sight.'

Colin pulled to a screeching stop behind their van. Without turning the engine off, he ran towards Beth. She cast a nervous glance towards the fisherman along the beach in case the sound of Colin's approach had carried that far. He was paying them no attention.

'Oh, Colin, thank God you're here.' Beth ran to him and flung herself into his arms. 'It was horrible. I thought he was going to hurt me.'

'Where is he? Where's he at?'

'It's okay, he's gone. I did as you said and the sound of my horn scared him away. Thanks for coming out.'

'Did you ring the police?'

'Yes, yes, they're on their way.'

'Huh,' remarked Colin. 'They're taking their time. You could have been raped and murdered by now.'

'Oh, don't. It's too horrible to think about.' She buried her head in his shoulder and gave a couple of dry sobs for good measure.

Colin, embarrassed by the display of emotion, cleared his throat and moved her gently away. 'Come on, then, let's have a look at this van. What's the trouble? What're you doing driving that thing, anyway? Where's your car?'

'I don't know what's wrong with it, it just won't start. I think the battery might be flat?'

'Okay, pop the lid and let's have a look. If we can't

get her going, I'll give you a lift home and come back with the tow truck.'

He already had his head under the bonnet so Beth didn't answer him. She heard him wiggling things and clanking things.

'What are you doing out here?' he asked.

That was a question that she didn't have an answer for. She signalled to Jennifer who came out of the bush, hunkering low to the ground. The plan was that Jennifer would get the pad of chloroform over his face while he was still under the van's bonnet. This would render his greater weight and strength useless. They hoped the chloroform would take effect before he could shrug Jennifer off his back.

Jennifer ran at him from behind. She was all but silent despite her heavy footwear and obstructive clothing. As she rose from her crouch to attack him, her shadow passed across the front of the van. Beth watched in horror as he reacted. The shadow, coupled with instinct—and possibly a warning whiff of the chloroform, alerted him to the fact that he was in danger. Jennifer flew at him and, as rehearsed, clamped the pad over his mouth and nose. In the same instant, Colin straightened, banging his head hard on the underside of the bonnet. He let out a muffled yell. Far from being compliant, he came out from under the van fighting. Jennifer was clinging to the back of his jacket with one hand while clamping the rag to his face with the other.

Once out from the restraints of the van, he shook Jennifer off easily. She went flying backwards, stumbling over the uneven ground and her own feet, and came to a stop in a muddy puddle on the track.

Colin took two steps towards Beth. He shook his head and Beth watched in wide-eyed horror as he tried to assemble the details of what was happening. He mumbled incoherently. His eyes were streaming and although the chloroform hadn't knocked him out as planned, it impeded his judgement. He shook his head again, trying to clear it, and the motion knocked him off balance. He fell forward onto his hands and knees. His arms refused support and shook beneath him. Beth just stared as he tried to regain his footing. His leg wouldn't come out from under him despite three attempts.

From the corner of her eye Beth saw Jennifer creeping up on them. Beth turned to look and saw that she had a rock in her hand. She was almost level with Colin. She raised the rock, aiming to bring it down on the back of his head.

'Jennifer, no!' screamed Beth. She lunged towards Jennifer. Colin turned and, retching from the effects of the chloroform, he wrapped his arms around Jennifer's legs. It took him off balance and the pair of them rolled on the track in a tangle of arms and legs. The rock fell from Jennifer's hand and Beth leant over and picked it up.

Colin and Jennifer were wrestling in the mud. Because of Colin's weakened and half-conscious state they were evenly matched. He aimed a punch at Jennifer's face, but his motion was slow and she saw it coming and deflected it. He used his weight to pin her to the ground and, lying on top of her, brought his arm back again. This time she couldn't move to escape his fist.

'Beth, do something,' yelled Jennifer. She turned her face to the side when Colin's bunched fist came at her.

The punch was weak and lacked any power but it was enough to bust her nose and blood ran from her nostrils as she struggled beneath him.

He was regaining his senses. With each breath of fresh air, his movements were more solid, his focus more aligned. He was bringing his fist back again. If he hurt Jennifer, Beth would be left alone with him. How would she explain the unprovoked attack on him? She had to do something. All the tension, all the stress, the feeling of weakness and the fury built within her in a seething mass of rage. She'd never felt this feeling before. Her body was tense and trembling from the static of adrenaline borne of aggression. Her fingers curled around the rock—the weapon—and she could feel the blood boiling in her veins as her world turned red. She wanted to smash and smash and not stop smashing until she was physically unable to raise the rock. She wasn't seeing, wasn't thinking. She had no awareness of what she was doing.

Taking a tighter hold of the rock in her hand, she cleared the two steps that distanced her from the twisting bodies on the ground. She took her arm behind her, the momentum of her fury carrying it back with force as she brought the rock down hard on somebody's head. She didn't know or care who the head belonged to, she had to expel the fury inside her with violence.

Colin slumped onto his face unconscious, a gash in the back of his head pouring blood that diluted on contact with the rain-wet path and spread in a darkening stain. Jennifer was climbing out from underneath him as Beth raised her arm for the second blow.

'Beth, stop. Give me the rock. You're going to kill

him.' The roles were reversed. Jennifer was calling for Beth to come to her senses, but Beth was beyond seeing the irony.

She wheeled to face Jennifer. 'You want the rock? You want the fucking rock?' she yelled, continuing the arc of her slam, this time with the rock directed at Jennifer's head. Jennifer rolled and scrambled to her feet. Beth was already preparing her next swing. She had never known a feeling of power like this. Her body was electrified. She felt super-human, stronger than she had ever felt before. She was hard and invincible. She was unyielding. She was powerful without having the capability of rational thought to bring her under control. She wasn't aware of what she'd done to Colin, or of what she was about to do to Jennifer. She only knew that her body was tingling and for the first time in her life—she felt big. It was good. It was primal and a violent ecstasy overcame her. It was akin to the strongest orgasm she'd ever had and she exulted in the thrill of the sensation. Without thinking, she reacted on impulse. Her mouth was open. She was gasping. A line of spittle dripped from her chin and her eyes were wild and unfocused. She let out a yell of rage and lunged towards Jennifer.

Jennifer scuttled out of her reach.

'Barry,' she screamed. 'Beth, we have to get Barry, now. Think of Barry. Think of Maggie's little boy.'

Beth hesitated. Her arm was in the downward swing. She was confused. Her eyes focused and she stared at Jennifer. It was as though she was awakening from a dream. Her arm was tired so she dropped it and let the stone fall to the ground. She had no idea what was happening but that wonderful feeling of being powerful and invincible was gone. She felt sad, as though she'd lost something very, very important to her. She looked at Colin. She saw him lying face down in the dirt and asked in a tired voice, 'Is he dead?'

Jennifer eyed her warily. She risked taking her eyes off Beth and glanced around the beach. The fisherman was looking in their direction. He had one hand up on his forehead shielding his eyes, he'd heard something. Jennifer waved at him and shouted, 'Hello,' at the top of her voice. Then she jumped around and laughed loud. She was shouting 'You're it, you're it.' She ran around the van. Beth just stood there. Confused.

'Is he dead?' she asked again. 'I need to know if he's dead.'

'Shut up,' hissed Jennifer. 'That bloke's looking over. Now start jumping around as though we're playing a game.'

A game, thought Beth. Yes, that's it, just two kids playing a game. She wanted to play, she wanted more than anything for the power to come back to her, but it was gone and Colin was lying in a bleeding heap on the ground and Jennifer was jumping and laughing—and Beth was so very tired.

The fisherman returned to his fishing. Jennifer stopped laughing. She dropped to her knees beside Colin. She tried to turn him over but he was too heavy.

'Oh, you shouldn't do that,' muttered Beth. 'Shouldn't move him. Need to wait for an ambulance to get here.'

'There is no ambulance, stupid,' Jennifer shot back. And then, realising that she'd insulted Beth, she looked up at her sharply, gauging her reaction. 'Sorry, I mean…

Look, you're the nurse. Can you, like, sort of snap out of it for a minute and come and see if you've killed him?'

Beth fell to her knees on the other side of Colin. She'd killed a man before. This time it wasn't as bad. One murder is very bad, the second is diluted. The song, *One Man Went to Mow* came into her head and she wanted to sing it, but it wouldn't be appropriate with dead Colin lying beside her. She felt the world returning to her and she was more normal. 'I want to kill you, too,' she said in a dry voice, 'but I'm too tired now. You'll have to wait.'

'Well, thank God for that,' muttered Jennifer. 'So, is he dead, or what? What are we going to do? Either way, we're going to have to stick to the original plan initially, we can't leave him like this.'

Beth tried to focus on what should be done but her thoughts were fuzzy and blurred as though she was the one who'd been clunked with a boulder. She took off her scarf and wrapped it around Colin's head to close the wound, keep dirt out and stem the bleeding. She waited for nurse mode to click in and to feel the buzz that a professional emergency brought on, but what she really wanted was the dark super power with an ability to crush bones in her bare fist. Even with the aid of a rock, it was still a thrill.

Between them they turned him onto his back. Beth checked his airway and ensured that it was open and clear of blockage, put her ear close to his mouth to check his breathing, and felt for his pulse to see if he had circulation. 'He's alive,' she said to Jennifer, but she didn't feel anything about it, one way or the other. She looked down on him and tried to remember that he was a human being, that they'd once been friendly, flirty even, although she'd never had a great deal of time for him. But she'd seen death and she'd seen cruelty and she'd inflicted hurt—and nothing mattered anymore except that one day she might feel the violent power again.

'Right let's get him loaded and get out of here. Grab his legs and we'll get him to his van,' Jennifer said. 'We'll leave our van here and hide his at the house. With a bit of luck, he won't have told anybody where he was going and the fisherman won't remember anything about a breakdown service later.'

By the time Jennifer finished speaking, they had him in the back of his van. Jennifer moved some tools and boxes to get him in. 'You get in the back with him and do your best to keep him alive until we get back.'

As an afterthought, Jennifer bent down and picked up the rock, still sticky with Colin's blood, and held it in her hand for a second. 'Beth, you are one psychotic bitch, do you know that?' She threw the rock in the back of the van beside her. 'I'm just glad that there's a wall between you and the driver's seat in this thing.'

Jennifer slammed the back doors of the van shut.

Beth prayed to God as she used to when she was a little girl. Jennifer held all the cards again.

Chapter Twenty

Maggie took the phone book to the kitchen table with a pen and note pad. She held the pen between her thumb and index finger and tapped it against her teeth. She didn't immediately thumb the book to find the listing she wanted, she was thinking. Why was she bothering with this? It was none of her business. She didn't even know what she was hoping to find. She knew that something was wrong. She was hurt that Beth had turned on her. They were lifelong friends and yet Beth had changed beyond recognition, into somebody that Maggie didn't want to know.

But she was still Beth—and Maggie loved her. She had no idea what was wrong. That alone was so wrong on so many levels. They shared everything, always had. Or they had until recently. Everything changed the day Jennifer appeared on the scene and whether Beth wanted her help or not, Maggie couldn't sit by and do nothing. Trouble was something that Maggie associated with young people and married people. Not the likes of Beth who had never even been caught smoking at school.

Beth wasn't the type of person who ever had trouble, caused trouble or got into trouble, but the word was thumping around Maggie's brain and it wouldn't let up.

She found the listings for Brown in the telephone directory. Luck was on her side, there weren't that many locally. Maggie was sure that sod's law would have turned against her and every Brown, nationwide, would have decided to move to the Lake District when the book was last updated. It was doable and with a bit of luck she wouldn't have to call too many people before she struck gold.

'Er, hello. Yes. Is that Mrs Brown? The thing is, I was wondering, do you know a Jennifer Brown? Is she maybe your daughter? I'm a friend of a friend and I'm trying to locate her family. No. Okay. Thank you. Sorry to bother you.' She hung up and keyed the next number.

'No, no, sweetheart it's not Nana. Can you get your mummy or daddy for me, please? Daddy's gone away? Oh, I'm sorry to hear that, love. Did she? Yes, that's a very bad word. I'm sure Mummy's just a little bit angry with him.'

Another call. 'Listen, buster, I already told you, I don't want to sell you anything. I'm a friend of a friend of hers. Do you know her? –Bastard, you didn't need to hang up on me.'

And another. 'You've just moved to the area and don't know anybody? No, I'm sorry, I can't help you there. Dorothy Perkins? No, not in Ulverston, but I think there's one in Barrow, but it might have shut down now.'

Twenty-two calls later she had spoken to the last person listed in the phone book. She had left messages on four answer machines and had five ring-outs that she'd call back later, but if the calls she'd made were anything to go by, she was out of luck. She only needed one call to be successful though, and she could locate Jennifer's family and get to the bottom of this mess.

Plan B had to be put into operation and Maggie rang the hospital, waiting five minutes on hold to be transferred to the personnel officer. 'Hello. I wonder if you can help me. I'm trying to get hold of one of your young nurses and I wondered if you could give me her number, please? Her name is Jennifer Brown. Of course, I understand that it's privileged information. Yes, yes, I know all about data protection but it's an emergency. I've had some bad news. It's her granddad, you see. I really need to contact her as soon as possible.'

The woman on the other end of the line sighed and asked for the name Maggie was looking for.

'Jennifer Brown. A trainee, I think, or maybe one of those care assistants, auxiliary maybe. I'm not entirely sure. I think she works on Ward Four.'

'She doesn't work here. I know all the staff personally. We did have a Jennifer Reid but she left to have a baby.'

'She must work there. It's not Jennifer Reid and I'm pretty sure she's never had a baby.'

'You must be mistaken, then, there is no Jennifer Brown on our staff.'

'Okay. Thanks for your help.'

Maggie disconnected the call and tried the ring-outs, managing to scribble a line through one of the numbers on her list. She had drawn a blank. Beth was the most honest and truthful person she had ever known. She must have a damned good reason for saying that Jennifer worked at the hospital when she doesn't. Maggie wanted to help her, but lies only made her curious. Why would Beth lie?

She placed a call to the only high school in Ulverston and was put through to the school secretary. 'Shelly, hi. How are you?'

'I'm fine,' Shelly said, pausing to figure out the voice speaking to her. 'Yes, good, thanks. How can I help you?'

'It's Maggie Johnson here, Jess and Ben's mum.'

'Oh, hello. Is something wrong?'

'No, no, not at all. Well, that's not true. I was trying to be polite.' She put on a feeble voice. 'There is a problem, actually. It's all been very upsetting, you see, and I was wondering if you could help me. It's our Jess, she's terribly upset.

'Oh dear, really? What is it?'

'It's not exactly a problem at school. She's being bullied. Very badly bullied. Too-frightened-to-leave-the-house, bullied. It's terrible.'

'That's awful. Poor Jess. Is it somebody in her form?'

'Ah well, that's the trouble, the ring-leader of this gang is a bit older, eighteen-ish maybe, and I don't think she's the sort to still be there doing A-levels unless they've brought out an exam on intimidation. But with you being there forever and knowing everybody, I hoped you could give me something to go on. Could you get me an address to give to the police, or maybe just tell me something about the family? You know, are they the approachable type? That sort of thing. I thought I might just give them a knock, see if we can sit down, civilised like and sort it out between us without having to involve the police and such.'

'I can certainly try. What's her name?'

'Jennifer Brown. She might have left school last year or maybe the year before. Her and her henchmen are making Jess' life a misery. Her schoolwork's bound to suffer and what with her GCSEs and stuff going on.'

'Jennifer, you say?'

'Brown. Weird looking thing, she is. All black clothes and self-mutilation, you know the type, gothic and a nut short of a squirrel stash. Strange appearance. Ugly, if you ask me. I blame the parents. Not for the ugliness of course—the bullying. Mind you, she didn't get those piggy little eyes from Asda.' Maggie chatted on, trying to lead the secretary into gossip, but her eyes were shrewd, pen poised ready to write as soon as she gleaned any information that would be useful.

She heard some keystrokes, Shelley was tapping on her computer, and then she said, 'No, nothing. I've never had the pleasure of having that duck in my pond.'

'But she must have gone to Vic High; it's the only high school in town.'

'Are you sure that's her name?'

'Yes, I've got the right name. Jess talks about her all the time. You've had absolutely no school leavers of that name in the last five years?'

'Sorry, love, none, and we're a small enough school that I know them all.'

'Okay, thank you.'

'Your best bet is to ring the police.'

'Yes, I will. That's going to have to be the next step. No, I'm sure there's no need to worry the head about it. So busy? Oh yes, I know you do, yes very seriously. Absolutely, I hold the school in the highest regard. I'll pass your best wishes on to her. Yes, yes, thank you now. Goodbye.'

The hospital had never heard of her and neither had the school. Maggie looked at her scribbling on the pad in a looped and uneven scrawl.

Phantom -- ghost-like -- able to pass by unnoticed.

She underlined the name Jennifer Brown. The rest of the page was blank.

Chapter Twenty-One

Beth was exhausted. Jennifer took charge of the situation as she always did. She barked orders and Beth complied meekly and obediently. Colin was unconscious throughout the journey to the house at the top of Rake Lane where Jennifer and Marc used to live. Beth knelt in the back of the van beside him. He was recumbent on the floor with Beth's jacket under his neck to immobilise it. Beth was on her knees to the side of him, neither touching nor ministering. She was just kneeling there, absorbing the motion of the van. Her state was the same as after Marc's death. She was detached and barely hanging on to the unravelling ribbons of her sanity. As they pulled into the driveway, she remembered Barry and pulled herself together enough to ask Jennifer about him. 'I've stuck to my side of the bargain. I've done everything you asked. You must let Barry go. Let me take him back home. He'll be terrified.'

'I haven't got him, never did have. Phone Maggie and check if you like. I said I'd tell you the truth—and that's it.'

'You really are one grade-A bitch. I only did all this,' she gestured weakly with her hand, 'because you said you had him.' She wanted to believe her and it was easiest just to take her statement as fact. That took the least effort and, after all, if Barry had been kidnapped from nursery, she'd hear about it. She could rock Maggie in her arms and talk about the wickedness of the world while offering platitudes and chocolate biscuits. For now, it was enough that she'd almost killed Maggie's ex-husband. She'd deal with one thing at a time. She had to keep Colin alive. She couldn't tell if he was alive or dead, but she was very tired and couldn't remember what to do to find out, so she looked once, and looked away. It didn't matter—nothing did.

'What are you going to do with Colin's van?'

'I've been thinking about that. I was going to dump it. Middle of Lancaster, or Preston even, but after your psycho-killer stunt, it's probably got tons of messy evidence all over it. Too risky. We'll leave it in my garage. It's the safest place for it. We can reassess later if we need to.' There were a lot of things to reassess later. 'How's he doing?'

'Okay, thanks,' Beth replied.

Jennifer laughed at Beth's innocuous reply. It sounded so ridiculously inept. 'Weirdo,' she muttered.

They struggled to get Colin out of the van and into the vault. Jennifer moaned at Marc's lack of thought in having the vault built into an upper storey of the house instead of at ground level. She was pale and looked frightened. She berated Beth for her part in the kidnapping. 'He was only supposed to be unconscious from the chloroform. Why did you have to hit him so hard?'

'I was aiming for you. I should have saved Colin and hit you. I could have told him everything. He'd have known what to do. I wish I'd got rid of you while I had the chance. I should have killed you.'

'I'm not sure I'm liking this new, aggressive side of you, Beth. You're freaking me out. You're supposed to be my stable guardian-type person. If you're going to go nut-loop on me, you really are going to be a headache.

What kind of a role model are you, waltzing around the place, clonking people with rocks like a Yeti? And Jesus, Beth, enjoying it the way you did. That's screwed, man, that's really screwed. Hold him steady, will you. No, not like that, he'll roll off the bed. You've got to support him. Christ he's heavy. Right he's on. Go on, do your nursey bit.'

Beth didn't know what to do. They had first aid equipment and enough morphine to put a nation to sleep, but not much more. She side-stepped Jennifer, who was putting up the cot-sides of the bed, and leaned over Colin. His skin was pale and clammy. She put two fingers to his throat and checked for the movement of his pulse against them. It was coming back to her, gradually, her vocation was leaking through the inertia fighting for supremacy over her psyche. His pulse, barely beating through the carotid artery was weak but tangible. Lifting an eyelid, she watched as his pupil contracted from the glare of the overhead light. She repeated with the other eye. 'He's stable, but poorly.'

Jennifer laughed at her again. 'I'm not his grieving mother, you know. Stable but poorly, that's funny. Poorly is having the chicken pox, love, not having your skull caved in with a bloody great boulder. You sound as though you're reading a *Casualty* script. Go on, tell me to get the crash cart, stat.'

Beth didn't reply. She looked at Jennifer who was still giggling. Jennifer's mascara had run onto her cheek. She was pale and looked shocked and although she still poked jibes at Beth, she seemed frightened and fidgeted with her fingers.

They were both frightened.

'Let's cover him up and leave him to sleep it off,' Jennifer said. 'We can come back and check on him later.'

'We can't leave him. His condition's serious. He could die, Jennifer. The next twelve hours are critical. He's not going to wake up from this with a headache, you know. He could have brain damage. We can't leave him for a second. What are we going to do? He needs to go to hospital. Let's just take him and leave him there. We don't have to let anybody see us. We can leave him on the pavement when it's dark. We can put him out of range of the security cameras. Somebody will raise the alarm. He needs proper care.'

'What, and just hope that when he wakes up, the memory of being clunked on the head by his ex-wife's best mate is going to be wiped away with a convenient bout of amnesia?'

'If he does wake up. What if he dies? He might die, Jennifer. Why have you brought him here? What are you going to do with him? What are we going to do?'

Jennifer didn't look up. She examined her boots in a sulky silence. 'I don't know. You weren't supposed to hurt him. I just wanted to see if we could do it. I wanted to get at Maggie, she's such a bitch, and now it's all gone wrong. It's all your fault.'

Beth was thinking more clearly. She turned her frustration back at Jennifer. 'My fault? Phantom, this isn't my fault. I hit him to save you. God knows why. All I've ever wanted is to get you out of my life. I just panicked in the heat of the moment. But you can't blame me for this. You got us into it. You thought you could kidnap a man, do whatever the hell it is that you thought you were going to do with him—rape him or whatever depraved rubbish you're planning, and then just let him go telling him it was all a joke and no hard feelings, mate? Is that it?'

'I don't know.'

'Jennifer, you must know. Why is he here? Were you going to try and blackmail Maggie?'

'No.'

'What then? And why Colin? How does kidnapping Col hurt Maggie? They've been divorced five years. I don't understand. How did you see this ending?'

'I don't know.' Jennifer shouted it this time. 'I just wanted to mess with him. I wanted to see if we could get away with it. I thought maybe I'd clear off afterwards. Go somewhere.'

'Well, you certainly messed with him, all right. Look at him.' The implication of what Jennifer said sank in. 'Hang on, so you were going to kidnap Colin, do whatever weirdness you had in mind and then take off leaving me to face the music? Is that it? You were just going to disappear and leave me to take the flak for—everything?'

Jennifer shrugged and then raised her eyes to meet Beth's. The look she gave her was filled with hatred. 'I still can. You killed my brother. I wanted you to pay.'

'You stupid little girl,' Beth yelled and Jennifer shrank away from her. 'You think I'm going to let you walk away from all this—this carnage that you've created with your sick games? You aren't going anywhere, sweetheart. Are you? Answer me, damn you. You aren't going anywhere, are you?'

'No,' replied Jennifer in a small voice. Beth felt a tiny jolt of the power return. She was incredibly thirsty and remembered how after cleaning up Marc's remains she couldn't stomach anything to drink from this house. She'd never been able to eat or drink here in all the times they'd returned to clean up and maintain the house. 'Go and make coffee while I attend to his wounds. Lots of it, strong, it's going to be a long night. And something to eat, too.'

'I want to watch what you do to him. I might be a nurse like you one day.'

Beth shook her head. 'Go,' she yelled.

When Jennifer left the room, Beth prepared what she could find while the kettle in the vault boiled. She poured water into a bowl and used cotton wool and gauze pads from the First Aid kit to clean the blood and matted hair from his wounds. Small shards of bone were sticking out of the open wound at the back of his head. She picked the loose pieces away with tweezers. On clearing the debris, it didn't look as bad as she feared it might, but it was bad enough and far more worrying was the deep depression in his skull where she'd hit him with the rock but hadn't broken bone. It was a large surface area and the potential for it to be a serious and debilitating trauma injury was massive. She cleaned the wounds with iodine and dressed them with a pressure bandage around his head. The bleeding was minimal and clots were forming and scabbing around the wound. His temperature was rising. His body had gone into clinical shock and a fever was showing the first signs of being severe. She stripped him to the waist, pulled the blankets back and set up a fan beside the bed to cool him. If his temperature rose too high he could have seizures and that could cause problems with his brain.

Glad that Jennifer wasn't looking over her shoulder, she catheterised him. Although he was unconscious, he didn't need Jennifer's curiosity and innuendo. Beth tried to afford him as much dignity as she could under the circumstances. After making him as comfortable as possible, she gave him a ten-mil shot of morphine to keep him in his sleeping state. She could do no more than sit and wait it out. She pulled one of the two straight-backed chairs in the vault up to the side of his bed and prepared herself for the night ahead.

Jennifer came back with coffee and sandwiches of potted meat made with bread taken from the freezer and not quite defrosted properly in the microwave. Beth found that she was starving and the sandwich seemed like the best she'd ever tasted. She devoured it and washed it down with coffee from the pot that Jennifer brought up. It was too hot and burned her throat. Jennifer ate daintily, nibbling in her mouse-like way at the corner of the bread. She cast her sandwich aside after two small bites and asked Beth if they could go to MacDonald's. Beth's cold stare was enough to stop her repeating the question but after sitting quietly for a little while, thumbing through a couple of out of date magazines left in the vault when it was kitted out, her boredom threshold reached its limit. And she peppered Beth with questions.

'When's he going to wake up?' she asked for the third time.

'Twenty past four next Thursday. I don't know, do I? We don't want him to wake up yet. While he's sleeping, his brain is quiet and can heal.'

'Is that what he's doing, just sleeping? Does that

mean he's getting better?'

'No, you fool, he's in a coma. It's a little bit further up the sleep scale than forty winks, in case you're wondering.'

'If he's in a coma can he still get a hard on?'

'Oh, shut up, you childish fool. I get so sick of your ridiculous incessant questions?'

'God, you get narky when you're stressing out. I only asked. He's not going to wake up or anything tonight, is he? Let's go home, Beth. Please. I want to watch *The X-Factor*.'

'You're not going anywhere. We're going to take turns in sleeping and watching him around the clock for however long it takes. Make up the bunks. We'll work in a military shift pattern of eight-four-four-eight.'

'What the hell does that mean?'

'Well, if you'll shut up and listen for a minute, I'll tell you. We work eight hours on then four hours off, four hours on and then eight hours off. It's the most efficient and energy saving way of maintaining a two-man shift for an extended period. I'll take the first eight-hour shift while you sleep.'

'I'm not tired,' Jennifer protested.

'You will be. Sleep.'

Jennifer ignored Beth and got up to turn on one of the television sets. She picked up a remote control to transfer the signal from CCTV mode onto Sky TV.

'Turn it off,' Beth snapped.

Jennifer's voice was petulant. 'If you're going to keep me locked up in here like a prisoner then you can't expect me to just sleep and watch him. I want to watch the *X-Factor*.'

Beth relented for a quiet life. 'Well, keep it low so I can hear if there's any change in Colin's status.'

Jennifer watched television until after midnight and fell asleep lying on top of the bunk less than three hours before she was due to take over the night vigil beside Colin's bed. At four o'clock in the morning when the alarm that Beth set went off, Jennifer continued to breathe evenly. Beth left Jennifer to sleep through her eight-hour shift.

Beth watched over Colin for sixteen hours straight. She moved only to replenish his morphine, to use the lavatory once, and to refill the coffeepot with water from the vault's kettle. In the coldest hours before dawn, she walked over to her bunk and pulled off one of the unzipped double sleeping bags and took it back to her chair to wrap around herself. She dozed, annoyed with herself every time she felt her eyes closing and her head drooping towards her chest. She'd get up, check Colin's stats and pour herself another coffee.

She'd fallen asleep properly. As she opened her eyes she was aware of movement at the side of Colin's bed. Jennifer was standing with her back almost to Beth. She'd woken while Beth slept. Beth's first though on waking was one of guilt for falling asleep when she was on night watch. The feeling passed as she took in the scene at the bedside. Jennifer had rolled the sheet down to Colin's knees. As Beth's eyes adjusted to the darkness, she saw that Jennifer was only wearing a pair of briefs and the vest top that she often wore in bed. Her left hand was moving rhythmically. She could hear Jennifer breathing and was horrified when it became clear what she was doing. Jennifer's right hand was busy too. She had taken Colin's penis from his pyjamas and was moving it furiously. Beth could see Jennifer's hand working the limp flesh and she was oblivious to Beth as she simultaneously masturbated herself and Colin.

Beth tried to leap from the chair but got caught in the sleeping bag. 'What the fuck do you think you're doing? Oh, my God.' She was trying to untangle herself and get to Jennifer.

At the first movement from Beth, Jennifer jumped. She extracted her hand from the front of her panties and Beth saw her wipe her fingers across the scant material half covering her backside. She took hold of the catheter tube and peered closely. 'Beth, Beth, wake up,' she said, 'I think this tube thingies, blocked or something. It doesn't look right to me.'

Beth grabbed Jennifer and flung her across the room. 'You're sick, do you know that? You are a sick twisted human being. I saw what you were doing. You disgust me. Get out, go on, get out.' Jennifer, seeing the rage on Beth's face, stopped long enough to pick up her trousers from where she'd removed them in front of the bunk. Her face was red and she ran from the vault. Beth checked Colin over before covering him and checking his stats. His catheter was fine with the waste flowing smoothly down the tube to collect in the measuring bag. She couldn't believe what she'd just seen.

An hour before the second shift ended at midday she washed Colin's torso and face to remove the slick sweat that lay in a sheen over his body. She checked his dressings and topped up his morphine and intravenous paracetamol.

The next thing she knew Jennifer was shaking her

awake. 'Huh, some night-nurse you are,' Jennifer chided, 'I bet you've been asleep all night and all morning. I suppose you want me to take over now?' It was as though the events of the night had never happened.

Beth stretched herself awake and turned to look at Colin. She rose and checked his pulse and his pupils. Satisfied that his condition had not altered while she'd dozed, she sat back down. She was stiff, her head pounding, and she was so tired that her thoughts seemed lazy and inarticulate. 'No,' she wiped spittle from the corner of her mouth. 'It'll mess up the shift pattern and I don't know if I can trust you alone with him. I'm okay for the next four hours. Go and get some fresh air. Go home, get a shower. Bring back some supplies with you, please. Clean clothes and bread for a start. I couldn't face another half-frozen butty. I'll sleep when we go into the next shift and for God's sake, Jennifer, don't be late back. I need you to pull your weight.'

'Yes, Mother,' Jennifer replied.

Jennifer was just short of an hour late coming back. Beth was so tired that she felt physically sick. She was grubby and wanted a shower before crawling into the bunk, but when she attempted to stand, she overbalanced and had to grab hold of the railing on Colin's bed to support herself. After giving Jennifer a lecture about behaving herself, she made it across the room and flopped on to the bed, dragging her sleeping bag with her. She didn't bother climbing between the sheets and she mumbled to Jennifer to be sure to wake her at eight o'clock for her shift and to wake her immediately if there was any change at all in Colin's condition. Almost before she'd finished the sentence, she was asleep. Forty minutes later Jennifer was screaming at her to wake up and shaking her roughly.

'Wake up. Come on, wake up, Beth. I think he's dying. Something's happening to him. And he's shit himself. It stinks.'

Beth came to full wakefulness instantly. She threw back the sleeping bag, got up, and shot across the room to the side of Colin's bed in a fluid movement. Colin's eyeballs were flickering from side to side beneath his closed lids. His arms and legs were jerking. The movements were small, he wasn't jumping around the bed like a marionette, but it was a classic trauma-induced seizure. His body was covered in a film of glistening sweat that smelled sweet and sickly. The sheet beneath him was soaking from the moisture seeping from his pores. The saline drip bag was emptying drop by drop into his vein via the cannula. His catheter night-bag was a third full so he was taking in and expelling fluids and the morphine feeding through his cannula was getting into his system.

Beth dropped the end of the bed and laid him flat. His finger and toe nails were blue. Something was causing circulatory problems with his blood flow. Beth knew what it was.

Jennifer hovered close.

'Move,' Beth said. 'Get back. Look, go and get me something to tie his legs down.' She had no intention of tying him, but she needed Jennifer out of her way.

Jennifer ran out of the vault.

At that moment, Colin stopped breathing.

Beth lifted one of his eyelids and then the other. His pupils were fixed and dilated. She needed a defibrillator.

His heart had to be jolted into starting by a high voltage electric shock. All she could do was administer basic cardio-pulmonary resuscitation. She screamed at the top of her voice for Jennifer to come back, she needed her to assist, but sound in the padded room wouldn't carry to Jennifer downstairs.

Beth swept his mouth with her finger to clear any vomit or debris from his airway. She checked that his tongue was in the correct position and clear of his throat. She listened to his chest for a heartbeat. Nothing. Making a fist she brought the side of her hand down into the middle of Colin's chest with all the force she could muster. Her little finger reacted painfully to the blow and she shook her hand out to ease the pain as she put her ear on his chest. There was no heartbeat. She laced her fingers and dragged her index finger along Colin's sternum until she hit the soft area in the middle of his chest where his organs were exposed from the protection of the bone. With her fingers on the wall of the sternum she put the heel of her left hand onto the skin above the organs. She rose onto her tiptoes. Locked her elbows and pumped the first fifteen cardiac compressions. Quickly, she pinched Colin's nostrils together, took a breath and, covering Colin's mouth with her own, she forced the air from her own lungs smoothly into his. She watched as his chest rose with the air filling his lungs. She put her ear to his chest to listen for a heartbeat. There was nothing. Working fifteen compressions to one exhalation, she gave Colin lifesaving CPR. She worked on him solidly, knowing that without a sudden shock to the heart, it wasn't going to leap into life. The breath she gave him, working in conjunction with the heart contractions, kept his brain fed with oxygen. She had to get his heart started. She was only slight; it needed more muscle to put pressure on the heart. She used every ounce of force that she could muster. Sweat droplets fell from her forehead onto Colin's chest. She was exhausted and panting with the exertion. She would not give up. She would not let this man die under her hands. But she was weakening. She couldn't keep going. Every muscle in her body ached. Knowing it was useless, she yelled out after every set of compressions for Jennifer to come and help her. Colin was dead, only her artificial attempts to keep his brain fed with oxygen was giving him the chance to come back. She'd had no sleep. She'd used all her stamina to keep the CPR going but she needed Jennifer to come or she was going to have to stop. In desperation, she made a fist. Putting all her frustration and need for him to live behind the blow, she brought the side of her fist down on his chest and listened for a response.

She felt the soft flicker of a heartbeat against her ear, waited, making sure more beats followed and, when they did, she dropped her head onto his chest and sobbed.

Sitting back in the chair she waited for her own heart rate to slow. She was aware of her body odour. She had sweated. Her hair hung in damp rat-tails, her armpits stank and she needed a shower and sleep. She knew that neither of those things were going to happen for her for many hours. Colin's brain was bleeding; pressure was building in his skull. He was a ticking time bomb and until that pressure was released, he could die at any second.

Colin was covered to his waist with a single sheet. After preparing a bowl to wash him Beth took the sheet. She had stolen plenty of clean bedding from the hospital in the previous weeks.

She washed his face first. He was calm. The fit had passed but she knew that another one wouldn't be long in coming and that his heart couldn't take the strain of another fit and would probably stop again. Next time she would be less likely to be able to bring him back.

She washed his torso and dried him. His lower body was a mess from the defecation. She removed his boxers and threw them to one side. Using gauze wipes she cleared away as much of the mess as she could. Putting her right hand onto his back she rolled him onto his side. She straightened his right leg and crossed it at the ankle against the left one so that he would roll fluidly and she pulled his left arm out from under his body to use as an anchor. Resting Colin against her own body, which she pressed tight up against the bed to keep him in a forward rolled position, she first rolled the soiled incontinence pad into a tube and pressed it under Colin's side. Then she did the same with the draw sheet. With Colin lying in this position she washed and dried his bottom and as much of his legs as she could reach. She prepared everything in advance while the kettle boiled and had what she would need to hand. She took a clean already-rolled draw-sheet with a continence pad in position inside it and pressed it underneath him to meet the laundry that was to be removed. She creamed his bottom and scrotum with vitamin-E aqueous cream as a barrier against bed sores and slid clean pyjama bottoms up his legs from a box that had been in the corner marked *Marc's Clothing*. Carefully, she rolled him onto his back, remembering to uncross his ankles so that the blood flow wouldn't be trapped. She checked his stats before circling to the other side of the bed and rolling him the other way. She took out the rolled and soiled bedding and smoothed out the clean draw sheet and conti-pad from underneath him, pulling his pyjamas up from this side so that his skin wouldn't be lying against rucked material. She had performed the clean-up operation with only one roll to each side, a task difficult enough with two experienced nurses.

Colin's appearance belied the severity of his condition. He looked peaceful, but that was far from the case. He needed help and he needed it now. Every second passed was a second wasted and the bleed in his brain was getting worse.

Beth cleared his bed before she picked up the soiled things on the floor. Cleanliness was paramount and everything had to be done to keep the spread of germs to a minimum. She washed her hands before separating the soiled laundry into disposable items and things to be washed. She sealed the rubbish into a bag and put the sheets into another bag. Jennifer walked in as she was finishing her task.

'Ugh,' she said covering her mouth and gagging, 'It stinks in here. Haven't you wiped his arse yet?'

'Where the fucking hell have you been?'

Jennifer held up a box with *Fetish Fantasy* written on it. 'I knew Marc had one of these in his room, but bloody hell it took some finding. I found a shoebox with these really cool photos.'

Beth was exasperated. 'What the hell is that?'

Jennifer looked at the box in her hand. 'It's a rope.

You told me to go and get something to tie him with. This is a top of the range bondage tie-up kit, I'll have you know.'

'Oh, shut up. Right, he's clean. The yellow bag of rubbish needs to go down to the bins and the stuff in the other bag has to go through the washer. Some of it may need soaking in a bucket to rinse the heavy soiling first.'

'Ugh,' said Jennifer again. 'And?'

'And what?'

'And you're telling me this, why?'

'Just go and do it will you, please?'

'No way. No way am I *ever* touching that stuff. Beth, he shit himself. I'm not cleaning up after him.'

'No, I already did that. But not before he died on me and I had to resuscitate him. He needs to go to a hospital now, Jennifer. If we don't get him to a hospital immediately his heart is going to stop and he is going to die. There's no avoiding it. He's got a bleed inside his head.'

'No hospitals, Beth. It's gone too far for that. Whatever needs doing, we do it here. Doesn't sound too bad, releasing a bit of blood from inside his head. We'll do it ourselves.'

'Are you completely mad? He needs an operation. This isn't a game of doctors and nurses. His life is hanging by a thread and any second now he's going to die.'

Jennifer looked scared.

Beth went on talking, 'Do I look like a fucking neurologist? I can't perform intricate brain surgery any more than you can. I wouldn't know where to start. And what do you expect me to use, toilet roll inners and some sticky-backed plastic? It's called a subdural haematoma. He needs the blood releasing. Brain surgery, Jennifer. He needs brain surgery now.'

'No hospital. If he dies, he dies. If we can save him, all the better. But we do it here, Beth. It's up to you. You can find out everything you need to know on the Internet. It tells you everything these days. Hey, I bet there's even a video that we can download that'll guide you. And anyway, you've been trained for this stuff. You told me that you've helped in brain operations before.'

'Yes, as a scrub nurse as part of my training many years ago. I passed metal things from a tray into the hand of a skilled surgeon and, I admit, I did have a special interest in neurology and read a few books, but that's all. Listen, you stupid child, this isn't putting a plaster on a grazed knee and waiting for it to heal. I am a nurse. I look after people *after* they've had surgery. I can't drill into somebody's head.'

'Well if he's going to die anyway, you might as well give it a go because we can't take him to hospital. It's him or us, Beth. Even if he died in hospital before he got the chance to say anything, too many questions are going to be asked. We can't take that chance.'

'But nobody has seen us with him. There's nothing to link him to us. Please, Jennifer, let's get him the help he needs. That's all we can do for him. In the time we've stood here debating it, more blood has escaped into his cranium and is increasing the pressure.'

'Oh, my God, he's not going to explode, is he?' shrieked Jennifer, looking truly horrified.

'No, not explode—just die.' Beth shook her head, exasperated, and Jennifer let out her breath in an audible rush.

'If he's going to die anyway, there's no harm in trying, is there? What do you need to do? I'll help. Maybe the bleeding will stop and he'll get better without having to cut his head open.'

'No, there's no doubt about it, without releasing the pressure from his brain he is going to die. Even if I had the skills to do this, which I don't, I haven't got any of the monitoring equipment. It's like spinning a globe, closing your eyes and pointing. You might be aiming for Africa but you're more likely to land in the sea. I need a... oh, it's a probe that you insert inside his head with a tiny camera on the end. It shows you where the pressure has built and where you need to put a shunt.'

'Oh, is that all? Well, go into work and nick one.'

'Jennifer. You have no idea. I don't have access to the operating theatres. They are kept sterile. They have cameras everywhere. And the theatres are on round-the-clock operating schedules. It would be impossible. I'd need a surgical drill, shunts, oh the list is endless. You're asking the impossible.'

'Well, what about in the olden days? They didn't have little cameras and all that then, did they?' Jennifer interjected in triumph. 'Tell you what, just imagine something. Right. Imagine Colin was your old man, yeah? You've been out climbing mountains in the snow, somewhere snowy and cold, right. Imagine that he falls over and hits his head and then there's a blizzard and you only just manage to get him back to your remote log cabin up the mountain. The telephone's dead so you can't get help but you have a tool box under the sink and he needs this operation or he's going to die. What would you do, just sit there?'

'Just shut up, will you?'

'Beth, it's a serious question. Come on, what would you do?'

Beth sighed. 'Of course, I'd try to save him, but that's different. We aren't snowed in and we can get Colin to the hospital and into professional hands.'

'No, we can't. Come on, what do we need and I'll get it ready?'

'Jennifer, it's impossible. I wouldn't know where to drill, or what size hole to make. What if I drilled into his skull on one side of his head to find that the pressure build was at the other? What then?'

'Then you drill another hole at the other bloody side, of course. He might leak like a colander, but what the hell if it saves him? Now, are we going to stand here talking while he dies—or are we going to try and save his life?'

Beth couldn't believe what she was about to do as they boiled pans of water, sterilising, as best they could, the things they had collected to use on Colin's makeshift brain surgery. She thought about waiting until Jennifer was distracted and making a call to the emergency service. She knew that's what she should do. But Jennifer was right. It had gone too far and would bring about the downfall of them. They couldn't move him. The ambulance team would have to come right up to the vault. The likelihood that Colin was going to die was great anyway, with or without professional help. Self-preservation kicked in hard and she was too far down the slippery slope to get him the help he needed to live. She was left with two choices. She could sit and watch him die – she estimated that would happen within hours. Or she could make a feeble attempt to save him and probably watch him die anyway. She had to try. She spent the next four hours poring over Jennifer's laptop, searching neurology papers by eminent surgeons and gleaning every bit of information that she thought might guide her.

Colin lay on his stomach. They had covered his head in swabs to absorb any lost fluids and had a large piece of cloth with a hole cut into the centre placed in position over the area where the hole would be drilled. Beth's hands shook and she gripped the drill tighter to stem the shaking. One slip and Colin was history. Jennifer stood beside Beth looking terrified but still craning her neck to better see what was going on. Beth put the drill in position, lining the bit against the centre of the cross that she marked on the back of Colin's skull. She told herself this was lunacy and made the first turn on the old-fashioned handle to connect the drill bit with Colin's skull.

Chapter Twenty-Two

Maggie rounded the corner of Acacia Drive onto Maple Avenue when she saw Jennifer coming out of Beth's house with a rucksack. She was on foot and acting on impulse, she pulled into the cover of an overhanging lilac tree.

Jennifer appeared to be leaving—as in leaving Beth's house for good, maybe even leaving the country. Hell, thought Maggie, she could leave the bloody planet as far as she was concerned. With a bit of luck, she was going forever. Hopefully Beth had come to her senses and thrown the freeloading freak out. She didn't look as though she was nipping to the shop for a pint of milk. Her backpack was bulging and she had a carrier bag in each hand. The rucksack appeared to be heavy because she readjusted it twice so that it sat more comfortably on her shoulders and she pulled on the two pieces of webbing strap fitting it on her slender frame. She went down the hill at an unhurried pace.

When Jennifer had gone far enough down the road for Maggie not to be noticed, she walked passed the two houses that would take her to Beth's gate. She opened it quietly even though Jennifer was too far away to hear it and slipped inside. She knocked on the front door three times, then twice more when she didn't get an answer. She bent over, flipped open the letterbox and whisper-shouted, 'Beth. Beth, are you in there?'

She was annoyed when Beth wasn't at home. Checking on Jennifer's progress from the front garden and seeing that she was nearly out of sight at the corner of Maple and starting up the hill of Central Drive, Maggie turned to the living room window and looked inside. The house was neat and tidy. The TV was off, the door closed. There was nobody home.

Beth may well have been at work and Maggie was disappointed that she didn't get the chance to confront her about the lies she'd told. She needed to get through to her friend. With the wind taken out of her sails, she was flummoxed what to do next. If Jennifer was going any distance, the quickest way into town, and indeed out of Ulverston, was down Birkett Drive. She couldn't walk far with all that baggage and Birkett was on the bus route. Why hadn't she gone that way and waited at the bus stop? Maggie followed her. Jennifer was out of sight but she'd seen her turn onto Central Drive. She crossed the road where there was more cover and followed the route that Jennifer took. When she rounded the first bend on Central Drive she saw Jennifer struggling up the hill and hung back, keeping close to the walls and trees so that if Jennifer looked back she wouldn't see her.

At the top of the hill, she peered around the corner. The distance between them wasn't so great and Jennifer wasn't far ahead. Jennifer never looked back until she got to the driveway of the big house on the corner of Rake Lane where she glanced behind her and to either side before going through the gate. Her movements were furtive and Maggie knew somebody up to no good when she saw it.

What the hell was she up to? That was where Beth said that flash git she met at the speed dating lived. Was there a connection between him and Jennifer? The only link she was aware of was between him and Beth. Maybe Beth had been seeing him all this time and she had thrust the lovely Phantom on him, too. Maggie couldn't help smiling; she couldn't see what's-his-face and Goth girl hitting it off.

Without the faintest idea of what she would say if she was caught snooping Maggie followed Jennifer up the drive. The grounds were overgrown, lush with trees and vegetation. She was surprised at the neglect. Remembering the bloke who lived here she'd have expected manicured lawns, neatly pruned bushes and doctor-attended trees. She remembered his name. Marc—with a C—He was all show, more front than Brenda Bigtits from number thirty-two.

Jennifer let herself in the front door with a key.

Nothing in this jigsaw fit.

Bolder, Maggie circled the house hoping to look through windows and spy through doors. Every door was solid and every window had closed horizontal blinds and any chinks were covered by heavy lined curtains. This Marc fella valued his privacy above natural sunlight. Maggie wondered if he was a direct descendent of Edward Cullen and spent his days in the dark.

Was Beth in the house, too? Should she knock and ask to speak to her? Having come here, that would be the logical thing to do, but she stopped herself. Instinctively, she knew that something was wrong. She'd known for weeks that Beth was in trouble. It tied into Jennifer somehow, but where did Marc fit into it? Maggie tried to rationalise what was stopping her from marching up to the front door, hammering on it with a taking-no-prisoners attitude, and demanding to speak to Beth. She'd never been a shrinking violet. The feeling she had was one of foreboding.

She had too many questions to let it drop. She would keep trying Beth at home until she caught her in—hopefully alone. But either way, she couldn't let go. She felt deflated as she left the grounds of the house and almost turned back, going against her instinct to proceed with caution. Then she remembered that Jess had a school friend across the road and a few doors down from Marc's house. The Reid family home was a small detached bungalow, an ordinary house, nothing anywhere near as grand as the big house on the corner. Sophie had been to Maggie's house for sleepovers and Maggie was friendly with her mum, Helen. She was still trying to formulate a valid reason for being there when she walked up the neat path and knocked on the door.

A man answered, presumably Helen's husband. 'Yes?' he asked, smiling.

'Oh, hiya. Is Helen in, please?'

'Ah… Yes.' He paused.

'It's Maggie. Maggie Johnson.'

'I'll just get her.' He smiled again and left the door ajar. She heard him walking towards the back of the house and said in a hushed tone, 'It's somebody called Maggie for you.'

'Who?' Helen sounded irritated.

'Maggie somebody-or-other.'

'What does she want?'

'I don't know, go and bloody ask her.'

Maggie heard footsteps coming up the hallway and the door was opened by Helen, drying her hands on a tea-towel. 'Oh, Maggie! Hello. What's up?'

'Hiya, Helen. I was just out for a walk and as I was passing your house anyway, I thought I'd give you a knock to ask about the girl's homework. Thing is, Jess keeps telling me that she hasn't got any and it seems unlikely. I wondered if Sophie has been bringing much home. You know how they get at this age.'

Helen looked bemused. 'Um, Sophie's out at the moment, so I don't know how much help I can be. I think she was doing a geography assignment last night, but I don't know if she's in the same geography group as your Jess. Do you want to come in a sec and I'll have a look in her schoolbag for you?'

'Oh, that'd be great, thank you.' She followed Helen down the hall and into a spacious and spotlessly tidy lounge. 'Hope it's no trouble.'

'Um, can I get you a cup of tea, or anything?' Helen asked, the offer sounded as though it was made reluctantly but it would have been rude not to have done so.

'A coffee would be great thanks,' Maggie replied. She wanted a cig, too, after trudging up that hill, but it didn't look like the kind of house where she'd be welcome to spark up in the lounge. Helen made coffee and ran upstairs to get her daughter's schoolbag. Maggie felt guilty about the invasion of privacy; Jess would go mad if her mother rooted through her possessions.

They talked about schoolwork and their daughters in general and then Maggie went in for the kill. 'I was looking at the big house on the corner. They've done a lot of work on it, haven't they? It's beautiful.'

'Yes,' Helen told her, 'It's been gutted inside and had a complete refurbishment. It was an old people's home for a while, you know, but this new owner has taken it back to a family house. I haven't been in it, of course, but I believe he's made a good job of it.'

'It's nice that it's a proper home again.' She kept her voice level to not show too much interest. 'I remember when I was a kid, two old ladies had it. Sisters I think. They were a creepy old pair. Who has it now? Do you know?'

'Not really. Some new people from out of town. Leeds. I think he's called Mister Robinson. I seem to remember that name from somewhere but don't quote me on it. I wouldn't be surprised if he's bought it to sell on. It's too big for just him and his daughter. Well, at least I think it's his daughter. I've seen them once or twice. Keep themselves to themselves. He's not the sociable type. I haven't seen either of them about for a while and I noticed the garden needs doing. A good lawn really ought to be kept trim don't you think? Maybe he's moved onto his next project and put it on the market already but he really should get somebody in to keep on top of the garden. It will make a big difference to the value.' She paused, her eyes going to the window as though she could see the old house from where she sat.

Maggie saw that the woman was itching to say more. 'Well, I expect they're nice people, having a house like that.'

'Actually,' said Helen, 'now you come to mention it, there was a rumour floating about, you know what this place is like.'

'Oh?'

'I'm not sure if there's any truth to it. It's all very

vague. You know what Henry Daly's like. Half-truths and lies, as my Mum would say. Apparently, there was a scandal and Mister Robinson had to leave Leeds in a hurry.'

'I wonder what happened,' Maggie said.

'From what I could gather at the time, I think the police were still wondering that, too.'

'Oh, that's awful. Do you know what it was about?'

Helen shrugged and stared into her mug. 'I think it was something to do with money, bad money if you know what I mean, dodgy dealings—that kind of thing. It's nothing to worry about, you can still let Jess come around here. Besides, the Community Action Group probed a bit at the time and none of us have had any problems with him.'

'Oh, I'm sure it's nothing more than a parking ticket.' Maggie agreed,' You know how people exaggerate.'

After that, Maggie steered the conversation onto different subjects. She'd wanted to ask about Marc in the middle of a range of subjects so that it wouldn't seem out of place. She prolonged her coffee for another five minutes and she bet that Helen was as relieved as she was when she stood up to leave. She wondered if Marc was Phantom's father, surely, he was too young. And if Phantom was living with Beth on the strength of one date with Marc, where was he now? If he'd gone away on business, he'd have put measures in place for the care of his daughter. Maggie had no idea what Beth had got herself involved with, but she knew with every fibre of her being, that it wasn't good.

Back at home she checked the phone book under the name of M. Robinson. There was no listing for Rake

Lane. She went onto the internet and looked up Robinson on the electoral roll. She drew a blank. However, the electoral roll threw up eleven Mark Robinsons in Leeds over the last five years—but only two Marc Robinsons with a C. Maggie took down the addresses.

She went to her search engine and typed 'Marc Robinson, phone number, Leeds.' Then a thought occurred to her, based on something Helen said. She deleted what she had typed and replaced it with 'Marc Robinson: Arrested.' A black man of that name, in America, had been arrested for shop lifting. There were several listings of this story but nothing else on anybody with the name Marc Robinson under any crime. He wasn't on the electoral roll. Google and Bing had no record of him. She kept refining her search terms, swapping as many relevant words and phrases as she could think of. She found nothing; it was as though the man had never existed. She did a search on 'Jennifer Robinson' and 'Marc and Jennifer Robinson', all with the same result: nothing. What were they running from? Maggie was determined to find out.

The next morning, Graham said she was mad. He said that if she wanted to know who they are and what they're about so badly, she should go and ask them instead of tearing off halfway across the country on a wild goose chase. He moaned that, for what his opinion was worth, she should keep out of it and mind her own sodding business. Maggie was stuffing things into her bag for the journey, but took the time to tell him that his opinion was superfluous and that she'd made up her mind. 'Come with me, if you like. It's a lovely day and we'll be back in time for the kids coming out of school.'

'What do I want to go to bloody Leeds for? The Bradford Bulls are on the telly and they are way better than Leeds.'

'Fine, I'll drop you in the centre of Bradford on the way down—and leave you there.'

Graham rolled his eyes, huffed, and said, 'I'll stay here and keep the beers company, cheers.'

'Drinking before ten? You're turning into your father.'

Graham laughed. 'You know I'm joking. The day we have enough money to keep beers in the fridge, is the day I get pissed at ten o'clock in the morning.'

Maggie kissed him, hoisted her bag, and left him to the beer-less fridge.

She enjoyed the three-hour drive and was determined to get to the bottom of whatever was going on with Beth. When she found the correct area on the outskirts of Leeds, the first house that she pulled up outside was a mid-terrace two-up two-down. She was lucky that the door was opened on her first knock. The man who answered was beyond middle age and walked with a limp. He was happy to chat and told her that he'd lived in the house three years. His brow furrowed in thought as he tried to recall the name of the previous occupant. 'No, love, no. It's gone. Doubt I could say it even if I could remember. Darkie, he was. Had one of them nappies round his head and wore a long dress. I couldn't tell you how long he lived here.'

The second address was more promising. It was a large detached town house with a decent sized garden front and rear and enough parking for three cars, at the back of Roundhay Park. It wasn't as grand as the Ulverston house, but would fit well with the profile she was compiling on Marc. She knocked but there was no answer. It was lunchtime. People would be working. She'd told Graham she'd be back in time for the kids coming in from school and had left him to pick up Barry at lunchtime. She hoped that she wouldn't have to wait until the evening to get somebody in, Graham wouldn't be pleased.

A couple of blocks down, on the same street as the house, was a pretty cafe. She went in and ordered a meat and potato pie, chips, peas and onion gravy with two slices of bread and butter, a cup of coffee and a humongous piece of chocolate cake served with double cream. The cafe was small with five tables that comfortably fit two people each and a couple of four-seater tables at one end. Only one table was occupied and the elderly proprietor wasn't busy. Maggie got into conversation with her. Phyllis made all her own cakes and pastries and everything was cooked from scratch on the premises. Maggie complimented the lady on her baking and after the other couple left, their table had been cleared and the crockery used had been washed and put away, the lady came back into the dining area to chat some more. Maggie being Maggie, soon had the old lady narrating her life story and persuaded her to bring a coffee over and join her.

'So, what brings you here, love? We haven't seen you about before.'

'Oh, I'm just here for the day, Phyllis. Hoping to look up a cousin from years ago but I haven't had a lot of luck so far. We were close as kids, but you know how it is, families separate and nobody asks the kids what they want.'

Sensing a bit of gossip, Phyllis pulled her chair in closer. 'What was she called? If she lives around here, there's a good chance we might know her. Me and my Arthur, we get most of the locals in for their breakfastses and a bit of a chat.'

Breakfastses, thought Maggie, what the fuck? But this was more like it. She might have struck gold. With a bit of luck, she'd stumbled on the perfect talking history book. 'It's a he, actually. Marc,' she told the woman. 'Marc Robinson. I've got an address for him as living at number fifty-three.'

Phyllis drummed her fingers on the table in thought and then used them to count down the numbers of houses on the street. Her eyes opened wider when she hit on the correct house and then she looked dejected. 'No, no love, the Bankseses live at number fifty-three. Lovely woman, Janet Banks is. Just had another baby; that's her third and him only working on the... Oh, oh, hang on though—yes, Robinson, of course, him and the lass. He had to look after his sister, you know. Sad story. Parents both killed in a car accident, but you being family and all, you'll know about all that. I never took to him, personally. Never came in here. Too grand for the likes of us. But oh my, that young'un; he had his hands full with that one. But they left here about two year ago now, maybe more. It was Sharon *I* felt sorry for.' Her eyes clouded with a faraway look as she remembered.

Maggie was excited. 'Sharon?'

'Yes, his girlfriend, Sharon. Ooh, let's think now—Sharon. Cabot—that was it. Sharon Cabot. What a lovely lass she was. Used to come in here reg'lar. Think she liked to get out of the house sometimes, you know. That little'un was hard work and her rambling round in the house on her own all day, I think she liked a bit of company. Oh, I liked Sharon, was sorry to see her go.'

Phyllis didn't need much encouragement to continue.

'Well, they came here when little Jennifer was about ten or eleven. Came from Coventry, I think. Yes, Shaz used to go back to visit her folks there sometimes. She wasn't here long. Homesick was part of it. She missed her friends. He kept her pretty isolated. Don't mean to speak ill of your relatives, love, but I think he was a bit of a bugger with her—if you know what I mean. Anyways, one thing and another, and then one day she comes in all teary and said that she was leaving him and had to get away. We kept in contact with a Christmas card and a couple of textses for a couple of years and then lost touch as you do. You know how it is.

'And then they left, too, there was some talk of the police looking to talk to him about something or other, nobody really knew what, went up north somewhere, and that was that. The Bankseses moved in. Mind they've had their troubles, too. Jonathan their lad, he got run over last year, was in a bad way. Then Don was made redundant and had to take any job he could find. We gave him a couple shifts here, washing dishes till he was back on his feet, poor soul. Big house to keep up, that one. Can't be easy for them.'

Maggie hardly dared ask, 'I don't suppose you've got a forwarding address for Sharon, have you?' She quickly amended herself, 'And one for Marc and little Jennifer too, of course, if you have it, please.'

'Well definitely not for him, no offence,' she sniffed

her distain. 'Like I said, I didn't have a lot of time for the bloke. As for her, the cheeky tyke, I was heart glad to see the back of her. But I do believe I've got Sharon's address in my book. You can have that if you like. Of course, I don't know if she's still there, haven't heard from her in, well, it must be three years now. If you'll mind the café for me, I'll nip upstairs to get it, but the schools will be kicking out soon and I'll have my mid-afternoon rush so will have to get on.' She left to get the address book, taking Maggie's used plates and their cups with her and leaving them in the kitchen area. Maggie liked Phyllis and mused at her trust in leaving her till unattended to help a stranger and almost gave her a warning about being so outwardly friendly with newcomers, she'd hate to think of the old lass being taken advantage of. When she came back, Phyllis handed over the address and asked Maggie to pass on her regards to Sharon. In return, Maggie promised to go back one day and 'bring the family.' Despite Phyllis' protestations she left her a ten-pound tip and thanked her for all her help. As she left, she saw Phyllis stuffing the tenner into the charity box on the counter.

Maggie had her next clue in the paper trail and knew her next move but she still wanted to try the unoccupied house again to see if she could get any further information. A lady answered this time and she heard a baby crying in the background. Janet Banks confirmed that somebody called Robinson had lived there before her, but she couldn't tell her much else. She said that nobody had ever come to collect the mail and that eventually they had put an elastic band around it and had given it back to the postman.

The only interesting thing that Janet had to add was that about three months after they had moved in, a policeman came looking for Marc. She hadn't been able to give him a forwarding address because the Robinsons hadn't left one. Maggie thanked her and left.

On the phone, Graham was exasperated. 'You what?' he yelled down the receiver, almost perforating Maggie's ear drum. 'I can't take the night off, just like that.'

'Oh, please, Graham. Please. Do this one little thing for me and I'll wear the French maid's outfit and make you very pleased that you did.' She could sense him relenting.

'You can't get around me like that.' She knew that she could. 'Okay. One night. I mean it, Maggie. You'd better be home tomorrow; this isn't fair on me, or the kids. You have responsibilities, you know—and don't spend too much.'

'Love you, Squishy.' Maggie was smiling when she hung up.

Chapter Twenty-Three

Beth gave Colin as much sedative and painkiller as she dared. She shaved a small area of his scalp and used a sharp craft knife, the closest thing to a scalpel that they'd found, to separate a five inch flap of his scalp. She'd staunched the blood flow by cauterising the capillaries in the open flaps of skin and applying a sterile gel to the wound to keep the area clean. As she turned the handle, the drill bit ground ineffectually on Colin's skull for the first couple of turns. She had no idea how much he'd bleed and they had no transfusable blood to hand to give him should he need it. The job was made harder because the drill she was using was an old-fashioned hand drill. They didn't have an electric one because Jennifer hadn't been able to find the key to Marc's tool cupboard and they had to make do with what they could find in the cellar. Beth tried not to think too hard about the implications of infection if their less than adequate sterilising procedure proved futile. The drill bit on the third turn of the handle and she was able to go faster in an attempt to get the job done quickly before either she fainted, or Colin died. Getting through the dense bone of the skull was hard and took more muscle than she'd expected and she was worried that she'd have to give up, leaving him with a Chinese-chequer board hole in his skull. 'Maggie always called him a thick-headed bugger,' she said with a mirthless laugh. She picked up more speed and was alarmed to see smoke coming off the bone – or was it bone dust? She couldn't be sure.

'Fuck me, he's setting on fire,' Jennifer said. It seemed she was intent on Colin either exploding from the head or going up in a blaze of flames.

'No, he's not, it's only bone dust,' Beth placated her, though she wasn't sure herself. Colin moaned and his legs stiffened, testament to the fact that even when unconscious, people can suffer extremes of pain. Beth hated what she was doing to him, and hated even more what she'd already done. When the bone gave way to the soft membranes beneath, it went suddenly. The drill lurched forward inside Colin's head and Beth panicked that she'd drilled right into his brain. She tried to pull the drill backwards but it wouldn't come.

'Shit. Shit, it's stuck,' she screamed. 'I can't get it out.' This came out in a high-pitched screech as fear overtook her.

'Go backwards.'

'What?' In her terror, she wondered if Jennifer meant that she should turn around.

'Drill backwards. I think you have to turn the handle the other way to release it.'

Beth did as Jennifer suggested and the drill came away from Colin's head. She had used an eight-millimetre drill bit but there was surprisingly little blood. A thick, clear serum leaked from the hole when the drill was removed. 'Swab it,' she ordered. And Jennifer cleaned the area around the hole with some Medi-Wipes doused in iodine. Then she leaned forward and peered into the hole.

'Ugh, is that his brain?'

'No, it's the protective membranes that stop the brain from rattling around in his head.' Before Beth could stop her, she took her index finger and poked it inside the hole.

'What the hell are you doing? You're going to kill him,' Beth screamed. She pulled Jennifer's arm away, swung her round and hit her hard across the face with a back-handed blow that split Jennifer's lip. Beth was incensed and screamed in Jennifer's face as Jennifer backed away from her. 'You've contaminated my gloves now. What are you playing at? Is this just a game to you?' Beth peeled off the latex gloves and put on another pair while trying her best not to contaminate the outside of them from the touch of her skin, before turning back to Colin. She was so enraged that she picked up one of the two bottles of iodine and threw it at Jennifer. It hit her on the side of her arm and she cried out in pain and fear. Beth was still ranting, she'd moved onto the subject of Colin's dignity and the liberties that Jennifer took with it.

Jennifer crouched against the door. She had her hand up rubbing the side of her face that was red and already coming up in welts from the force of the back of Beth's fist. Her tongue licked tentatively at the rivulet of blood trickling from her split-lip. Her eyes brimmed with tears. 'I only wanted to know what a brain feels like,' she whimpered. 'You said he's probably going to die anyway, so what does it matter?'

'Get out. I can do this better on my own. You're a liability.' She heard the door close as Jennifer left.

Before doing anything else, Beth closed her eyes and took several deep breaths to steady herself. She hoped that the build-up of fluid causing the pressure was in one of the three layers of membranes on the outside of the brain and not in the brain itself. She was working blind and had no clue as to the true diagnosis. She took a fine reed catheter tube from the tray beside her and focused to quell her shaking. This was the moment of truth. She didn't know if the chiselled reed on the end of the tube would be strong enough to slice through the membranes or if it would buckle and bend. The tubing was fine, as thin as a piece of cotton. She took hold of the tube and fed it through the hole, adding more pressure when she came up against the resistance of the tissue underneath. She inserted the tube to a depth of two inches then took the other end, lowered it so that the fluid would flow downwards and put the end in a measuring jug. She could have cried with joy when she saw fluid rise up the tubing and empty in an almost clear, slightly thicker than water, trickle. There wasn't much, less than three ounces but she hoped that it was the cause of the fits. She took a moment to compose herself and checked his stats. His pulse was feeble but that would be partly due to the levels of sedative keeping his bodily functions slow. His pupils were reacting to the light and that was the vital she was most interested in. On first examination, it didn't look as though she'd caused further brain damage. He'd need a bone graft to fill the hole in his head with fresh bone shards that would knit together to make a new piece of skull. For now, all she could do was use the pieces of bone dust that came away as she worked and the bone shards from the initial wound. She fixed them to a thin piece of dissolvable gauze to keep them in place and packed it around the hole in Colin's head. She sutured the flaps of his scalp with tiny stitches that would dissolve in six weeks. She left the drainage tube in, between two stitches so that it would continue to drain any fluid from around his brain. She washed the area of his scalp in iodine and dressed the wound. And she could do no more. It was up to Colin now.

After clearing up, she poured herself a cup of coffee from the flask that Jennifer had replenished and sat back in the uncomfortable chair to continue her vigil. She was wired, her body surging with adrenaline and she became her alter-ego, the superhero, it was the same surge of power that she'd had when she had hit Colin over the head with the rock. She liked it.

After taking a few moments to revel in what she'd achieved, she went in search of Jennifer. She hadn't been in Jennifer's room before. She'd had no reason to, so she knocked on several doors before she found the right one.

'Go to hell.' Jennifer was sulking and Beth couldn't help but smile. She turned the handle on the door. It wasn't locked so she pushed it open and went inside. The room was beautiful. There was no hint of Goth and it was a grown-up and sophisticated bedroom for a teenager, complete with a four-poster bed and an open door in the far corner of the room that Beth could see led to en-suite facilities. She guessed that the room had been designed to Marc's specifications and taste. Jennifer sprawled on the big bed and was dwarfed by frills and encased in goose-feathers. Beth didn't know what to say. She looked down at her hands the fingers twisting and entwining, hardly the actions of a superhero. Her hands were streaked with blood and she felt that neither she nor they belonged in this opulent room. 'He seems to be okay, he's hanging in there' she ventured, 'well, as well as can be expected, as they say,' she ended with a chuckle.

'Stupid bastard, it would be better if he'd died.'

Beth sat on the edge of Jennifer's bed, 'Better for whom?'

'Did I say you could sit down?'

'Did I say I wouldn't hit you again if you don't snap out of it?'

'Why are you being so nasty to me?' Jennifer's tone was whiny, 'what have I ever done to you?' Beth felt something roll and shift in her stomach, it rose, it was coming out and Beth had no idea until it left her mouth if it was going to be vomit, or a barrage of verbal rage and ranting that may never stop. It was neither. She laughed until she was hysterical. She fell onto her back and brought her knees up onto her chest and she laughed until tears rolled down her cheeks and dropped onto the bed beside her. She laughed until she was separately aware of every rib in her rack, each one ached independently. Jennifer was laughing too, nervously at first, not sure what was happening, but Beth's cackle was infectious and soon Jennifer was laughing hard too. Beth sat up to speak to her, but she was laughing so hard that she could only spray spittle towards Jennifer. It was her third attempt at speech before she could half-coherently mutter, 'What have you ever done to me? Oh Phantom, where do I ever begin to tell you.'

'Freak.'

Nice room,' Beth stated, trying to keep Jennifer from sinking back into her sulk. She looked around, taking in the chintz and knick-knacks. She looked at everything and stopped at the shrivelled man's finger sitting on the bedside table beside her. Jennifer kept the keepsake three inches from where her head lay when she slept that first night. The finger was black, the nail the colour of aged parchment. Beth was amazed that she was neither surprised nor repulsed. She had seen so much, been through so much, that she was desensitized to this horror to the point of indifference.

'You kept it then,' she said, picking up the dry finger and turning it in her hand as though it was a tiny ornament she was lifting from the girl's bedside. She picked up a dead man's finger without flinching, or giving thought to how much she'd changed in six months. 'And you have the nerve to call me a freak. You said that you had a reason for hacking it off. Why'd you do it?' Her tone was curious; there wasn't a hint of revulsion or disdain. She just wanted to know why Jennifer had decided to hack off the finger.

'Ah see, I still have secrets. The question is, do I want to share them with you?' her tone was teasing. She was playing in true Jennifer style. 'Oh, go on then, come with me and I'll show you. Prepare to be amazed.' She snatched the finger out of Beth's hand, flung herself off the bed and left the room in a hurry, leaving Beth to follow in her wake. She went into the next bedroom and Beth knew on entering that it was Marc's room. Although it had no smell other than that of a musty room that hadn't been used in a while, it reeked of Marc. His personality and character was stamped into every inch of it.

'Two bathrooms.' Jennifer pointed in turn to two doors leading off the bedroom. 'That one's his. His lair, full of man-stuff and shit. And that one, is... ours... the same one that's in my room, interconnecting doors, easy access, I'll let you work out why. He used to hurt me...there...' She looked down to indicate her private place. 'I took his finger for two reasons, the first is that he's going to be doing no more girl-caving with that digit—not in this life or the next. And the second...' Like so often before, her mood changed in an instant, '...come on, this is what I want to show you.' She was excited. Beth wasn't surprised when she rolled part of the wall out of the way with a secret mechanism. She only wondered how many other secret rooms and compartments were hidden in this crazy house of secrets. The cavity exposed a wall safe. It wasn't locked and Jennifer opened the door simply by turning the handle. She stood back to allow Beth to stand in front of the safe. She had never seen so much money in her life.

'Touch it if you like, go on, pick it up and throw it over your head like they do on telly.' Jennifer's voice quivered with pride. 'It's mine now, mine. My inheritance if you like, and all thanks to you.'

'I've never seen so much money.' Beth reached in and picked up a wad the weight and thickness of a house brick. 'How much is there?'

'Enough.'

'More than enough,' said Beth in a reverent whisper. 'If Colin gets better we can let him go and then leave. She continued. We can go...anywhere. This money can save us, maybe. There's enough here to buy us passage to anywhere in the world. New identities. New lives. There may be a way out of this after all, Jennifer. We might be all right.'

'Yeah, yeah. God, you're boring me now. Have you

any idea how predictable you are. You have no vision Beth. You go for the obvious, every fucking time.'

'Well what are you going to do with it then, Miss Fucking Superior, give it to the starving children of Africa?'

'I don't know yet, but it's going to be something spectacular.'

Beth's voice was droll, 'I don't doubt that for a second. But I don't get it. Where does Marc's finger come into it?' Jennifer took the wad of money from her hand and put it back in the safe closing the door after her and replacing the wall.

'Haven't you worked that out? Beth, for a bright woman you can be so thick. It's disappointing because it doesn't work anymore so I've had to permanently deactivate the lock. I only had to open it with the finger once and could disengage the locking mechanism from the inside. It's a good job I got to it the same night he died. The bloody finger all shrivelled up on me in less than twenty-four hours and would have been useless. Fingerprint recognition,' she explained to Beth's blank expression and saw the penny drop. 'I needed big bro's fingerprint to open the safe. I didn't know if it would work without a life supply, so to speak, but it worked a treat. Otherwise all this lovely lolly would have been lost forever.'

Beth found something to be shocked by. Within an hour or so of his death, Jennifer had taken a knife and removed her dead brother's finger with her mind only on one thing, the money locked away in the safe out of her reach. 'You took his finger for money. That's disgusting.'

Jennifer laughed, 'Think yourself lucky the safe isn't activated by retinal recognition or it would have been his eyes—both of them.'

Beth went back to check on Colin, struggling to get that image out of her mind.

For the next three days Colin remained unconscious. His temperature fluctuated between dangerous highs and acceptable levels. His blood pressure was low. His pulse was often erratic. They watched over him day and night. Jennifer did few of her shifts and bored easily. Beth took the brunt of the workload but she got time to shower and enough sleep and food to sustain her.

On the third night after having his skull drilled, and five days after being kidnapped, Colin stirred. Beth was asleep and woke when Jennifer shook her, yelling at her to wake up. 'Quick, quick, he's waking up. He's waking up.' She shouted excitedly.

Beth was at his bedside in a second, Jennifer at the other side. Colin was moaning and twitching. His hand was moving on the quilt beside him. He brought it up to his face and swept his cheek. His eyes flickered open and then closed again. He mumbled something incoherent, possibly not even formulated words, just sounds borne either of pain or confusion, probably both. And then his body relaxed and he was unconscious again.

'Is that it?' Jennifer said, unimpressed. 'Is that all he's going to do?'

'Well what do you want him to do, three verses of the halleluiah chorus and the can-can? Yes, that's probably your lot for now, but its great progress. It's the first time that I've felt that he might pull through, but we've still got a long way to go until he's in the clear. And even if he does wake up properly, we don't know what state he's going to be in.'

'But he didn't say anything.'

Beth grinned, 'I would say that's a blessing, wouldn't you? Do you think you're going to like what he's got to say when he does come round?'

'You said "when,"' said Jennifer. 'Cool.'

'Fingers crossed, eh?'

Colin didn't move again for another fifteen hours. After the first time he'd shown signs of waking, Beth had lowered the dosage of morphine to allow him to wake naturally. He was only on a dose high enough to control his pain and keep him very lightly sedated. Nothing artificial was preventing him from waking. The second time he stirred was similar to the time before. He woke four times over the next five hours, each time for less than a minute. He never said anything and only made noises. While he was unconscious he was moving, thrashing sometimes. Beth would cool his forehead with a cool flannel and wet the inside of his mouth with lemon swabs. She talked to him, soothingly, repeating his name and telling him it was going to be all right. He grabbed the swabs with his mouth and sucked on them. She introduced ice cubes and then tiny sips of water. He was swallowing involuntarily – another huge step towards the possibility of normal brain function. The next day, she spooned thin soup into his mouth and, though he gave no indication that he was awake, he'd take it. The next time he woke up, he retched violently and brought back all the soup he'd taken. It was the medication, morphine. She injected him with an anti-emetic. Jennifer didn't have the knowledge to ask her to steal this, but the two went together and after stealing the Morphine, she'd figured that somebody would need an anti-emetic too. His fever was coming down and he seemed calmer in his sleep. He was moving less but more deliberately and his vital signs were stronger.

She hadn't been to work, hadn't called them. She had simply dropped off the planet. Work would have been ringing her; they'd need some explanation of her absence. She had none to give them. She had no intention of ever going back. She wasn't worthy of her profession.

She had saved Colin's life, after almost taking it from him. With every passing hour, Beth was more hopeful that he was going to make it. At the same time, she grew more terrified of what the outcome would be if he did.

Chapter Twenty-Four

Maggie drove from her investigations in Leeds to Coventry, arriving at teatime. She booked into a bed and breakfast and stopped at a garage for a brew, a sandwich, and enough chocolate to sustain her for a few hours, she decided that the people of Coventry sell rancid coffee and talk funny. It took her some time, and much misdirection, to find the flat where Sharon Cabot lived. She hardly dared hope that anybody would be in and rang the doorbell without being aware that she was holding her breath. If she could talk to this Cabot woman, she might shed light on the situation; she'd lived with the Robinsons. Finding out that Jennifer was Marc's sister—and not his daughter—made more sense, but it still didn't feel right. There was more to be discovered.

'Oh, hello. I'm sorry to bother you but are you Sharon? Sharon Cabot? My name's Maggie Johnson.'

'Yes?'

'Oh heck, now that I'm here, I'm not sure where to start. I really need to talk to you. I have this friend, you see, and she's in trouble. Phyllis from the café in Leeds sent me to you.' The young woman looked blank. 'Damn, I'm waffling. I always do when I'm nervous. Do you think I could come in please and I'll tell you what this is all about?'

The inquisitive smile left the woman's face and she frowned. 'I'm sorry, I don't mean to be rude, but who are you? Could you tell me what this is about first, please? I'm rather busy...'she tailed off.

Maggie would rather have laid her cards out inside the flat, and preferably over a decent cuppa, she knew that if somebody rocked up on her doorstep asking questions about her former partners, she'd tell them to mind their own business and get stuffed. 'Actually, I want to ask you about Marc Robinson, I believe you used to live with him in Leeds?'

Maggie watched her reaction. Sharon gasped and her knuckles went white as she clutched the door more firmly. 'That's a long time ago. I'm sorry. I don't know what this is about, but I don't want to talk about him. I've moved on. She went to close the door in Maggie's face and then stopped. 'Oh God, he doesn't know where I am, does he? Is he with you?' The colour left her face and she looked terrified.

'No, no it's okay, he doesn't know anything about this, and I'm not about to tell him. Look love, your reaction has just terrified me. I know somebody who could be in a lot of trouble, and if you can tell me anything at all that might help my friend, I'd be very grateful. She's the nicest person I know. You'd like her, everybody does. See, there I go waffling again, please talk to me. I promise, anything you say will stay between the two of us and he'll never find out about it.'

'What sort of trouble is your friend in?'

'Well, she's got herself mixed up with Marc and this Jennifer girl and—'

Sharon reluctantly opened the door. 'You'd better come in, but I hope you're as good as your word. I had to move three times before he'd leave me alone. I don't want anything to do with him. I haven't got long. My flatmate will be back soon and she tends to be a bit anxious. I don't want her knowing about my life back then.'

Maggie assured her that she wouldn't take up much of her time. She saw the possibility of a welcome cup of coffee fading. Sharon led her into a neat living room. The flat was pokey and a bit shabby, but with throws and bright colours the women had made it homely. As she sat on the lumpy sofa, her attention strayed to a framed photo on the unit by the window. It showed two women in walking gear, one was Sharon and the other an older brunette. The flat didn't appear to be separated in style by two flat-sharing tastes, it was warm and intimate. Maggie guessed that the women were lovers.

'How is Phyllis? She never could keep her bloody mouth shut, the old cow.' The words held no malice; she smiled as she asked after the cafe owner.

'Well, she makes one hell of a chocolate cake,' said Maggie, 'and she speaks fondly of you. More than can be said for her opinion of Marc Robinson. I can't stand him either. Didn't like him from the second I set eyes on him, the flash git.' This wasn't quite true as Maggie had only turned against Marc when he had chosen Beth over her.

Sharon grinned, 'Yes, he's an acquired taste. So, what did you want to know? You already know that he is my ex-partner and I don't see what relevance that can have on anybody nearly ten years later. Why are you here?'

'To be honest it's not just Marc that I'm interested in. It's more his sister. I want to find out anything that you can tell me about them. My friend, Beth, she went out with this Marc guy. I think she might still be seeing him. Anyway, she saw him for one date and the next morning she's beaten black and blue, said she was mugged, then this crazy girl shows up, and the next thing is, Beth's taken her in and she seems to have some kind of twisted power over her. I know that something is horribly wrong.'

'Look, Maggie, is it? Sorry, Maggie, I can't say much. I'm done with all that now. I'm happy.' Her eyes strayed to the photo and then back to Maggie's face. 'I don't want to rake the past up, it's done. All I will say is get your mate the hell out of there, no good will come of it. They're damaged, the pair of them, and anybody in contact with them will end up damaged, too.' She glanced at the clock. 'I'm sorry; I do have to get on, now. I'm sorry I couldn't be any more help.'

Maggie felt there was a lot more that Sharon could tell her that might help. If she'd arrived earlier she might have been able to get more out of the woman but she was clearly nervous about Maggie being there when the other woman was due home. Maggie wondered if that was because there was a strange woman in their flat, or because questions about Sharon's past would be asked. She couldn't help wondering if Sharon Cabot had lurched from one controlling relationship straight into another. At the door, she fished a piece of paper and a pen out of her bag and, using her knee to lean on, she scrawled her mobile number on it. 'Look, I'm staying at a bed and breakfast not far from here, if you can think of anything else that might help me, please ring. I don't care what time it is. I'm seriously worried for my friend's safety, so please. Ring me, yes?'

Sharon crumpled the paper in her hand. Maggie thought that she was going to throw it back at her, but she shoved it into her jeans pocket. She nodded and mumbled, 'Yes. I'll ring if I think of anything that might help, but it'll be late, when Annie's asleep.' Maggie wanted to tell her that her life didn't have to revolve around controlling partners, but it wasn't her place. She smiled, squeezed Sharon's arm in thanks and left.

She ate pizza in her room with her mobile phone on the bed beside her. Graham rang to let Barry speak to his mummy before bedtime. Then Ben came on the line to have Maggie intervene in a fight between him and his sister. Maggie couldn't get them off the line fast enough. Sharon might only ring once, and she didn't want to miss the call—if it came. She watched television but was restless and couldn't settle. It was long past midnight when she went to bed.

The following morning, she woke late. The phone by the side of her bed was ringing but it was only the irate owner telling her that she was late checking out of her room. She contemplated going back to Sharon's house and shaking her until she told her every detail of her life with the Robinsons. The trip had led her this far, but what had she learned from it? Marc and Jennifer were brother and sister, that was handy to know, but other than that, and the fact that he's a bastard, she was no further forward, and at a loss how to help Beth and get rid of Jennifer.

She drove all morning and was only an hour from home when her mobile rang. She expected it to be Graham moaning that she wasn't back yet and wanting to know how to cook fish fingers for the kid's lunch. She answered her phone on the hands free. It was Sharon.

'Maggie? Hi. I must be mad getting involved in this but I've thought of somebody who might be able to give you more information than I could. She's Jennifer and

Marc's nanny from years ago. I searched the directory for a number for you. You need to ring first; but I have the number. The last I heard she was living in this nursing home in Chester. She might be dead by now, for all I know, but it's the best I can do. I can't remember her exact name. Marc called her Nanny Nettles. I think her name might have been Cynthia, but don't quote me on that. Marc used to send money. I hope I'm doing the right thing.' She gave Maggie the phone number for the nursing home. 'Good luck. Oh, and please don't contact me again. I've done all that I can for you.'

Maggie didn't have the opportunity to thank her before the line disconnected. She rang the number that Sharon had given her and despite a poor line, due to her driving through hills, Maggie spoke to a member of staff who put her through to the matron of the sheltered accommodation. They established that the lady that Maggie wanted to see was a woman in her late seventies called Cynthia Thistle. The matron wasted no time in telling Maggie that the old woman's account was in arrears and that they had a long waiting list for rooms in *Tranquil Meadows* retirement accommodation. Maggie turned the car around at the next junction and headed for Chester. Graham was going to kill her.

Chapter Twenty-Five

After dealing with a furious Graham, Maggie felt guilty for what she was putting her family through. It wasn't fair scuttling off across the country on a whim and leaving Graham to deal with the kids. She hoped that one day Beth would come back to her and appreciate what she was risking for her.

The matron made it quite clear on the phone that Miss Thistle was a recluse and that she never received visitors. Well, to hell with that. If this old bat held the key to the weirdoes, then Maggie was going to talk to her. It was with firm resolve that she rang the doorbell.

The place was old but well cared for. She was admitted by a young girl in a nurse's uniform. Fresh flowers were arranged all over the foyer, but although Maggie tried to be polite, she couldn't help wrinkling her nose at the smell of old people and incontinence, that they tried so hard to mask.

Maggie asked to see the matron and the girl enquired as to whether she had an appointment. Maggie told her that she didn't, but that the Matron would be sure to see her as she had come to discuss Miss Thistle's overdue account. Maggie flashed her sweetest smile. Shrugging her shoulders, the nurse led Maggie down a corridor and tapped on a door marked *Office*.

'Come in.'

'Somebody to see you about Nanny Nettles, Matron.' She held the door wider for Maggie to enter and left, closing it behind her. The woman behind a cluttered desk rose.

'Good day to you, Mrs, um, I assume you're the lady that I spoke to on the phone earlier. I really must insist that Miss Thistle's account be brought up to date today, or I'm afraid her position here can no longer be sustained. I have the balance on this print out ready for you.'

This mercenary bitch wasted no time, straight down to business and not a chocolate biscuit sweetener in sight. 'I haven't come to pay her account. I need to speak to her.'

'I'm sorry, but in that case, you've had a wasted journey. As I explained to you, Miss Thistle has no interest in seeing anybody. I did ask her on your behalf, but she was adamant. Now, if you'll excuse me,' she indicated her desk and the papers that she was writing, 'I'm very busy. I'll be writing to Mr Robinson today and Miss Thistle's room will have to be vacated by the end of the week. Good day to you.'

Ignoring her, Maggie pulled out the chair on the other side of the desk and sat down. 'I thought you wanted to discuss her account.'

The matron stopped on her way to the door to show Maggie out. 'And you said you weren't here to clear it. Are you a relative of Mister Robinson? You didn't say earlier. She's never mentioned you and I'm sure you've never visited.' The last was thrown as an accusation.

'I came as soon as I could, I've been living overseas in—' she had been going to say Ceylon, then remembered, as her tongue was forming the word, that it wasn't called that anymore, and she didn't have a tan. '—Sweden. Well, when I came back and found out that poor Nanny Nettles had been abandoned in this hell hole, I had to come and see her.'

The Matron bristled, 'Let me assure you, Mrs, um, yes, Miss Thistle, has the best care here, she'd tell you herself, she's very happy. It will be such a shame if we must let her go. Her account, you see…' she tailed off.

'It's Maggie, love, the name's Maggie. Now then, this account that you're all worked up about. How overdue is it? How much is outstanding? And how are the payments usually made?' Sharon had already told her that Marc paid for the old woman's keep. It seemed a strange loyalty to have to what was only an ex-employee.

'Well, of course Mr Robinson always took care of those things, dear. Now, I'm not saying anything untoward. He's a very charming man, set the standing order up years ago and up until very recently there was never a problem. Never visited, of course,' she looked disapproving, 'but we spoke on the phone occasionally. Sometimes, she needed little extras you know, things that weren't covered in the bill. He never questioned it; the money was always transferred the same day.'

I bet it was, thought Maggie, and how many of the 'little extras' she wondered, did her charge benefit from?

'Then,' the woman continued, 'last month, the payment was refused and the account lapsed into arrears. I haven't been able to contact Mr Robinson, and now, well, it's almost time for the next payment to go through. I've tried ringing him, of course, but there's no answer. I've left several messages, and well, it's very serious, we have a waiting list. I've spoken to Social Services, you see. I'm sure Mr Robinson would be most upset to have…'

The woman was breaking Maggie's heart. She interrupted the matron's spiel, 'How much?'

She saw a glint of greed in the green eyes, or maybe it was just the light. 'You can settle the account? Oh, how wonderful, Miss Thistle will be pleased. The outstanding balance for last month—and of course this coming month, because we like to keep a month in advance is due. Miss Thistle receives round the clock, qualified nursing care—and she is resident in one of our deluxe suites, you see.'

'How much?'

'The balance is three thousand, two hundred and sixty-eight pounds. We accept cards, dear.'

Maggie spluttered at the size of the bill, sixteen hundred quid a month to stay in this dump. Okay it wasn't bad, but it was hardly The Ritz. She felt a twinge of guilt. She couldn't care less about deceiving the grave robber with her hand out, but she felt bad when she thought about the old lady going to rot and being haggled over. 'I'll have to see her first.'

'Of course, dear, anything you require. I'll have one of the staff take you straight up.' She pressed a button on the intercom on her desk.

Bastard, thought Maggie as she smiled sweetly.

The same nurse who answered the door led her up two flights of stairs that made Maggie pant and which were hardly conducive to making life easy for little old ladies. Maggie envied them the Stannah stair lift. After a maze of corridors, at least one of which Maggie was sure she walked down twice, the girl stopped and tapped on a door. Without waiting for an answer, she opened it and walked in.

It was only mid-afternoon but the room was in almost complete darkness. The curtains were closed and despite a low-lit bedside lamp, the light didn't extend as far as any of the corners of the room. Motioning with her finger against her lips for Maggie to be quiet, she ushered her in and closed the door behind her. The gloom enveloped her, and as the girl walked towards a huddled figure in an orthopaedic chair by the closed curtains, Maggie went to follow, but was frightened of falling over something. She groped along the wall for a light switch.

'Don't turn the light on,' the nurse snapped at her, and then more softly she said, 'Nanny doesn't like it.'

'Who's there? Who is it?' A reedy but sharp voice issued from the wing-backed chair that was turned away from them. The old lady sounded terrified but feisty. 'Claire, who have you brought in? Is it a new member of staff? Make them go away. What are you thinking of, girl? I won't have anybody new, I won't.' Maggie decided that she was wasting her time talking to the old crone because she sounded nuts.

'It's okay, Nanny,' said the nurse, 'it's your niece. It's Mrs Johnson come to visit you. Isn't that nice, now?'

'Don't be so ridiculous, I don't have a niece. And stop talking to me as though I'm a three-year-old. Have you any idea how lacking in intelligence you sound?'

Maggie cut in. 'It's me, Aunty Cynthia, remember? Maggie, Marc Robinson's sister.' She turned to address the nurse, 'I'm not a real niece, of course, we were her wards. Miss Thistle was our nanny, years ago.'

There was a moment's silence before the crone in the chair spoke again. 'Of course, I remember you, you stupid woman. Why does everybody around here think that I've lost my faculties? Are you an imbecile?' Maggie grinned and moved a step towards the voice.

'Did I say you could come over to me? Sit there on the bed,' Maggie saw a withered arm come out from a blanket and motion in the direction of the single bed behind her. 'And you girl, get out of here. Haven't you got any work to do? Do they pay you to stand around and look gormless?'

The nurse left the room and only when the door closed did the woman speak again. 'So, *niece*, you have two minutes to tell me what all this subterfuge is about before I ring to have you removed.'

Maggie smiled. The old lass was gutsy. 'Hello, Miss Thistle. Nanny Nettles, isn't it? I really need your help. A friend of mine is in danger and you might be able to spread some light on what I'm dealing with.'

'Well, if it has anything to do with the Robinson family, I'd advise you to get your friend, walk away, and keep on walking until you can't smell the evil any longer. They're no good, either of them. Sick in a way that it's hard to describe. You frightened me for a moment. When you said you're his sister, I thought you were the girl, here to finish me off. But from your voice, I knew you're not her. They feed from each other like succubus, and sometimes it's hard to tell which of them is leading the other.' The old dear didn't hold back, it didn't look as though Maggie was going to have to drag information from her. As she spoke, the old woman's voice took on a reflective tone, as though she was in a different place in her mind, still talking from behind the wings of the huge chair, she said, 'Evil, no other word can describe her.'

'Her?' questioned Maggie, 'Are you talking about Jennifer? Please go on.' She felt her heart beating faster.

'How much do you know?'

Maggie thought about her answer for a second, wondering whether to play another bluff. She decided to be completely honest, 'Very little. Almost nothing.'

'I'd better ring for tea then, hadn't I?'

Maggie rose to move closer to her.

'Stay where you are. Did I tell you to move?'

'I'm sorry, didn't mean to overstep the mark. Actually that's a lie, I'm not sorry. Look, Miss Thistle, now that we're acquainted, would you mind if I pulled that chair up so that we can talk properly? It's difficult talking to you through a Chesterfield and I've got so much to ask you.'

'I'd rather you didn't, but I suppose you better had. Just give me a second.' Maggie's eyes were accustomed to the gloom and she saw the old lady pulling something around her shoulders.

'Come along then, we haven't got all day, pull up the chair and we can talk. I must warn you, though; I'm not much of a looker.'

Maggie pulled the pink Dralon chair beside the bed up to sit beside the old lady. 'It's okay, my mirror demands that I pay it danger money before looking into it.' Maggie had to force herself to remain impassive and not register any noises of either revulsion or pity. The poor woman had no nose or lips and that was only part of the Halloween mask facing Maggie. Little wisps of fluffy white hair poked from a bald pate covered with thick scar tissue. Even though Cynthia had pulled a lace shawl about her head and face, it didn't do much to cover the wreckage. Her bald scalp was covered in thick burn scars. Her right eye socket hung down onto what was left of her cheekbone, the inner rim red and watery. The eyeballs were damaged. One had been removed leaving a line of stitching where the socket was sewn closed. Beneath the filmy cataract of the remaining eye, was a shrewd and intimate appraising gaze. Her nose was gone, leaving only the open nasal channel and a sharp cliff of bone, her lips lost to the burning, only a ridge of hard scar tissue remaining. Maggie could see that the burns travelled from her neck into the material of her dress. Cynthia pulled her cardigan around her and said bitterly, 'There, so now you have it.'

Maggie was at a loss of how to answer, but she had to fill the uncomfortable void with something, 'What happened?' she asked simply.

'All in valuable time, dear. Have a good stare and let's get beyond it. I can see that it's making you uncomfortable. You came here for information. Well, I've got a story to tell you, but first I need to whet my whistle, it'll give us a few minutes to be easy with each other. We'll have a cup of tea and a sliver of cake. The cook's meagre on portions, but she does an acceptable sponge. We'll have our tea and you can tell me all about yourself, because once I start, I don't want to be interrupted.'

Cynthia rang twice more before the tea arrived. It was ten minutes since she first asked for it. 'And tell Cook that I don't want any burnt edges on the cake,' she said to the closing door after the third time her bell was answered. When the afternoon tea arrived, Cynthia berated the girl because one of the paper doilies had a small brown stain where a cup had marked it. 'I will not have second-hand doilies. The amount I pay to stay here, I expect to be given a new doily with every cup of tea.' Maggie exchanged a sympathetic glance with Claire – she was sure that she had better things to do than play room-service to a cantankerous old woman. 'And never mind you two rolling your eyes at me. I'm old; I'm entitled to be difficult. You'll have your day when I'm dead, but this one—my dears, is mine.'

'Get away with you, Nanny Nettles,' said Claire. 'You know it's a pleasure to bow and scrape to your every whim.' She smiled at Cynthia and Maggie realised that, even though she was particular and demanding, there was a fondness between them.

'And don't come back until you learn some manners,' shot Cynthia to Claire's retreating back. While they ate what Maggie thought was excellent cake, but Cynthia declared too dry, and drank their tea, Maggie gave the old woman chapter and verse of her life to date. Cynthia probed and questioned and although it was only light chit-chat about nothing much, by the time Maggie had picked up the last crumbs from her plate and wished that there was another slice on offer, she felt as though she'd been interrogated by the Gestapo. Cynthia was sharp and as they talked, Maggie found that she was less sensitive to the horrendous burns of the old woman.

'There, dear. Now that we're comfortable with each other, we can discuss what you came here for.' Maggie wasn't sure, but she thought Cynthia tried for a wink, but the tight skin at the corners of her eye wouldn't allow it.

'Once upon a time there were two beautiful little girls,' Cynthia began.

Maggie butted in. 'Miss Thistle, please, I'm sure this is going to be very interesting, but can I just ask you some relevant questions about Marc and Jennifer Robinson?' Not for the first time, she wondered if this had been a fool's errand after all, and the old hag was as batty as she first thought.

'You may not. You have chosen to come and invade my space, young woman, so please, indulge me. I have a tale to tell and if it's to be told then I will do it my way, from the beginning and concisely. When I conclude, you will have the opportunity to decide for yourself if there is any credence to it, or if I'm just a lonely disfigured old fool with too much time to play with my addled imagination.' Maggie held up her hands in resignation and wondered how far Graham's temper had risen by this point.

'As I said, two little girls. Twins. And if this were indeed a fairy tale, I could say that one little girl was very, very good, while the other was very, very bad, but that isn't the case. Melissa was an easier child to deal with. She was cheerful, biddable and easily entertained. But you see, Jennifer, she was a different kettle of fish altogether.

'Wait,' said Maggie, 'Jennifer is one of twins? She has a sister?'

A cloud passed over Cynthia's face. She ignored Maggie's question and continued. Her voice took the same tone that she used earlier when she spoke about her charges. It sounded softer, as though she was reliving another time. 'I was always there, you see. I was employed first as nurse and then, later, as governess to the boy, Marc. He was older. A bright child, a handful sometimes as most small boys are, but he had a quick intelligence and was eager to learn. He was a good bit older than the girls. I think he was approaching seven when the girls came along. I was going to have to look for new charges, a new family when they outgrew my services, but it didn't work out like that. If only things were different.' Her hand came up to the side of her face and she fingered some of the wreckage below her left eye. 'I gave up my life for the Robinsons. I left it too late to marry and then after... well, after the accident there was nothing left for me. I was finished. But that comes later.'

The bitterness left her voice and she was reflective again. 'I'm not one to talk of matters of a delicate nature, I'm sure, but I don't think having the twins was part of the plan for the Robinsons. I assume that the news of first one and then two new babies was as much a surprise to them as it was to me. James Robinson was a self-indulgent man. He worked away a lot and dragged his poor wife from Whey to Fen, and often overseas, too. Miranda was a genteel woman, given to a nervous disposition. Far be it from me to speak ill, but I always felt that she was apt to pander to the man, she appeased him too much, but it wasn't my place to say so, of course. The children didn't see a lot of their parents. It was a lonely childhood for Marc. The girls had each other, you see, but he was such a speculative little boy.

'When the girls came along it was a lively household, they breathed new life into it. They kept me on my toes almost from the day they were born. Later, I often looked back at the early years, tried to make sense of it all, pinpoint the exact moment when... Perhaps we'll never know, but the chickenpox played a big part.'

'Chickenpox?'

'Oh, most inopportune. It couldn't have happened at a worse time. Jennifer was a bright little thing, but she was always into mischief, always the first to be told off. I called her White Phantom. It's the definition of her name in Hebrew. She was like a little ghost appearing all over the place when you least expected it, listening at doors and getting into trouble. She felt that Melissa was favoured. Complete rubbish, of course. I loved both equally, we all did, but she was always vying for attention and fighting with her sister to steal the limelight. She was what you'd call a livewire. A right little monkey, she was. They both were. Oh, and how she loved her big brother. She trailed after him day and night—she idolised him. But to him she was just a silly little girl who would get in his way. He teased her mercilessly.

'Well, the chickenpox, which I've always felt was the catalyst that turned everything upside down, was a terrible blow for Jennifer.

'Joanna – that's Miranda's younger sister – was getting married. They were to have the reception in the grounds of Swarthdale Hall, the family home. It was a fine affair. No expense spared. I'd never seen the like. And the girls in their bridesmaid dresses, my little angels. You have never seen a child as beautiful as those identical twins.

'But then, less than a week before the wedding, Jennifer came home from school with chickenpox. The spots didn't come for a couple of days but, oh my goodness, when they did the poor mite was driven insane with them. I had her coated head to toe in calamine lotion, but it did no good. She scratched and scratched.

'I disapproved of their decision over the wedding. I thought it was wrong, damaging for the child, but they wouldn't listen to me. This wedding had to be perfect and never mind the feelings of a hurt little girl. She was told that she wouldn't be allowed to attend. It started when the rash broke out. Gosh they all flew into a flap. Jennifer was taken to a separate wing of the house and was expected to sleep there alone. I wasn't going to agree to that, she was terrified the poor mite. I went to her isolation room in my dressing gown and slippers and crept into that ridiculous cot-bed with her. They didn't want her to have any contact with Melissa, you see. The child had shown no symptoms and they wanted to keep it that way so that they still had one good looking child to walk up the aisle.

'The day before the wedding, my little Phantom looked a sight. Her face was a mass of angry spots, but she was feeling a lot better. The thing is, you see, she could have taken part in that wedding—the period of contagion had past. She should have been included. But they knew best. I was only Nanny Nettles who was expected to do as she was told. It all came down to their silly, egotistical photographs. Joanna, who I always felt was a spoiled child in adult clothing, screamed and cried and said how Jennifer would ruin her photographs and how everything had to be perfect. She refused to have her at the wedding at all and said that she had to be kept away from the guests at all costs, even though the incubation period was over.

'I have to say, though, that young devil Marc didn't help. I remember the screaming tantrum in that kitchen to this day. He came into the room and teased Jennifer the way he always did. I can remember it clearly. He kept calling her Zitzilla and pinching her. I told him to leave her be, that it was all going to end in tears. Nobody could ever have predicted just how those tears would fall. My accident was nothing compared to…'

Cynthia was tiring. She leaned back in her chair and took several shallow breaths. Her chest wheezed and Maggie asked her if she wanted to stop.

'Stop, dear? Why, I've barely started. You want to know the horrible truth and I'm going to give it to you, no holds barred. There's no proof of course. No proof of any of it, but I was an observer. I saw things that others didn't. I saw pure evil. I watched it grow in that child and saw it swell within her until it was all that was left. I blame myself for it, too. I should have done something sooner. I saw it happening and I knew, but I hoped that she'd come right, that something could be done for the child before it was too late. I can only imagine what she's become.'

'I have my suspicions,' said Maggie. 'But I don't know what's going on. All I know is that my friend's in trouble and these Robinsons are at the bottom of it.'

'Fruit and barley, dear. Like the juice. Listen, what I'm going to tell you next, if you believe me – and that's entirely up to you – is not going to make you feel any better about things. Are you sure you want me to open this box? It's been closed tight for a long time.'

Maggie nodded.

'I missed the wedding, too,' Cynthia said. 'Not that it was any great loss in my book, all that pomp and finery wasted on one day when there're so many starving children in the world. I stayed at home with my Jennifer. I had pleaded with Miranda to relent and let the child put on her pretty frock, but there was no talking to them, so taken up with this wedding and the perfection of it, they were. I will never forget how they broke that little girl's heart. She put her head into her folded arms on the wooden kitchen table and she sobbed for three hours. There was nothing I could do to make it any better for her. She cried until the wedding party arrived by horse and carriage and then, with big wet eyes all a-stare, she went and had one little look out of the window before she took herself off to her room.

'Miranda said that under no circumstances was Jennifer to be anywhere near the guests. "Looking like that," she'd added, too, in front of the child. I had no intention of locking the pitiful thing up, I'd keep her in the playroom with me and we'd have a picnic. But Jennifer wouldn't be placated and while my back was turned she sloped off to her room and locked the door.

'I felt that she'd come out when she was good and ready. I thought it best to let her cry. I went to the playroom and laid out a picnic, anyway, in case she changed her mind later. She must have been hungry with all that sobbing. I was in there, standing by the window when she made her way into the garden with the guests. I had a ringside view. I saw more than anybody else. I was higher up, you see. I saw what was going to happen. I knocked on the window, hammered on it to try and draw somebody's attention, but I was too late. Could you get me some water, please? I'm a little hoarse.'

'Of course,' said Maggie. 'Can I get you anything else?'

Cynthia patted her hand, and sipped at the glass that Maggie poured and held out to her. 'No, let's get this out and have it done with. Maybe I can sleep at night then. I will never forget the look of determination on that child's face as she walked out of the door and towards the brazier where some of the guests had gathered. She had on her bridesmaid dress. She was going to attend the party, and may the good Lord help anybody who tried to stop her. I remember that day as one of three expressions: determination, hatred, and curiosity, each one worse than the one before. My poor little raggedy Phantom walked over the lawn with her dress hanging open at the back because she couldn't do it up herself. She was tripping over the hem in her little silver wedding shoes, and the yellow of that big, poufy dress only served to bring out the redness of her spots. But that little minx held her head up high and walked right into the middle of them.

'I remember the ice-cream cone. She snatched it out of her sister's hand. Melissa was breath-taking, the dress was beautiful—but together, for that split second, standing by the brazier and lit by the flames of the fire, my little darlings should have been a picture. Why did they do that to her? She stood with her little body proud and the dress hanging off one shoulder. That's when the tragedy happened. Everybody else calls it an accident. It wasn't. It was a loathsome tragedy.

'Melissa was too close to the brazier. The adults should have been watching her by an open fire like that. I saw, clear as day, what was going to happen. Jennifer stepped on the hem of Melissa's dress. That part may have been an accident; after all, she'd been stepping all over her own.

'One little push, that's all it took, all that taffeta and lace. The poor mite had no chance. Jennifer pushed her beautiful sister into the open fire and I was the only witness. Melissa was a ball of flame. Somebody pulled Jennifer to safety. And I saw her looking at Melissa, her face a mask of sheer malevolent hatred.

'She was dragged further away from the heat of the fire. Somebody tried for a moment to shield her from watching her sister burn, but they were too engrossed in the burning pyre themselves to take her right away.

'I watched my little Phantom glide back to the drama playing out in front of her. People were screaming and crying; the men snatched their hired jackets off and tried to swat Melissa with them to put the fire out. And that's when I saw Jennifer's third expression, the worst one of them all. She stood on the side-lines, her ice-cream cone still in her hand, forgotten, a sticky mess melting down her fingers. Jennifer's eyes were open wide. She had a glimmer of a smile on her face, just the merest hint, but her overall expression was one of open curiosity as she watched her sister's face melt before her.' Cynthia touched her own face again. 'They say once a murderer has perfected their M.O. they stick to it.'

Maggie couldn't take it in. 'Did Melissa survive? Is she all right?'

'No dear, I'm afraid she died. Her injuries were horrific. The child suffered a terrible death but luckily, she didn't survive past the hour. She died in the ambulance on the way to the hospital. It was merciful. I wouldn't have wanted her to live like this.'

'But Jennifer wilfully and knowingly murdered her

twin sister. That's horrific.'

'It is. That's true. But how culpable can a jealous eight-year-old be? Should I have stood up and informed the authorities then? What proof did I have, a couple of odd looks from an exasperated child? No, it was said by all to be an accident. It was best left at that. And that's something I've had to live with since that terrible day, because it didn't stop there.'

'What do you mean?'

'There were others, Maggie. After Melissa's death, things returned to something akin to normal. The parents resumed their trips, I was left with Marc and Jennifer, and what had happened to poor Melissa was never mentioned. Jennifer was withdrawn. She would lock herself away for hours, reading. The only one who could ever get through to her was Marc. He was growing into such a big, strong boy. When he was ten he'd decided that he was going to be a mechanic.' Cynthia chuckled. 'You should have seen his father's face. I thought he was going to explode. All that private tuition and his son wanted to be a mechanic. Indulging the whim and hoping that it wouldn't last, his father bought him cars to tinker with. Marc was a determined child, he pored over books and manuals for days and then he'd climb into his overalls and get greasy in his garage. Jennifer had her own little set of overalls, and she'd be there, too, handing him spanners and getting technical and oily. In the two years between his fourteenth and sixteenth birthday, the lad became very proficient. He was good enough to work on the family cars, sometimes with a hired mechanic to oversee him, and then later, on his own initiative. When he first began, he had to stand on a box to reach into the engine. He turned into a man while his head was in an old oil tank. He began with beaten up Minis and Volkswagens and then his interest took a more highbrow turn. Marc always had an eye for money. He enjoyed the feel of it in his hands right from being a little boy. "Pennies, Nanny, pennies," he'd say, never sweeties or toys, like other children, always pennies. He got his first classic car when he was sixteen. It was an old Aston Martin, a beaten up and neglected old thing, but he took it apart piece by piece and restored it with love. Before his parents'… accident, he was as good as any grease monkey twice his age.

'That day, Jennifer was being difficult. She was just shy of ten, if I remember correctly. Her parents had come back from Japan hours earlier and that night they were going out again to a party. Jennifer was crying for attention from Miranda, she wanted to spend time with her mother. Don't get me wrong, when Miranda had time she doted on Jennifer, it's just that she doted on James more. His needs always came first. That night they were going out for cocktails and then on to a restaurant for dinner. They were schmoozing some new clients that James was hoping to snare. It was all very tense. Miranda spent most of the day having beauty treatments and her hair done and then came home to get ready. James asked Marc to look at the brakes on his Jaguar. They were sticking and Marc said they needed replacing. He was working on them that day. They could have gone out in one of the other cars but James was out to impress and was keen to go in that one, sleek executive green thing it was, too big if you ask me. Marc had taken the old brakes off and with Jennifer's help they'd replaced them with new ones. He was very specific afterwards that he'd told Jennifer to come into the house and tell James that the breaks had been done, but light was fading and he hadn't managed to finish the job. The car wasn't safe to drive. Marc insisted that he told Jennifer to say that.

'I was in the kitchen when she came in, wiping oil from her hands on her overalls. I only remember the conversation so succinctly because it was important, otherwise I wouldn't have given it a thought. Jennifer skipped into the room and went straight over to Miranda to fling her arms around her waist. Miranda pushed her away, she was in overalls. Jennifer was never a demonstrative child, she wasn't one for kissing and cuddling, I put it down to the continued absence of her parents. She was a distant child, but it wasn't just the unusual cuddle that struck me. It was out of character for her to come out of a sulk so quickly. When she'd gone to the garage, she was furious with Miranda. She came skipping in and over her shoulder she said to James, "Daddy, Marc says the car's safe to drive." Marc was in the shower when they left. They had only been gone twenty minutes when the policeman knocked at the door. He had his hat in his hands, just like in the films. Jennifer was quiet; she said she'd made a mistake. The inquest said it was a horrible accident. It had a terrible effect on Marc. He got into trouble with local thugs, petty thievery, and he was put away in a special place for naughty boys. He was there for two years. He never blamed Jennifer as far as I could tell, but he came back a different person. He had a nasty turn to him, anger at the world boiled inside him.

After that I was all that they had. I couldn't leave them, though there were times when I felt like it. Jennifer grew into an unpleasant child. She was sly and sneaky. Marc was surly and aggressive. What had once been such a cheerful home was just a shell. We had to move, Marc was the man of the house, he had inherited his parent's fortune. Gossip was rife in the village after Marc returned from his stint away. That was the first house move. Marc was eighteen and became Jennifer's legal guardian. Jennifer was twelve.' Maggie hadn't butted in; she was enthralled in the story as it unfolded.

Now she had questions.' Cynthia, was Phantom really so evil that she could kill three members of her family? Did she understand the simple facts of right and wrong? When my kids were five they already knew that it was wrong to hurt people. Surely she knew what she was doing?'

'Oh yes, she knew exactly what she was doing. I blame myself dear, after Melissa, I should have spoken out. I should have done something. Possibly even before Melissa, I could have done something. Even then I knew that she had an unnatural jealousy towards her sister.' She motioned to her face, 'They say that what goes around comes around.'

'What happened?' Maggie asked for the second time.

'Jennifer happened, simple as that. She wanted chips cooking in one of those awful deep fryer contraptions. Jennifer asked for sweets before her meal. I told her no. I had my back to her; she was sitting at the dining-room table drawing. We were arguing, the child would never take no for an answer. In a rage, she stood up from the table and scraped her chair into my legs. It hit me at the back of my knees and they went from under me. I've had many years to think about it, it all happened so fast, but I swear that, if that's all that happened, my knees would have buckled and I'd have let go of the frying handle and would have simply slumped downwards, but something pushed me forwards immediately after the chair hit my legs. My head was pushed towards the fryer, I reached out to shield myself from it with my arm and the whole lot came over on top of me. Jennifer was burned too, but it was minor. She spent a night in hospital and was released the following day.

I was in hospital for eighteen months, I had operations, but what could be done about this? I was scared to go back, but I had no choice. I have no family, they were all I had. The Robinson's paid me generously for my years in their employ, and I'd spent little, but how could I live independently with this face?

I went back, but I couldn't face the world. I lived alone in a room at the back of the house. Jennifer was never put off by my face. She'd come and talk to me and it would be like the old days before she became twisted, but other times she'd just come to taunt me. Jennifer was drawing a picture when the ambulance arrived. It was a picture of me, dead. She told me about it herself, bragged about it. She screamed that she wanted me dead and would make a better job of it next time. I've been waiting for her to come ever since. There was nothing more that she could do to hurt me. Death would be preferable to this. I wasn't scared of her—not for me, at least.

I wasn't there long. There were other things, things that I can't bring myself to talk about even now. Bad, dirty things. I heard them together at night sometimes; please don't ask me for details. I confronted Marc. I told him that I was going to go to the police. He begged me not to. They were like my own bairns, once. It was as though I'd borne them of my own body. He promised me that the dirty stuff would stop.

We came to a mutual decision that I'd be happier somewhere else. He promised to look after me, and by goodness, he has. This isn't my first home, there was another one for three years and I've been here five now. Marc pays the bills in return for my silence, or at least he did, until recently I believe. I don't know what's going to become of me now.'

'Is that why you've spoken to me?'

'Good Lord no, this isn't malicious. Not at all. I'm worried about Marc. I thought maybe he'd done something wrong, been sent to prison, or worse. He has never missed a single payment. He's been very generous. I've been looked after well. But they have a twisted gene, the pair of them. They are capable of incredible evil. I had to warn you, I couldn't face another death on my conscience.' She gripped Maggie's arm. 'Whatever happens make them stop, Maggie. I'm relying on you to do what's right.'

'So, if Jennifer was twelve when she did this to you, how old is she now?'

'She was ten dear, it happened while Marc was away in that place, they let him out early because of it. Jennifer spent a little time away in foster care, but it didn't last long, something happened, something bad, but I don't know the details. She was released into Marc's care. They moved shortly afterwards to escape the probing eyes of social services.

'What can I do? Can I go to the police, will you talk to them?'

'There's no proof of anything Maggie, everything that Jennifer did was investigated and found to be a run of horrible accidents.'

'Yes, but they were never investigated as one case before. Seen one at a time, they could be passed off as accidents but together, three deaths and your terrible accident in two years, it's far too coincidental.'

'She's canny, that one, and he's as slippery as an eel. They'll talk their way out of it and then they'll disappear. There's nothing concrete to get them on. You need to find something on them. I'm sure if you dig hard enough, something will stick.'

'What about the abuse that you hinted at?'

'Their word against mine, dear. I'm a bitter old lady with an axe to grind. My best advice to you, Maggie, is to dig and dig hard my girl.'

They talked for a while longer, but Maggie could see that their afternoon had tired Cynthia. She shook the old lady's hand and crept out of the room, down the stairs, and out of the door before anybody could stop her.

All the way home she worried about Cynthia. When she told Beth what she knew, it would put the old nanny in danger. And then there was her tenuous position at the rest home. Maggie felt responsible for her. She'd told the matron that she'd pay Cynthia's bill, but there was no way she could afford that kind of money. She had to do something to help her...but what? She drove home to face World War Three with Graham and her head was spinning with thoughts and unanswered questions.

Chapter Twenty-Six

The pain was incredible. He'd woken several times that he was aware of, he had cognitive memory of being alive, but he knew little more than that he was in a very bad place. He was tied to a bed. Why was he tied? Had he been violent to somebody? Up to this point, attempts to open his eyes were futile. He tried again but his eyelids felt crusted to the lower rim of his socket. The other times he hadn't been able to stay awake long, there was always a deep pull back into either sleep or unconsciousness—he wasn't sure which.

He thought he might be in some kind of heavy sedation, sometimes the pain in his head was different, it came down his nerve receptors in waves, but not as intense pain, he was high, morphine maybe, and he was aware of it as a noise, a building, horrendous noise in his skull that only allowed him moments of wakefulness at a time. He must be in hospital.

The pain in his head was bad, but he could feel something else, a new ill that hadn't been there before. He had a heavy intense weight on his chest. He felt as though his sternum was caving in, he couldn't breathe. Every time he inhaled it felt as though something was squeezing down on his chest trapping the air inside him and not letting it out again. It took him several breaths to realise that this wasn't internal pressure. He hadn't broken every rib in his body and cracked his chest open, there was something cold and heavy on top of him. He needed see what it was. He tried to move and the thing adjusted its position. It moved too, but not with him, it moved independently of him. It was alive. When it shifted, the warmth where it was lying left and a rush of frigid air blew over his sweating body. The thing repositioned and, where it had touched him it felt warm, but the new areas of it meeting his hot body were cold. It was a sensation unlike anything he'd felt before, and it was so heavy.

He forced his closed eyelids to move upwards. He felt them un-stick. The movement of opening his gluey eyes caused a new wave of pain in his head. He felt as though he might vomit, and fought down the rising nausea.

His vision was blurry, wherever he was, it was light—harsh fluorescent light burned the back of his eyes and caused the headache to intensify so much that he was forced to close them again.

The thing on him shifted. He felt the movement. The bulk of it stayed in place, but he felt some part of it moving towards his face. Although he'd never felt anything like it before, a primal instinct knew what it was. His mind was screaming at him that there was a huge snake crawling up his body. But that was ridiculous. If this was a hospital, why was there a snake lying on top of him? He was delirious. He couldn't make any sense of it, but he needed to see.

Aware of the light this time, and prepared for it, he opened his eyes. His vision was blurry, but it came into focus as he demanded it. His mind knew that he was in terrible danger and ordered his eyes to put some effort into working.

When his vision came into part focus, he saw the giant head of a huge brown snake inches from his mouth.

Its amber eyes with the elliptical cat-like—no, snake-like—black pupils bored into him. The holes along its nose were open and went right inside its head. Its tongue slithered out between the horrible fleshless lips and touched him on the chin. He tried to inch up the bed, he tried to jump out, run away, but he was tied fast, with metal. His mind made the next leap towards understanding his circumstances. He was handcuffed to the bed, so that was it, he'd been arrested, but that didn't explain the enormous weight of the snake on top of him, pinning him down. He was hallucinating.

It was lunacy, he was insane. It couldn't be happening, but since when did hallucinations feel so heavy? He opened his mouth and screamed. The effort was too much for his injured body to take and he felt the darkness calling him back. The snake moved an inch further up and put the tip of its hideous nose into Colin's mouth to investigate the warm, damp darkness there. Colin closed his mouth, fast, and the snake jerked back, startled. Colin dropped his eyelids and drifted into unconsciousness.

He felt the sting of a hard slap across his face. This wasn't the gentle tap of a nurse to rouse him back into consciousness, or even a duty police officer come to question him. It was a hard, brutal, welt-raising slap that made his face sting and his eyes water.

'No, you don't. Not again. I'm sick of you sleeping all fucking day, wake up.' A hand came into view, a slender hand, small, like a child's. It lifted the snake's head and wafted it in front of his face. 'Don't you like my baby,' the voice crooned. He screamed again, but this time it didn't carry him into the murky world where even snakes and the creatures of nightmares didn't prowl.

He was aware of a door opening in front and to the left of him. Somebody ran into the room. 'Jennifer, oh my God, What the hell do you think you're doing? What's going on, get that thing out of here. Why have you brought it? Get it away. Are you trying to scare him back into a coma? Jesus Christ.' The voice rose in pitch on every word until it was a scream. He was aware of a scuffle; the second person was yelling and swearing. The great heaviness was lifted from his body and where it had been, the sweat on his torso was cold and wet, the sheets beneath him drenched. He heard the door open.

'I'll take him back home then. I don't see what you're making such a fuss about. I was only showing him Darklord. I thought you'd be pleased that I'm being friendly.' The door closed and the horrific snake was gone.

His vision was hazy, the second person was moving towards him. He couldn't see very well; the light was so bright and he had to squint to keep his eyes partially open. They were water-filled and sore.

'Colin? Colin, can you hear me?'

He steadied his head. It wasn't moving but it felt as though it was rocking from side to side in nauseating waves. He concentrated his attention on focussing. 'Beth,' it was a croak, hardly recognisable as a word.

'Yes, it's me. Don't worry, it's going to be all right.' She was wiping his face with a soft cloth, it felt nice, soothing after the harsh slap.

'Where…?'

'You're safe, that's all you need to know for now.'

'Tied up?'

'Yes, I'm so sorry about that, but it's unavoidable, you see. I really am sorry Colin, about everything.'

Was it fine? After all, Beth was a nurse, wasn't she? 'Hospital?' he croaked, his voice rising in question. How could this be safe?

'No. Not hospital. Look, don't you worry. Everything's going to sort itself out.' The room was coming into focus. This was no hospital ward. Where the hell was he?

'What the fuck?' He tried to sit up. He fought against the bonds holding him down.' Untie me, fucking untie me. Where am I? What's happening to me? How…'

He felt the sharp prick of a hypodermic needle in the crook of his arm, on the inside of his elbow. He was thrashing, trying to get loose and then, ten seconds later, a blanket of wooziness started in his stomach and spread up to his head. He fell back onto the pillow, tried to force his eyes to stay open—to not close. And then he was gone.

Chapter Twenty-Seven

Maggie spent every spare moment that she could steal from her days sitting outside Beth's house. The pretty little semi was in a state of perpetual neglect. Like a crazed bunny-boiler she staked out the house on the hill where she suspected that Beth spent her days and nights. Was she still working? The hospital wouldn't give out any information other than to say that Beth had taken some leave and hadn't been in for some time, they didn't know, or wouldn't say when she'd be back. Maggie didn't know if Beth had left her little house to live in the big house. She hadn't seen her at either residence, though twice she saw Jennifer going into the big house. She hadn't seen Marc at all.

Maggie came so close to pounding on the door, but instinct told her that to show her hand would be damaging. She had to see Beth on her own, to be able to tell her what she knew. The people that she was involved with were dangerous; above all else, she had to make Beth aware of that. If there needed to be a showdown, if she had to call the police, that was all well and good, but first she had to talk to Beth.

As well as staking out the two houses, appeasing her man, who was convinced that she was one step away from the nut house, and looking after the kids, she trawled the internet with her phone by her side. Maggie armed herself with facts, lots of them. The deaths that Nanny Nettles had spoken of had all occurred. There was no blame laid at anybody's door, they were three reported, unconnected, completely disassociated terrible accidents. The little girl who fell into the brazier, made the front pages, but a week later, after her televised funeral, she hovered around page seven of the local newspaper for a day or two before she was forgotten. Among all the other sentimentality, her obituary spoke of the sister who would always love her and would never forget her. The inquest was opened and closed in fifteen minutes. A verdict of accidental death was announced, typed and stamped on any official papers that had to be filed.

The death of Marc and Jennifer's parents was reported in greater depth, but only made the second page of the newspaper. Marc had been questioned extensively by the police in relation to the tragedy. The newspaper report pulled at the heart-strings of the reader by telling of the poor motherless child who had been left behind. There was no mention of the fact that she had already lost a sister in another terrible accident

After the death of their parents, Marc and Jennifer fell between the nets of the Social Service's beady eyes. Maggie made phone calls to the school that Jennifer had attended. She spoke to Jennifer's form teacher. The woman remembered the child. She said that she was bright, but difficult. To the best of her memory, she had never had a day's absence, was always well presented for school with her uniform and kit in order and she had no cause for concern regarding her home life. Maggie spoke to a lady from Social Services who investigated the Robinson's at the time. She said that the family nanny had been retained and was in-situ. There had been no need for further involvement by the agency. Maggie ended the call abruptly when the social worker was suspicious and asked for her credentials and why she was poking around in a long-dead case file.

Maggie spoke to the police but as her only excuse for phoning was a family interest—her being a second cousin of the deceased back from overseas; the police had little to tell her. The desk sergeant suggested she contact the local library to ascertain the facts from old newspaper reports. She'd spent several days in the library, once with a fractious Barry perched on her knee. She alternated between doing the voices of Thomas the Tank Engine and investigating murder. Barry refused to be entertained and she left, after less than an hour, under the pointed glare of the librarian.

While she never found a single piece of evidence that said that either Marc or Jennifer were murdering psychopaths, she had made three pages of notes. She was armed with times and dates and cold hard facts, that Miss Jennifer Robinson couldn't wriggle away from.

Maggie tried to catch Beth in half a dozen times, she knocked on her door after tentatively peeking through the curtains first, the house was empty and abandoned. When she did catch somebody in, she couldn't believe her luck. She rounded the corner and saw that a light shone in Beth's living room, her bedroom light was also on. While it looked as though somebody was in, she doubted that her luck would hold enough for her to find Beth in alone. By this point she didn't care. Her dander was so far up that it had altitude sickness. If she had to face Beth, and confront Marc and Jennifer at the same time, then that's how it would be. She was more than ready for a fight after psyching herself up over several fruitless visits.

Maggie hammered on the door. This wasn't a friendly social call and she might as well make that damned clear from the get-go. When the door wasn't answered, she rapped again.

'Just a minute,' the voice on the other side of the door was Beth's. So far, Maggie's luck was holding. Beth opened the door and Maggie was horrified by her appearance. She looked gaunt, tired—older. Her hair had grown and was pulled back from her face and held in a lank ponytail with an elastic band. Her blonde dye had grown out by over an inch and darker roots were visible. Beth had always been meticulous about her grooming. She had on a pair of old track pants and a washed-out T-shirt that looked as haggard and tired as she did. For a fragment of a second, Beth's eyes lit up when she saw Maggie standing on her doorstep, but the look didn't last and was cowered as a shadow crossed her face, Maggie watched her close down all expression. Beth stared at her for a couple of seconds and replaced the empty look with an equally empty smile. It was cold and devoid of any emotion, the same expression that Maggie kept on a hook behind the door, to fix in place when the Jehovah's witnesses called.

'Maggie, hiya, what are you…' Maggie wasn't about to be fobbed off with any feeble excuses.

'Hiya mate, remember me? It's time we had a catch up. Call it for old time's sake, if you like.' She pushed past Beth and walked into the living room and straight through to the kitchen. She scrutinised both rooms as she entered them. 'I'd like to tell you that you look good. That's what old acquaintances say to each other when they're being polite, but I'd be lying. You look like shit. How've you been? Judging purely on appearances, I'd say, not great.' She said all of this in a harsh tone, not quite a shout, but pointed enough that Beth knew that she'd come here to kick arse and wasn't going to leave until she saw a boot print on Beth's behind. Maggie had picked up the kettle and filled it at the sink while she talked, before putting it on to boil.

'Yeah, I'm good thanks. Thing is though, you've caught me at a bad time. I'm busy with some stuff and…'

'Bollocks. You can cut that out right now, because I'm going nowhere. Got that?' Beth nodded and Maggie opened the cupboard and took down two mugs. 'Just the two of us for coffee is it, or am I making for the malignant goth and her brother, too?' She didn't wait for an answer and spooned coffee into the mugs before turning to the fridge and taking out the milk. Her lip curled as she shook it and watched the cheesy curd, churn against the side of the plastic bottle. 'Well, it looks as though you haven't been drinking much coffee lately.'

'No, I've been, um … busy.'

'Yeah, you said, not buying it though Beth. It's time you and I had a good old heart to heart. I've taken so much shit from you that I'm seriously about ready to punch you out. Don't mess with me Beth. One last word of warning, I'm on, and I'm bleeding like a stuck pig, so you really don't want to pick today to take me on.'

'If I can't get rid of you, then we might as well open this.' Beth grinned and Maggie saw a glimmer of her former friend in the smile. Embarrassed under scrutiny, Beth turned to the carrier bag that she'd brought into the kitchen with her and pulled out a fresh two litre bottle of semi-skimmed. 'I haven't been in long and was just about to have a cuppa myself.'

'Got any biscuits in that bag?' Maggie was still as mad as fuck but couldn't help grinning back.

'Didn't know you were coming.'

'You could have called, Beth.' Maggie couldn't hide her bitterness.' At any point Beth, you could have rung me. We're supposed to be friends.'

'I know, it's just been difficult, that's all.' Beth picked up an ashtray and put it on the kitchen table. Then she added water and milk to the mugs and brought them over before sitting down opposite Maggie. They sat at the table as they had a thousand times before, but they'd never had a brick wall between them as they did now. Maggie had so much to say, but she didn't know where to start. Beth threw her a cigarette and flashed another grin. Coffee and cigarettes was old, it was familiar, it's what they did and the only thing that stopped them from being strangers.

Maggie intended to shout. She was going to confront her friend with her notes, facts, and stories—everything she'd learned. She was prepared to shake Beth if she had to knock some sense into her. She just wanted her friend back and the strange people she'd taken up with, out of her life so that things could be like they used to be. She opened her mouth to speak and then closed it again.

Beth's eyes filled with tears. Maggie watched as she tried to blink them away. Beth took a puff on her cigarette and exhaled along with an escaped sob. The tears broke free from their confinement and rolled down Beth's cheek. Maggie was up from her seat and had her arm around Beth's shoulder in an instant. 'Oh sweetheart, come on tell me. It can't be that bad, it's nothing we can't sort out, you and me. We're like the A-team—just with more cellulite and less gold.'

Beth wiped snot on her sleeve, 'Oh Maggie, you have no idea.'

'So, talk to me, tell me what's wrong. Let's sort it out. We can you know, whatever it is Beth, no matter how bad it seems we can sort it out.' Beth laughed but didn't say anything.

'Beth love. It's clear you aren't happy with this Marc bloke. I know he's got you playing nursemaid to his wacko sister. Yes, I know that Jennifer's his sister, don't look so surprised. You know me when I feel that somebody's hiding something.' She paused to gauge her friend's reaction. 'That's not all I know about them. I've been digging. Fuck Beth you wouldn't believe where I've been. I know a lot of crazy stuff. Maybe I even know things that you don't. I know what they're capable of. If he's hurting you, you have to talk about it. I'll help you. I promise.' Beth had pulled away from her. She was frightened, startled. Her eyes were terrified.

'He's not hurting me, Maggie. You have no right. You don't understand. You have to back off. Don't get involved.' She stood and stubbed out her cigarette.' You have to go.'

'I'm not going anywhere. Sit down.'

Beth sat and Maggie threw her another cigarette. 'Here have some more lung cancer. I don't care if we have to sit here and smoke our way through a hundred cigarettes. You are going to hear what I've come to say, at least. I can't make you talk, but I hope to God you'll listen and take heed. I know you're in trouble.'

Beth sat complacently at first, all the fight left her and she was shutting down on herself and her emotions. Maggie started at the beginning with her following Jennifer to the big house and how that led her to the neighbour's place, which in turn led to her research and her following adventures. By the time she got to the part about her visit to Sharon, Beth was sitting upright in her chair, puffing hard on her cigarette and hanging on Maggie's every word. She interrupted often with questions and interjections, but mostly she just let Maggie tell her tale. When Maggie recounted everything that Nanny Nettles had told her, and gave her own account of the old lady's appearance, all the colour left Beth's face. She was cold and trembling as the shock of what she was hearing sank in. She looked as though she was about to vomit. Maggie finished, stubbed out her cigarette and lit another one.

'Have you heard enough to cut that poison out of your life?'

'I can't.'

'Even after everything I've told you, it doesn't make any difference?'

'It makes a world of difference, and at the same time—none at all.'

'What's he got over you Beth, what can possibly be as bad as murder, for God's sake?'

'It's not Marc. He's not even here. He's had to go away on business... China... conference, meetings and....stuff.'

'China? What does he do, run a karaoke night and roll a few sushis on the side?'

'That's Japan.'

'Same difference, so is that it? He's swanning off building his empire and you've been left at home minding the baby? Why Beth? I don't get it. Just walk away. She's old enough, and Christ knows she's ugly enough, to take care of herself. Hell, she'll probably murder a few babies to feed on till her wacko brother gets back. Walk away.'

'I can't. I'm tied…responsible.'

'Responsible for what?'

'How are the kids?'

'Fuck off. Responsible for what?'

'How's Graham? Have you had your fanny waxed, recently?'

Maggie didn't crack a smile. 'I wish I had a photo of that old lady to show you Beth.'

'Leave it Maggie.'

'Like you keep saying, I can't. If you saw what I saw in that nursing home, that old lady's face, Beth, it was… gone. And she had this burned plate of melted cheese where her face should have been. God, it was awful.'

'There's nothing you can do. Don't get involved. You could get hurt.'

'Is that a threat?'

Beth laughed but the sound was false and hollow. 'Of course not. Don't be stupid.' Her eyes filled with tears again, 'Please Maggie, there's nothing you can do, just leave it.'

'Okay, I'll drop it for now, seems you've got enough people bullying you without me joining in. But, I'm not having you cutting me out. We've been friends too long Beth. Make time for me. I need you, Beth. I'm worried sick about you and I've got all this stuff going on with Colin. You've heard about that right?' She didn't stop to wait for an answer. 'Him deciding to swan off to God knows where. I had the police around last night asking if I'd seen him. I told them he'll be lying on some Mediterranean beach with a woman half his age. The kids are upset and asking all kinds of questions that I can't answer and I'm ready for murdering him as well as you. I'm at the end of my rope and I can't take much more.'

Beth tried to deflect Maggie's attention away from her face, she was red. She could feel the shame burning her cheeks. She made a show of busying herself collecting up the mugs and dirty ashtray. Three months earlier Maggie would have been on to her guilty look in a heartbeat, but things had changed a lot since then. They had drifted and Beth had undergone a major crash course in deception. 'How's the investigation going?' she asked, 'I saw the appeal on the news last night.'

'But you didn't think to come around and be there for me, Beth?' the bitterness in her voice was tinged with disappointment and some acceptance of the fact.'

'I thought about it, but what could I do to help? I'd only be in the way.'

'You know Beth, if I had a quid for the amount of times I've told that man to go and jump off a cliff, and now, what if he has? The kids saw the news; all the kids at school are talking. They keep asking questions. And fucking hell Beth, it breaks my heart that I have no answers for them. I'm going to kill the bastard when he shows up for putting them through this.'

'He'll be okay,' Beth mumbled,' 'You know he will. It's Colin we're talking about. He could talk himself out of any hole and he's just not the type to... well you know. He'll have gone off somewhere on a whim. Maybe they don't have Granada telly in outer Mongolia or wherever he is and he's oblivious to all the fuss he's caused. It will be okay. You just wait and see.' She tried to smile but knew that her expression was shifty and insincere.

'So, where's his van?'

'Eh,' Beth was thrown by the question.

'His van. Where is his van? If he's off living the high-life somewhere, why isn't his van sitting in Manchester airport car park stinking of cheap perfume and bimbo? His passport was in his flat. His bank account hasn't been touched in over two weeks. He went off to a job in the morning on the third of last month. He vanished into thin air, van and all, and he hasn't been seen or heard from since. Explain that.

'I can't.'

Maggie smiled and touched her hand, 'No of course you can't, but you can just be my friend. The kids miss you. Hell, I miss you. I'm going now, but when can I see you again. Let's go out for a drink Friday, or just stay in if you prefer. Something. Anything.'

'Okay.'

'Promise.'

'Promise.'

Chapter Twenty-Eight

After Maggie left, Beth's head was swimming. She had so many things going around and around and couldn't make sense of any of them. At the forefront of her mind was something that Jennifer said on the day she met her. 'Have you ever watched somebody burn?' She'd gone on to say, 'I have.' Beth had to talk to Jennifer to find out the truth, or her warped version of it. She had to have both sides in front of her so that she could think, but she was terrified of the showdown. How would Jennifer react to the accusations, or even to the fact that Beth had spent time alone with Maggie? It was one rule that Beth didn't need to have hammered home. Because her friend was so sharp, she was happy to keep distance between herself and Maggie. But she missed her like missing a limb.

Jennifer was supposed to be on Colin watch but, as usual, she'd sloped off at the first opportunity. Beth was angry and frustrated. Jennifer couldn't be trusted with the simplest of instructions. Colin may have been left unattended for hours and anything could have happened to him.

She knew Jennifer wasn't there before she entered the vault, her jacket wasn't slung over the dowel of the stairs, but Beth called her name anyway.

Colin was awake; she could see that he was more alert; his condition was improving with each awakening. He was out of danger and was going to make it. It was the best news in the world—and the most damning evidence for her spending the rest of her life in prison. His head turned as she came into the room and let the heavy vault door slam shut behind her. His eyes were wide open and fully focused; he barely winced with the movement of his head. Beth made a note to herself to be cautious. Even though he was restrained at ankle and wrist, he could still be dangerous. She added the ankle cuffs that day as he was stronger and more alert and unpredictable. As she fastened the metal cuffs to the bed Colin realised that Beth was not a prisoner alongside him—but his captor.

'Hello Col, how are you feeling?'

'Beth.' It was a hostile greeting. They were like two family members meeting at a mutual friend's party after a bitter row. If only Beth could apologise, pass him a vol-au-vent and let that be an end to it. Beth approached the side of his bed. She saw that both of his wrists had deep lacerations and were bleeding from his attempts to escape. He said one word, but she heard that his voice was raw from shouting. He should have been protected from hurting himself. Oh, the irony. She was furious with Jennifer for leaving him. It looked as though he'd been alone for hours. She busied herself getting dressings to seal and protect his wrists from further damage. The silence between them was deafening.

'There's no point in screaming, we're soundproofed. You need to conserve your energy.'

Colin watched her ministrations. 'And of course, there's absolutely no point in asking you to release me from these things,' he motioned towards his bonds with his eyes. Beth bit her bottom lip and shook her head.

'What the fuck's going on, Beth?'

She couldn't reply, she looked in his eyes and hers filled with tears.

'Well, I think it's time we had a catch up don't you, Beth. Call it a gossip, if you like. Now who's going first? You? Me? I know, here's an idea. Why don't you go first? No. No, I insist. I bet you've got some really interesting things to tell me.' His voice dripped sarcasm but rose on every word until he was thrashing his head and straining against the handcuffs. Beth took a step away from the bed. His fight was impressive and his body arched from the sheet. He turned from side to side, his voice ragged with pain and his language was foul. He was weak and quickly spent himself. He flopped back onto the pillow, exhausted. 'Talk to me, Beth. At least make me understand what the fuck's going on. How did a nice person like you turn into a kidnapper?'

Beth was crying. She was too choked up to speak and even if she could, there was nothing she could say to make this mess better.

'Okay, don't bother telling me why I'm handcuffed to a bed in some kind of fucking dungeon, and my ex-missuses' best mate is torturing me. Let's start with something easy and we'll come back to the big stuff in a second. Keep that fucking psycho kid away from me, okay? She's been back, you know.'

Beth's eyes widened but she didn't say anything.

'She came creeping in just after you left. She's mental. You do know that, don't you? She touched me Beth. I'm lying here trussed up like a fucking Christmas Turkey, helpless, and she's there copping a feel and then flashing her underdeveloped tits at me.'

'Oh no,' Beth groaned.'

Come on, Beth. Let me go. You can do that, right? You can just unlock these things,' he jiggled his wrist, 'and get me out of here.'

Beth shook her head and looked at her feet like a naughty twelve-year-old.

'Why? Why not? Why am I here? What do you want from me? Tell me and I'll get it. Let's sort this and then I can get out of here and see my kids. Jesus what day is it? I don't even know what day it is. How long have I been here?

Beth didn't answer. She didn't dare tell him that he'd been captive in the vault for three weeks and two days, or that there was a National appeal out for news of his whereabouts.

'Beth let me go. You have got the keys, right? You can let me go.'

'I can't,' she snuffled miserably.

'Why?'

She didn't answer.

'For fuck's sake, Beth.' He laid his head on the pillow and closed his eyes, his brow creased in pain. Beth risked going to the bed and putting her hand on his forehead. It was cool, no fever.

'Is the pain bad? Do you need something? I can give you morphine; it'll help to make you comfortable.'

'No, Beth. I don't want fucking morphine. How the hell can I ever be comfortable when I'm stuck in the same fucking position and can't even move to scratch my own arse? I want to go home. Please girl, just let me go.' Beth looked at him. There was nothing she could say and she had no answers. She'd finished dressing his wrists. The cuffs rested on thick gauze and wouldn't do any more damage, but Beth feared that he'd carry the scars from the deep wounds for the rest of his life. They needed stitching, but that would have to wait until he was calmer. She picked up a beaker and offered him a drink. She put her arm under his head and lifted it. He glared at her but accepted the straw into his mouth. He sucked up a mouthful of the juice and spat it in Beth's face.

She lowered his head and wiped her face on a cloth that was on his tray table beside the bed and without speaking—because there was nothing to say, she turned and walked towards the door.

'Wait. Beth, stop. Don't go. Please. Don't leave me.'

She turned and pivoted towards him. 'I have some things to do. I won't be long. You're stronger now, but you've lost a lot of weight. I'm going to go and make you some food. We'll see if you can manage a little.' The words were forced and mechanical.

'Don't bother. I won't eat it. Until I get out of here I'm on hunger strike. I won't eat anything.'

'I'll make it anyway. We'll see.'

'Beth?'

'Yes,' she answered him dully. She was exhausted by the emotional exchange and she could see that he was in pain, but she wasn't going to force any more morphine on him. The healing process was a slow one, and she didn't want to deprive him of his free will and choice, any more than she had done already.

'I am going to get out of here alive, aren't I? I'm not going to die here?'

Her reassurances went from her brain to her throat and got stuck. She wanted to tell him that of course he was getting out. That very soon he'd be released and to try and be patient until they worked out the details. But the truth was that she didn't know whether Colin was ever going to be set free. She said nothing, but the look in her eyes told him that she couldn't be sure.

'Oh shit. Oh, Jesus Christ, help me. You're insane, you know that?' He struggled against the cuffs and he lay back, terrified and exhausted. He squeezed his eyes shut and tears leaked from the corners and ran along the lines of the wrinkles at the side of his face. 'Help me, Beth, please. Tell me what's going on. You were the steady one. You kept Maggie in line. You were bright, sensible, reliable. How did you come to this?'

She went to him and took his hand. He didn't resist and squeezed her palm in his, taking something, though God knows what, from the physical contact with his captor. He carried on talking, 'You've always been a good person. I can't get a grasp on why you'd do this to me. I've never done anything to you.' He considered her eyes. 'We've got history, Beth. We've never said this out loud, but there've been moments. You know that as well as I do. That party when the kids were little, remember? You felt it too. I know you did. We were in the kitchen; you were tidying up, like you do. All you could hear was Maggie's voice; she was on that damned karaoke machine, again. We came close to kissing.' He had a faraway expression on his face as he remembered a simpler past. 'But I was married—and you were loyal. The moment passed and it never got as far as us having to blame the alcohol. But it was there. You wanted me, and, God knows, I wanted you. I always fancied you, but I ended up with Maggie, and I don't regret that 'cause, for a long time it worked, you know?' Beth was crying and couldn't say a word. Colin changed the subject. Why am I here, Beth? Explain it to me, please.'

Beth's mind was working. Why shouldn't she tell him? She could pull up the chair to the side of his bed, open her mouth and not shut it again until she'd purged every foul word from her body. The thought of telling somebody, anybody, every sordid detail from start to end was overpowering. To say what she'd done, what she knew, what she'd been told by Maggie even, and the potential danger to Maggie if she got too involved, everything. She had nothing to lose. Colin was tied and captive. Either he was going to die in that room, in which case anything she said would go to the grave with him, or he was going to get out of there. If that was possible, then she was as good as done for anyway. She had nobody to talk to. She ached to be able to get it out. She didn't want to make excuses, or cry, 'Poor me,' but being able to talk would be wonderful. No matter how badly Colin reacted to her afterwards.

'Colin I...' she stopped unable to continue.

'Just tell me.'

'I murdered someone.' He examined Beth's expression to see if what she was saying was true, but her face was blank and her eyes dull beneath the tears that were still spilling down her cheeks.

'Fuck. Who was it? What happened? Are you going to kill me, too?'

The first statement was out there and free. The rest of the words were fighting to tumble out of her mouth. She sighed and got the chair and pulled it to the bed before sinking into it. 'I'll tell you Colin. I'll tell you everything, but are you sure you're up to it? You can sleep and I'll come back later?' If she left that room without saying anything, she never would.

Colin's eyes were wide open and alert. He was ignoring any pain that he had and whereas five minutes earlier he looked weary and on the verge of sleeping, now he was with it and eager to hear what she had to say.

'Tell me.'

Beth talked. She was at the speed dating event, meeting Marc and setting this whole mess in motion. She talked slowly and methodically, telling every detail just as it was. Colin interjected with questions and passed comment at various points, such as telling Beth that Maggie would never have gone to the dating thing while she was with him and, what was that soft bloke she was with now, thinking of. When she got to the attempted rape, Colin said that she'd been stupid to go back to his house. As she progressed with her tale to Marc's death Colin's eyes grew wide and he shut up. He was riveted to what Beth was saying and only butted in with questions when he didn't understand something. She got to the meeting with Jennifer and her agreeing to Jennifer's help in hiding the body.

'You fucking idiot. Why didn't you just go to the police?'

'I was scared.'

'You fool. There isn't a court in the country that would convict you after what he did.'

'I killed a man. I couldn't think straight. I went along with what she said.'

And she continued. As she told him about hiding

Marc's body, Colin tried to sit up in the bed. 'Ugh, he's here? He's in this room? You moved him, right? Oh, dear God, tell me that I'm not sharing this nightmare with a fucking rotting corpse?' Beth motioned with her eyes to the side of the room and the roll of carpet. Colin strained to see, but it was a blessing that his vision didn't rotate that far. He struggled again. 'Get me out of here. Fucking get me out of here, now. I'm not bed-sitting with that thing.'

'Lie back down and relax. I don't think he's about to jump up and bite you.' Colin ranted but Beth continued her story. There was some heated debate when she got to the part where they'd robbed the old lady, which led onto Colin's attack. He paled when she told him how they'd had to perform Do-It-Yourself brain surgery on him to keep him alive.

'My God, you drilled into my fucking brain with a rusty old tool? It's a miracle I'm still alive. I can't take this shit in, Beth. It's too crazy.'

Beth ended with what Maggie told her about Jennifer's past. And she stopped.

They sat in silence for over a minute.

'So, let me get this straight. I'm only here because that little freak wanted to play a game at my expense? That's it? That's the sole motive for me being bonked on the bastard nut, having my fucking brain drilled and being tied up here? And you went along with it, like some dumbstruck fucking sheep.'

'Beth nodded.'

'So, what happens next?'

'I don't know. I honestly don't know.' Beth hung her head, letting everything that had been said sink in. They talked in circles and round the houses. Colin took a moment to think and then reached for Beth's hand. 'Let me go, Beth.' He spoke steadily, never breaking eye contact with her. 'Let me go and I promise you. I give you my solemn promise that I'll go with you to Maggie's. We'll talk this whole mess through and then Maggie and I will go with you to the police and support you.' Beth was terrified and shook her head. 'There's no doubt about it, you've been a bloody fool. But with us standing alongside you, it's bound to help. We'll make them see that you've been a victim of circumstance and then blackmail and manipulation.'

'It won't work,' Beth cried and a fresh batch of tears sprang from her eyes. 'I can't go to prison. I know I deserve it. I know I killed a man—and nearly killed you, too. I've been guilty of terrible things. But they can't let me go.' She wrapped her arms around her knees. 'Even if they wanted to go easy on me, they would have to put me away for years just for this part, for keeping you here against your will—and then there's the hospital and the drugs, and poor Mary. They'd have no alternative. There are guidelines.'

'Please let me go. Come with me. We can be at Maggie's house in ten minutes. We'll help you to go on the run.'

And what happens the second I undo your cuffs? You'll overpower me and go straight to the police. And who could blame you? You're telling me what I want to hear.'

'I won't. I promise I won't. I swear to you that I can see how this came about. I'll help you in any way I can. Trust me, Beth.'

Beth laughed mirthlessly. 'Colin, I've seen you swear to things on your children's lives, and then turn out to not be telling the truth. How can I trust you?'

'Yeah, hands up. You know me well. And I could be blagging. But, doesn't that mean something? We have history, Beth. Let me help you.'

What he said made sense. She had the power to bring everything that happened to a close. Maybe he would do everything he could to get her off. She knew Maggie would fight her corner, at least, she hoped she would stand by her. But there was no getting away from the fact that she had a list of convictions that couldn't be walked away from. Nothing had changed. Colin was waving a juicy carrot and it would be tempting to put her faith in him and let him take over whichever way it went. She told him she'd think about it. He was crying in pain and he agreed to an injection of morphine, 'I don't even care if I can trust you. So what if it's the lethal dose that kills me,' he told Beth, 'anything would be better than this. Please Beth, think on it hard and do the right thing, it's not too late. We can sort this.'

Chapter Twenty-Nine

Beth was making soup in the kitchen when Jenifer came in. They rarely went to Beth's house and spent all their time at the big house. Beth hated being there, but necessity made her make the best of a dire situation. She still slept in the chair at the side of Colin's bed, but she had moved some personal things into the small spare bedroom and would be sleeping in there now that Colin didn't need a twenty-four-hour bedside vigil.

Jennifer threw her duffel bag onto the stainless-steel centre isle and commented that the soup smelled good. Beth told her that it was for Colin and that she'd made a curry for them that just needed heating. She stirred the soup, while Jennifer, attuned to her apprehension, gauged her mood.

'What's up?'

It was now or never and Beth was at a loss how to begin.

'I saw Maggie today.'

'Oh yes. Did she come to you, or did you go to her?'

Beth was quick to defend herself. 'She came to me, of course.'

'I hope you got rid of her and didn't let her in.'

'It wasn't that easy.'

'Oh, my God, you are so bloody dim-witted, can't you do anything right? What was it, coffee three dozen cancer-sticks and bosom to bosom sympathy?'

'Something like that.'

'Well the police aren't here, so she didn't drag much

out of you.'

'It wasn't me doing the talking. She had a lot to say. She's been away.'

'Good, pity she didn't stay away.'

'She's been visiting an old lady in Coventry.' Beth watched Jennifer for a reaction. Jennifer either saw her past as no threat to her immediate future, or didn't know where Miss Thistle had retired.

'So?'

'She went to visit your old nanny.'

Jennifer was motionless as she took over thirty seconds to process this information and mentally debate the ramifications. Her facial expression didn't alter, she looked cast in stone, the only visible symptom of distress was the pulse in her neck that moved in time with her accelerated heartbeat. When she replied, she was in control.

'Ugh gross. Who'd want to go and see that old waxwork? I suppose Maggie came back full of gory details about how I did that to her. The old bat's senile. Why do you think Marc had her put away? She's nuts. She doesn't know what she's talking about. And what's more, there is not a policeman in the land who would listen to her. 'I did it,' she admitted, hanging her head and putting on a puppy dog expression, 'but it was proven at the time that it was a terrible, terrible, horrible, awful accident that has haunted me since I was a child. Is it any wonder that I'm odd, after having to live with the guilt of what I accidentally did to that old lady?'

Maggie had seen her acting skills many times and didn't react. 'Actually, she told Maggie a lot more than that. She told her what happened to your sister and your parents. Nanny Nettles says that you murdered all three of them in cold blood.

'Hearsay and vile deluded accusation from a bitter old lady, M'laird. I put it to the prosecution to provide one piece of evidence in support of their accusations—or stand down.'

Beth tightened her hold on the wooden spoon after stirring the soup to death and beyond—and still stirred it. She told Jennifer as word perfect as she could remember, minus the insults towards Jennifer, what Maggie had told her and waited for Jennifer's response.

'I've got enough on you to take you down ten times over, Beth, and unless you're wired and you're recording this, which let's face it, you wouldn't have the forethought to arrange—anything that's said in this room is only words.' She grinned and behind her eyes Beth saw the glint of evil. 'Do you want me to tell you all about it? Not my dear old Nanny's diluted version, but the real deal, straight from the loco horse's mouth?'

'Will it be the truth?'

'And nothing but, M'laird.'

'Don't mess with me, Phantom.'

'Wouldn't dream of it, sweetheart. Here you go then, the whole truth. I suppose you could say I just got a taste for killing people,' Jennifer began. Once started the words came fast, each one turning Beth's stomach more than the last. She was horrified but glued to what the girl was saying. 'Melissa was my first. And I liked it. God, I hated her. She was always so perfect, so sweet, so pretty. Pushing her into that brazier and watching her burn was the most exciting thing that had ever happened to me. I wasn't even out of primary school and I'd committed murder in front of sixty people and got away with it. I'm glad Maggie told you. I've been dying to tell you myself for ages, but you weren't ready to take it. You need to know how clever I am, Beth. Some would say I'm a genius. You should appreciate me. I could have taken up with anybody but I chose you. You're so lucky to have me. There were some others that never even came to light because I'm that good at it. About a year after Melissa, things got really quiet and boring. Our gardener had an asthma attack. I stood in front of him and, one squirt at a time, I emptied his inhaler before wiping my fingerprints off the canister, I was nine, but I loved Agatha Christie, she taught me a lot. When he was really bad and slumped over a rhododendron bush, I put the canister in his hand and watched him die trying to suck dregs from the empty puffer. So simple, quite boring really, but it was fun watching him choke.'

'My God, you're a monster.'

'It takes one to know one, X-O-X-O.'

'X-O-X-O? What the fucking hell are you talking about?'

'Never mind. Do you want to know the highlights of my murder back catalogue, or not? Because the next one was a stroke of genius.'

'Your parents?'

'Oh, yeah, they were next, weren't they? I forgot about them. But that was dull as ditch; I never even got to see it happen. I was just pissed off with them, so it wasn't really murder, not a proper one. After Melissa, the one after my folks was my favourite—I like killing children best.' Beth put her hands to her face in horror and Jennifer laughed, delighted by her reaction. 'I was walking through the park one day. It was busy, big crowd again, you see a theme emerging? I killed this ugly little kid right in front of its mother. Not that she noticed. She was too busy sitting on a bench and gossiping with her mate. The kid—he was about three—was just there looking gormless. It had a big head, nearly no hair and it was dribbling down its disgusting, dirty bib. It offended me, so I stuffed its gob full of sand and walked away. There were a couple of other kids in the sandpit, my little accomplices, they just sat there staring and didn't say a word. The boy died right there with his mother not thirty yards away. I was a bit further on out of the way by this point. I heard him making these snuffling noises and flinging his arms around a bit before he fell over. The mother and her crony never looked up once. Eventually one of the other little brats must have figured that this wasn't good and started screaming and they ran over, some other people came too, including me, Phantom to the rescue. And that was a huge risk with the other kids in the sandpit knowing that I'd done it. I saw one of them staring right at me with these freaking big eyes. She tugged on her mum's hoodie and pointed at me, but her mother ignored her. Man that was a buzz. It was too late, of course, the kid was already dead.'

'Shut up,' Beth's voice couldn't hold her words steady and she half croaked half screamed at Jennifer. 'Shut up, I don't want to hear any more.'

'Oh, don't stop me, there's more. Funny thing about that kid was, once the brat was dead, the mother decided that she loved him.'

'How many people have you killed?'

'Well after that there was the incident with the nanny, that didn't exactly go to plan and I had to stop for a bit. I didn't kill anybody for another six years. Let's just say I found a new game that kept me occupied for a while. I do like killing people though, you've been lucky, Beth, it's a good job I like you.'

'I've got to go to the police. You've got to be stopped and what happens to me doesn't matter.'

'So, brave. So, self-sacrificing. So, full of shit. You know why I didn't kill you? In fact, do you know why I took to you? Why I chose you to be my only friend? It's because you know what it's like. You're just the same as me.'

'I'm nothing like you.'

'You reckon? Have you searched your conscience lately? How many times have you thought about killing me?'

'Hundreds. But I'd never…'

'How many times have you actually considered the possibility of having to kill Colin to save your own skin?'

Beth blushed and bit her lip without saying anything.

'I've watched you change. That day when you hit Colin, you felt it too, just the same as me, go on deny it. Tell me you didn't feel the thrill and get one hell of a buzz out of it.'

It was true. 'I'm nothing like you.'

'You're everything like me. When it comes to it, you would kill rather than suffer. Colin will be easier than Marc, you'll see.'

'Don't be ridiculous. After everything we've gone through to save his life, we aren't going to kill him. It's absurd. You're just trying to frighten me. Stop talking shit.'

'And the alternative is?'

'I don't know, we'll think of something.'

'Well you'd better get a move on, sister, because he's getting better all the time. In fact, I'd say there's not a lot wrong with him now, if his cock's anything to go by. Did he tell you we had a bit of fun today?'

'He told me you molested him, and told me to keep you out of his way.'

'Well the fucking lying bastard. I admit he complained a bit at first. Told me to get off and stuff like that, but after a couple of seconds he rose to the occasion. I jacked him off and he liked it plenty.'

'Oh, stop lying. He told me exactly what happened.'

'He's the liar. Let's go up and ask him.' Jennifer was shouting, furious at not being believed. 'In fact, I'll get the baby wipe from the bin that I used to clean his spunk off my hand. Will that be proof enough for you? You can have it DNA tested, if you like.' She was gesticulating like an angry child and was red in the face. 'God I hate being called a liar when I'm telling the truth.'

She felt sorry for Colin. He must be embarrassed that his body had betrayed him. But it was Colin after all, and maybe he'd enjoyed it, too. Beth felt a flash of jealousy and realised that, as accused, she was fast becoming just as fucked up as Jennifer.

Jennifer was ready for going up and confronting Colin but Beth didn't want him being disturbed. She was frightened that he might blab their conversation and wanted to keep Jennifer away from him until she decided what to do. 'Okay, I believe you,' she said, trying to calm Jennifer who was still ranting at the injustice of

Colin denying her. 'And anyway, what did you mean when you said that you found something new to do instead of killing?'

As if a switch had been flicked, Jennifer's mood changed and she smiled. Come upstairs, I want to show you something, you haven't been in Marc's room since the night I showed you the money, have you?'

'No, it's kept locked.'

Jennifer laughed, 'Oh you've tried then?'

'Once, out of curiosity. I've watched you going in and out and you always lock the door behind you. I wondered what you were up to locking yourself in there for hours on end. I tried the door once on the off chance that it might be open.'

'Well, you're about to find out, what I've been doing.' They'd reached the door to Marc's bedroom and Jennifer unlocked it with a key that she took from around her neck. She flung the door wide for Beth to enter. Being in Marc's room again made her shudder. The bedroom screamed male. It was his lair. She wondered how many women he'd entertained in the big bed. And she wondered if things might have turned out different if she'd been a willing participant that first night. Her head turned towards a wall with no furniture against it. It was dominated by a huge mural and was a picture of Jennifer as a child. She was beautiful, absolutely stunning. It was a head and shoulders portrait; her hair was blonde then and hung in perfectly formed ringlets down to the end of the picture. Her eyes were sapphire blue and her smile was sweet, and looked so innocent. Beth was sure the mural wasn't there the last time she'd been in this room, but she'd been so mesmerised by all that money that she couldn't be sure.

'Oh, Phantom, that's lovely,' said Beth, 'It's a beautiful picture of you,'

'Not me,' answered Jennifer, 'it's Melissa.'

'But the likeness, I don't understand.'

'We were identical, but she was the pretty one. She was pretty with goodness. She was the one that Marc liked best.' Her voice took such a tone of anger that Beth looked up sharply. You asked me what I wanted Marc's money for. Go on step closer.'

Beth moved to the picture. She noticed a few tiny pieces of coloured paper on the floor at the foot of the picture. 'I only finished it this morning,' said Jennifer, what do you think?'

The perception and artistry in the picture was fantastic. Jennifer had a real talent as an artist. 'I think it's…' Beth stopped as she realised what she was looking at. The mosaic was made up of literally thousands of pieces of coloured paper, blues, browns, purples. The paper was perfectly cut, half inch square pieces of five, ten, twenty and fifty pound notes. 'My God, it's the money. You ripped all of Marc's money into little pieces.' Beth took in the size of the picture, predominantly made up of fifties that took up most of the wall. 'So much money, you were rich and you did this with it? That money could have secured us a future—false passports, maybe. I don't know.' So that's what Jennifer had been doing every time she left the vault. It must have taken her hundreds of hours to complete while Beth was sitting with Colin.

'Marc was obsessed by money,' Jennifer said, in a calm and distracted voice. Using it to buy our freedom would have been too easy. Think how much more exciting it will be to get out of this situation by using our brains, or not maybe, if that's what fate decrees.'

'You're mad, you really are completely loopy.'

'Not at all. I wanted to put this money to the best use. I wanted to do something with it that would really piss Marc off. What better way than by making a picture of his little princess, a shrine to the golden one.' The bitterness was back in her voice. She sat down and patted the side of the bed for Beth to join her. Beth looked distastefully at the quilt and sat down. 'You know I said that Marc had sexually abused me?'

'Yes,' said Beth, wondering where this new tack was leading.

'I lied. Actually, that was one big fat lie.'

'For God's sake, Phantom. I held you sobbing in my arms, when you told me how awful it had been for you as a child.'

'I know, good, aren't I?' Jennifer replied with a grin.

'So he never forced himself on you night after night?'

'Oh yes, that's bit's very true.'

'I don't understand. God Phantom, you tell me so many lies that I don't know what to believe. '

'Well shut up and listen, will you. I'm about to tell you the truth, if you want to hear it.'

'I don't have time for this. I never know what to believe with you. I'm going to get dinner ready. She turned and walked to the door.

'I raped him.'

Beth stopped in her tracks and turned around.

'Well kind of. I certainly seduced him, as they would say in polite circles.' Beth wanted to walk away but she couldn't stop listening. She had no idea what was truth and what was lies. What was true one day was the opposite the next. But she was compelled to listen to every disgusting sentence and couldn't break away.

'It took months to get his attention. I'd been reading some pretty sexy books. I was about eleven and wanted to know what this sex stuff was about. I tried just throwing myself at him. But he slapped me and pushed me away. I had to be subtle, so I messed with his head. I'd leave the bathroom door open a crack when I was drying myself after a shower. I'd pretend not to notice that he was there watching me. One day I glimpsed his hand moving, I couldn't see exactly what he was doing, but I had a good idea. Bingo, I had him. I left my bedroom door open once when I was playing with myself naked on the bed. Afterwards, I burst into his bedroom and caught him in the middle of a similar pursuit; he had his cock in his hand and was wanking it for all he was worth. I had him so confused that he didn't know which way was up. He yelled at me to get out and threw his pillow at the door. But I knew it was only a matter of time. I haven't got much in the chest department and I had even less then, but I'd make a point of leaning over him to reach for things, whenever I could. I'd rub my chest in his face. Any chance I got to rub up against him, I took it. I drove him mad. One night, when I felt that I'd waited long enough, I crawled into bed with him. He was a deep sleeper. He was lying on his back, naked, and his cock was easy to get at. He was just about to come when he woke up. He was as angry as hell and let out this noise, it was part anger, part lust. He was crazy mad. He flung me onto my back and had his hands around my neck strangling me, and then he couldn't stop himself. He wanted to—but couldn't. He thrust his hips and plunged his cock deep inside me. He was massive, thick and long. I thought I was going to split and bleed to death, I did bleed all over his sheets.'

'Stop,' said Beth, 'I don't want to hear any more.'

'No wait, we're getting to the funny bit. After that night, we were at it like rabbits. I could get him hard just by looking at him. I used to do it when he'd be in the kitchen having a conversation with Nanny Nettles. I'd stand behind her and give him a flash of my crotch, or sometimes just look at him in a certain way, and within seconds he'd have a massive bonk on. She knew. Nanny knew exactly what was going on. She tried to keep us apart, but she had no chance, we were like two dogs on heat.'

Beth was disgusted by the depravity of what she was hearing. She told Jennifer to stop again but was powerless to walk away. As horrible as it was, she needed to hear the entire story. Marc had abused Beth and mocked her over the size of her breasts, was this some sick throwback to his obsession with having sex with his eleven-year-old sister?

'It wasn't all fun and games though. He stopped after six years, when he got me pregnant. It was as though he hated me, was repulsed by me. I'd been lucky. I didn't start my periods until late. I was turned fourteen, and then we got away with it for another six months. I was just turned fifteen when I found out I was pregnant. He sorted it out for me with one of Nanny's knitting needles.'

Beth flung her hands up, 'Oh my God, no. That's horrible,' and then her face hardened and she dropped her hands. 'No. No way, you're making it up. That can't be true; you'd have bled to death.'

'It is the truth. I swear to you. Far from bleeding to death it was no big deal really. It hurt a lot but was over in one night. I bled a lot, but there was nothing there to see, just a blood clot when I went to the toilet. If you don't believe me go and see that bitch, Thistle. She knew. She heard me screaming. Marc had gone out. He couldn't cope with it. Nanny Nettles saw the bloody knitting needle by my bed and put it all together. She ran me a hot bath and gave me some horrible liquid stuff that she kept in her room; I don't know what it was. She sat with me all night.

'What a horrible story.'

'Tell you what though; you've got to admire the old girl. She gave Marc what for, threatened him with the police and all sorts.' Jenifer laughed. Funny thing was, she totally blamed Marc for it all. I don't think he stopped because of what she said. He wasn't bothered about her. He just went off me. He wouldn't let me near him and once he physically gagged when I brushed up against him. He pinned me up against the wall and told me that if I went near him, like that, again, he'd kill me. A few months later he started seeing this other girl, only just legal. I hated her—so I killed her.' Jennifer went on talking, as though Beth wasn't there. 'I stabbed her in Marc's bedroom. He found her. We hid the body together in the woods. See the irony, of that Beth,' she said, as if remembering that Beth was there. When we hid Marc's body, I'd already done the self-same thing before. Funny eh?'

'Hilarious.'

'Obvs. They never found the body but we moved anyway and I had to lay low after that. And then I've only killed one more person. Last year, actually. I went to a party and got off with this dude. He took me back to his flat for sex, which was cool but then he tried to give me drugs. Do I look that fucking stupid? I don't do drugs. I was offended that he'd think it of me. I waited until he was high and then refilled his syringe. He was already out of it when I plunged it into his arm. Accidental overdose, they said. Unsatisfactory murder, unsatisfactory outcome. That one was a complete waste of effort. There was no excitement and it left me hungry for more. And Beth, here we are. Can you feel it coming to a head? I can. I wonder who will live, and who will die?'

Beth had no answer. She didn't know what to say. Jennifer's words were swirling around and around in her head but only one sentence made sense. Yes. She could feel it coming to a head, and it terrified her. 'Dinner in half an hour,' she said turning and leaving the room.

Chapter Thirty

The curry was good and Jenifer dove into it as though she hadn't eaten for a week. Beth forked hers through but barely managed to eat any. She had no idea how much of what Jennifer said was the truth. Jennifer cleared her plate in less than five minutes and said that she was going to her room to watch a DVD. Beth knew that she'd be lying flat on her bed with earphones glued to her head without a care in the world, but Beth's mind was blurring with so many thoughts and mixed emotions. The overriding feeling that she couldn't push away was fear. She felt as though a clock was ticking in her head. Jennifer was right about one thing, things were coming to a head. She stood at the sink washing up. If she could get a good night's sleep, maybe she could clear her mind and think of a way out for all of them. She felt as though her head was overfilled with information. There was too much in and no way to let it out. And then, just when she needed time for peace and contemplation, there was a loud hammering at the front door.

Nobody ever came here. She snuck into the hall and tried sliding up the wall to get closer to the door to see who was there through the leaded glass panel without being seen, but it was no good.

'I can see you, Beth, open this fucking door, now, or I'm going to call the police.' Beth didn't know whether to be terrified or relieved that it was Maggie. She went to the door and shouted in a whisper. 'Maggie, go away, Jennifer's here. I'll come to your house, when I can get away.'

'I'm not going anywhere. Where is he? I know you know something, Beth, open this door now. Or I swear…'

Beth opened the door and Maggie pushed her way in striding down the hall. She burst into the living room and checked that it was empty before coming out of there and moving to the kitchen, where she did the same.

'I know you've got something to do with Colin going missing. Where the hell is he?'

Beth's blood ran cold. After everything that had happened that day she felt that she couldn't cope with any more and she felt herself shaking. 'Maggie, what the hell's got into you? What are you talking about? I don't know where Colin is.'

'Liar,' Maggie spat at her. She raised her finger and pointed it at Beth. 'You forget I know you. I know you inside out. Nobody understands you like I do. I should have seen it straight away. As soon as I mentioned Colin's disappearance, you got jittery and acted shifty. I know when you're lying, Beth. I knew it when you took that freak in, and I know it now.'

'Maggie, you'd just spent an hour trying to tell me that Jennifer's some kind of whacked-out murderer, and then you think I'm hiding something when I act a bit strained. Jesus Maggie. You want to get your facts straight before you go making accusations like that. '

'I don't believe you. Look at you, even now you're shaking. You're drying the pots in the middle of a life-important conversation, for God's sake. It's because you can't keep your hands still. You can't look me in the eye.

You can't stop your body from telling me that you are lying through your teeth.'

'Look Maggie, you're upset over Colin. I can understand that, so I'm not going to hold it against you, but you really need to go now. Think about what you're saying, it's ludicrous. Why the hell would I know where he is? I've hardly seen him since you two split up.'

'So why is that cup more interesting than this conversation? Look at me, Beth. See, one quick glance and your eyes are back to the floor.' Maggie marched over to stand beside Beth and Beth cringed away from her. Maggie picked up a cup and smashed it against the far wall. 'You need to start talking to me, Beth.'

'Have you gone bloody mad? Stop it.' Beth looked towards the door and her eyes rose upwards as she listened.

'Maggie picked up a plate and slammed it to the floor. 'What's the matter, Beth? Who's upstairs that you don't want to know I'm here. Just Jennifer, or Marc, as well? What do they know about my ex-husband's disappearance? She picked up another plate and threw it. A door slammed upstairs and was followed by feet pounding down the stairs.

Maggie cupped her hands and shouted into them, 'Marc, c'mon. Be a man get yourself down here and face me. Where's Colin, Marc. I'm going to call the police in ten seconds if you aren't down here.

The door flew open and Jennifer burst though it in her stocking feet. 'What the hell is going—' she saw Maggie. 'What's she doing here? Get out.' Her voice rose as Maggie strode towards her. 'Get out of my house, now.'

'Where's Colin.'

'Get out of my house, you mad cow. How do I know where he is?'

They were screaming at each other. Maggie grabbed Jennifer by the shirt and slammed her into the wall. She used her greater strength against the girl to punctuate each word by pulling Jennifer away from the wall and slamming her hard back into it, banging her head against the wall with each thrust. 'What have you done with Colin?'

Jennifer was terrified. She'd had the wind knocked out of her and was gasping hard. 'I don't know,' she croaked, 'Beth get her off me.'

Beth was behind Maggie, pulling ineffectually at her shoulder, trying to get her to loosen her grip on Jennifer. Maggie was like a steel door.' You'd better start talking or, so help me, I'm going to call the cops.' She pushed Jennifer away and the girl slumped to the floor in a heap, gasping for breath. Maggie reached into her jacket pocket and pulled out her phone.

'Maggie, don't. Wait,' said Beth.

Maggie stopped. Beth didn't know what the hell to say to follow it up. But Maggie was staring at Jennifer's feet. She ran over to her and the girl flinched back against the wall. Maggie picked up her leg and literally tore one of the socks off her foot.

'Where did you get these socks?'

'You crazy bitch, want a pair just like them, do you? Well you only had to ask.'

'These are Colin's socks. Where is he?' Maggie whirled around and grabbed a knife from the draining board. She was staring at the motif on the ankle of the sock. There was no mistake. 'Look, Beth—and try telling me that I'm wrong. You remember the year after we married we went to the ice hotel in Jukkasjarvi, in Sweden? The socks were souvenirs from their gift shop. Now you two had better tell me. Where is my children's father?'

Maggie dragged Jennifer up by her throat. 'Where is he?'

Something snapped in Jennifer. She'd recovered from the initial shock of finding Maggie there. Her temper flipped but she was cool and calculating. The end game was on, and much like her damned snake, Jennifer was going to play with her prey. 'Chill, woman, He lent me his socks when we got out of bed this morning. That's after we spent all night having sex and he kept telling me what a fat ugly cow, you are. What's the big deal?'

Maggie had the knife up against her throat. She stared at the blade; saw it indenting Jennifer's flesh. She threw the knife behind her and punched Jennifer in the face. There was a crack of bone, and blood flew from Jennifer's nose. Jennifer shook her head to clear it of stars. She licked some blood from the stream flowing from her broken nose. 'Mm, blood. Tastes good. Go on, hit me again, baby, that's just how I like it.' Her voice was brave but her legs were buckling. 'Want to know where your precious Colin is, he's strapped to a bed in a hidden vault upstairs.'

Maggie punched her again. 'Where's Co—' She released her hold on Jennifer and they fell to the floor. Jennifer landed on her hands and knees and she held steady gasping, trying to regain her breath and clear her head. The second blow had landed in her right eye; she could feel it swelling.

Maggie slumped to the floor in a swish of escaping breath as it left her body like a gasp in a wind tunnel and she lay unconscious on the floor. Beth hadn't intended to hit her. She had the frying pan in her hand. She'd hit her lifelong best friend, but she had no recollection of doing it. She stood over Maggie watching blood spill from a gash in her forehead.

Jennifer rose behind Maggie and came from nowhere with the large kitchen knife in her hand. She brought it down in an overhand stabbing motion and sunk it to the hilt in Maggie's side. She grunted as she pulled it out and brought it down again, and then again, and again, and again.

Beth held the frying pan limp in her hands. She made whimpering noises. 'What are you doing? What are you doing?' She muttered. 'This is terrible. I'm going to get Colin. He'll know what to do. He'll help us. Maggie will be all right.'

'No,' Jennifer screamed. She pulled the knife from inside Maggie's chest and rose to her feet. She turned to face Beth and moved towards her. Raising the knife above her head, she brought it down in a swift motion, towards Beth's head. Galvanised into action Beth made a dash for the door. 'Stop, don't you dare go to the vault. Get back here, now.' Jennifer was slow from the multiple bangs to her head and her facial injuries. Her right eye was closed and she bounced into the wall as her balance failed her. Beth was already halfway up the first flight of stairs. She was fast on her feet, but her mind was in trouble. She kept muttering Colin's name like a mantra, over and over. She fumbled over the vault lock. As she burst into the room, Jennifer was only feet behind her.

Beth ran over to Colin screaming his name. She already had the key for the cuffs in her hand and she tried to get them into the lock. Her fingers were all thumbs and she sobbed as she tried to fill Colin in on what had just happened. 'She's killed Maggie, stabbed her, stabbed her over and over,' she screamed.

'Hurry,' yelled Colin turning his hands to help her get them undone. Jennifer made it to the bed and Beth backed away, she hadn't managed to unlock the handcuffs. Jennifer put her face close to Colin's, sneering. 'It wasn't me who killed your precious wife. Beth, hit her over the head with a frying pan.' As she talked, Colin brought his arm up. Despite being cuffed to the bed he managed to raise his elbow far enough to grab Jennifer's head in the crook of his arm. He used every ounce of his strength to lift her and drop his arm to her throat with a grimace on his face. He squeezed. Colin lifted his face to Beth's. His expression was pained. He stared at Beth with hatred on his face. 'You killed Maggie?' He asked. 'You…killed…Maggie.' He punctuated each word by squeezing down harder on Jennifer's windpipe. 'I'm going to kill her,' he said motioning with his head down to Jennifer. '…And then I'm going to kill you.'

As Colin squeezed the life out of Jennifer, her tongue protruded from her mouth, she made noises from her nose and her eyes bulged in their sockets as her face turned red and swelled with the trapped blood. A fresh stream of new blood ran from her nose. She looked towards Beth and raised one hand, begging her to help. Her other hand grabbed uselessly at Colin's forearm, trying to get loose. And then she stopped trying. Her body was limp and she slumped against Colin's forearm. He looked at the top of her head and raised his elbow to release her. Jennifer fell to the floor and didn't move again.

Beth had been trying to get the key in the handcuffs to release Colin, but he kept moving as he grabbed for her. She'd dropped the keys and bent to pick them up, still trying to free him. And then he was killing Jennifer. And then he said he was going to kill Beth. And then Beth stopped. She stepped away from the bed and watched as Jennifer's eyes bulged. Jennifer fell to the floor and Colin turned his head to look at her. 'He's going to kill me,' she muttered detached from reality and gabbling to herself.

Colin saw her phasing out. 'C'mon now, Beth, don't be stupid. Come on, it's going to be all right. You know me. You know I didn't mean it. I was just angry. I'll make everything all right. It's over now sweetheart. You've got to let me go. We can get out of here.'

Beth had had enough. She had to get away from all of them. She turned and walked out of the room. She slammed the door behind her. The last thing she heard before the door locked on the soundproofed room was Colin screaming for her to let him go.

She walked along the corridor and down the first flight of stairs. She rounded the bend and walked down the second flight of stairs and along the downstairs hall. Beth opened the front door, walked out and slammed it to lock behind her.

Chapter Thirty-One

She walked down Springfield Road, passed two schools and went by the train station. Her mind was riddled with thoughts and questions. Her best friend was dead, lying in the kitchen of the big house. Maggie was in full view of anybody walking in to find her in hours, days, weeks or months. She thought about Maggie's children. She knew Maggie was dead. Maybe she killed her—maybe Jennifer did, it didn't matter. Their father had vanished. Now their mother had done the same. It could be a long time before Maggie was found. Unless she'd told Graham where she was going, that would speed things up. Beth doubted that she'd said anything; Graham wouldn't have let her go alone. Beth should feel guilty about the children, but she didn't feel anything. She thought about Colin strangling Jennifer. She hadn't checked to see if she was dead, but she looked as dead as any fish she'd ever seen on a monger's block. She tried to analyse how she should feel about Jennifer's death. She felt nothing at all. The girl had held her to ransom for over six months and she taught Beth just what hatred meant, and yet, at times, Beth had felt close to her. It was a classic case of Stockholm syndrome. Jennifer taught her what it was like to feel alive. She didn't know for sure that Jennifer was dead. She turned left onto the main road around Ulverston town. She'd walked out of the vault and left Colin handcuffed to the bed. He'd starve to death, lying in his own filth. Beth wondered how long that would take. Dehydration would get him long before the lack of food. She remembered the story of a man trapped in a mountain crevice when a rock had fallen on his hand. He'd hung there for days before hacking through his arm with a penknife to escape. She tried to remember if there was anything to hand that Colin could cut off his arm with. Maybe as he emaciated, his hand would be wasted enough for him to slip it through the cuff, but surely, without food or water, he'd be dead long before that time came. Marc, Maggie, Jennifer and Colin were all in that house, already dead or slowly dying and she had walked away and closed the door behind her. Things were dulling. She was tired, but wasn't aware of it. As she passed the canal, she considered suicide again, she knew it was for the best, but she just kept walking. If her feet had stopped while she considered it, she would have drowned herself, but they continued—one in front of the other, and the canal was gone. In space, nobody can hear you scream. It occurred to Beth that if nobody found the bodies for a long time, then maybe it never happened. On her next question, when she asked herself if anything really did happen, she knew her mind was broken. She imagined a hole in her brain where all the nastiness was leaking out. The thoughts were calming, and stopping altogether, leaving her mind one by one. She embraced the emptiness. She hummed. It wasn't a song, just a droning, tuneless noise. She walked and hummed and eventually the humming stopped. Her mind was blank and only the walking remained.

At Greenodd it rained. She had walked over ten miles, but she didn't notice either rain or distance. She put one foot in front of the other and walked. Hours later a car drove along the darkened road. She was close to Milnthorpe; the road had no pavement and no street lighting. Cars had to rely on cat's eyes to guide them on that piece of country road. The man saw her at the last second when he was almost on top of her. He swerved to miss her and his tyres squealed. She didn't notice. She kept her gaze ahead of her, on the horizon, and continued to walk. The man drove ahead and pulled into a lay-by a hundred yards further on. He was shaken and his legs nearly gave way beneath him when he got out of his car to confront the stupid person in the road.

As soon as she came close enough, he shouted at her. 'Hey you. Are you mad? You nearly got us both killed.'

She kept on walking towards him. 'You lady. What the—' The woman walked towards him. He spoke to her but she seemed not to notice. She walked by without so much as glancing his way. He wondered if she was sleepwalking, she gave that impression. 'Jesus Christ, this is crazy,' he said aloud. He reached out his arm to grab her, but she just kept on walking out of his grasp. She seemed to be in some kind of trance. 'Hey lady,' he yelled after her,' Hey you, you're going to be run over. Oh shit.' He rummaged in his pocket for his phone and rang 999.

Chapter Thirty-Two

Cheryl prided herself on always being cheerful. It didn't help the nuts if you were all solemn and down on yourself, now did it? Today she was especially happy because it was Friday and she was going clubbing. She only had one teensy little eight-hour shift to get through first. She had the job of breaking in a new temp, who was due to arrive at any minute, and she was already behind on morning routine. If she didn't begin the drug round in the next ten minutes, the doctors would be coming and she'd be for it. 'There now, dear,' she said to the mute in the wheelchair. 'That's you all washed and clean. Not that you care one way or the other. Shall we take you out to the conservatory and let you look out of the window. It's too cold to go in the garden today, but the sun's trying its best, it'll be nice for you in the sun room.' She wheeled the patient into the conservatory and parked her in front of the window overlooking the front of the hospital. At least this one wouldn't be any trouble. The world could come to an end and this one wouldn't notice. She'd been at Dane Garth for four months and hadn't said one word. She was a nurse herself, apparently, and a damned good one, according to her colleagues. Took time off work one day and just never returned. Then a few weeks later, she was found wandering alone in the middle of the night, in the pouring rain. What could be so hard about her life, she wondered? She had a good job, a nice house and car. Some people had it all. Cheryl would never understand some people.

Beth slumped in her wheelchair and gazed straight ahead. She didn't see. She didn't look. She just gazed.

A figure walked up the drive, a nurse, in a short pink uniform. She had black spiky hair, cut severely. She carried a satchel style rucksack over her shoulder with a lightning design and the words *White Phantom* emblazoned across the front in spiky writing.

Beth hadn't made a sound in months. She opened her mouth and screamed. Cheryl was parking another patient in the opposite corner of the room. She jumped out of her skin. Running to the side of Beth's wheelchair, she crouched down beside her. The woman's eyes were wide and bulging. She pointed, the only hand movement she'd made voluntarily in all the time she'd been there. She looked terrified. Cheryl followed her gaze into the garden. 'There, there love,' she soothed. 'There's nobody there.'

Made in United States
Orlando, FL
06 March 2022

15451844R00204